Sign up for our newsletter to hear
about new and upcoming releases.

www.ylva-publishing.com

Other Books by Jae

Standalone Romances:
Perfect Rhythm
Falling Hard
Heart Trouble
Under a Falling Star
Something in the Wine
Shaken to the Core

The Hollywood Series:
Departure from the Script
Damage Control
Just Physical

Portland Police Bureau Series:
Conflict of Interest
Next of Kin

The Vampire Diet Series:
Good Enough to Eat

The Oregon Series:
Backwards to Oregon
Beyond the Trail
Hidden Truths

The Shape-Shifter Series:
Second Nature
Natural Family Disasters
Manhattan Moon
True Nature

Just
FOR
SHOW

JAE

Acknowledgments

While my name is on the cover, writing and publishing a book is always a team effort. First and foremost, I want to thank my wonderful team of beta readers, who are reading every chapter as I go. Anne-France, Christiane, Claire, Danielle, Erin, Trish, and Melanie, you are worth your weight in ice cream!

Thanks also to my editor, Robin Samuels, to my proofreader, Laina Villeneuve, and to Glendon for the great cover.

Last but certainly not least, thank you to my readers. Your enthusiasm for my stories and my characters keeps me writing.

Chapter 1

"WE NEED TO TALK," ABBY said from somewhere behind her.

Claire barely heard her over the rattle of plates she was stacking on the buffet table. She threw a glance over her shoulder and laughed. "You might want to check out my latest podcast, honey. I just told my listeners never to start conversations with their spouses using those four little words. They make it sound as if something bad is going on."

"But we *really* need to talk," Abby said.

"One second, honey." Claire slid the flower arrangement in the middle of the table more to the right. "Can you see if the bartender has everything he needs?"

"Claire, please."

Something in Abby's tone made the hairs on Claire's neck stand on end, but she shook off the feeling. It was the day of their engagement party. Nothing unpleasant was allowed to intrude. She turned around.

Abby stood in the middle of their dining room, her back ramrod straight, her face pale, and the cocktail dress Claire had picked out for her to wear to the party suspiciously absent.

Claire tensed. "What's wrong? Why aren't you dressed yet? Our guests will be arriving any moment."

"I know, but I…" Abby's gaze darted to the bartender and to the cellist they had hired to provide unobtrusive background music. "Can we talk in the kitchen for a second?"

After one last glance back at the buffet table to make sure everything was the way she wanted it, Claire nodded and followed her.

Abby pulled out a stool from the kitchen island. "Sit."

That strange sense of dread niggled at the back of Claire's mind again. She eyed the stool. "We don't have time right now. Can't this wait?"

"No," Abby said, stony-faced. "It can't. I've tried to talk to you all day, but you haven't sat still even for a second."

Heat suffused Claire's face. "I want to make sure everything is perfect."

Abby squeezed her eyes shut and then opened them again. For the first time in seven years, Claire couldn't read the look in the familiar blue irises. "Listen, Claire. I love you."

Claire beamed. "I love you too." She chuckled. "Which is a good thing since we're planning to get married."

"But I'm not in love with you anymore," Abby added.

The floor tilted beneath Claire's feet. She swayed and grabbed hold of the stool. "W-what? D-did you just say…?"

"I can't marry you."

A whooshing sound started to pulse in Claire's ears. "You don't mean that!"

Abby looked at her with a grave expression. "I'm afraid I do." Her voice was low and shaky, yet there was conviction in her tone too.

"But…but w-why? Is there someone else?" The thought stabbed her in the chest like a dagger.

"No. But going through with this would make us both unhappy."

"Unhappy?" Claire echoed. That was something her clients said during their couples therapy sessions. It didn't apply to her and Abby. "How can you say that? We're perfect together!"

"Perfect?" Abby laughed, a sound bare of any humor. "We rarely see each other. That's not perfect in my book."

"So we both have demanding jobs."

"No, Claire." Abby roughly shook her head. "I have a demanding job. You have an obsession. I'm tired of playing second fiddle to your job."

Claire bit her lip. "I could tell our office assistant not to fill my six o'clocks anymore and come home an hour early."

Abby's closed body language never changed. Her arms were folded over her chest so tightly that Claire wondered how she could even breathe. "Yeah, but that's the thing. Even when you're home, you never stop. You do a lot of things that your job doesn't really require. You're either recording a podcast, planning the next seminar, or working on your book. Other psychologists don't do all that stuff."

"Yeah, but other psychologists also don't want to take over a counseling center one day. I have to get my name out there, so just counseling clients isn't enough." Claire struggled to keep the defensiveness from her tone but had a feeling she was failing. "Besides, I'm done with the book now, so there's nothing stopping us from spending more time together."

Abby sighed. "I'm not sure that's what I want any longer. Even in your private life, you micromanage every little detail." She waved her hand in the direction of the buffet in the dining room. "It's exhausting!"

The words and Abby's tone were like a slap to the face. Stung, Claire flinched back. "I'm trying to create a nice home…a nice life for both of us."

"It's not working for me, Claire. I don't want to hurt you, but…it just isn't working."

"And you realize that now—five minutes before our engagement party? If you had any doubts about us, why didn't you talk to me when I first proposed to you?"

"I…I…I wanted to. Really. But…" Abby shrugged and stared off into space. "I guess I didn't know how to bring it up, so I tried to ignore it and hoped everything would get better."

It sounded like a bad joke. Here she was—a successful therapist who gave seminars on communication in relationships, and her own fiancée couldn't even talk to her?

Claire stared at the three-carat engagement ring on her finger. This had to be a bad dream. She would wake up any second, and then Abby and she would laugh about her stupid nightmare.

"Okay, so you have your doubts." She swallowed heavily. "But that's no reason to throw it all away. Maybe it's just wedding jitters or the stress of planning the party and the wedding. Just a rough patch. Every relationship has them."

That was what she always told her clients, but she had never believed that she would one day experience one too. There hadn't been any signs.

Or had she just not seen them?

"We can make it work." Claire tried to reach out and touch her, but Abby pulled her arm away before she could make contact. "We could go to couples therapy. I'm sure Renata could recommend a good thera—"

"No. The last thing we need is for you to tell our therapist what methods to use or how to do her job."

"I wouldn't do that."

Abby snorted. "Yes, you would. I'm done, Claire. I'll move out first thing tomorrow morning."

Done. Move out. The words echoed through Claire, filling spaces that had been overflowing with happiness and anticipation only five minutes earlier.

The doorbell rang.

Claire woke from her daze. *Our guests!* She pressed both hands to her mouth. "Oh God! What are we supposed to tell our friends and colleagues… and my parents?"

"You are the one who cares about appearances. You figure it out." Abby pushed past her and walked out, stopping at the bar to down a glass of champagne.

Claire sank onto the stool and stared after her.

Chapter 2

Two months later

THE RINGING OF HER CELL phone made Claire look up from the patient file she had been reviewing. She had been staring at the same sentence for twenty minutes without registering a word. It seemed that was all she'd been doing for the past two months: staring. She had stared at the movers who had carried out boxes upon boxes of Abby's things, stared at Abby when she had handed over her key and her engagement ring, and stared at Abby's photo that she couldn't bring herself to remove from her desk.

She swallowed down the lump those memories had formed in her throat and squared her shoulders. *Come on. Pick up.* It could be a client in a crisis. But a glance at the display revealed that it was Mercedes, her friend and agent.

Oh, great. Mercedes was traveling a lot, so they hadn't talked in a while—since before Abby had called off the engagement, actually. Had Mercedes heard about the breakup now that she was back from Europe?

For a second, Claire considered not picking up. She wanted to forget about her failed relationship, not recount the painful details again, but she forced herself to be an adult and lifted the phone to her ear. "Hi, Mercedes."

"Guess what?"

Claire wasn't in the mood for guessing games, but she was used to keeping her own emotions in check, so she patiently said, "You won the lottery and are moving to the Bahamas?"

Mercedes snorted. "I wish. Not quite, but I've got good news anyway."

"I could use some good news," Claire muttered under her breath and then asked more loudly, "What is it?"

"Remember that publisher I pitched your manuscript to?"

Claire clutched the phone. "They want it?"

"It's not a definite yes, but based on your outline and the first five chapters we sent them, they think it might be a good fit for them. If we play our cards right, that book deal is yours, my friend."

"Wow, that's...wow." She had been working on the book for the past two years, first writing it and then trying to get it published. Now it was finally happening. At least one thing in her life wasn't falling apart. "So, how do we get the ball rolling?"

"Well, how does your schedule look at the end of June? Ms. Huge, their acquisitions editor, wants to read the rest of the manuscript and then meet you, so if you could take a few days off to fly to New York..."

Claire reached for her planner and leafed through it. The end of June... That would give her two months to clear her schedule. "That should be doable."

"Great. Then I'll let Ms. Huge know you and Abby will gladly meet her, provided that Abby will be able to take off a few days too."

"Sure." Then it hit her. "Uh, Abby?"

"Yeah. Ms. Huge said she's looking forward to meeting you and your fiancée." Mercedes chuckled. "Guess she wants to meet the woman who inspired the book about thriving love lives."

Claire took off her glasses and kneaded the bridge of her nose. She stared at the slightly out-of-focus version of Abby, who smiled at her from behind the glass of the picture frame on her desk. "There's, um, a problem with that. Abby and I..." She breathed in through her nose and out through her mouth. No matter how often she had to say it, it wasn't getting any easier. "We called off the engagement."

A gasp filtered through the line. Then there was only silence for a few moments.

"What did you just say?"

Claire refused to repeat it. Having to say it once was bad enough.

"Jesus, Claire! When did that happen? Your engagement party was barely two months ago, when I was in London!"

"Um, yeah. It happened around that time."

"Why didn't you tell me?"

"I…I guess I wasn't ready to talk about it." So far, she had kept the breakup on a need-to-know basis.

"I'm so sorry." Mercedes groaned. "Dammit. That might be a deal breaker for the guys from Wishing Tree Publishing."

"What? But that changes nothing!"

"It changes everything. In the nonfiction sector, the author and her marketability are as important as the book's content. You're lucky they didn't bat an eye at you being gay. But if they find out you're single, they won't be happy."

"So we'll tell them I'm focusing on my career and the book right now. What's wrong with that?"

"Nothing—if you're writing a book on how to achieve your career goals. But last year, I pitched them a really good book on parenting. It was the best thing I have ever read on that topic. But they rejected it, just because the author doesn't have kids herself. It's about believability. How can they expect their readers to buy a book called *The Art of Lasting Relationships* if the author can't even make her own relationship last?"

Claire sucked in a sharp breath and rubbed her breastbone. That was the crux of the matter, wasn't it? With her decision to call off the engagement, Abby had changed much more than just Claire's relationship status. Now her work life was in tatters too.

The silence stretched between them until Mercedes cleared her throat and said, "I'm sorry."

"Isn't there anything we can do?" Claire's dream of having her book published had been within her grasp, and she wasn't ready to have that part of her life crumble the way her relationship had.

"Unless you have a replacement fiancée lying around somewhere, I'm afraid that ship has sailed." Mercedes paused. "Oooh, wait a minute! That could actually work."

"What could work?" Claire hadn't heard any workable plan.

"If we find someone who'll fly to New York with you and pretend to be your fiancée…"

Claire shook her head. "You're insane."

"I thought psychologists aren't allowed to use words like that to label people."

"The APA would make an exception for this crazy suggestion. Really, Mercedes! How would we even find someone who'd be willing to go along with something like that? Put out an ad on Craigslist? *Fake fiancée needed, no wifely duties required.*"

"No," Mercedes said. "Working with an amateur in such a delicate situation wouldn't be a good idea. We'd enlist a pro."

"You want me to hire an escort?" Claire blurted. *Oops.* That had come out a little too loudly. She pressed a hand to her mouth and glanced at the door, hoping no one in the counseling center's reception area had heard her. She didn't need any rumors about her hiring call girls on top of all her other problems.

"Not that kind of pro," Mercedes said. "This is LA, the city of smog and unemployed actors. I bet we could find someone who'd be willing to take over the lead role as your fiancée."

For a second, Claire was tempted. A business arrangement with clear roles and expectations would be so much easier to handle than messy relationships. But true chemistry couldn't be faked. No one would fall for it, and even if they did, it was completely unethical. "No, it would never work."

"Trust me, with the right person, it would."

Trust me, Claire repeated to herself. That was the problem. She could no longer trust anyone, not even her own judgment. *Especially* not her own judgment. "No," she said again. "I guess we'll just have to keep pitching it to other publishers."

A knock came at the door. Tanya, the center's office assistant, stuck her head into the room. "Dr. Renshaw, your ten o'clock is here."

Claire gave her a nod. "Tell them to come in, please." To Mercedes, she said, "I have to go."

Thankfully, her ten o'clock appointment didn't require much therapeutic finesse. The Varneys had been her clients for half a year, and today was their final session.

Claire sat in her oversized leather chair facing the couch and regarded them across the low coffee table. What a difference compared to their very first session! Back then, both had clung to the armrests on either end of the couch, sitting as far apart as possible. Now they were holding hands, their legs touching from hip to ankle.

Normally, Claire would have been overjoyed. She lived for moments like this, when she realized she had made a difference in her patients' lives. But today it drove home the failure of her own relationship. Why couldn't she and Abby have fought for their relationship the way the Varneys had? Had Abby considered it not worth fighting for? Tears burned in her eyes.

"Are you okay?" Mrs. Varney asked.

God, how unprofessional! Letting her emotions leak through like this had never happened to her before. She forced a smile, took a tissue from the box she kept on the table for her clients, and dashed it over her eyes. "Yes, of course. I'm just so happy for both of you. You did it. You really did it."

"Well, we had the best therapist in LA to help us." Mr. Varney grinned at her.

Claire smiled. "Thank you, but you two did all of the hard work."

The Varneys beamed at her, then at each other.

Their look of pure happiness hurt, but this time Claire had braced herself against it and was able to switch into therapist mode. "So," she looked from one to the other, "what do you think needs to happen for your relationship to continue to thrive instead of returning to the way it was when you first came to see me?"

***

Forty-five minutes later, the small, silver clock on the end table next to Claire indicated that the session was coming to an end. She wished the Varneys all the best and walked them to the door.

When they left the center, she slumped against the doorjamb and stared after them. God, she really needed to get a grip and stop all that staring!

"Hi, Claire."

A low voice next to her made Claire jump. When she whirled around, she came face-to-face with the last person she wanted to see: Dr. Vanessa West, one of the center's nine psychologists—and her biggest rival for clinical director once Renata retired in a couple of years.

Claire put on her best professional mask. "Hi, Vanessa."

Vanessa stepped closer and reached out to touch her arm.

What the heck? Claire stared at the hand on her arm. *What's up with her?* They weren't exactly friends.

"I'm so sorry to hear about your breakup."

Vanessa sounded sincere, but Claire stiffened. How on earth had Vanessa found out? Claire hadn't wanted it to become common knowledge at the center. Here she was supposed to be the one others came to for help, not the one with the problem. She hadn't even taken a day off so she could hole up at home and cry her eyes out. "Thanks," she forced out. "But it's okay, really."

"You're allowed to be heartbroken, you know? You need to let yourself feel it."

Claire didn't appreciate having that therapist voice used on her. "And I would, if I were heartbroken."

Vanessa blinked. "You aren't? But Linda said Abby was the one who ended it."

Dammit, Linda! Why did Abby's best friend have to run her big mouth and embarrass her in front of everyone? Claire struggled to keep her expression neutral. "It was an amicable breakup, and it happened two months ago. We have both moved on."

Vanessa raised her perfectly sculpted eyebrows and pierced her with that all-knowing therapist look. "Really?"

"Yes, really," Claire said. "In fact, I've already started seeing someone else."

They stared at each other.

Claire was just as surprised as Vanessa. Why had she said that? She wasn't normally one to blurt out ridiculous stuff like that, but now she couldn't take it back, at least not without humiliating herself even more—and she would rather die than to do that. Her therapist mask firmly in place, she held Vanessa's gaze.

"Well," Vanessa finally said, "good for you, I guess. But if you ever need to talk, let me know."

Hell would freeze over before that happened. Vanessa would use any sign of weakness on her part to gain an advantage. "Thanks. But my girlfriend is a wonderful listener."

"You'll have to introduce us sometime." Vanessa patted Claire's arm. "Why don't you bring her to Renata's party?"

"Uh, I'll see if she can make it. Now if you'll excuse me. I've got paperwork to do before my next clients arrive." She stepped back and closed her office door firmly between them before slumping into the chair behind her desk.

God, what had she been thinking? Now Vanessa expected her to show up at the party with a doting girlfriend, and Claire wasn't even ready for a casual date. She had painted herself into a corner with no way out but forward.

Her gaze went to the phone. Should she call Mercedes and…? *No.* It was silly. Ridiculous. Dangerous. If any of her clients entertained an idea like that, she would definitely advise against it.

But if she didn't present a new girlfriend or even fiancée soon, she'd lose the book deal and would go from being a respected couples therapist to the poor woman her colleagues pitied because she couldn't keep her own relationship going—much less anyone else's.

She reached for the phone.

As soon as Mercedes picked up, she blurted out, "I'll do it," so she wouldn't have time to back out.

"Uh, do what?" Mercedes asked.

Abby's blue eyes seemed to watch her from the framed photo, judging her, taunting her.

Claire reached out and picked up the photo. She traced the familiar features with her thumb, but it didn't bring her the feeling of comfort and safety it had evoked in the past.

"Do what?" Mercedes asked again.

After one last second of hesitation, Claire dropped the photo into the wastebasket with a resounding *thud* and took a deep breath. "Get a fake fiancée."

Chapter 3

Two days later, Claire jumped up from the visitor's chair in Mercedes's office. "You did what?"

"I put out a casting call."

"Do I need to remind you that you are not Steven Spielberg? This is my life, not a blockbuster movie!"

Mercedes held up her hands in a placating way. "How long have we known each other?"

"Um, ever since you helped Renata get her book published, so about… five years, I guess."

"And in those five years, have I ever steered you wrong?" Mercedes continued without waiting for a reply. "There's a reason directors put out casting calls. If they are trying to fill the role of the love interest, they have actors come in to do a chemistry test."

An image of Bunsen burners and bubbling chemicals rose in Claire's mind's eye. "Chemistry test?"

"Yeah, you know. To see if the actors have a connection that will convince the audience they're really in love."

Like Bogart and Bacall or Powell and Loy. Claire nodded to herself. That actually made sense. Kind of. "So you told your contacts in the movie industry…what?" *That you're looking for an actress willing to play the fiancée of a pathetic couples therapist who couldn't even save her own relationship?*

"I kept it as vague as possible," Mercedes said. "Basically, I told them it's a special project that needs absolute discretion."

Discretion was good. Claire's tension eased. "So how many actresses have you lined up out there?" She pointed to the reception area of Mercedes's literary agency.

"Just one for today. If this one doesn't work out, I have a couple of others that look promising. But I thought we should keep the circle small for now and start with the one my friend Jill recommended."

"Anyone I'd know?" Claire asked.

Mercedes shook her head. "If you would recognize her from a movie, Ms. Huge or someone else at the publishing house might too. We need someone with acting experience, but not a recognizable TV personality. Plus even you can't afford to hire Angelina Jolie."

"Right." Claire squinted over at her agent. "Have you done this before?" Usually, Claire was the one with the detailed battle plan, but now Mercedes seemed to have thought of everything.

"Held auditions for a fake fiancée?" Mercedes chuckled. "Nope. But it's kinda fun, don't you think?"

"Fun?" Claire's idea of fun was a bubble bath and a glass of Pinot Noir, not trying to stop her tattered life from fraying even more by coming up with a harebrained scheme.

"Yeah. Come on." Mercedes patted her on the back. "Let's go watch her make googly eyes at you."

"What?"

"Chemistry test, remember?"

"Oh Christ." Why the hell had she ever thought this was a good idea?

How strange. Lana looked around the waiting room, then glanced at her wristwatch. She was only a couple of minutes early, so where were the other actresses? If an assistant hadn't told her to wait right here, she would have thought she was in the wrong place.

Usually, at auditions, she was surrounded by at least a dozen actresses who looked like her, all full-figured brunettes in their late twenties who were nervously studying their lines and eyeing the competition.

But this time, she was waiting alone, and there was no script to study. Did the casting director want her to do a cold read?

Her friend Jill hadn't told her much—or anything, really—about this movie. Apparently, the person Jill had talked to had been pretty secretive and had revealed only that they needed an "unconventional actress for an unconventional project," preferably a lesbian or bisexual woman.

It was probably some small independent film that no one had ever heard of. But at this point, Lana wasn't picky about her roles.

In the two years since the accident, her sole claim to stardom had been playing a corpse on a crime show. With just a handful of commercials and her job at the coffee shop, she could barely make ends meet.

"Ms. Henderson?"

Lana looked up. "Yes?"

A Latin American woman in her forties stood before her. "I'm Mercedes Soto. Thanks for coming."

"My pleasure." Lana stood and focused on not limping as she followed her down the hall to the audition room.

The first thing she noticed after entering was that there was no camera and no camera operator. Apparently, they weren't taping the audition. Just how low-budget was this production?

But a badly paid acting gig was better than none.

Lana gripped the folder with her headshot and her admittedly modest acting resume and smiled at the only other person in the room, a woman she guessed to be a few years older than her own twenty-nine. Was she the casting director's assistant?

No, Lana decided. She was too well-dressed for that. Everything about the woman was refined: her blonde hair secured in an elegant chignon, the turquoise silk scarf knotted around her neck that gave her pale gray eyes a greenish tint, and the formfitting pencil skirt hugging her slim hips.

When the woman crossed the room to shake Lana's hand, Lana noticed her shoes. The modestly heeled pumps looked as if they had cost more than Lana's rent.

Definitely not an assistant. Maybe someone sponsoring the movie?

Whoever she was, her expression didn't bode well for Lana's chances of getting the part. The woman stared at her with obvious dismay. Had she wanted to cast a different type of actress? Maybe one of those size-zero stick figures? Or was it the scar or the tattoo peeking out from the short sleeve of the blouse she'd bought for the audition?

Lana held her head up high and looked her square in the eyes. She had encountered that attitude hundreds of times in showbiz and refused to let it intimidate her—or let it make her hate the way she looked.

As if she had guessed what Lana was thinking, the woman's expression cleared. "Hi, I'm Claire Renshaw." Her tone was carefully neutral, and she didn't add anything that told Lana what role she played in the production.

"Lana Henderson. Nice to meet you."

The woman's hand was slender and felt pleasant—if a little damp—in her own. Why the hell was she so nervous? Was she an actress reading for a role in the movie too?

Lana glanced around. No script on the table. Apparently, they wanted her to do improv. No problem. Lana had learned to work with unexpected situations and could improvise at a moment's notice.

"Here's what I want you to do," Ms. Soto said. "Make me believe you're madly in love with Claire. You're comfortable being, um, close to a woman, right?"

Lana smiled. For once, being a lesbian worked in her favor. "Very comfortable." Playing a romantic scene with Claire Renshaw definitely wouldn't be a hardship. Even if she was too stuffy and uptight to be Lana's type, she was undeniably attractive. "Any directions?"

"No," Ms. Soto said. "Just show me how you'd sell the two of you being deeply in love."

"All right." Lana took a moment to center herself, pushed back all thoughts of rent and medical bills, and slipped into the role of Claire's lover. "Claire." She dropped her voice to a sexy murmur.

Claire's gaze flicked to her. A frown wrinkled her smooth brow.

Oh man. That looks like indigestion, not infatuation! Whoever Claire was, she wasn't a fellow actress. She didn't give Lana much to work with. *God, I hate working with amateurs.* But she was determined to land this role, so she took a step closer, right into Claire's personal space.

The other woman's body heat engulfed her, and a light, springlike fragrance teased Lana's nose. *Hmm. Nice.* She allowed herself to react to it and lean even closer, using her body's instinctive response to sell them being in love.

If circumstances had been different, Lana might have tried to get the casting director's attention with a hot kiss, but she had a feeling if she tried

15

that, it would earn her a slap instead of the role. So she gently took Claire's hand and lifted it to her lips.

Claire watched her with wide eyes, her hand limp in Lana's grasp.

Definitely not one for improvisation.

Lana turned Claire's hand around and teased the fair skin at the inside of her wrist with her breath before whispering a kiss on the pulse throbbing beneath her lips.

A visible shudder went through Claire. "Uh, I think that's enough." She tugged her hand free and stepped away.

Enough? They hadn't even improvised a conversation.

"Would you mind waiting outside for a second?" Ms. Soto asked.

Lana perked up. That wasn't the "don't call us, we'll call you" she had expected. Had she done so well that they would now bring in the real actor or actress she'd star with in the movie and test them together?

"Sure. I'll be right outside." Lana nearly skipped to the door, despite her protesting leg. In her mind's eye, she could already see her name rolling down the screen in the closing credits of a romance flick.

<hr />

Mercedes beamed at her. "What do you think? She was perfect, wasn't she?"

"Perfect?" Claire echoed. Then, suddenly reminded of that conversation when Abby had broken up with her, she paused and inhaled deeply, trying to wrestle down the rising nausea. "She's about as far from perfect as you can get! No one will believe for even a second that I'm engaged to someone like her!"

"Why? What's wrong with her?"

"What isn't?" Claire shot back. "She's not my type at all." She liked women who were successful, sophisticated, and reliable. Someone like Abby. Claire sighed. Lana Henderson couldn't be more different from Abby if she'd tried. "Did you see the tattoo?"

The short sleeves of the actress's blouse revealed a tattoo of what looked like a bird of prey. Its wings and long tail feathers were inked in all the colors of the rainbow, while its head and body glowed in hues of red and orange, almost as if the bird were on fire.

"Did you see the scar?" Mercedes asked softly.

Claire's anger deflated, and she lowered her gaze. "Yes, I did."

A jagged, purple scar zigzagged horizontally across Lana's left arm, just above the bend of her elbow. The inked bird spread its wings above it, gripping the scar in its claws as if it were a snake.

If Claire had been in her shoes, she would have chosen a tattoo that concealed the scar rather than one that called attention to it—not that she was the type to get a tattoo. She also wouldn't have worn a short-sleeved blouse that revealed the scar during an audition.

Why on earth had Mercedes thought a woman like Lana Henderson would be a good fit for the role of her fiancée?

Claire blew out a breath. "Listen, I'm not trying to be mean."

The poor actress didn't deserve to be judged this harshly. She might actually be a nice person, and with her sun-kissed skin, her dazzling girl-next-door smile, and her wavy, light brown hair, she was definitely pretty. Her voice was sexy, reminding Claire of Lauren Bacall or another sultry movie star from an old black-and-white movie. If she paid more attention to what she wore, Claire thought she'd be downright stunning.

"But she's not what we're looking for. We need someone…classy. She had the price tag still sticking out from the back of her blouse, for Christ's sake!"

"That's exactly why she's perfect for the role of your fiancée." Mercedes held her gaze. "No offense, Claire, but you can be a little…intimidating to other women."

Claire crossed her arms. "What's that supposed to mean?"

"You're so put-together. So perfect. A stinking rich family, a doctorate from an expensive private university, and a house that looks like a feature in *Architectural Digest*… Few women can live up to that. What we need is someone more approachable at your side. Someone your readers will be able to relate to. Someone who's curvy, tattooed, and having the occasional wardrobe malfunction."

Claire loosened her stance. "You're the expert. But please tell me you at least ran a background check on her."

"Of course. There are no skeletons hiding in her closet—and she isn't either. Jill says she's out and proud, so no one will bat an eye when she suddenly announces her engagement to a woman."

"Good, but that's not really what I'm worried about."

"I checked her out, Claire. Really. I wouldn't make you live with an ax murderer."

A heavy feeling settled in the pit of Claire's stomach. "Live with...? Wait a minute! Who said anything about living together?"

"If you want people to think you're in love and committed to each other, you can't keep separate houses."

"Who says we can't be a happily committed couple who enjoys having our own space?"

"Actually, you do." Mercedes opened a desk drawer and pulled out a stack of paper. "Chapter five." She opened the manuscript, leafed through it, and then read, "Moving in together before getting married will give you a realistic idea about cute and not-so-cute little quirks and will teach you to work as a team in everyday life." She slapped the manuscript onto her desk in front of Claire. "Those are your words, Claire. If you want people to take you seriously, you've got to practice what you preach."

"Can't I rewrite that chapter instead?" Claire grumbled.

Mercedes just gave her a look.

Oh God. This is a nightmare. Claire rubbed her face with both hands and groaned into her palms. "Okay," she said from behind her fingers. "I'll do it."

Mercedes put the manuscript back into the drawer. "So I can tell her she's got the job?"

Claire sighed. Maybe picking someone who wasn't her type had its advantages. At least there was no danger of her falling in love with this actress. This would be a mutually beneficial business arrangement, nothing more. "Yes. I guess she'll do."

Lana drilled her nails into her palms as she followed Ms. Soto into the audition room. *Oh, please, please, please...* She looked at the two women, trying to read their expressions.

Ms. Soto smiled at her, but Claire looked about as happy as someone who had just received a prison sentence.

Was that a good or a bad sign?

"Please take a seat, Ms. Henderson," Ms. Soto said.

"Lana, please."

"Then please call me Mercedes."

Lana nodded and took the chair next to Claire, facing Mercedes, who sat behind the desk.

"Before we tell you anything else, we need you to sign this." Mercedes slid two sheets of paper across the desk.

Lana couldn't help grinning. "Does that mean I've got the role?"

"Yes."

A flare of elation rushed through Lana. She barely held herself back from pumping her fist. "Great." She nodded in Claire's direction. "So will she be my co-star?"

"I guess you could say that."

"That's…uh, wonderful." Lana pasted an enthusiastic smile on her face. "Working with new actresses is always so…exciting!" She flicked her gaze to Claire and gave her an encouraging nod. "I mean, we've all been where you are with your acting, just starting out. Don't worry, I'll give you some pointers. Unless, of course, you really aren't comfortable starring in a lesbian movie." Maybe that was why her fellow actress had been so wooden. She turned back toward Mercedes and tried not to look hopeful when she added, "In that case, maybe recasting my co-star might be a good idea."

As soon as she'd said it, she scolded herself. An actress with no real roles in the past two years couldn't afford to be picky about her co-star. What if Claire was friends with the producer or something, and that was how she'd gotten the role?

Claire scowled at her. Somehow, her elegant features still managed to look refined.

Mercedes giggled. "I'm afraid recasting is not an option."

"I wish it were," Claire muttered.

"No problem." Lana had worked with untalented actresses before. It beat having no acting work at all. "So, where do I sign?"

"Um, hold your horses," Mercedes said. "You might not want the role after hearing all the details."

Why wouldn't she? Roles for more curvaceous actresses weren't exactly in abundant supply in Hollywood, so she would say yes to pretty much any gig. Unless…

"This isn't a porn production, is it?"

Claire started to sputter, then cough. Her fair cheeks flushed. "No! Nothing like that."

"There's actually even a celibacy clause in the contract," Mercedes added.

A celibacy clause? What the hell? This wasn't some kind of Christian production, was it?

"I'll explain in a second. But first, I need you to sign this." Mercedes nodded down at the papers on her desk.

Lana leaned forward and picked up the top sheet, expecting it to be the contract. Instead, the paper said *non-disclosure agreement.* They wanted her to sign an NDA? She looked from Mercedes to Claire and back. Jeez, what kind of movie were they filming?

Well, I guess you'll find out once you sign it. She took the pen Mercedes handed her, signed on the dotted line, and slid the agreement across the desk.

Mercedes took it and put it in a drawer. "Do you want to explain your situation, Claire?"

Claire slid her palms over her black pencil skirt as if wanting to remove invisible wrinkles. "I'm actually not an actress."

No shit, Sherlock. Lana smiled. "I kinda guessed that. But we've all got to start somewhere."

"No, you don't understand. I don't have any ambition to become an actress. I'm a psychologist."

"Oh. So this is some kind of documentary or a reality TV show? Please tell me you don't want me to play a patient. Because I've got to tell you, ladies, that's pretty much the only couch that I avoid at all costs—well, that and casting couches." Lana managed to lighten her tone and make it sound like a joke, but she was actually serious.

Claire shook her head. "No, don't worry. I don't want you to be my patient." She inhaled and exhaled deeply, as if she needed to brace herself for what she was about to say next. "I want you to be my girlfriend."

For a moment, all Lana could do was stare at her. Was this some kind of joke? Then the humor of the situation overcame her. "Shouldn't you at least buy me dinner first?"

Mercedes muffled a giggle behind her palm.

Claire wasn't laughing, though. She glared at Lana.

20

"Would someone please tell me what this is all about?" Lana asked.

"Claire is trying to get her relationship-advice book published," Mercedes finally said.

Lana nearly groaned out loud. *Oh man.* So Claire was one of those. A self-appointed relationship guru who made money off vulnerable people. People like Lana's mother. "What exactly would my role be in this scenario?"

"Well, you see, Claire's fiancée recently broke up with her, and if the publisher finds out, her book deal could be in trouble. If you want to sell a book on lasting relationships, you need to actually be in one."

"That makes sense, I guess." Lana turned her head to look at Claire, who was white-knuckling the armrests of her chair. "So let me get this straight, Ms. Renshaw...or not so straight, in this case. You want me to be your fake girlfriend."

"Fake fiancée, actually," Claire said. "And it's *Dr.* Renshaw."

"Wow. I don't know if I want to contribute to that."

"I can understand your concern," Mercedes said. "I mean, it's a highly unusual situation and not exactly what you were expecting when you came here today."

That wasn't what made Lana hesitate. But did she really want to help Claire get her self-help book published? One more book that told women like her mother that they needed to be in a relationship and shell out hundreds or thousands of dollars for intimacy workshops and get-in-touch-with-your-feelings retreats in order to be happy.

But then again, her landlord wouldn't care about her personal opinion on self-help books when her rent was overdue.

"What kind of compensation would I receive?"

Mercedes took another document from a drawer and handed it to her. "You'll find that information on page two of the contract."

Lana turned the top page and found the number. *Holy crap. Fifty thousand?* That was more than she had earned with her acting in the past two years. If Claire could drop that amount of money on a ruse like this, therapists were definitely overpaid.

"Plus I'll pay for all expenses such as any new articles of clothing you might need," Claire added.

Was that a snipe at her style of dress? Lana chose to ignore it. "What exactly do you expect me to do for that kind of money? We wouldn't actually have to get married, would we?"

Claire's eyes went wide. "No!"

Jeez, how about making the idea of getting married to me not sound quite so horrible?

"No," Claire repeated more softly. "I guess we could just have a long engagement. That would be pretty believable, actually, since I'm very busy with my job."

"How long exactly are we talking?" Lana asked.

Claire shrugged. "For however long it takes for me to get the book deal. I'm meeting with the acquisitions editor at the end of June, so my guess is two or three months at the most. Once the contract is signed, we could quietly dissolve our engagement."

That didn't sound so bad. It wasn't as if she had any exciting roles lined up for the next couple of months anyway. "That works for me. If it takes longer, I could make myself available." For some extra payment, of course.

"Great, but I'm hoping that won't be necessary," Claire said.

"What would my duties as your fiancée be during that time? You don't expect any bedroom privileges, do you?" She made good use of her acting skills and lent her tone an almost horrified note, just to get back at Claire for sounding so appalled at the idea of marrying her.

"No, of course not! It would be purely a business arrangement, a relationship only on paper, not when we're alone."

"Plus we'd also expect you to not sleep with or date anyone else during the length of the contract," Mercedes added. "We can't have anyone think that you're cheating on Claire. Is that a problem for you?"

"Not in the least." Lana had been single for two years and had no intention of changing that anytime soon. She read over the rest of the contract—the celibacy clause, the compensation, the demand for twenty-four/seven availability. All were fine with her. Then she paused and looked up. "Cohabitation?"

Claire sighed. "It would be best if you'd move in with me to prove that we're a happily committed couple."

"Couldn't we be a happily committed couple who decides to wait to share a bedroom—and a house—until we're married?"

Mercedes laughed. "I think you two will get along just fine."

Lana and Claire glanced at each other.

Claire looked as unconvinced as Lana felt. Finally, Claire said, "It's not as if we'll be living together forever." She sounded as if she needed to convince herself as much as Lana. "Once I sign the contract, you can move out right away, and I will tell everyone we broke up because I realized I'm not over my fiancée...ex-fiancée."

Lana considered it. Fifty thousand dollars was a lot of money, and it was an acting gig...kind of...even if she wouldn't be able to put it on her resume. She would even save on utilities for a couple of months while she lived with Claire.

Before she could talk herself out of it, she picked up the pen again and signed the contract. "Congratulations, sweetheart." She batted her lashes at Claire. "You got yourself a fiancée."

Chapter 4

LANA SLID HER ROLLER SKATES into a moving box, closed it, and watched as her friend Jill taped it shut.

"How did the audition go last week?" Jill asked when they started on the next box.

"It was a disaster." Lana drew on her acting skills to keep her face impassive and not give away that it hadn't been an ordinary audition. "My co-star was as talented as a piece of wood, and when I got home, I discovered that the price tag was still sticking out from my blouse."

"So you didn't get the part?"

Lana gave a noncommittal grunt that could mean yes or no.

"I'm sorry. I thought for sure they'd take you. The description of what my acquaintance said they were looking for fit you to a T—someone unconventional, not a cookie-cutter Hollywood starlet."

"It's okay," Lana said lightly. She didn't want Jill to feel bad. "At least this way, I'll have more time for my new relationship."

Jill straightened from where she'd been bent over a box. "You know, I didn't want to say anything, considering I'm always pushing you to go out and date, but this is crazy." She swiped a strand of her red hair out of her face and regarded Lana with a shake of her head. "Up until a couple of days ago, I had never heard of this woman, and you're already moving in with her! How long have you even known her?"

Lana ignored the question. "Hey, you and Crash moved in together pretty fast too, didn't you?"

Crash, Jill's girlfriend, squeezed past them with a moving box. "Not as fast as I wanted to because this beautiful woman was too busy trying to convince both of us that what we had was just a physical thing." She paused behind Jill and pressed a kiss to the back of her neck.

Jill shuddered and leaned in to her. "Well, I didn't think there could be a happy ending for us, but I've never been so glad to be proven wrong."

When Jill turned around and they kissed, Lana looked away to give them some privacy.

Finally, Crash tore herself away to carry the moving box outside.

Jill fanned herself, flushed from Crash's kisses. "If your new girlfriend is anything like Crash, I guess I can't blame you too much for falling head over heels."

They both turned and watched Crash as she slipped out the door.

Sweat gleamed on her bare arms, which were well muscled from her work as a stuntwoman. Crash threw a glance back over her shoulder and flashed Jill one of her confident, sexy grins. In her ripped jeans and faded tank top, she looked as different from Claire as possible while still belonging to the same species.

"No," Lana said. "She's nothing like Crash. She's..." *Straitlaced and posh.* "...hard to describe." She let out a dreamy sigh. "Words can't really do her justice."

"Do you have a picture of Wonder Woman?"

Damn. She should have thought of that before she had told Jill about her supposed new relationship. But then again, she didn't have much experience in lying to her friends. She really hated deceiving them, but she had signed a non-disclosure agreement, and if she told anyone about this fake fiancée deal, Claire would probably sue her ass faster than she could say *breach of confidentiality.*

"She's not Wonder Woman," Lana said to buy herself some time.

"She is if she finally got you to believe in love again after what Katrina did to you."

Lana didn't want to talk about her ex, so she pulled her smartphone from the back pocket of her jeans. Therapists like Claire usually had a website, didn't they? She googled *Claire Renshaw, couples therapist.*

Bingo! There she was.

Dressed all in pastel colors, Claire certainly looked the part of the compassionate, but reserved counselor as she smiled into the camera.

25

Lana scanned her bio. *LMFT, PsyD...* Claire—or, rather, Dr. Renshaw—had more letters behind her name than the alphabet. She had graduated summa cum laude from USC, a university Lana would have never been able to afford, even if she'd been interested in getting a degree.

Jill perched on a moving box and pulled down Lana's hand so she could see the display of the smartphone. "Is that her?"

"Yes, that's Claire."

Jill looked at the picture and let out a wolf whistle. "She's hot! Well, if you go for the more...um..."

"...uptight type?" Lana chuckled.

"Um, something like that. No offense."

"None taken. I know she's not my usual type, but..." Lana faltered and searched for a believable excuse.

"Well, sometimes the person we least expect to turns out to be exactly what we need," Jill said softly, her gaze on the door.

Lana suppressed a snort. Claire Renshaw certainly didn't have anything she needed—except for her money. "Yeah, I guess."

Jill turned her head to look at her. Her green eyes seemed to drill into Lana. "Is everything okay?"

"Yeah, why wouldn't it be?"

"Maybe because you're answering a question with a question? My therapist calls that deflection."

"You've got a therapist? You?" Her friend came across as an eternal optimist. When they had first met on the set of a TV show four years ago, that was what had immediately impressed Lana. Jill had always been quick to make a joke or a witty comment, even after a grueling fourteen-hour day on set.

Jill shrugged and studied the tips of her sneakers. "You know how things are in Tinseltown. Cattle calls are hell on the self-esteem, even for perfectly healthy people. But if you're an actress with MS..."

She didn't finish her sentence. She didn't need to.

Lana absentmindedly fingered the scar on her arm.

They looked at each other in silent understanding.

Then Jill pushed to her feet. "Let's get the rest of those boxes packed." She paused. "Oh, what about your furniture? That won't fit into Crash's SUV."

"Um…" Lana's mind raced as she searched for a good excuse. She couldn't very well tell her friend that she wasn't really moving out. She had told her roommate that she'd be gone for a couple of months because of a role—which was the truth, kind of. "I sold most of it to my roomie since I won't need it anymore. Claire has a bed and everything else I need."

Jill grinned. "I bet she does." When Lana poked her in the ribs, she just laughed. "Come on. The sooner we get all of the boxes packed, the sooner you can introduce us to Wonder Woman."

Oh shit. Lana didn't want to drag her friends into this charade, but how could she refuse without having Jill smell a rat?

Let's hope that Claire worked on her improv skills since last week. Apparently, they would have to start their acting sooner than expected.

———⟨∼∽∼⟩———

Lana had lived in LA for more than ten years, but she'd never been in this part of the city. Not that she'd ever have reason to be in such an upscale neighborhood. Palm trees and elegant homes lined the street. Her beat-up Volkswagen Rabbit stuck out like a sore thumb among the BMWs, Audis, Bentleys, and other luxury cars when she parked at the curb.

She glanced at her phone on the passenger seat to double-check the address Claire had emailed her.

This was it.

Lana peeked through the side window.

Behind a manicured lawn lay a sprawling Spanish-style one-story house. The reddish-brown terra-cotta tiles on the arcaded front patio gleamed in the afternoon sun and made the snow-white walls seem even whiter. Arched columns flanked the front door.

Wow. Maybe that cohabitation clause in the contract wasn't such a bad thing after all if she got to live in a house like this. It certainly beat the tiny apartment that she shared with a roommate.

Lana took a deep breath and climbed out of the car.

Crash let out a low whistle as she jumped down from behind the wheel of her midnight-blue SUV. "Wow! Looks like Lana's got herself a sugar momma!"

"Crash!" Jill came around the SUV and slapped her shoulder.

Lana winced but said nothing. Crash's joking remark hit a little too close to home since Claire was indeed paying her. But it was too late for moral scruples. She'd made her bed; now she'd have to lie in it. *Hopefully not literally.* From what Claire had said, they'd have separate bedrooms.

Each of them took a moving box and carried it along the tiled path, with Lana in the lead. She didn't allow herself to look around much, trying to pretend she'd walked that path a hundred times already.

Well, if she had, she would have known that the sprinkler system on the lawn was set to go off at this time.

A sudden hiss warned her, but with the moving box weighing her down, she couldn't duck out of the way. The spray of water hit her front, drenching her T-shirt and soaking the cardboard. She stood there for a second, frozen. When the next spray hit her, she let out a yelp and ran up the three steps to seek cover on the porch.

Water dripped onto the tiles. She shook herself. "What a welcome!"

Laughing, Jill and Crash joined her on the porch.

The moving box pressed to her chest with one arm, Lana willed her fingers not to tremble as she reached out and rang the doorbell.

"You don't have a key?" Jill asked.

"Uh, not yet."

The door swung open.

Claire was two inches shorter than Lana's five-foot nine, but there was one more step leading into the house, so Claire had a slight height advantage. For several seconds, she looked down at Lana and her drenched T-shirt as if Lana were delivering a package she had never ordered.

Lana gave her an Oscar-worthy infatuated smile. "Hi, honey."

"Uh, hi." Claire's gaze traveled over Lana.

Was is just Lana's imagination, or had she lingered on her breasts for a second?

Lana peeked over her shoulder at Jill and Crash. No time like the present to test her faking-a-relationship skills. She put down the box on the porch and wrapped her arms around Claire in what she hoped looked like a tender embrace.

Claire's slim body tensed in her arms, so Lana decided not to try to kiss her. Getting slapped would destroy the illusion of them as a couple. But she couldn't resist pressing close—not because of how surprisingly good Claire

28

felt against her but because she wanted to make Claire's shirt wet too, as a little punishment for not playing along.

When Lana finally let go, Claire stepped back and pulled her now-damp white blouse away from her skin with two fingers. "Uh, you're wet. What happened?"

Lana couldn't help herself. Teasing someone as uptight as Claire was just too much fun. She leaned forward with an impish grin and whispered just loud enough for Jill and Crash to hear, "That's what happens every time you're close."

Claire narrowed her eyes. Her lips twitched into something that looked more like a facial spasm than a smile.

Oh boy. If she doesn't lighten up and play along, it'll be a long two or three months!

Luckily, Jill cleared her throat before the silence could become awkward. "Actually, your sprinkler thought my smitten friend here needed to cool off." She stepped next to Lana and studied Claire. "So you are Wonde... I mean, Claire. I'm Jill, and this is my girlfriend, Kristine. But please call her Crash, or she won't answer."

Claire's eyebrows rose up her smooth forehead, but she didn't comment on the nickname. "Nice to meet you."

"I'd shake your hand, but..." Jill nodded down at the moving box in her arms.

"Oh. Sorry. Come on in, please." Belatedly, Claire moved aside to let them in.

Lana was the first one to enter. Her wet sneakers squelched over the cream-colored tiles. The entryway opened up into a spacious living area, which in turn flowed into a dining room.

She tilted her head back and stared up at the high vaulted ceiling. A skylight and two huge arched windows made the living room look even larger than it was. A burgundy leather couch and a matching recliner faced a seventy-inch flat-screen TV mounted to the wall. Two bookcases flanked a stone fireplace, and a sliding glass door led to the backyard.

Somehow, this open, airy house didn't seem to fit Claire, who stood by stiffly while her guests took in the living room.

Oops. Lana realized she wasn't doing a very good job playing the unimpressed girlfriend who'd been here many times before. Thankfully, Jill and Crash were just as busy staring and hadn't noticed.

Under the pretext of putting down the moving box, Lana looked around some more. Jeez, this place was as clean and tidy as a museum. The only things lying around were a few copies of the *Journal of Couples Therapy* on the coffee table.

Claire used the toes of her stylish loafers to push the sodden moving box out of the living room and onto the tiles of the entryway. "Um, would you mind taking off your shoes?" She pointed at Lana's sneakers, which had left drips of water all over the immaculate hardwood floor.

"Oh. Sorry." Lana toed off her wet sneakers and set them down next to the moving box. "I should go change." She glanced around. Where the hell was the bathroom…or her bedroom for that matter?

"Why don't I come with you and, um, say hello in private?" Claire said.

Lana grinned. *Nice rescue.* Maybe Claire wasn't totally useless when it came to this charade. "Good idea, honey." To Jill and Crash she said, "She's a little shy when it comes to PDAs."

Claire looked as if she wanted to kick her. "Um, if you'll excuse us for a minute. Put down those boxes wherever you want, and make yourself comfortable. We'll be right back." She grabbed Lana's hand and dragged her through an arched doorway.

As soon as the door of the guest room closed behind them, Claire dropped Lana's hand.

How could a little spray from the sprinkler do so much damage? Claire could only hope that her fake fiancée wasn't always so accident-prone, or she would embarrass her in front of the Wishing Tree Publishing staff. With her locks plastered to her head, Lana looked like a drowned rat.

Okay, admittedly, she looked more attractive than a drowned rat. Her white, nearly see-through T-shirt clung to her ample chest. Droplets of water dripped from her tangled hair and onto the floor. A single drop slid down her throat and pooled in the V of her shirt before sliding down into her cleavage.

When Claire noticed that her gaze had followed its path, she tore her eyes away. Heat climbed into her cheeks. She tried to tell herself it was just annoyance at the careless way Lana had treated her pristine hardwood floor.

It certainly wasn't that she was in any way attracted to her fake fiancée. She liked sophisticated women like Abby who kept fit and dressed well.

"I'll, uh, get you a towel." She ducked into the guest room's bath and used the few seconds alone to get herself together.

"Thanks." Lana took the towel she handed her.

Claire tried not to watch as she dabbed it over her scarred arm and the front of her almost transparent shirt. "I'd get you some dry clothes, but I don't think any of mine would fit you."

"Well, I brought my clothes. I just have to figure out which box has my T-shirts."

"You didn't label the boxes?"

Lana shook her head, spattering the mirror above the dresser with drops of water. She didn't even seem to notice.

Claire grimaced. *Ignore it.* They had more important things to focus on than a bit of water. "Why didn't you hire movers, like I suggested?"

"Why waste money? It's just a few boxes. My friends and I can handle it."

"I would have paid for the movers. Dragging your friends into this," Claire waved her hand back and forth between them, "wasn't necessary. The fewer people who know, the better."

"What was I supposed to do—move away without telling them?"

She's got a point there. Claire rubbed her chin. "No, of course not. But you didn't tell them about our…arrangement, did you?"

"I signed a non-disclosure agreement, didn't I?"

"You're deflecting."

Lana groaned. "Not you too. Can we amend the contract? No psychobabble while we're living together. You're supposed to be my lover, not my therapist."

"Deflection is not necessarily a psychological term. It's—" She snapped her mouth shut. Arguing about terminology wouldn't get them anywhere. "All right. I'll try to tone it down. So, what did you tell them?"

Lana hung the towel across her shoulders. She didn't try to finger-comb her messy locks, but somehow, this tousled, carefree look suited her. "That we're madly in love and can't stand to be separated for even a second, so you asked me to move in with you."

Claire stared at her. "And they bought that?"

31

"They were surprised, but...yeah."

So Lana had a history of falling in love at the drop of a hat and making rash decisions? They'd have to come up with a different story for her own circle of friends because Claire wasn't like that at all. "You didn't tell them we're engaged, did you?"

"No. I doubt they'd buy that."

Claire exhaled. So Lana did have some common sense. "Good. My friends and colleagues wouldn't buy it either. I think we should use the fiancée story only with the publisher and simply introduce you as my girlfriend to everyone else."

"Um, Lana? Claire?" came Jill's voice from outside. "We brought in the rest of the boxes. Could you maybe wait with the moving-in sex and show us where to put them? Do you want them in the living room, with the others?"

The tips of Claire's ears went hot. They stared at each other.

Of course, Lana's friends assumed they would share a bed, so she couldn't direct them to the guest room. "I'll show them to the master bedroom. We'll move the boxes over here later."

As they slipped from the guest room, Claire had the feeling that her life would never be the same again—at least not for the next few months.

~∼∽∾~

Jeez, what did I put into this box? If she hadn't known any better, Lana would have thought it held several bars of gold. Huffing and puffing, she lugged the box down the hall toward the master bedroom—and nearly collided with Claire, who stepped through the doorway.

"Oh. Excuse me." Claire circled around her, giving her and the moving box a wide berth.

Lana stared after her, and the contrast to earlier, in her apartment, hit her. The way she and her fake fiancée interacted was so different from the way Crash had kissed Jill's neck before squeezing past her.

They really had to step up their game, or no one would believe they were a happy couple.

Jill was already throwing questioning gazes her way when she entered the bedroom with another box. "You okay?"

"I'm fine."

"Are you sure? You look…ambivalent about moving in."

They stacked their boxes next to the neatly made, king-sized bed. The satin sheets were free of any wrinkles, as if they were freshly ironed.

"It's just a little overwhelming, you know? Living here will take some getting used to." While she liked the house, it was full of things she could never afford. She glanced around the room with the lush oriental carpet, the French doors leading to the backyard, and two oak nightstands that matched the bed.

Then her gaze fell on the photo on one of the nightstands. It showed a slender, blue-eyed woman with flowing, blonde hair beaming into the camera, clearly enamored with the person who'd taken the picture.

Oh shit. Why the hell did Claire still keep a picture of her ex around? If Jill saw it, it would be game over. No way could she explain away the photo of another woman on her supposed girlfriend's nightstand.

Under the pretense of needing a break, she flopped down onto the bed, glanced at Jill to make sure she wasn't looking, and then shoved the picture beneath the pillow.

Phew! Her heart thumped against her ribs, and she fought against the urge to press her hand to her chest.

Jill finished her perusal of the room and turned back toward her. She laughed. "I'd be afraid I'd break something. You know how clumsy I get when the MS acts up."

"Speaking of which…" Crash joined them, put down her own box, and wrapped one arm around Jill. "You really should take a break, or you'll overheat—and not just because of my sexy presence."

Lana had expected Jill to protest, but instead she leaned heavily against Crash's strong body and sighed. "I know, I know."

Claire rushed into the room as if an army of fire ants were after her. She was carrying Mr. Cuddles, and she plopped the pink plush bear down on the bed hastily, as if she couldn't wait to get rid of him. "You really don't need to stay. We can finish the rest of the boxes ourselves."

Crash and Jill exchanged gazes.

"Are you sure?" Jill asked.

"Of course," Claire said. "Just put the rest of the boxes at the curb. No one will steal them in this neighborhood. The two of us can handle carrying them in and unpacking without a problem."

It would have been more believable if she'd been dressed for moving day. For the past twenty minutes, she had lugged around moving boxes in tailored slacks and a crisp, white blouse. Lana was starting to wonder if the woman even owned a pair of jeans and a T-shirt.

But at least she was helping, even though she probably did it only to hold up the impression of the loving girlfriend.

"She's right. We'll manage." It was better to get Jill and Crash out of here, just in case there were more pictures of Claire's former fiancée lurking around the house.

Lana got up from the bed and wrapped one arm around Claire, mirroring Jill and Crash's loose embrace. "Right, honey?"

Claire stiffened, but then she put on a smile and put her arm around Lana too. "Right."

Should she kiss her cheek or something, to make it look more believable?

Just as Lana leaned in to kiss the fair cheek, Claire seemed to have gotten the same idea and turned her head. Their lips nearly collided, and both flinched back at the last second, ending up with an awkward brush of Lana's lips against Claire's cheekbone.

Oh boy.

If Jill and Crash hadn't been busy staring deeply into each other's eyes, their little charade would have been over before it really began.

"Okay, then," Jill finally said. "We'll leave you two lovebirds alone. Call if you need anything." They walked to the door, and Jill added back over her shoulder, "Don't be a stranger, and let's have dinner sometime so we can get to know Claire."

"Uh, sure."

Their steps faded down the hall, and then the front door fell closed.

Lana and Claire dropped their arms from around each other and stepped back.

"Finally alone," Lana said to interrupt the awkward silence.

Claire grimaced. "God, that was awful. I should have thought this through much better. I suddenly remembered Abby's photo on the nightstand. That's why I came charging in." She looked around for the photo.

"I hid it before Jill could see it. Look beneath Mr. Cuddles."

"Uh, Mr. Cuddles?"

34

Heat rose up Lana's neck. "My plush bear."

"Let me guess… A gift from a former girlfriend?"

Lana shook her head. "My father gave it to me when I was two." It was the only thing she had from him. She lifted the bear and pulled out the framed photo from beneath the pillow.

"Phew. Thank you. I wanted to put it away weeks ago, but then, um, kind of forgot." Claire took it from her and looked down at the picture before putting it into the bottom drawer of her dresser, sliding it beneath a stack of neatly folded socks.

"So, when will our first big performance be?" Lana asked.

"Excuse me?"

Lana hefted Mr. Cuddles onto her hip. "You mentioned a meeting with an editor at the end of June. Is there any event before that, or will we just… play house until then?"

"My boss, the clinical director of the Renewed Spark Counseling Center, is having a party the week after next. I'll need you to come with me, plus maybe one or two other events. All of them should be in the evening. I can email you the details."

"Email?" Lana grinned. "We live in the same house now. Why not just talk about it over breakfast?"

Claire shook her head. "I don't normally eat breakfast. So, does that schedule work for you?"

"Yeah, sure. Evening events are not a problem since I usually work the early shift."

A fine line formed on Claire's brow, and Lana realized she was wearing makeup. "Work? I thought we agreed on no other gigs during the length of this agreement."

"This isn't acting work. I rarely have enough gigs, so I work in a coffee shop four or five shifts a week."

"But the contract stipulates twenty-four/seven availability."

"My sister actually owns the coffee shop, so I could be available whenever you need me. Just say the word, and I can easily get someone to take over my shift. But I can't sit at home all day while you work for twelve hours."

The line on Claire's forehead deepened. "What if one of my colleagues or acquaintances sees you in that coffee shop?"

Wow. I can't believe she said that! Lana struggled to keep her voice down. "They have something against coffee?" she asked innocently.

"No, of course not. It's just… Being a waitress isn't exactly…"

"It's called a barista, and it's a perfectly fine job."

Claire lifted both hands. "I didn't mean to imply otherwise. I just don't think… If you need the money, I could pay you a little more. I don't want people to think my fiancée or girlfriend needs to work in a coffee shop because I can't—or won't—support her."

And here I thought only men could be chauvinistic assholes. Lana gave her a disbelieving look. "You think I'll give up my job for appearance's sake? This is the twenty-first century. Women can hold jobs—even jobs in coffee shops. They don't need someone to support them. That's what you should tell your friends if they comment on my job." She grabbed one of the moving boxes, piled Mr. Cuddles on top, and carried it past Claire.

She was halfway to the guest room when steps behind her announced that Claire had followed her.

"I didn't mean to sound like a snob," she said when she put down a box next to the one Lana had carried. "If it's important to you, fine. Keep the job."

Lana bit back a sarcastic *thank you very much for your permission, milady.* No wonder Claire's fiancée had run for the hills. Good thing their engagement was just for show. She could never be in a relationship with someone like Claire, and no amount of therapy or self-help books would change that.

Chapter 5

WHEN CLAIRE CAME HOME FROM work on Monday evening, loud music blared from the living room. She closed the door, hung her keys on their hook in the entryway, and slipped out of her heels. "Sorry I'm late, hon—"

She cut herself off when she entered the living room and caught sight of the person lounging on the couch.

It wasn't Abby.

No, of course not.

Abby would never play music as loud as this. And she would never put a glass on the coffee table without using a coaster. She also didn't leave dishes in the sink, like the ones Claire had found when she had entered the kitchen this morning.

Lana sat up and grinned at her. "Practicing already, *hon*?"

Claire sighed. She crossed the room and turned the volume down and the temperature up. God, it was freezing in here. "Ms. Henderson…"

"Lana. If we want to make everyone believe that we're madly in love, we'd better call each other by our first names." She tilted her head, and a mischievous twinkle entered her hazel eyes. "Or do you prefer pet names? Honey bunny? Babycakes? Snugglebutt?"

Claire grimaced. "No, thank you. Claire will do." Well, at least Lana didn't seem to hold a grudge because of Saturday, when she had implied being a barista wasn't a desirable job. She settled into the recliner and flicked her gaze over at Lana. "Poopsie."

Lana's eyes widened, and her jaw slackened.

"What?" Claire asked. "You think I don't have a sense of humor?"

"Um, no, of course not."

Claire didn't need a doctorate in psychology to see through the lie. She shouldn't care what Lana thought of her, but for some reason she did. "This might be fun and games to you, just another adventure in the life of an actress, but to me, this is serious. I want that book deal." She *needed* that book deal. If she wanted to take over the center one day, she needed to establish herself as LA's go-to expert on relationships before Vanessa could do it.

"I get that," Lana said. "But what's so bad about having a little fun while we're working toward that goal?"

"Nothing, I guess. As long as you're taking it seriously." She eyed the condensation ring on the coffee table. "And using a coaster."

Lana used the edge of her shirt to wipe down the table, making Claire wince. "I'll try," she said, without clarifying which she meant.

Claire gave her a nod and got up from the recliner. She needed a shower—a long, hot shower. This entire fake fiancée situation had made her so tense that every muscle hurt. Lugging around heavy moving boxes all weekend hadn't helped.

"There's some leftover lasagna in the kitchen," Lana called after her.

Claire paused in the doorway. "You cooked?"

"Yes. My apartment only comes with a mini fridge and a hot plate, so I took advantage of having a real kitchen. I hope that was okay."

Oh God. Claire didn't dare imagine how her poor kitchen might look. "Uh, no, that's fine. It'll come in handy if you know your way around my house, in case I have guests over."

"True. So, help yourself to the lasagna if you're hungry."

Her stomach growled at the thought of homemade lasagna, but she ignored it. "Thank you, but I try not to eat carbs after six."

"I tried that." Lana laughed. "It lasted all of four days." She patted her full hips and the feminine curve of her belly without a hint of regret.

Even though Claire was proud of her self-discipline, she couldn't help admiring Lana's positive attitude about herself and her body. It had to be nice to be so relaxed about everything.

That thought lasted for exactly ten seconds—until she passed by the kitchen and saw the dirty pans stacked up next to the stove. Groaning, she ducked into the bathroom to soak away her frustration.

The next day, Claire paced the floor in her bedroom, her cell phone tightly pressed to her ear. "I want her out of here, Mercedes! Now!"

Mercedes sighed. "Claire..."

"Do you have any idea what my house looks like? Her stuff is everywhere! Earlier, I found cookie crumbs and pieces of chocolate all over my couch... my four-thousand-dollar designer couch. Can you believe it? And don't even get me started on what she's doing to my kitchen. It's like living with a teenager...or a toddler!"

"So hire a cleaning lady," Mercedes said when Claire paused to breathe.

"I already have a cleaning lady. When I got home today, she and Lana were sitting in the kitchen, chatting."

Mercedes laughed. "So she's a people person. Isn't that exactly what you'd want in a fiancée?"

"*Pretend* fiancée," Claire said. "I have nothing against her being a people person. She's just so...so...so unpredictable. You never know what's going to come out of her mouth next. Renata's party is next week. What if she embarrasses me in front of my colleagues?"

"Jesus, Claire, would you relax? Maybe some of the breathing exercises from your bonus chapter would help."

Claire grimaced but pushed her shoulders back and took a deep breath, then another. She perched on the edge of the bed and freed her hair of its chignon.

Okay, maybe it wasn't all Lana's fault, even though she really was driving her up the wall. Maybe part of it was that it felt strange to share the house with someone again. Abby had always been so quiet she'd barely known she was there most of the time. Lana definitely made her presence known.

Claire sighed. "I can't relax until this is over."

"I can't believe I'm saying this, but it's just a book deal, Claire. It's not worth—"

"There's much more on the line for me." The moment she said it, she realized how true it was. This wasn't merely about the book any longer. There was much more at stake. If she got caught in such a massive lie while advertising honesty in her book, her podcast, and her workshops, she would lose her credibility—and that was everything in her job.

Nausea swept over her. She bent over and clutched her stomach with her free hand. *Oh my God, what have I done?*

"I get it," Mercedes said. "And that's exactly why you and Lana have to work as a team."

A team. Like in the team-building workshops Dad does. I can do that. Claire went through another cycle of breathing exercises. *I can do this. I won't allow this to destroy my career.*

"Go talk to her instead of hiding out in your home office," Mercedes said.

"I'm not in my office," Claire grumbled, even knowing it was beside the point. "And I talk to people all day. The last thing I want to do in the evening is deal with someone else's issues too."

"I said talk, not play therapist. Come on. Go talk to her. You need to get to know her if you want to convince people you're a couple. At least it'll take your mind off Abby."

Admittedly, she'd barely thought of Abby since they had started this crazy charade. "Okay, okay. I'm going." Claire lowered the phone to end the call but then moved it back to her ear. "Mercedes? Thank you."

"You're welcome. Talk to you later."

Claire put her cell phone down on her nightstand and got up from the bed. Quietly, she opened the door and peeked out.

Every single light in the house was on. No wonder Lana had trouble making ends meet if she ran up her electricity bill like this. At least Claire assumed Lana had financial problems. Why else would she have agreed to take over the role of her fake fiancée?

Pots clanked in the kitchen, and someone was whistling off-key.

It took Claire a few seconds to recognize the song as "Can't Buy Me Love" from the Beatles. Despite her tension, she had to smile because the song somehow fit their fake engagement deal. Not that she was trying to buy Lana's love, of course. Her acting skills were what she was after.

Then her smile faded as a line from the song went through her mind. *Buy you a diamond ring... Oh shit. Am I supposed to get her one?*

They really had a lot to talk about. With a deep sigh, Claire forced herself to march toward the kitchen.

40

When Claire entered the kitchen, Lana had just washed the last pot. "Oh, hi." They had lived together for three days now but so far had spent less than half an hour in the same room, so Lana still wasn't quite sure how to act around Claire.

"Hi," Claire said.

Lana expected her to stride to the fridge, get herself a bottle of water, and leave the room, as seemed to be her routine whenever she entered the kitchen.

But instead, Claire stood in the middle of the kitchen, looking as out of place as Lana had felt in this luxury home on her first day.

"There's rice and curry in the fridge," Lana said.

"No, thanks. I'm sure you're a great cook, but I don't eat—"

"Carbs after six," Lana finished for her.

Claire nodded. Her gaze traveled over the counters.

"I wiped them down," Lana said.

"I appreciate it." Claire walked over, wrung out the wet rag Lana had left in the sink, folded it, and hung it over the faucet.

OCD much? Lana managed not to shake her head at her.

Claire turned and leaned against the sink. "We need to talk." She squeezed her eyes shut. "Great, now I'm forgetting my own advice not to start a conversation like this. What I wanted to say is that we should talk about how we're going to pull this off." She pointed back and forth between them.

"Sounds like a good idea."

Claire went over to the wine rack that took up the entire length of the counter. "Do you want a glass of Pinot Noir while we talk? Or do you prefer white wine?"

"Um, actually, I'm more of a Blue Moon girl."

When Claire just looked at her, Lana added, "Beer."

"I know what it is. But I don't have any beer. Sorry."

"Well, *we* do. I went grocery shopping today." Lana walked past her to the fridge, opened it, and pulled out a beer. "Want one too?"

"No, thanks." Claire peered around her into the fridge. It was the closest they had been since that semi-embrace show they had put on for Jill and Crash's sake. "Are those peanut butter cups?"

"Yep. Want some?"

A low moan escaped Claire.

Lana's cheeks flushed at the unexpected sensuality of the sound. Who knew that Ms. Uptight could sound like this?

But instead of accepting the chocolate Lana held out to her, Claire shook her head. "I shouldn't. No—"

"Carbs after six."

"Exactly."

Lana eyed the bottle of wine Claire had opened. "Doesn't wine have carbs too?"

Claire froze, and an almost adorable wrinkle formed on her forehead. "Uh, I suppose it does." She turned the bottle to read the label.

Lana took the bottle from her and poured her a glass. "We're supposed to practice pretending, right? So let's pretend we don't know about the carbs in the wine."

"Denial doesn't change the fact that—"

"Nuh-huh! No psychobabble, remember?"

Claire sighed and took the glass of wine from her. "Let's go to the living room."

Lana took a seat on the couch while Claire sat in her leather recliner with a notepad and a Mont Blanc pen on her lap. Except for the glass of wine in her other hand, she looked the picture of the attentive psychologist about to take notes during a session. "So, tell me about yourself."

"Um…" Lana shifted uncomfortably. This was too much like therapy for her liking. "Is that really necessary?" She forced a grin. "You know, I usually try not to talk too much about myself on the first date."

"This isn't a date. It's a business arrangement. If we want to convince my colleagues and the publisher's acquisitions editor that we're a happily in love couple, we need to know more about each other."

"Can't we just make stuff up as we go?"

Claire shook her head. "I've never liked going into important situations without some kind of preparation."

"Okay, okay." Lana stabbed her index finger in her direction. "But no psychoanalyzing."

"I'm trained in cognitive behavioral and systemic therapy, not psychoanalysis."

Lana rolled her eyes, not caring how immature it might come across.

Claire tapped the notepad with the end of her pen. "So?"

"What do you want to know?"

"How about...hobbies?"

That seemed harmless enough. "I love to cook, like you probably already guessed."

"Are you any good at it?"

"You'd know if you didn't always refuse to try my food."

Claire shook her head. "Not this late in the day. I'll take your word for it. Any other hobbies?"

"Yeah. I roller-skate."

"Roller-skate?" Claire's eyebrows nearly reached her hairline.

Lana stretched out on the couch and turned onto her side to stare her down. "What? You think someone who looks like me can't be into any kind of sports?"

"No, that's not what I...Isn't it kind of dangerous?"

"Dangerous? No, it's fun. I'm not doing any crazy tricks like the ones Crash can do. I just skate." She studied Claire. "How about you?"

"Uh, me?"

Lana laughed at the startled expression on her face. "Yes, you. If you think preparation is key, I need to know a few things about you too. What do you like to do in your free time? I already know you don't cook and you don't eat."

"I do eat. Just not..."

"Carbs after six," they said in unison.

Claire laughed along with her, and Lana marveled at how much that transformed her entire face from beautiful but rigid Ice Queen to a stunning woman. She opened her mouth to tell her she should laugh more often but then snapped it shut without saying anything. It wasn't her place. After all, their engagement was only pretend.

"I guess I don't really have much time for hobbies," Claire said. "Well, other than dining out and seeing the occasional movie."

"Let me guess... You like socially critical movies and documentaries."

"Um, no. I like the old black-and-white classics. *Casablanca*, *The Philadelphia Story*, and *It Happened One Night*. That kind of thing." Claire fingered the clip of her pen as if embarrassed by that admission.

Lana held back a smile. *Aww. What do you know? A romantic at heart.*

43

"Why are you grinning?"

"I'm not grinning."

"I've got three degrees in psychology. I'm trained to read body language. I know when someone is grinning—and you are."

"Maybe I'm just in a good mood, Dr. Freud."

Claire squinted over at her but then seemed to decide to move on. "Favorite food?"

"Pizza. No, wait. Ice cream. Or cheesecake. Yours?"

"Anything with shrimp."

Shrimp and pizza. Lana shook her head. *God, we couldn't be more different if we tried.*

They went through a dozen more questions and answers until Claire had filled two pages. For Lana, it was a bit like memorizing lines for a movie. Who would have thought that she'd ever star in the role of the fake fiancée? Usually, she was cast as the comic-relief sidekick, never the love interest.

Finally, Claire looked up from her notepad. "What do we say when people ask about us? Us as a couple, I mean. And trust me, they will. My colleagues are a curious bunch."

"Do you think I will meet them?"

"Oh yeah. My boss is having a party next week, remember?"

A party with a bunch of psychologists. Fun. Lana somehow managed not to grimace.

"So what's our story?" Claire asked. "Where did we meet?"

"Maybe I mowed you down in the park when I was roller-skating."

"That would certainly get my attention." Claire scribbled it down. "And who made the first move?"

"I did," Lana said.

"Why do you get to be the one who made the first move?" Claire asked. "Most of the time, I was the one who asked out women instead of the other way around. I don't know why, but women sometimes seem hesitant to approach me."

A sip of beer went down the wrong pipe. Lana coughed. *Oh yeah. I wonder why?* "Yeah, but if I ran you down with my roller skates, I would have invited you for a coffee or something."

"That's an apology, not a date."

"It could be a date if I asked with romantic intentions."

Claire tilted her head. "So it was love at first sight?"

"Of course." Lana batted her lashes at her. "Wasn't it for you, lover girl?"

Claire threw the cap of her pen at her.

Caught off guard, Lana didn't catch it. The missile bounced off her shoulder, ricocheted across the living room, and landed on the floor near the fireplace.

Claire got up and retrieved it as if she couldn't stand even that tiny bit of a mess on the floor. When she bent to pick it up, her formfitting skirt tightened across her trim butt.

Lana didn't even try to avert her gaze. It was all for getting into her role, of course. As Claire's fiancée, she was supposed to stare at her ass, right?

"I'm not one for whirlwind romances," Claire said when she was back in her recliner. She curled her nylon-stockinged feet under her. "Abby and I—" She bit her lip.

"Abby?"

"My fiancée. Um, former fiancée. She and I knew each other for a while before we started dating."

"Okay, so you and I were friends first, and then, when the two of you broke up, we got involved. We could tell people I was there for you after the breakup, and that's how we grew close so fast."

Claire rubbed her chin, leaving an ink stain behind on her fair skin. Somehow, that tiny imperfection made her more human, so Lana decided not to tell her for now. "Won't people think you're my rebound girl?" Claire asked.

Lana winced. Unfortunately, that was a role she had plenty of experience with. Katrina had left her not long after her accident, claiming she'd never gotten over her ex and wanted another chance with her.

"I guess we'll just have to convince them that we're really into each other," Lana said.

"At least you're not a carbon copy of her, so no one will think I'm trying to recreate what I had with Abby."

A snort escaped Lana. From what she had seen of the thin blonde in the photo that had been on Claire's bedside table, she and Abby couldn't even be distant cousins, much less carbon copies. "We also need an engagement story for when we meet with the publishing people. Who proposed?"

"I did," Claire said immediately. "If you get to be the one who made the first move, I get to be the one who proposed."

Lana shrugged. "Fine with me. So you went down on one knee in some romantic place?"

"Of course. Should Ms. Huge—the acquisitions editor—ask, we've been together for seven years. Last December, we went to an excellent French restaurant, then took a stroll along the pier on a moonlit night, and I asked you to marry me."

Had that been how it had happened between Claire and her ex-fiancée, or had Claire made up these details? Not that it really mattered.

Claire capped her pen and clipped it to the top of her notepad, apparently done with the conversation.

"Can I ask you something?" Lana asked before Claire could decide to call it a night.

A wary expression settled on Claire's face. "Um, sure."

"Why pay someone to pretend to be your girlfriend? Why not date someone for real?" Lana had asked herself that question since finding out about this unusual arrangement. "I mean, look at you." She gestured at Claire, who, even curled up in the recliner, her bare feet tucked under, exuded an air of elegance. "You're gorgeous. A woman like you shouldn't have any problem attracting dates."

A blush climbed up Claire's neck. "I hope flattery is included in what I'm paying you."

Stung, Lana stared at her. Yes, Claire was paying her for pretending to be her fiancée, but did she have to be an ass about it? "I have a feeling you psychologist types have a word for what you just did."

"Excuse me?"

"Someone who gets sarcastic when they're being complimented. There's probably some shrink term for that."

Claire sighed. "I'm sorry. I guess I'm not feeling very attractive after—" She cut herself off. "Anyway, the last thing I need right now is the complication of a real relationship."

"I get that. I'm happily single myself. I just didn't expect a love guru to be so…anti-love."

"I'm not."

"Not a love guru or not anti-love?" Lana asked with a slight smile.

"Neither. I'm a psychologist specializing in couples therapy, and I believe in love. Just…"

"Just not for yourself?" Lana finished when Claire fell silent.

Claire shrugged and took a long sip of wine. When she looked up, she studied Lana over the rim of her glass. "What about you? Why did you agree to our arrangement?"

Lana looked her in the eyes. No reason to lie about it. "Oh, I've got a very good reason. Fifty thousand reasons, to be exact. I'm not kidding myself. This is probably the most I'll ever get paid for a role, and I'd be a fool to turn it down."

"I couldn't live like that…month to month, never knowing if I'll be able to make rent…"

"What if being a psychologist were like that?" Lana asked. "Barely paying enough to get by. Would you still want to do your job, or would you look for another?"

Claire circled the rim of her wine glass with the tip of her index finger, a gesture that was strangely hypnotic. Lana couldn't look away.

"I don't know," Claire said after a while. "I'd like to believe that I'd do it anyway. I never considered doing anything else."

"Not even as a kid? You never wanted to be a princess or a doctor or a dragon slayer?"

Claire raised her eyebrows at that last one. "Is that what you wanted to be when you were growing up?"

Lana laughed. "No. I wanted to become a famous artist. But the problem is that I can't even draw a stick figure."

"So you settled for becoming an actress," Claire said.

"It's not about settling. It's about finding something that fit me better."

"Hmm." Claire stared into the depth of her red wine.

Silence settled between them, and for the first time, it wasn't awkward. Lana was hesitant to disturb that newfound peace, but there was one last thing she needed to know if she wanted to play her role as Claire's fiancée convincingly. "Your colleagues…did they know Abby? I mean, I take it you're out at work, right?"

"Oh, yes, of course. The counseling center is very LGBT-affirmative. Abby and I were together for seven years, so my colleagues met her several times."

Lana let out a low whistle. So at least that detail about their fake engagement was based on Claire's relationship with her ex-fiancée. "Seven years? Wow. I've never been with anyone for that long. What happened? I mean, after such a long time, you don't just break up, especially if you're engaged to be married…do you?"

Claire snorted and mumbled something Lana didn't catch into her nearly empty glass.

"Oh no. Don't tell me… You caught her cheating?" Lana couldn't see it happening the other way around. Claire seemed like a woman who wouldn't betray her principles.

"What? No! It wasn't that. It was…nothing you need to concern yourself with."

"But won't people expect me to know?"

"The people from Wishing Tree Publishing don't know there's been a breakup, and if anyone else asks, tell them you don't want to betray my confidence by talking about it." Claire emptied her glass with two big gulps and stood. "Now excuse me. I'm tired. Let's continue this another time."

Before Lana could think of anything to say, Claire had disappeared down the hall and her bedroom door clicked shut behind her.

Lana took a long swig of beer. *Damn.* Just when Claire had begun to loosen up a little, she'd chased her back into her ivory tower. If they continued like this, this entire arrangement would fail the very first time they pretended to be a couple in public.

Chapter 6

THE NEXT MONDAY, CLAIRE WAS counseling a couple that reminded her a bit of herself and Lana.

Mr. Greyson slumped against the back of Claire's couch. "Why do we have to talk about this over and over and over again?"

"We wouldn't have to if you listened and stopped being such a slob," his wife fired back. "Would it really be so hard to put your mug into the dishwasher instead of leaving it in the sink?"

"I would, just not the moment you want me to do it. You're so anal that you—"

"Anal? It's not anal to expect some help with simple household chores, is it?" Mrs. Greyson turned toward Claire. "Do you think it's too much to ask that he contribute a little?"

Oh no. Claire knew that game. She wouldn't take sides. She was a therapist, not a referee. "Let's pause here and think about what's really going on in your relationship." She looked from one to the other, but neither jumped in, so she continued. "First of all, could you try to use more neutral terms when you talk about each other? I can't imagine it makes you feel positive toward each other if you hear yourself called *slob* or *anal*, right?"

Both lowered their gazes to the floor. "Right."

"Okay." Claire turned toward Mrs. Greyson. "How do you feel when you get up in the morning and find dishes in the sink?" Not that she really needed to ask. She knew how it felt since she'd found dirty dishes in the sink this morning too.

"Angry," Mrs. Greyson answered without hesitation.

Claire could empathize, but she kept her face neutral. No taking sides. "It makes you angry because...?"

"Because he's not contributing!"

"Can you try to use *I* statements?" Claire asked before the cycle of mutual accusations could start again. "What is it that you feel when he's not contributing?"

"I...I feel taken for granted."

Claire gave her an encouraging nod.

"I feel...unloved. Like he doesn't even care enough to do this one simple thing for me."

"You feel unloved because I leave one damn mug in the sink?" Mr. Greyson looked genuinely puzzled.

"It's not about the mug. It's about..." His wife looked to Claire for help.

"About being seen and heard?" Claire gently suggested.

"Yes! I feel like he doesn't see or listen to what I need."

"Can you tell Brian?"

Mrs. Greyson turned on the couch to face her husband. "When you leave dishes in the sink, it makes me feel like you don't see or care about my needs."

He vehemently shook his head. "That's not true. I just figure why bother if I already know the way I put the dishes in the dishwasher won't be good enough for you?" He looked at Claire and added, "She always takes them out again and restacks them the way she wants it done."

Claire scribbled down "not good enough for you" without glancing down at her notepad. She kept her gaze on Mrs. Greyson. "Have you tried telling Brian how you feel?"

"Um, no."

"So instead of talking about your feelings, what do you usually do?"

"I nag him until he does the dishes," Mrs. Greyson said.

Claire turned toward him. "How do you feel when she does that?"

"How do you think? It annoys the hell out of me!"

"It makes you feel...?"

"Annoyed?"

"What else?" Claire prompted.

He shrugged. "I don't know."

"Can you think about it for a second?" The way he clasped his hand around his wedding ring made her think there was something more behind it.

"When she starts her nagging, it makes me want to run."

"Run?" Claire wrote it down too.

"Yeah. Because it's annoying."

Now they were back to that word. Apparently, he needed a little help to see beyond it. "People don't usually run when they're annoyed, Brian. Most people run when they're afraid."

He went very still. His hand around the wedding ring tightened.

Bingo. Claire waited, not wanting to pressure him any further.

"Afraid?" He repeated it as if tasting the word and not liking it much. "Why would I be afraid?"

"I don't know. You tell me."

He shifted on the couch. His feet pointed at the door as if he wanted to jump up and flee. Just when Claire thought she might have pushed him too far, he said, "Sometimes I feel like I can't do anything right, not even the damn dishes."

"Like you'll never be good enough for her," Claire said quietly, glancing down at the words on her notepad.

"Yeah. Like she'll have enough of me one day and move on to someone better."

"So what you're afraid of is…losing her?"

He hung his head. "Yeah."

Mrs. Greyson slid toward him on the couch and put her hand over his. It was the first time they had touched since starting their sessions with Claire.

She let them sit like this for a moment before asking, "So whenever you feel this fear, what do you do?"

"I turn on the Xbox and ignore her nagging."

"Remember those negative cycles we talked about last time?" She waited until both of them nodded. "This sounds like one. The more you ignore her, the more Sally feels unheard and unappreciated."

"And the more unappreciated I feel, the more I nag and the more he gets scared and withdraws," Mrs. Greyson said.

"Exactly." She put her notepad down and leaned forward. "So what can we do to turn it into a positive cycle instead?"

"Maybe instead of criticizing I could praise him if he loads the dishwasher the right way?"

Claire tapped her pen against her lips. "Hmm. Is there a right way to load the dishwasher?"

Mrs. Greyson blushed.

"She means *her* way," Mr. Greyson grumbled.

His wife took her hand off his.

Come on, guys, don't destroy our progress. "Can you think of a compromise that meets both of your needs? Brian?"

"I'll try to remember to put the dishes in the dishwasher, and she'll accept that I'll do it my way."

"How does that sound to you, Sally?"

Mrs. Greyson smiled and put her hand back on his. "Sounds great."

Five minutes later, Claire walked them to the door and watched them leave. They were holding hands. *Hmm. Maybe I should ease up on Lana about the dishes in the sink too.* As she had said in her book, every relationship required a certain amount of compromise—apparently even fake ones.

Renata crossed the reception area, carrying a stack of files. "What did you do to them?" She tilted her silver-haired head toward the door, where the Greysons had disappeared. "When I saw them last week, they were arguing in the waiting room. I was afraid we'd have to repaint because they were going to slit each other's throats."

Claire smiled and pretended to sprinkle fairy dust. "Therapy magic."

Renata laughed and patted her shoulder in passing. "I'm glad you're feeling better. Your new girlfriend seems to be good for you."

Apparently, Vanessa had already spread the news. "Um, yeah. She's great."

"Make sure to bring her on Friday," Renata said before stepping into her office. "I want to meet the woman who put the smile back on your face."

Claire swallowed. No way out now.

Lana jerked awake with a hammering heart. The sweat-dampened sheet stuck to her body as she tried to sit up. She drew in a shaky breath and looked around.

It was still dark. Only the slightest hint of dawn lit up the horizon. The room was quiet, the only sound her own ragged breathing. Even when her eyes adjusted to the darkness, it took her several seconds to remember where she was.

The guest room. She was in Claire's house. Not in the car.

Next to her, the alarm clock glowed in the dark. Four fifty-seven. Lana knew she wouldn't be able to go back to sleep now.

She untangled herself from the sheets, swung her legs out of bed, and sat on the edge. Cool air from the air conditioner chilled her damp skin, making her shiver. She pressed her palms to her eyes and tried to shut out the vivid images of shattered glass and gushing blood. But the horrible sounds couldn't be pushed back that easily. The honking of horns, the squealing of brakes, and the almost human groan of metal as it bent out of shape...

Lana tried to shake it off. She hadn't had the dream in a while. What had triggered its return? Had it been the stress of her strange arrangement with Claire?

"I'm okay," she said into the darkness. "Everything's okay." Her voice was hoarse. Had she been screaming?

God, she hoped she hadn't woken up Claire. The last thing she needed was her questions and that piercing therapist's gaze directed at her.

With a groan, she got up from the bed. Every joint and muscle was stiff, probably because she'd tensed up during her nightmare, and her scars ached.

She limped into the bathroom and splashed cold water onto her face. In the mirror above the sink, she watched the color slowly return to her face. She smiled at herself. *That's it. A lot better now.*

She went back to the bedroom for a sip of water, but the glass on her nightstand was empty. Without turning on the hallway light so she wouldn't wake Claire, she tiptoed through the hall toward the kitchen to get herself some water.

Claire was tossing and turning. An hour ago, she had climbed out of the too-big bed and dragged her pillow and covers to the couch, where she had ended up sleeping most nights since Abby had moved out. She had dozed a little, but real sleep eluded her.

Too many things kept going through her mind.

To her surprise, it wasn't images of Abby telling her it was over that played through her mind's eye. Instead, what had kept her awake was her mind conjuring up possible scenarios of what might happen when she took Lana to Renata's party and the meeting with the acquisitions editor.

A sound from the hall swept away the last remainder of sleepiness.

Was that a floorboard creaking?

Claire tensed, even though she reminded herself that she had a security system.

The sound of the fridge being opened and closed drifted over, and Claire sank back against her pillow. A burglar would check out the expensive art works on the walls, not the contents of her fridge. It had to be Lana.

The thought brought back some of her tension as she imagined Lana messing up her kitchen again.

Hey, you wanted to be more tolerant about that, remember?

A glance at the illuminated hands of her wristwatch revealed that it was five o'clock anyway, so she might as well get up. She carried her pillow and covers back into the bedroom so Lana wouldn't realize where she'd slept, then padded toward the kitchen.

"Good morning," she said from the doorway.

Lana dropped the plastic bottle she'd been holding and whirled around. Water splashed all over the kitchen floor as the open bottle rolled around. "Jesus! You scared the crap out of me!" She pressed one hand to her heaving chest.

Claire lifted both hands. "Sorry. I…" She squinted at Lana, who looked pale and rattled. "Are you okay?"

"I'm fine. You just startled me." Lana bent, picked up the bottle, and started to mop up the water with the rag that had been hanging over the faucet.

Her therapist instincts propelled Claire closer. Was it just her imagination, or were Lana's hands trembling? She walked over, careful not to step into any of the puddles, knelt next to Lana, and stopped her with a touch to her knee.

Only when Lana flinched did she realize her leg was bare; she was wearing some kind of sleep shorts.

Claire snatched her hand away. *Wow.* What an intense reaction from Lana. It wasn't as if she was trying to feel her up or something. Without touching her again, she pointed at the rag in Lana's hands. "Want me to do that?"

Lana paused in her attempts to mop up the spilled water and stared at her. "You really are a control freak, aren't you?"

"What? No! It's not about me wanting to take over. All I wanted was…" Claire stopped herself. She didn't need this, especially not before she'd had her first cup of coffee. "You know what? Forget it." She jumped to her feet and strode to the door.

"Claire, wait!" Lana's voice stopped her. "I… I'm sorry. I just… I didn't sleep very well. Of course, that's not an excuse for being an ass."

Her blatant honesty made Claire's annoyance melt away. She turned back around. "It's okay. I… I didn't sleep very well either." Normally, she wasn't one to share such things, but now it felt right to bare that little bit of herself too.

"How about we make a deal?" Lana said. "You mop up the floor while I make us some pancakes."

Claire hesitated, about to point out that she wasn't a breakfast person and just wanted coffee and some peace and quiet in the morning.

But now that familiar twinkle was back in Lana's eyes. "Come on," Lana said. "It's before six, so a few carbs won't kill you."

"All right. I'll have one." Claire held up her index finger.

"That's what you think." Lana grinned. "Once you've tasted my world-famous pancakes, you won't be able to stop yourself from taking a second and then a third and…"

Claire gave her a look.

"Okay, okay. One pancake it is." She went to the fridge for some ingredients while Claire mopped up the rest of the floor.

Then she sat at the kitchen island and watched Lana make pancakes.

Thankfully, Lana didn't seem to feel the urge to make conversation while she broke eggs in a one-handed flourish. She moved with unexpected grace as she whisked the ingredients together.

55

It occurred to Claire that she'd never watched Abby cook, not even once in their seven-year relationship. Aside from occasionally dining out, they hadn't shared many meals.

Lana ladled batter into a hot pan. Once bubbles started to form, she turned the pancake with a quick flip of her wrist.

Just when Claire was beginning to admire her cooking skills, the pancake flopped back into the pan, sending spatters of oil and batter across the backsplash and the stove.

Lana continued without seeming to notice.

Ignore it. It's just a little batter. Claire bit her tongue and got up to make coffee.

A few minutes later, both the coffee and the pancakes were ready. Lana placed a stack of perfectly round, golden-brown pancakes on the island in front of her. They smelled heavenly, making Claire's mouth water.

Lana slid one pancake onto Claire's plate before climbing onto the stool next to her. "Go on, try it."

Under Lana's expectant gaze, Claire cut off a bit of pancake with the side of her fork, blew on it, and put the bite into her mouth.

The fluffy piece of pancake seemed to melt on her tongue. The aroma of chocolate and peanut butter exploded across her taste buds. Forgetting her manners and the state of her kitchen, she moaned around a mouthful of pancake. The question she had asked Lana last week was definitely answered: Lana was a fantastic cook.

"Oh my God," she said once she had swallowed. "What did you put in there?"

"Pieces of peanut butter cups." Lana grinned proudly.

Claire eyed the pancake on her plate. "They probably have a thousand calories each."

"Probably." Unrepentantly, Lana took a big bite of pancake.

Well, there was no use spoiling food that was already on her plate, so Claire ate the rest of her pancake…and then started eyeing the stack between her and Lana. *Oh no. Forget it. One of them is more than enough.*

Instead of staring at the calorie bombs within easy reach, she forced herself to focus on the woman who had made them and on what had happened between them a few minutes ago. "Earlier, when I touched your knee…"

Lana looked up from her own pancake. A dusting of flour smudged her tan cheeks. "Yes?"

"Well, my boss's party is on Friday, and we'll have to convince everyone we're newly in love and can't keep our hands off each other. If we avoid touching, my colleagues will immediately know something is up. They are trained to notice that kind of thing. So if you've got a problem with me touching you, you'd better tell me now."

"I don't have a problem with that," Lana said.

Oh yeah? It sure looked like it earlier. Claire knew she couldn't afford to let this go. "Just to make it crystal clear, I wasn't trying to take advantage. It wasn't meant to be a sexual touch at all. Our contract specifically excludes that kind of, um, thing."

Lana sighed and put down her fork. "I know. That wasn't why I flinched away. I just…" She gestured toward her leg, drawing Claire's gaze down.

What the…? Claire nearly dropped her fork.

Lana's sleep shorts left the lower parts of her soft thighs bare. On her left leg, a pink, slightly raised scar ran from the edge of the shorts to the top of her knee.

"My leg is bothering me today," Lana said.

The pancake sat like a clump of mud in Claire's stomach. "Did I hurt you?"

"No!" Lana put her hand on Claire's.

Her skin was warm against Claire's suddenly clammy fingers, making her relax her grip on the fork.

Lana took her hand away. "You didn't. Really. It just felt weird for a second to have someone touch it."

Did that mean no one else had ever touched the scar? Claire ignored the question. It was none of her business. "I'm sorry. I had no idea."

"Why would you?" Lana started eating again. "It's no big deal."

Claire had to stop herself from calling her on that obvious lie. Lana was clearly sensitive about being "psychoanalyzed," but Claire couldn't completely let it go. "Do you want to talk about what happened?" she asked quietly.

"And spoil my perfect pancakes?" Lana shook her head. "It happened, I survived and moved on and don't want to keep talking about it. I guess you can relate."

Was she talking about Claire's refusal to talk about her breakup? "What if one of my colleagues notices and asks me about it?"

"What if they ask me about what happened between you and Abby?"

Claire sighed. *Touché.*

"Just tell them it's an old injury that acts up every now and then," Lana said.

"All right." She watched Lana finish her pancake in silence.

When Lana got up to carry the plates to the sink, Claire waved her away. "You cooked, I'll clean up."

Lana didn't protest. "Thanks."

Claire leaned against the sink. Her gaze followed Lana to the door. She hadn't noticed it before, but now she detected a slight limp. "Lana?"

Lana turned. A bit of wariness lurked in her usually open gaze.

"Thanks for breakfast. And, um, if you want to use my bathtub, you can. It comes with massage jets. Maybe they could help with your leg."

Lana smiled, which chased away the wariness in her eyes. "You'd really share your pristine bathroom with me?"

Claire gave her a mock glare. "Only if you promise to wipe down the fixtures afterward."

"Aye-aye, ma'am." Lana fired off a salute. Then her comical face softened into another smile. "Thank you."

"You're welcome," Claire said quietly and stared after her as she walked away.

Chapter 7

EVEN IF CLAIRE HAD PAID her more, Lana would have refused to give up her job at the Mean Bean. Claire had clearly judged her job as a barista as not impressive enough, but Lana loved the hiss of the espresso machine, the soothing murmur of voices, and the clinking of dishes. Nothing beat the scent of freshly brewed coffee, hazelnut, and caramel either.

Well, she admitted to herself, she could do without customers like the one who had just stepped up to the counter and ordered, "A medium vanilla latte, please, but in an extra-large cup."

Lana didn't bat an eye. "Coming right up."

The woman turned to the customer behind her. "That lets the coffee breathe, you know?"

Lana held back a grin. She could imagine Claire ordering something like that—without the vanilla syrup, of course.

"Oh, and please make the milk half skim, half soy, with a dollop of whipped cream on top," the customer added.

Okay, even Claire wouldn't order her latte like that. Lana exchanged a glance with Avery, who was restacking the towers of paper cups and lids.

Once half-skim-half-soy woman was gone and they had served the two customers in line behind her, Avery leaned against the gleaming espresso machine and shook her head. "She is definitely a few beans short of an espresso."

"Well, as a wise woman taught me, the customer is always right—even when she's wrong," Lana said with a smile.

They kept their voices down so that the customers sipping coffee at the small tables lining the wall opposite the counter couldn't hear them.

Avery eyed her. "What's up with you, sis? You're in a good mood today."

"Nothing's up. I'm always in a good mood."

"Yeah, but today it's with an extra dash of good on top."

Lana shrugged. For once, she didn't need to worry about where the money for her rent and the medical bills would come from. She'd also enjoyed a long soak in Claire's bathtub last night, so her leg didn't bother her today.

"Ah, I get it now. That new girlfriend of yours must be pretty good in bed."

"Avery!" Lana started coughing and looked around to see if any of the customers at the tables had heard. Thankfully, they were all focused on their beverages. "Isn't there some kind of law that prevents employers from asking about an employee's sex life?"

Avery grinned unrepentantly. "Not when your boss is also your favorite sister."

"Stepsister. Are we even still stepsisters since our parents are divorced?"

"Think you can get rid of me so you don't have to tell me about your sex life?" Avery flicked a coffee bean at her. "Come on. Tell me."

"There's nothing to tell. How do you even know I have a new girlfriend?" Lana had barely told her anything. She didn't want to draw the only family member she was still in contact with into this crazy charade.

"I saw that you changed your address in your employee file this morning, and I know I'm not paying you enough to even rent a bird house in that neighborhood. So, is she rich?" Avery waggled her brows. "Hot?" She nudged her. "Come on. Spill the beans."

"Would you lay off the coffee metaphors?"

"I will—if you show me a photo of your girl."

"She's not a girl...and I don't have a photo of her." If she showed Avery the same photo from Claire's therapist website she had shown Jill, Avery would instantly know something strange was going on. She knew Lana avoided therapists like vampires avoided holy water and, unlike her mother, would never get involved with one.

Avery frowned. "No photo? Not even one?" She leaned her hip against the counter and regarded Lana. A shadow of hurt passed over her face. "You know, I thought we could tell each other everything. That's how it's always been, from the moment my dad started dating your mom. Why are you suddenly keeping secrets from me?"

"I'm not. Not really." *Damn.* She should have thought about this sooner. Of course her fake relationship would affect the people in her life and make them think she was shutting them out. "I just…"

"Oh hell," Avery said. "Don't tell me you're dating someone on the rebound, and that's why you want to keep it from me. Come on, Lana! After Katrina, you really should know better."

"No, that's not it. Really." Although, technically, Claire *was* on the rebound. Even if not for her slightly uptight personality and OCD tendencies, Claire wasn't someone Lana would have ever dated. Having her heart ripped out once when her girlfriend had decided to go back to her ex was enough. "What Claire and I have is…special and very much unlike all of my past relationships. I guess I just don't want to jinx it by telling people about it too soon."

That wasn't a lie, she told herself. A fake fiancée arrangement certainly wasn't her usual style.

"People?" Avery repeated. "I'm not people. I'm family. When are you going to introduce me to her?"

"Um, Claire's a pretty busy wo—"

The jingle of the bell over the door announced a new customer.

Phew. Saved by the bell. She hated lying to her sister, so the less she said, the better.

"Lucky you," Avery said. "Okay, back to the grind."

Lana rolled her eyes at yet another coffee metaphor and turned to greet the customer with a smile. "What can I get you today?"

When Lana got home later that afternoon, Claire's Audi A6 was already in its spot in the two-car garage.

Strange. What is Claire doing home so early?

Lana parked next to the gleaming silver vehicle, climbed out of her battered Volkswagen Rabbit, and paused.

Wait a sec! Did I just think of Claire's house as home?

She shrugged and took it as a sign that she was starting to get into her role, which was a good thing, considering they had their first big show in front of Claire's colleagues in three days.

She unlocked the front door.

No beep from the security system since it had already been disarmed.

"Claire?" she called out.

"Yes, I'm here," came Claire's voice from somewhere down the hall.

Lana dropped her keys on the table next to the door, then, already two steps down the hall, she turned back around and hung them on a hook next to Claire's. She found Claire in her home office next to the master bedroom, sitting at a desk with a high-end computer that looked as if it could steer an army of spaceships.

"Hi," Lana said. "You're home early."

"I never schedule sessions with patients on Tuesday afternoons, remember?" Claire answered without taking her fingers off the keyboard.

When they had talked about their work schedules, Claire had said that she took off Tuesday afternoons to work on her book.

"But I thought you were already done with the book."

"I am. I'm just getting a head start on the editing process by polishing it a little."

Lana bit back a grin. If she looked up perfectionist in the dictionary, there would probably be a picture of Claire next to the entry. Knowing her, she would still be fiddling with her book two seconds before the printer started the presses. Lana stepped closer and leaned forward to get a glimpse of the manuscript over Claire's shoulder.

The subtitle of the chapter caught her attention. *Sex Begins in the Kitchen.* Lana raised her brows. "Wow. I didn't know you were writing that kind of book."

"What?"

Lana pointed at the subheading.

"Oh, no, no." Claire vehemently shook her head. "It's not what you think. I mean, yes, a healthy sex life is part of a good relationship, but this chapter isn't about sex. It's about making your partner feel loved by sharing household chores. The subtitle is merely meant to grab the reader's attention."

"Oh. It definitely worked."

Claire laughed. "You sound disappointed."

"Yeah, well, sex on the kitchen table sounds way more interesting than taking out the garbage."

Claire smacked her lips as if her mouth had gone dry.

Lana couldn't see her face because she was looking at the screen, but she had a feeling Claire was blushing.

"So…" Claire cleared her throat. "Was there something you needed?"

"Photos."

When Claire turned around in her leather office chair, the color of her face had either gone back to normal or she hadn't blushed after all. "Photos?"

"Yes. We need photos. My sister asked to see a photo of you, and I didn't have one I could show her. There's also not a single photo of us in the entire house. Don't you think people will find that strange?"

Claire rubbed her chin. "You might be right. It won't be long before Vanessa will start eyeing that empty spot on my desk where Abby's photo used to be, wondering why I haven't replaced it with one of you."

"Vanessa?" Lana asked.

"She's a colleague of mine." Claire looked the way Lana's childhood dog had when he'd accidentally bitten into an olive.

"Why do I get the feeling you don't like her?"

"Because I don't." A bit of heat entered Claire's usually neutral voice. "She's the most career-focused, arrogant b…person you can imagine."

That's rich, coming from a workaholic like Claire. Lana struggled to keep a straight face.

"She always pretends to be nice to me, but I know she'd love nothing better than to see me humiliated in front of the entire staff," Claire continued. "If she ever finds out about our arrangement…"

Lana put her hand on Claire's shoulder. The slim muscles beneath her fingers were tense like tightly wound springs. "We won't let that happen." She withdrew her hand and pulled her phone from her pocket. "Want me to snap a few selfies of us?"

Claire stopped her before she could try to perch on the chair next to her. "Uh, I don't think that's going to cut it. Wishing Tree's marketing department might also want a photo of the two of us."

That sounded like a job for a professional. A thought occurred to Lana, and she opened the contact list on her phone.

"What are you doing?" Claire asked.

"Jill knows this photographer who helps out actresses by doing their headshots for free. She did mine last year, and they got me that role as a corpse on *Central Precinct*."

"Uh, I don't know if that's such a high compliment."

"Trust me, it is." Lana was already making the call and lifted the phone to her ear. "Besides, this photographer is hot."

"Hey!" Claire's indignant cry followed her out of the office. "You're supposed to be my fiancée, remember? No flirting with hot photographers allowed!"

The next day, Claire was home early again because Lana had somehow managed to talk the photographer into coming over to take photos of them on short notice.

When Lana stepped into the living room, Claire looked up from the journal article on empty-nest couples she'd been reading.

"This is what you're wearing for the photo shoot?" She pointed at Lana's faded jean shorts, her bare feet, and the pink T-shirt that said *abs are great, but have you tried chocolate-chip cookies?* in big, black letters.

Lana glanced down at herself. "Um, yes. Why? Something wrong with it?"

How could she answer without hurting Lana's feelings? "Oh no, it's fine. I just thought…"

Lana laughed. "Relax. I was about to get changed."

Claire gave her a stern look. "You enjoy teasing me, don't you?"

"Just a little." Grinning, Lana held her thumb and index finger a fraction of an inch apart. "Sorry. I grew up in a household where teasing each other mercilessly was our favorite sport. I hope it doesn't bother you."

"Um, no. I'm just not used to it."

"So there wasn't any teasing at la Casa de Renshaw?"

It occurred to Claire that they hadn't talked about their families so far. "Not much, no. My parents always thought that teasing and sarcasm came too close to being passive-aggressive."

"True. My second stepfather had that down to an art form."

"Second?" The journal slid from Claire's grasp. "How many do you have?"

"Four and counting," Lana answered with a big smile.

Claire didn't need her degrees in psychology to sense that Lana's grin hid her discomfort with the topic, so she decided to curb her curiosity and not to ask any more questions for the time being. "So, do you need any help deciding what to wear?"

"I'll let you pick what I'll be wearing if I get to pick your outfit," Lana said.

"Um, I was planning on wearing this." Claire gestured at her Armani skirt suit.

"Seriously?"

Now Claire was the one who stared down at herself. "What's wrong with this outfit?"

"Don't get me wrong, I think women in power suits are hot, but..."

Heat rushed into Claire's cheeks. Sometimes, she got the feeling that Lana said stuff like that only to see her blush. "But?"

"I think we should be going for a more relaxed look. Two women newly in love lounging around at home, you know?"

Claire pointed to where she was sitting in the recliner. "I am lounging."

"Then you're doing it wrong." Lana grabbed her hand and pulled her up. "Come on." As she dragged her down the hall, she didn't let go of Claire's hand.

Claire stared down at their hands, then shrugged it off. Lana was obviously a person comfortable with touching others, or maybe she was preparing herself for the role she'd have to play once the photographer arrived in twenty minutes.

"First stop: Lana Henderson's modest closet," Lana announced and led her into the guest room.

Only some of her clothes had made it into the closet, though. Others were still stacked in messy piles on top of two unpacked moving boxes.

Claire looked over her choices. For an actress, Lana was amazingly unglamorous when it came to her fashion choices. T-shirts, shorts, and capris dominated her wardrobe. They'd definitely have to go shopping before their trip to New York.

"How about this?" Claire laid out a nice pair of white capris on the bed. They were long enough to cover Lana's scar, and the color would complement Lana's tan. She draped a burgundy blouse with three-quarter sleeves over it and looked at Lana for approval.

"Why not? The blouse is a little tight, but if you've got it, why not flaunt it?" Grinning, Lana slid down the zipper of her shorts.

The tips of Claire's ears burned. She whirled around.

Lana chuckled. "You're too cute." Clothes rustled, then Lana said, "Okay, you can look now. I'm decent—or as decent as I'm going to get in this top."

Claire turned around.

The blouse clung to Lana's full breasts, and the two top buttons were undone, showing off a hint of cleavage.

"Is this okay?" Lana asked, and for the first time, a bit of insecurity crept into her voice.

Claire forced her gaze up and looked her in the eyes. "You look great."

This time, Lana was the one blushing.

Claire smiled and decided to go easy on her. "Come on. Let's go pick my outfit."

Lana discreetly adjusted the cups of her bra while she followed Claire to her bedroom. Did Claire really think she looked good in this top, or had she just said that to be polite? With her carefully neutral therapist voice, it was sometimes hard to tell.

That was probably why Lana liked teasing her: to get behind that polished facade.

Claire crossed her bedroom, opened the door to her walk-in closet, and turned on the light.

Lana joined her. Side by side, they peered into the closet. *Wow. This thing is larger than my apartment!*

Three walls were lined with full-length mirrors. Half of the closet was empty, probably where Abby's clothes had once been. The other half was filled with rows of blazers, pencil skirts, slacks, and an army of silk blouses, all neatly sorted by color. A three-shelf shoe rack ran the entire length of one wall.

"If you're putting on any of these, we won't be looking as if we're going to the same event."

"That's a problem," Claire said. "Couples usually have a matching style."

Lana raised herself on her tiptoes and peeked into the upper compartment of the closet, hoping to find more casual clothes there. Instead, she encountered silk camisoles. *Ooh. Sexy. But not what we need.*

She turned toward Claire. "Don't you have any cargo shorts? No flannel shirts? What kind of lesbian are you?"

"A well-dressed one," Claire answered.

Lana laughed. "We really need to get you a pair of jeans."

"Oh, I have a pair of those."

"Let me see."

Claire reached into the very back of her closet and presented Lana with a pair of designer jeans that looked as if they had never been worn.

Lana wouldn't have been surprised if they still had the tags on them. "Put them on. I'll find you a top." She managed not to peek as clothing rustled behind her. When she finally found a top that would do, she whirled around and triumphantly held it out to Claire. "I think this will...um..."

Growing up with seven stepsiblings and then later, as an actress in commercials, Lana had quickly learned not to be shy about nudity, but she hadn't been prepared to see Claire standing there clad in a pair of skinny jeans and a black lace bra.

Claire looked like a statue carved from white marble, her fair skin as smooth and flawless as the silk blouses she normally wore. She wasn't overly muscular, but with barely any excess fat on her body, a hint of abs played beneath her skin.

Wow. Maybe I should cut out carbs after six too. Lana gave herself a mental kick.

Luckily, Claire was busy threading a belt through the loops of her jeans and hadn't caught her ogling.

When Claire looked up, Lana thrust the top at her. "Um, here. Put this on." *Now.*

Claire slipped into the sleeveless V-neck silk shirt that showed off her slim arms. Its turquoise color matched the frame of her glasses and made her eyes appear more green than gray. She slid her hands over her jeans-clad hips and regarded her reflection. "Is this okay?" she asked, making eye contact with Lana in the mirror.

"It'll do," Lana said.

Claire turned and just looked at her.

Jeez, I bet her patients never get away with even a little bit of evasion. "You look great. Really. I like you in jeans. But you've got to stop looking at them like a lumberjack someone put in a dress."

Claire laughed.

The sound made Lana smile reflexively. "Now all we've got to do is find you some sneakers." She pointed at Claire's bare feet.

The doorbell interrupted them.

They looked at each other, all laughter now gone.

Lana tugged on the front of her blouse one final time. "Showtime."

Lana had been right, Claire had to admit. Michelle Osinski, their photographer, was hot, at least if you went for butch women, which Claire usually didn't.

Michelle ran one strong hand through her short, brown hair, several shades darker than Lana's, as she looked around the house. "There," she finally said with a decisive nod toward the backyard. "We'll do it out there. Do you have some cheese and grapes or something?"

"Sure," Claire said. "Good thinking." They would sit at the dining table next to the outdoor kitchen with the integrated bar, eat cheese and grapes, and sip wine while Michelle took a few pictures.

Claire still wasn't wearing shoes, but when she wanted to go find a pair, Michelle stopped her. "No need. Barefoot is great."

The grass tickled her toes as Claire crossed the lawn, and it occurred to her that she'd never been barefoot in her own backyard. Heck, it must have been weeks or even months since she had last been out here. Maybe Abby hadn't been completely wrong about her working too much.

They sat on rattan chairs in the shade of a large umbrella.

"Can you slide the chairs closer to each other?" Michelle asked. "And maybe put an arm around each other or something?"

Claire dragged her chair a few inches closer and put her arm around Lana's shoulders, overly aware that her fingers were resting on Lana's left arm, right where her scar was. Did this look as awkward as it felt?

"Come on, you two. Is this what you call a hug? You look like complete strangers."

They turned their heads and glanced at each other.

That's because we are complete strangers.

A twitch at the corner of Lana's mouth revealed that she was probably thinking the same.

Okay, maybe they weren't *complete* strangers if she could guess what Lana was thinking.

"Don't be shy on my account. It's not like I've never seen two women being, um, affectionate with each other." Michelle winked at them. "You should see me with my fiancée."

The mention of a fiancée didn't help Claire relax at all, reminding her of how crazy this entire arrangement was.

"Okay, let's get you two moving a little," Michelle said.

Moving? Claire eyed her nervously.

"Claire, can you feed Lana some of the grapes?"

Feed her the grapes? She could do that. Claire took one piece of fruit and unceremoniously popped it between Lana's slightly parted lips.

Michelle hadn't taken a single photograph yet. "Uh, that looks about as sexy as me feeding my little nieces and nephews." She sighed. "You know what? Let's start with something else." She gestured for them to get up and led them over to the lawn. "Let's do a tickle fight."

Claire stared at her. "A...a tickle fight?"

"Yeah. It's great for photos that you don't want to look rehearsed or artificial. It gets you laughing, and it's very intimate, so it'll give the photos that romantic touch that Lana said you wanted." Michelle looked from Claire to Lana and back. A tiny scar at the corner of her left eye made her look as if she were constantly winking. "Right?"

Claire stared at Lana, who stared back but then shrugged. "Sure, why not. It'll get you out of your uptight mode."

"Hey!"

"Just teasing, honey." Lana sidled up to her and put one arm around her. "You know I love you."

69

Claire glared at her through narrowed eyes. "It won't work. I'm not even ticklish."

"Oh yeah?" Lana snuck her fingers up Claire's side. "Not ticklish at all?"

"No!" Claire twitched and struggled to escape.

"Oh yeah, this is great." Michelle lifted her camera to eye level and started snapping away. "Can you put your other arm around her too?"

Lana followed orders. She stood half behind Claire, half to the side, and wrapped both arms around her, trapping her in the circle of her arms. Her fingers pressed into her ribs and tickled up her sensitive sides.

Claire let out an undignified squeak and tried to squirm away, but Lana was amazingly strong. "Why...do I...have to...be the one...being... tickled?" In between bursts of protest, helpless laughter exploded from her. She tried to fight it, tried to keep it in, but couldn't.

"Because I have seven younger siblings." Lana was pressed against her, both arms looped around her, so her words and her laughter vibrated through Claire. "I'm a master at finding ticklish spots." She proved it by running her fingers along the curve of Claire's waist.

Oh God. Claire laughed so hard that she felt as if she would pee her pants any moment. She bent and twirled in a circle, trying to toss her off, but Lana hung on to her from behind like a cowgirl on a bucking mustang.

Her fingers somehow ended up beneath Claire's top, finding even more skin to tickle.

Claire gasped, yelped, and laughed uncontrollably. "S-stop!"

Lana paused. Her chin rested on Claire's shoulder, their cheeks pressed together so that Claire could feel the heat emanating from Lana's flushed face. Out of the corner of her eye, she glimpsed the mischief sparking in Lana's hazel eyes. "I thought you weren't ticklish?"

"I didn't...think...I was." Claire's chest was heaving in an attempt to suck enough air into her lungs. "No one ever...tried."

"No one?" Lana ran her fingers over the bend of Claire's elbow, which suddenly was ticklish too.

Claire squeaked and tried to pull away.

"Okay, okay." Michelle laughed and lowered the camera. "You can let her up now."

Let me up? Only now did Claire notice that they'd both dropped to their knees in the middle of the lawn, with Lana's front flush against her back. When Lana let go, Claire shakily got to her feet. Her sides hurt from laughing so much, and now her brand-new jeans had large grass stains on them. "Um, I think I need to go change."

"No, no, that's fine," Michelle called after her. "That natural look is exactly what I'm after."

But Claire didn't listen. She needed a break. She pushed past them through the French doors and stormed to her bathroom for some much-needed cold water.

For several seconds, Lana knelt on the lawn, frozen, and stared after Claire.

"Is she okay?" Michelle asked.

"I...I don't know." As her fiancée, she probably should know—and she should go after her. "Help yourself to the grapes and the cheese. We'll be right back." She jumped up and hurried after Claire.

The master bedroom was empty, but water splashed in the adjoining bathroom.

Lana pressed her ear to the door and listened for a second, then knocked softly. "Claire?"

The water was shut off, and the door swung open a few inches. Claire peeked out, her face wet and pale. She had removed her makeup, as if deciding that the photo shoot was over.

"You okay?" Lana asked.

"I'm fine."

Lana leaned against the doorframe and studied her. "What was that?" She used her thumb to point in the direction of the backyard.

"That was our photographer having the dumbest idea ever." Claire grabbed a towel and rubbed it over her face several times, not bothering to be gentle.

"You hate being tickled that much?" Lana asked quietly.

Claire lowered the towel slowly, as if she was hesitant to give up its cover. "I didn't say that. It's just... It was a weird feeling, being so..." She gestured helplessly.

"Out of control?"

When Claire neatly hung the towel on its holder and turned toward Lana, her eyes were a stormy gray. "Who's playing psychologist now?"

A faint smile tugged on Lana's lips. "Maybe living with you is rubbing off on me."

Claire didn't say anything, but her guarded expression gentled.

"Ready for more photos?" Lana asked.

"Ready." Claire gave a decisive nod, as if she had to convince herself. "As soon as I reapply my makeup. Just no more tickling."

Lana chuckled. "No more tickling, I promise. And forget about the makeup. Who wears that when they're hanging out in the backyard, goofing around with their lover?" Not giving her time to object, she hooked her arm through Claire's and pulled her back to the yard.

~~~~~~~

"Okay." Michelle looked around the backyard as if searching for a promising photo op. "Why don't you," she pointed at Lana, "hop on there?"

Lana eyed the round granite table the photographer indicated. It looked sturdy enough to carry her weight, so she slid onto the table and dangled her legs.

Michelle snapped a photo. "You're a natural. Did anyone ever tell you that?"

Lana flushed. It wasn't too often that she got complimented by a hot butch. *She's got a fiancée, remember? And supposedly, so do you.*

Right on cue, Claire cleared her throat behind them. "Where do you want me?"

"Come over here, facing Lana." Michelle pulled her forward. "And step between her legs."

Before either of them could blink, Michelle had them positioned with Claire standing in the V of Lana's thighs.

"Great." Michelle adjusted some setting on her camera. "Now hold that pose."

Claire looked at Lana as wide-eyed as a field mouse who'd realized it had been spotted by a circling hawk. She shifted uncomfortably, which brought them even closer.

The soft clicking of the camera shutter interrupted the awkward silence. "Oh yeah. This is great," Michelle murmured from behind her camera. "Keep looking at each other like that. Pretend nothing else in the world exists except the two of you. Now move even closer and part your lips, like you're about to kiss."

Lana stared into Claire's wide, gray eyes. Clearly, she'd have to take the lead. *You can do this. You've had to play intimate scenes with people you barely knew before.* She leaned forward the tiniest bit until she could feel Claire's breath bathing her face. A hint of lilacs and spring teased Lana's nose as Claire came even closer. Heat seemed to flicker between them like waves rising from asphalt. They stared at each other with only inches of space between them. Lana found herself holding her breath.

"Okay, that was great," Michelle said. "Let's try a different pose. Lana, move your legs a little farther apart. Claire, lean closer, as if you're about to bend and kiss her neck."

"Jeez, did she have to pick this scenario that could be straight out of your sex-on-the-kitchen-table chapter?" Lana whispered.

A wrinkle formed between Claire's brows. "It's not a chapter on sex on the kitchen table," she whispered back as she leaned closer, as instructed. With every word, her breath fanned over the sensitive skin on Lana's neck.

Lana's own breathing hitched, and heat spread from her neck to her toes. Okay, maybe it didn't quite reach her toes. That heat went straight to her core. *Oh hell. I've definitely been single for too long.*

She tried to get a glimpse into Claire's eyes. Was this affecting her too?

Claire's irises were still a stormy gray, but Lana couldn't tell if it was from their closeness or if she was still upset because of the tickle incident.

Michelle pressed the shutter release button again and again, circling around them for different angles. "Claire, can you put one hand on her hip?"

When Claire lifted her hand, her fingers bumped Lana's knee. "Oh God, I'm sorry."

Before Claire could jump back, Lana grabbed her bare elbow and held on. "It's okay. I'm not going to break. Besides, it was the good knee."

"Oh." Claire blew out a breath, which sent goose bumps all over the skin of Lana's neck, and placed her hand on Lana's hip.

Through the fabric of Lana's capris, Claire's fingers felt much too cold for LA at the end of May.

"Good," Michelle said. "Lana, can you try leaning back on your palms and tilting your head back?"

Lana decided to pretend she was on a set and followed the instructions of the person behind the camera. The movement thrust out her breasts, and she imagined she could hear the top button on her blouse groan as the fabric stretched to the max. Or maybe she was the one groaning as Claire's hips pressed between her thighs. She dug her hands into the rough granite of the table, not sure if she wanted this photo op to end now or to last forever.

Finally, with one last click of the shutter, Michelle stepped back and lowered the camera. "That's a wrap, as you movie people say."

Claire pulled back fast, as if she couldn't wait to get away from Lana. She busied herself picking blades of grass from her jeans.

Lana adjusted her blouse and checked the top button to make sure it had held.

Michelle studied them with a grin. "You two haven't been together for very long, have you?"

Both of them froze and stopped adjusting their clothes. They exchanged a glance.

"Uh, no." Lana stepped next to Claire and lightly bumped her hip. "Still in that honeymoon phase, right, sweetie?"

"Um, right."

Michelle chuckled. "I could tell. Claire touched you so carefully like she was afraid to lose control and rip off your clothes in front of me."

"What?" Claire sputtered, her face as red as if she was about to blow a fuse. "I have never—"

"Oh, honey, don't be embarrassed because she saw right through us." Lana wrapped one arm around her and squeezed hard to get her to play along.

"Yeah, okay, I admit it. Clothes ripping. Totally me," Claire said with a straight face.

Lana struggled not to burst into laughter. *Yeah, right.*

Chapter 8

CLAIRE CLICKED THROUGH THE NEXT few days in her digital planner. Maybe she should do what she had offered Abby: not fill the last slot of the day anymore so she could spend more time at home. If she and Lana wanted to be a convincing couple, they had to get to know each other better.

Just as she was about to boot down her computer, a familiar chime announced an incoming email.

She clicked over to her email program.

Ooh. Michelle, the photographer, had already sent them the photos she'd taken yesterday.

Claire glanced at her watch. She still had fifteen minutes before her next appointment, so she downloaded the attachments and opened the first one.

Oh wow.

In the photo, Lana was sitting on the granite table, dangling her feet, looking as if she didn't have a care in the world. The May wind tousled her wavy hair. Her hazel eyes twinkled, and her sensual lips curved up into a smile.

Claire decided then and there that this photo would go on her desk. After regarding it for a few seconds longer, she clicked to the next picture.

Again, she couldn't help staring. It was one of the *tickling* photos. Lana had her arms wrapped around her from behind, both of them bending forward at the waist, hair flying everywhere as they laughed hysterically.

Claire hadn't believed that she'd ever think so, but maybe Mercedes had been right. They complemented each other well. It wasn't just the visually appealing contrast between her own fair skin and Lana's tan. The way her slim figure fit against Lana's curves seemed…real.

Yeah, well. It was probably Photoshop.

She clicked to the third photo in the small collection that Michelle had pronounced the best ones.

It was the photo that Lana would undoubtedly dub the sex-on-the-kitchen-table picture, and admittedly, it looked a lot like that. Claire picked up a folder and fanned herself with it while she stared at the photo.

Lana had her head thrown back, baring the curve of her neck, and was arching up against Claire, who seemed to be pulling her closer with her hand on Lana's hip. From the look on Lana's face, Claire could have easily believed that she was a woman in love…or at least in lust.

She slowly exhaled. *Guess she's a better actress than I've given her credit for.* She picked a couple of photos of them together—not the sex-on-the-kitchen-table one—and sent them to Mercedes so she could decide if she wanted to forward them to the publisher's marketing department.

"Dr. Renshaw?"

The voice through the intercom made her flinch. She hastily closed the photo like a teenager being caught looking at porn. "Um, yes?"

"There's a Lana Henderson on line one for you," Tanya said through the intercom.

"That's my girlfriend," Claire said, pleased how smoothly that had come out of her mouth. "Whenever she calls and I'm not with a patient, please put her through directly to me."

"Will do," Tanya said. "I'll put her through now."

After a second, the line clicked. "Hi, Claire. Sorry to disturb you at work," Lana's voice came through the phone.

"No problem. I'm between patients." Claire leaned back in her office chair. "Did you get the photos too?"

"Yes, I did—and I was right. Didn't I tell you you'd look great in jeans?"

"Um, I guess." Truth be told, Claire hadn't paid attention to how she looked in the photos, other than that unfamiliar expression of unrestrained laughter on her face.

"I really should get you another pair for your birthday. Hey, when is your birthday?"

"October twenty-ninth," Claire answered, then fell silent when she realized that by then, they would no longer be in contact. Their arrangement would end long before her birthday.

Lana was quiet for a while too. Finally, she cleared her throat. "Um, anyway, I called because Jill just texted me. She and Crash want to have dinner with us and a couple of friends sometime this week. Do you want to go, or should I make up some excuse?"

"Ask them if they're free tonight."

"Tonight?" Lana echoed.

"Yes. It can be our final rehearsal before the party tomorrow. If we can convince an actress that we're a real couple, we might stand a chance of convincing eight therapists too."

Lana gulped audibly but then gamely said, "Sounds like a plan."

"See you tonight, then."

"See you tonight."

When they ended the call, Claire went into her calendar and blocked any six o'clock appointment that wasn't already booked for the next two months, resisting the urge to click over to her download folder to look at the photos again.

Claire had stopped on her way home to pick up another pair of jeans. It wasn't because Lana had commented on how good she looked in jeans, she told herself. Jill and Crash had both worn jeans when they'd been at her house, and she didn't want to stick out like a sore thumb among Lana's friends; that was all.

"Is this okay?" she asked as she stepped out of her bedroom and gestured at her jeans and the short-sleeved emerald green blouse.

Lana looked up from the strappy sandals she'd just put on. She was wearing a cream-colored pair of capris and the burgundy blouse Claire had picked for the photo shoot. Thin leather strips crisscrossed over her sturdy calves, making her look like a Roman soldier—only sexier.

Sexier? Claire arched her brows at herself. Since when did she find full-figured women sexy? Apparently, she was growing into her role as Lana's pretend fiancée too.

"Um…" Lana said.

"Not good?" Claire peered down at her outfit. She hadn't spent so much time thinking about what to wear since she'd first started dating women.

"Oh, no, don't worry. It's great, but..." Lana tied off her sandal straps and came over to her. She reached up and pulled the silver clip from the back of Claire's head, making Claire's hair tumble down around her shoulders. "There. Now it's perfect."

Claire ran a hand through her slightly tangled strands. "Are you sure?"

"Positive."

"Okay." Claire took her car keys off their hook next to the door. "Then let's go."

―――⁓―――

"Wow, this looks really nice," Claire said as Lana guided her toward the Glendale restaurant where they were meeting her friends.

Two palm trees flanked the entrance of the red brick building, and small tables were set discreet distances apart beneath striped awnings on the large outdoor patio. Soft music drifted over, and as they crossed the street, the aroma of grilled chicken and saffron rice wafted over, making Claire's mouth water.

Lana laughed. "What? You thought I'd take you to some fast-food place or something?"

"No! It just looks a little..." Claire bit her lip. She couldn't very well tell Lana that the restaurant seemed to be out of the price range of an out-of-work actress, could she?

"Out of my wallet's league?" Lana said with a laugh. "Yes, it is. But it doesn't matter because we're never allowed to pay here. The restaurant belongs to Jill's friend Laleh. Well, to her family, really."

Claire was grateful that, thanks to her job, she was used to meeting new people.

As they approached the patio, Lana's step faltered. "Um, should we hold hands?"

Claire paused and stared down at her hand. Why hadn't that simple gesture occurred to her? Of course Lana's friends would expect them to hold hands. "Good idea."

After the sex-on-the-kitchen-table position the photographer had arranged them in, something as innocent as holding hands should have been easy, but for some reason Claire's cheeks warmed as she reached out and clasped Lana's hand. Somehow, the casual gesture felt very intimate.

Lana's fingers were warm and soft and engulfed hers securely.

It felt so completely different from holding Abby's hand that Claire could hardly believe it was the same sensation. *Of course it feels different. Abby was the woman you wanted to marry. Lana is an actress you're paying to pretend she's in love with you.*

But the difference wasn't a bad one, just one she couldn't put her finger on.

Just hold her damn hand and stop overthinking.

As they stepped onto the patio, Lana's friends waved from a table next to the wall, which was decorated with a mural of a scenic seascape. Jill, Crash, and a beautiful, slim woman with long, black hair rose and took turns hugging Lana so Claire had to let go of her hand.

Her fingers suddenly felt cold, and she rubbed them as she stood next to the table, shuffling her feet.

"Everyone, this is Claire Renshaw…my girlfriend."

Lana's hesitation had been so short that Claire hoped only she had noticed.

"Claire, this is my friend Laleh Samadi, and, of course, you already know Jill and Crash."

Just when Claire was about to offer her hand, the black-haired beauty named Laleh gave her a short hug.

Wow. That wouldn't have happened in Claire's circle of friends, which, come to think of it, was mostly Abby's circle of friends, so she had stayed clear of most of them since the breakup.

"Where's Hope?" Lana asked as she and Claire sat next to each other, across the table from Jill and her girlfriend. She turned toward Claire and said, "Hope is Laleh's partner."

Laleh sighed. "She called to say she'll be running late. There was a bad accident near the 101/405 interchange, so they had several patients rushed in just as she was about to leave."

"Hope is an ER doctor at Griffith Memorial," Jill explained, but Claire barely heard her. She was focused on Lana, who had gone pale beneath her tan.

Claire leaned toward her. "Hey, you okay?" she asked quietly.

Lana nodded, but her full lips formed a tight line.

"Oh God, Lana, I'm so sorry." Laleh reached across the corner of the table to clasp Lana's shoulder. "I shouldn't have mentioned..."

Everyone exchanged knowing looks, while Claire sat there, her gaze darting from one woman to the next. Why the heck was she the only one who didn't have a clue what was up with Lana? She couldn't even ask because they thought she was Lana's girlfriend. Everyone looked at her, clearly expecting her to know what was going on—and to do something about it.

Her hands bunched into fists beneath the table. God, she hated being unable to help or to say anything that would ease the sudden tension. Would a comforting touch be welcome, or would it make Lana flinch and stiffen up even more?

Carefully, Claire reached out and put her hand on Lana's, which lay on the table. For once, Lana's fingers were cold, so she rubbed them gently.

"It's okay." Lana smiled, but Claire had a feeling she was drawing heavily on her acting skills. She gave Claire's hand a squeeze before withdrawing hers and returning her attention to her friend. "So Hope will be missing her beloved *adas polo* today?"

"Oh, don't worry." Slowly, Laleh's smile returned too. "I'm sure Aunt Nasrin will send some home with me if Hope doesn't get here in time."

As if on cue, a stocky, salt-and-pepper-haired woman appeared, introduced herself to Claire as Laleh's aunt, and took everyone's order.

Claire was still more focused on Lana than on the menu, so when it was her turn to order, she chose the first thing that caught her attention—the chicken soltani—and handed back the menu with a "*kheyli mamnoon.*"

Laleh regarded her with interest. "You speak Farsi?"

"Oh no, only a few words I picked up from a Persian couple I counseled a few years ago."

"Claire is a psychologist." Lana leaned toward her and slid her hand onto Claire's thigh, high up, where at least Laleh could see it.

Claire flinched at the unexpected move. When Lana started to withdraw her hand, she quickly covered it with her own so they wouldn't draw attention. The move pressed Lana's hand more intimately against her thigh, making Claire's belly quiver and her skin heat beneath the jeans. Her body clearly hadn't gotten the message that this was just pretend.

"What else did you pick up from your patients?" Laleh asked.

"Only a few basics like *salaam* and *khoda hafez*," Claire said. She hesitated and then added, "But actually, the Farsi words I heard most often from them were *harum zadeh* and *kos maghz*."

Laleh laughed, and the Middle Eastern family at the next table looked over.

"Let me guess," Laleh said when she stopped laughing. "That couple ended up divorcing."

"Actually," Claire allowed herself a proud grin, "they just celebrated their tenth wedding anniversary."

Lana patted Claire's thigh, making more tingles shoot through her body. "Claire's an excellent therapist. Did I tell you that the American Association for Marriage and Family Therapy honored her with an award last month?"

Claire blinked at her. Apparently, Lana had done some research.

"Congratulations," Jill said. "So that's your secret."

Claire looked over at her. "Secret?" Had she missed something? That hand on her thigh was far too distracting.

Jill flashed them a grin. "The secret of how you made Lana fall for you like this." She snapped her fingers. "After that whole Katrina disaster, I didn't think Lana would ever move in with anyone again, especially not that fast."

Katrina disaster? She wasn't talking about the hurricane, was she? *Great, here I go again, sitting here like a complete idiot.*

Laleh's aunt returned to the table with their drinks, bread, plates of fresh herbs, and bowls of hummus and yogurt-cucumber dip. Lana took her hand away from Claire's leg to help reorder things on the table.

Finally, Claire could breathe again.

Everyone was still looking at her expectantly, waiting for her to tell them how she had won Lana over so quickly.

"Yeah, well, what can I say…?" That was the question: What could she say when everyone else at the table knew more about her supposed girlfriend than she did? She smiled at Lana, hoping it looked like a loving smile, not like a disgruntled animal baring its teeth.

Lana lifted her hand and cradled Claire's cheek in her palm. Looking deeply into Claire's eyes, she said, "From the moment we first met, it was like magic. We just…clicked."

Claire struggled to suppress the twitching of her lips. During that first meeting, the only thing that had clicked had been the dollar signs in Lana's head when she'd heard the offer of fifty thousand dollars.

"Wasn't it like that for you and Crash too?" Lana asked, directing her gaze away from Claire.

Good. Get their attention off us.

Jill laughed. She and Crash traded a long look.

"Not exactly," Crash said with a fond smile. "I thought Jill was a spoiled Hollywood diva because they hired me to stumble over a bedpan for her."

"Hey, I wanted to shoot that scene myself, but the director wouldn't let me."

"I know." Crash lifted Jill's hand to her mouth and kissed her knuckles.

Claire frowned. "Why wouldn't the director let you do it yourself?" Stumbling over a bedpan wasn't exactly dangerous, was it?

Silence spread over their table.

Claire looked from one woman to the next. *Oh great.* Clearly, she had put her foot in her mouth again.

"Because I have MS," Jill said. Her tone was light, but Claire had often heard such deceptively easy statements during therapy sessions, so she knew Jill must have struggled quite a bit until she'd reached that kind of acceptance.

For a few seconds, words deserted Claire. Lana should have told her so that she wouldn't have been caught unawares. What was the right thing to say? I'm sorry? I couldn't tell? Finally, Claire decided on, "Thank you for telling me."

Jill nodded. "It's getting easier, thanks to my therapist—and Crash."

The two looked at each other again and seemed to forget everything around them.

Claire averted her gaze so she wouldn't intrude on their private moment.

Laleh's attention wasn't on her friends either. She stared at something behind Claire, and the biggest smile Claire had ever seen appeared on her face.

Claire turned.

An athletic stranger with tousled, chin-length, brown hair strode toward them, not glancing left or right even once. The gaze of her intense blue eyes was on Laleh alone. She stopped next to Laleh's chair, bent, and kissed her softly. "Hi."

Darkness had slowly descended on the patio, so now the candle in the glass globe in the middle of the table threw shadows across their faces, and the lights wrapped around the trees lining the patio twinkled like stars. A love song was playing in the background.

Claire leaned back in her chair. *Great.* Here they were, in a romantic little restaurant, with two couples who could have been poster children for her thriving relationships book. *How awkward.*

She sent Lana a glance, but she just shrugged and said, "Hi, Hope."

Maybe they should try a romantic gesture of their own, to fit in with the other infatuated couples at the table. Quickly, Claire went over chapter seven of her book—*Making an Effort: Little Gestures That Keep Your Romance Alive.*

Taking a bath together and making out in an elevator were definitely out, but tip number eight might work: feeding each other dinner. She submerged a piece of bread into the yogurt dip and held it out for Lana to eat.

Lana looked from the morsel to Claire's eyes with both brows drawn up, but then she seemed to realize what Claire was trying to do. Just as she leaned forward and was about to close her lips around the bread, a drop of yogurt splashed onto her blouse.

The tips of Claire's ears went hot. *Great.* She should have listened to Michelle, who had commented that her trying to feed Lana was about as sexy as feeding a toddler. Hastily, she looked away as Lana dabbed a napkin over her chest.

Claire slumped against the back of her seat. *I really hope my tips work better for my readers than they do for me.*

<hr>

Lana pulled the seat belt away from her belly and popped open the button on her capris. "God, I'm so full."

Claire didn't answer, maybe because she was fully focused on pulling the Audi out into the light evening traffic.

"The 101 might still be closed," Lana said. "We should take Brand."

Again no reply from Claire, but she headed south on Brand Avenue.

Lana peered at her, trying to make out her features in the lights of an oncoming car.

Claire had that therapist look on her face, which Lana knew by now meant she was holding back her emotions. "What is it? I thought it went really well tonight. Didn't you think so?"

To be honest, she hadn't been sure how prim and proper Claire would fit in with her more laid-back friends, but to her surprise, Claire had gotten along with everyone. She had seemed genuinely interested in Crash's anecdotes about life as a stuntwoman, and she had made everyone laugh when she'd recounted a hilarious story about shopping for her office couch.

"Oh yeah. Really well." Claire's voice was dripping with sarcasm. "Especially the parts where I looked like an idiot!"

What the hell was she talking about? "You mean when you dripped yogurt all over me? That was no big deal."

Claire braked a little too abruptly at a red light, making Lana press a hand against the dashboard, and turned her head to glare at Lana. "I'm not talking about that."

"What then?"

"I'm talking about when you suddenly got all quiet and pale and Laleh apologized for…I don't even know what!"

The light turned green, and Claire accelerated across the intersection.

Nausea swirled through the pit of Lana's stomach. She clutched the door handle. Was Claire speeding, or did it just feel like it to her? "That's bullshit! No one thought you looked like an idiot."

"Oh no? I was the only one who had no clue about something that obviously upset you."

"At the moment, you are the one upsetting me!" Cold sweat dotted her brow. She stared through the side window at the buildings that seemed to fly by much too fast.

"Oh, now you are upset when you were the one making me look stupid in front of all your friends? Couldn't you have at least told me about Jill's MS or this Katrina person?"

"You mean the way you told me everything about Abby and your breakup?"

They glared at each other.

Lana swallowed down the rising bile in her throat. "Could you please keep your eyes on the road?"

With a grunt, Claire returned her attention to the street ahead. "Me not telling you every little detail about Abby… That's different."

"Oh yeah? How?"

"It's different because…because…because I'm the one paying you, not the other way around!"

The words hit Lana like a punch in the stomach, adding to her nausea. "Oh wow. Way to make me feel like a prostitute," she muttered.

Claire didn't seem to hear—or care. "I'm paying you to save me from public humiliation, not to make me look stupid."

"Is that all you care about? How you look to other people? You know what, Claire? For a psychologist, you sure have a lot of hang-ups!"

Claire winced as if Lana had slapped her. "Says the one who's sitting in a car, trembling and refusing to talk about it!" she shot back.

"You'd love that, wouldn't you? So you could focus on what's wrong with me instead of your own problems."

Claire white-knuckled the steering wheel. "Nonsense. If I want to convince others I'm your loving partner, I need to know what's going on with you." Her voice softened as she added, "And I want to help you."

"I don't need help—and certainly not yours. Now drive slower, dammit, before you kill us both!"

"I'm doing the speed limit," Claire said but eased up on the gas anyway.

They spent the rest of the forty-minute drive in silence.

When Claire pulled into the garage, Lana got out of the car on trembling legs. Without waiting for Claire, she stomped to the door and stabbed the security code into the keypad.

A red light flashed across the panel. *Wrong code. Dammit.*

Claire pushed past her. "Let me."

Lana gritted her teeth, hating the feeling of standing there like a helpless child who couldn't even open a door by herself. But if she didn't want to stand there half of the night, she had to move aside.

As soon as the door opened, they both stepped forward, nearly colliding.

They glared at each other, then Claire waved her through and stomped into the house behind her. Their bedroom doors fell closed behind them without them exchanging another word.

Lana sank against the door. *Great. And tomorrow we'll have to convince half a dozen therapists that we're happily in love… If Claire doesn't want to cancel our arrangement.* She stripped off her stained blouse, threw it across the room, and dropped face-first onto the bed. "Fuck," she groaned into the pillow.

Chapter 9

CLAIRE HAD NEVER BEEN SO glad that the counseling center, where Renata's party was being held, was just a six-minute drive from her home. Even those few minutes seemed to stretch forever.

Silence reigned between them since they'd left the house. They hadn't exchanged more than a few words all day.

She peeked over at Lana, who didn't make eye contact but instead stared straight ahead through the windshield.

Claire sighed. Their chances of pulling off looking like a couple in love were practically zero.

"The most important person to convince is Renata, my mentor and boss," Claire said, to fill the strained silence. "So try to impress her, okay?"

Lana grunted a reply.

"Remember to introduce yourself as my girlfriend, not my fiancée. And whatever you do, try not to let Vanessa corner you alone."

Another grunt came from Lana.

Claire glanced over at her. "You're not going to give me the cold shoulder during the party, are you?"

"Don't worry. I'm a professional, and I know how to act. I won't embarrass you," Lana said without looking at her. "After all, you're paying me."

Claire bit back a sharp reply. Another hurtful back-and-forth like the one yesterday wouldn't help. She pulled into the parking garage that was attached to the three-story office building housing the counseling center.

With the silence between them, the clacking of their heels sounded overly loud as they climbed out of the car and made their way to the entrance. At the last moment before entering, Claire remembered what she'd forgotten yesterday too. "Uh, hands."

"What?"

"We're supposed to be holding hands," Claire said.

Lana frowned but then offered her hand. As always, her fingers were warm, so unlike her attitude toward Claire right now that it startled her.

Clinging to Lana's hand as if it were a lifeline, she pulled her into the building and past the exotic plants and the koi pond in the courtyard without giving her much of a chance to marvel at her surroundings. The shades on the floor-to-ceiling windows to either side of the path were up for a change, giving her a glimpse of her colleagues mingling in the reception area.

"Great," Claire muttered. "Vanessa is already there, parading around her husband and probably her book."

"Which one is she?" Lana asked.

"The redhead with the toothpaste-ad-white smile and the James Bond look-alike pasted to her side."

Lana craned her neck. "She looks nice."

Claire arched her brows at her. Had Lana just said that to aggravate her? "Oh, she is nice. At least to your face. But if it serves her purposes, she'll bad-mouth you behind your back."

"Maybe you're just paranoid," Lana said.

Before Claire could answer, Vanessa saw them through the window and gave an exaggerated wave.

Claire groaned. "Here we go." She pulled Lana through the door.

"Claire, welcome," Vanessa said as she dragged her husband over to them. He was a lean, clean-shaven guy who indeed looked like James Bond in his custom-tailored tux.

What the heck? Why is she acting like she's the hostess? Claire looked around. Where was Renata?

Vanessa turned her attention to Lana and eyed her from head to toe with a gaze that made Claire itch and want to push between them. "And this must be the charming...?"

"Lana Henderson." Lana shook her hand with a pleasant smile. "And you must be Vanessa. Claire has told me so much about you."

"Um, she did?"

"Of course! She talks about her favorite colleagues all the time."

Claire warningly squeezed her hand. *Don't overdo it.*

Lana pulled her hand free and pointed at the reception desk, where a buffet and a tray of champagne glasses had been set up. "I think I'll go get myself a drink. Do you want a glass of champagne too, honey?"

"Um, no, thanks." Maybe Claire could have used some alcohol to calm her nerves, but she wanted to keep her wits about her.

"Would you mind getting me a glass too, sweetie?" Vanessa asked her husband.

"Of course." He kissed her hand and then let it go with some hesitation, as if he could barely stand to be separated from her for even a second.

Christ. Their lovey-dovey behavior was getting on Claire's nerves. Maybe it was just bitterness and jealousy since her own relationship hadn't worked out, but somehow, she found their displays of affection fake. *Says the woman who's paying an actress to play her girlfriend!*

When her husband and Lana walked off, Vanessa turned toward Claire. "So that's your new girlfriend."

"That's Lana." Claire infused as much pride into her tone as she could.

"I have to say, I'm a little surprised," Vanessa said.

"That I'm with someone else that fast after...?" She didn't say Abby's name.

"That too, but mostly because she doesn't seem to be your type." Vanessa turned and swept her gaze over Lana, who was just reaching for a glass of champagne.

Claire looked over at her too. Lana's dress was off-the-rack and couldn't keep up with her own mauve satin dress or the designer gown Vanessa wore, but she looked stunning in it anyway. The lavender faux wrap dress hugged her full hips and breasts, while a wide sash concealed her belly. The hem brushed her knees, and with the three-quarter-length sleeves, both scars and the tattoo were covered.

"Not my type?" Claire blinked at Vanessa as if she had no idea what she meant.

"Well, no offense, but she doesn't seem anything like Abby."

"Thank God," Claire said, and to her surprise, she didn't even have to act. "I like Lana just the way she is." *Damn. I should have said love, not like.*

Then she tried to relax. No one would expect her to declare her love after such a short time, would they?

"Good for you." Vanessa smiled and patted her arm. "I'd hate for you to settle just to avoid being single."

Claire wanted nothing more than to grip the hand on her arm and rip it off. "It's not about settling. It's about finding someone that fit me better."

Lana rejoined them, with Vanessa's husband in tow. Her glass of champagne was already half empty, and Claire suddenly wished she had requested one too. Instead, she accepted the glass of orange juice Lana handed her.

"Thanks, honey," she said to Lana.

Vanessa's curious gaze rested on them, heavy like an anvil. Like Claire, her colleague was trained to observe the body language and physical interaction of couples. Under Vanessa's watchful eyes, she leaned toward Lana. Considering they hadn't exchanged one civil word in the past twenty-four hours, she didn't dare aim for her lips but instead pecked her cheek.

Vanessa, however, laid a passionate kiss on her husband when he handed her a glass of champagne.

Great. Claire secretly rolled her eyes. Did Vanessa have to outdo her at every step?

When the lip-lock ended, Vanessa turned toward Lana. "So, Claire tells me you're a lawyer."

"Did she now?" Lana drawled.

Oh shit. Had she forgotten to tell Lana about that?

Lana wrapped one arm around her and lovingly trailed her hand over Claire's hip.

Her palm was warm, even through the satin of Claire's dress, leaving a trail of fire in the wake of her touch.

Under the pretense of caressing her hip, Lana pinched her—hard.

The pleasant tingles gave way to a flare of pain. *Ouch.* Somehow, Claire managed to conceal her flinch.

"Honey, you know I don't like it when you brag about me," Lana said.

"Can I help it if I'm so proud of you?"

Vanessa sipped her champagne and studied Lana over the rim of her flute. "So what kind of law do you practice?"

A drop of sweat pooled at the base of Claire's spine. She should have listened to Lana and told her colleagues that Lana was a barista. No shame in that, right? But no, she'd had to make up a more impressive job for her fake girlfriend. If they crashed and burned now, it was her own fault.

"Oh, my firm handles pretty much everything you can think of," Lana answered with only minimal hesitation.

She was good at improvising; Claire had to give her that.

But Vanessa wasn't done digging. "How about you personally? What kind of cases do you handle? Tax evasion? Corporate stuff?"

"No," Lana said with a sweet smile. "Divorces."

They all stared at her, including Claire; then Vanessa started to laugh. "Oh my God. That's hilarious! A couples therapist and a divorce lawyer!"

"Most of my dates were pretty freaked out when I told them what I do for a living, but not Claire, of course." Lana wrapped her other arm around Claire too and squeezed a little too hard. "She doesn't have any prejudices about my job."

Okay, okay. Message received. Claire gave her a nod of grudging respect.

"Oh, I didn't mean to imply that I have anything against divorce lawyers," Vanessa said.

"Of course not," Lana answered. "Our jobs are not that different, after all."

"Uh, they aren't?"

"Well, we're both helping couples through an emotionally raw time."

"True." Now that Vanessa no longer had the upper hand in the conversation, she looked around. "Oh, there's Renata. I haven't seen her yet. If you'll excuse me, I have to show her my book. The copies I ordered arrived today. How exciting, right? I'll have to sign a copy for you later."

"Uh, sure." Claire somehow managed not to scoff. Of course Vanessa had to bring her book to the party, making sure everyone took notice of it. Well, if Claire had chosen to self-publish too, she could have had an entire series of books out by now. But she'd held out for a traditional publishing deal because she'd wanted the prestige of a New York publisher. Hopefully, Vanessa would stop her obnoxious showing-off once Claire's book was out.

With a touch to Claire's arm, Vanessa was gone, dragging her husband off with her.

Claire blew out a breath and downed half of her orange juice as if it were a shot of liquor. "Divorce lawyer?" she whispered out of the corner of her mouth. "You've got to be kidding me! That's like the natural enemy of couples therapists! Why the heck didn't you say you're a tax lawyer or something?"

"I went through three divorces with my mother, so I know a thing or two about what divorce lawyers do. Besides, it's the only type of law that I was sure she wouldn't want advice on."

Claire had to give her that. "All right. I've got to admit you handled it well."

"I wouldn't have to handle it if you hadn't lied about my job," Lana hissed, her voice low so that no one else could hear.

"I couldn't very well tell them you're an actress."

"Why not? Actresses aren't exactly out of the ordinary in LA."

"Yeah, but what if anyone gets the wrong...or, in this case, the right idea and figures out that," Claire lowered her voice to a whisper, "you're only playing the part of my girlfriend?"

"Okay, I'll give you that. But then why not tell them I'm a barista? Just because Vanessa has a stick up her ass the size of a sequoia doesn't mean you have to play her game."

Claire had just taken another sip of orange juice. Now it shot back out of her nose as she started to laugh, then cough.

"Good evening, ladies." Of course, Renata chose that moment to join them. She patted Claire on the back in a motherly way. Her warm gaze went from Claire to Lana. "You must be Lana."

So Vanessa had already told her Lana's name. Claire's hackles rose as she wondered what else she might have said about Lana.

"And you must be Renata," Lana said as she shook Renata's hand. "Claire speaks very highly of you."

"Well, she hasn't told me much about you, but that's our Claire for you." Renata patted Claire's back again. "She's always been very tight-lipped about her private life, preferring to suffer her heartache over the breakup in silence. It's great to see her laugh again, so thank you for performing that miracle."

Claire wiped a drop of orange juice from her nose and hid her blush behind a tissue. She felt like a heel for lying to Renata, who was almost like a second mother to her. But she had started this, so now she had to stick to the script.

"Oh, Claire is a very easy woman to please," Lana said with a smile.

The last sip of orange juice nearly shot through Claire's nose too. She sent Lana a hidden glare. *What did I tell you about not embarrassing me?*

Lana gave her an affectionate hip bump. "Get your mind out of the gutter, tiger." She made good use of her sexy actress voice. "I didn't mean it like that. I meant that all it takes to make Claire happy is some coconut-lime shrimp, a glass of Pinot Noir, and cuddling up on the couch to watch *The Philadelphia Story* for the fifty-third time."

She said it so convincingly that Claire could almost imagine them spending every evening like that. It was a surprisingly nice thought, even though they'd done nothing but argue for the past twenty-four hours.

"I'm glad to hear that you're getting her to relax at home," Renata said. "She's too much of a workaholic at times."

Renata and Lana exchanged knowing glances.

"Said the pot to the kettle," Claire murmured.

Renata gave her a pat on the shoulder. "Well, this is a classic case of 'do as I say, not as I do.' I want you to have a long, successful career and achieve everything you want, but not at the price of your personal happiness."

The warmth and sincerity in her eyes made Claire feel even worse. "Don't worry. I'm very happy with my personal life."

Lana slid an arm around her waist as if to prove it.

"To happiness and new beginnings, then." Renata lifted her glass and toasted them both.

Claire was glad that she'd already emptied her glass so she didn't have to add to her deception. But Renata was right about one thing: a new beginning was in order. With the trip to New York coming up next month, she and Lana couldn't continue like this, arguing whenever they were alone and pretending to be head over heels whenever someone else joined them. With her acting background, Lana might have been able to pull it off, but it was giving Claire emotional whiplash.

As soon as Renata moved on to the next group of guests, Claire lightly clasped Lana's elbow. "Can we talk?"

"What did I do now?"

"Nothing. I just… I'd like to talk to you alone." She led Lana in the direction of her office.

"You know they are totally thinking you're dragging me to your office so you can have your way with me on your desk, right?" Lana commented.

Claire stopped abruptly. "What? Nonsense. No one is thinking any such thing!"

"If you say so."

Claire huffed, but just to make sure no one could accuse her of unprofessional behavior in her office, she pulled Lana into the courtyard instead. The gurgling of the small waterfall feeding the koi pond would drown out their conversation, so no one could overhear them, and maybe the serene surroundings would soothe Lana and make her more willing to forgive her.

A turtle lifted its head out of the water, took one look at them, and dove back beneath the surface, disappearing between the ferns reaching into the water.

Claire wished she could do the same, but she knew there was no hiding from this conversation. "Listen." She took a deep breath. "I wanted to…" Before she could say *apologize*, movement caught her attention out of the corner of her eye.

Vanessa stood by the entrance, leaning against the metal gate, a cigarette dangling from her fingers. She was watching the smoke curl up, so she hadn't seen Claire and Lana yet, but if she turned her head a bit or went back inside, she would discover them. The cigarette was smoked almost down to the filter, so it could happen any moment.

Shit. Claire's gaze darted around, but the slender palm trees and ferns wouldn't provide any cover.

Vanessa would catch sight of them any second, and she would know immediately that Claire and Lana were arguing. Their body language—facing each other with their arms stiffly by their sides and their shoulders up—screamed arguing couple. Besides, what other reason could they have for sneaking away from the party? At least Vanessa with her cigarette had a good excuse.

No doubt Vanessa would offer them relationship counseling or recommend a chapter from her book—unless Claire could convince her that she hadn't dragged Lana here to argue.

Lana's words echoed through her mind. *You know they are totally thinking you're dragging me to your office so you can have your way with me on your desk, right?*

Vanessa threw her cigarette stump down and crushed it with a twist of her nine-hundred-dollar stilettos—the same way she would crush Claire's reputation if Claire didn't stop her.

Just as Vanessa turned around, Claire stepped forward, right into Lana's personal space.

Lana's hazel eyes widened. "Wh—?"

No time for long explanations. "Please don't slap me," was all Claire whispered before she dipped Lana back against a palm tree and kissed her.

Lana went rigid.

For a moment, Claire thought she'd get punched or at least pushed away, but then Lana parted her lips and kissed her back, and all thoughts stopped.

Lana's lips were so incredibly soft and warm and pliant against hers.

A breathy gasp escaped Claire as Lana's tongue stroked along her bottom lip then gently touched her own. Lana tasted of champagne and something fruity. Her body melted against Claire's, all hints of resistance gone.

Lana slid her hands up Claire's back. Her fingertips grazed Claire's neck, sending shivers down Claire's spine, and then her fingers tangled in Claire's hair so she could deepen the kiss.

Several strands came loose from Claire's pinned updo. Not that she cared at the moment. The warm glide of Lana's tongue against hers sent spirals of sensation through her entire body. Her mind spun, and she gripped Lana's hips with both hands to keep her balance. *Oh holy...*

Someone cleared her throat next to them.

Reality washed over Claire like a bucket of ice-cold water. *Vanessa. Right.* That was why she'd kissed Lana.

She backed away from Lana, but it took several seconds before she could tear her gaze from her.

Lana stared back, her lips red and her cheeks flushed.

Was it a physical reaction to their kiss, or was part of it anger at being ambushed like that?

Claire didn't have time to figure it out.

"Well, well," Vanessa said. "Looks like you two made up."

"Who says that we were arguing?" With trembling fingers, Claire tried to pin her hair back up. Her scalp still tingled where Lana had touched her.

Vanessa let out a huff. "Please. If you'd read my book, you'd know it was obvious."

"And if you'd read Claire's book, you'd know that the best part of arguing with your lover is the making up," Lana said, her voice low and seductive. She stepped next to Claire and pressed against her side, her body hot and soft against Claire's. "Right, honey?"

"Right." Claire's own voice was husky without her having to act.

They turned their heads and looked at each other, their gazes catching and not letting go. What was going on behind those hazel eyes? For once, even three degrees in psychology weren't going to help Claire figure it out.

"Well, good for you," Vanessa said stiffly. "As you probably know, our target audience doesn't like self-help authors who don't practice what they preach."

Claire narrowed her eyes. What was that supposed to mean? It sounded almost like a threat. Did Vanessa suspect something?

But that was impossible. Their kiss had been entirely convincing. Claire's libido had certainly bought it, hook, line, and sinker.

"You'll have to excuse me now. I bet Daniel is already looking for me." Vanessa strode past them, back toward the party, leaving them staring after her, hesitant to look at each other.

As soon as Vanessa disappeared around the corner, Lana slumped against the palm tree Claire had pressed her against. Her senses were still reeling. Where the hell had that come from? She hadn't thought of Claire as a passionate person, but if this was how she kissed when it was fake, Lana had a feeling she wouldn't survive a real kiss.

Not that she and Claire would ever share one, of course.

"Oh God." Claire rubbed both palms across her face, then stopped abruptly as if remembering that it might smudge her makeup. "I'm so, so sorry. I shouldn't have ambushed you like that, but I saw Vanessa standing there and knew she'd assume we were arguing and then she turned around and I didn't know what else to do..."

95

"No, no, that was good." *Really, really good, actually.* "Um, I mean, it was a good thing to do to convince her we're happy together and not in need of her services as a couples therapist."

Claire exhaled and leaned against the palm tree next to hers. "I also, um…" Ferns rustled as she shuffled her feet. "I think I also owe you an apology for last night."

Lana was speechless for the second time within minutes. She certainly hadn't expected an apology from Ms. I'm-always-right. "An apology for what?"

"You're going to make me spell it out, aren't you?"

"Yes." Lana held her gaze. "An apology is not an apology if you don't have the guts to admit to what you did wrong."

Claire fiddled with the pins that held up her hair, trying to tame an escaped strand. "I apologize for possibly overreacting a little when we were at the restaurant…and in the car."

"Possibly?" Lana gave her the look she had perfected playing a strict governess in a B movie.

"Okay. I did overreact. And I'm really sorry if I upset you in the car… or scared you. That wasn't my intention. It's just… I don't like feeling humiliated in front of people."

"You weren't—"

"I know," Claire said. "I said *feeling*." She sighed and gave up on trying to secure the stubborn strand of hair. "Maybe I'm overly sensitive right now because of this whole situation." She swept her arm in a gesture that included Lana, the office building, and the party guests. "It's really important to me to have the respect of my colleagues and not look like a fool in front of them."

Lana's anger, fueled by that spike of fear she'd felt in the car last night, dissipated like fog in the California sun. But she still struggled to understand why Claire had reacted so strongly. "Is it really that important to you what people think?"

If nearly dying had taught her one thing, it was that she needed to live her life without worrying what people might think.

Claire sighed. "I know it shouldn't be. But I can't help it."

That admission and the look of vulnerability on her face made Lana want to reach out and hug her, but she held herself back. The memory of Claire's body against hers was still imprinted on her mind.

"I care about what people think." Claire glanced down and smoothed her hands over the wrinkle-free satin of her dress before peeking back up. "Especially these people." She nodded toward the party.

"But why? They don't even seem like close friends."

"They aren't." Claire hesitated. "Well, maybe Renata is. She's been my mentor from the very beginning. I want her to know that the counseling center will be in good hands with me once she retires."

"So you'll take over one day?" Lana asked.

"We never actually discussed it, but I know Renata and everyone else always thought I'd be the perfect person for it. I mean, I had it all: a doctorate, a flourishing career, a great house, a loving relationship, and the prospect of having my book published with a prestigious publishing house. But now…" Claire spread her fingers as if she could feel everything slipping through her grasp. "Now it's all falling apart. I can't let them see the cracks."

"Bullshit," Lana said fiercely.

Claire's eyes widened.

"Yeah, you're not in a relationship anymore." Lana lowered her voice. "So what? Everything else is still true. Well, maybe your house doesn't look quite as great whenever I use the kitchen…"

The corners of Claire's mouth twitched. She started chuckling, then laughing.

Lana watched her and smiled. She liked the way Claire's usually serious features relaxed when she laughed.

When Claire finally sobered, they looked at each other.

"I, um…" Lana gave herself a mental nudge. "I think I owe you an apology too. I should have given you a bit more background on my friends before we met with them."

"Why didn't you at least tell me about Jill having MS?" Claire asked.

"It's not my story to tell. I didn't want to take the choice away from Jill."

Claire seemed to consider that for a moment before nodding. "Apology accepted. So, are we okay?"

"We're okay," Lana said. A weight lifted off her chest, and only now did she realize how stressful the last twenty-four hours of arguing had been. She cracked a smile. "So now that we made up, does that mean we get to enjoy the benefits you describe in your book?"

It was supposed to be a joke, something to lighten the mood some more, but her body hadn't gotten the message. Heat pooled in Lana's belly as she flashed back to the feeling of Claire's body pressing into hers and that smooth, warm tongue stroking her own.

Claire's flush was obvious, even beneath her makeup. "How did you even know about that? You haven't read the manuscript, have you?"

Lana shrugged. "No. But don't all relationship books have a chapter on making up and making out?"

"So you read a lot of them?" Claire studied her with a curious gaze.

"Me? God, no." Lana grimaced. "But my mother devoured books like that when I was growing up. Probably still does." Not that it did her any good. Her fourth marriage was, in Lana's opinion, the worst of all—and that was saying something after catastrophic marriage number three. Why did Claire put so much effort and money into this ruse, all for a book that wouldn't help anyone? Lana didn't get it.

"Probably?" Claire repeated. "You don't know if she's still reading them?"

"I haven't talked to her in years." Not since her mother had chosen to turn her therapist number nine into husband number four, refusing to listen to anything Lana had said.

"Do you want to talk about it?" Claire studied her with that too-deep-seeing psychologist's gaze. It was gentled by genuine compassion, but Lana still didn't like that look directed at her.

"No, thanks. This isn't the right place or time." Most of all, Claire wasn't the right person to spill her guts to. The last thing Lana needed was another therapist poking into her life.

"Okay. But if you ever want to talk, I'm here. I even promise to omit the psychobabble," Claire said with a slight smile.

"Thanks." Lana returned the smile and pushed away from the palm tree. "Should we head back inside?"

"Yeah, we'd better, before my colleagues really start thinking that we are...um..."

Lana's smile grew into a grin. "Traumatizing the koi by having a quickie next to their pond?"

The flush creeping up Claire's neck was just too cute. "Um, yeah, something like that."

Side by side, they stepped back onto the path and walked toward the party. Simultaneously, they reached for each other's hand.

As Claire's fingers entwined with her own, Lana ignored the flutter in her belly. It was only a physical reaction, part of getting into her role a little too much.

"There you are," Renata greeted them when they rejoined the party guests. "I was wondering where you two had disappeared to." Her gaze swept Claire's slightly disheveled updo and her subtly smudged lipstick, and a knowing grin spread over her face, deepening the lines around her eyes and mouth.

Claire's face took on the color of the strawberries on the buffet table. "I just…um, showed Lana around." She squeezed Lana's hand in a silent call for help.

Renata turned to Lana with an amused smile. "So, did you like what you saw?"

"Oh yeah," Lana said, with a bit too much enthusiasm. Her cheeks heated too. "The office is very, um, impressive. Not what I expected at all." That was definitely true for Claire's kiss too. She had expected the kiss to be more precise and controlled, something that was meant to achieve only one goal: make Vanessa believe they were a couple. The gentleness of Claire's lips and the hint of passion had been a surprise—as had been her own reaction.

"No?" Renata tilted her head. "What did you expect?"

"Something a little more…uh…" Now Lana was the one who squeezed Claire's hand, hoping she would jump in and help her out.

"Austere," Claire said with a smile.

Thanks a lot. That wasn't exactly the word she would have chosen to make a good impression.

Claire reached out and tucked a strand of hair behind Lana's ear. "I'm afraid moving in with me might have given Lana the impression that all psychologists are a little…"

"OCD," Lana said at the same time as Claire said, "overly meticulous."

Renata laughed, then sobered. "Wait. Did you just say… You already moved in together? Why didn't you tell me?" A shadow of hurt ghosted across her face.

Claire put a hand on Renata's forearm. "I'm sorry. I wanted to, but… It's a rather recent development, and I didn't want you to think that it's too soon after, you know, Abby and everything."

"Claire." Renata slid her hand on top of Claire's. "I'd never judge you. You should know that by now. It is a little soon, but if it's right, it's right. I'm happy if you are happy."

"Thanks," Claire answered, her voice hoarse.

"You'll have to excuse me now. I promised Vanessa she could sign my copy of her book." A slight raise of Renata's eyebrows gave away what she thought of Vanessa's showing-off. With a smile and a wave, she walked away.

Her departure left behind a slightly awkward silence. Lana didn't know what to say to Claire after their kiss. Finally, she settled on, "I like her. She seems nice."

"She is," Claire said. "We met when I did an internship as an undergrad, and she has become almost like a second mother. I hate lying to her."

"Why not tell her the truth, then?" Lana asked. "You heard what she said—she'd never judge you."

Claire snorted. "How could she not?" She lowered her voice so that Lana had to strain to understand her. "Hiring an actress to play the part of your girlfriend is kind of crazy."

Lana couldn't argue against it. "Come on." She looped her arm through Claire's. "Let's check out the buffet. I hear some shrimp salad calling your name."

The sound of their laughter filled the entryway as they stepped into the house.

Claire closed the door behind them and put her purse down on the hall table. "Did you see Daniel's face when you told him Vanessa had been smoking?"

Lana flashed an unrepentant grin. "How was I supposed to know she was keeping that little habit from him? Does she really believe he can't smell it on her?"

"So much for practicing what you preach." Claire held up the copy of Vanessa's book, which Vanessa had insisted on signing for her. "I bet she has a passage on not keeping secrets in relationships."

"See?" Lana kicked off her heels and wiggled her toes. "Even Vanessa isn't perfect, no matter what she wants people to believe. Maybe you should ease up on yourself."

Claire sighed. If only it were that easy. "Maybe."

In the momentary silence, her stomach rumbled loudly.

Lana laughed. "Oh my God, that sounds like an entire pack of wolves. Why didn't you eat something at the party? I told you to try the shrimp salad. It was great, and so were the spinach dip bites."

"It all looked good, but I was too tense to eat." To her surprise, she didn't mind admitting that much to Lana.

Lana grabbed her hand, which felt like a natural extension of their evening, and dragged her into the kitchen, leaving her just enough time to kick off her heels.

"Um, what are you doing?"

"Don't worry, we're not trying that kitchen-sex advice from your book. I'm just making you something to eat." Lana steered her toward one of the stools. "Sit."

Claire remained standing. "It's much too late to eat a big meal."

"Then only eat a little. Sit," Lana repeated, as if it were her kitchen, not Claire's.

With a sigh, Claire sank onto the stool and watched as Lana took what looked like leftovers of a tuna noodle casserole out of the fridge. "Oh, no, no, no. You know I don't eat carbs after six."

Lana put the casserole into the microwave, turned toward her, and reached for Claire's arm.

"Um, what are you...?"

Lana clasped Claire's wrist with one hand and turned back the hands of her watch to five o'clock with the other. "There."

"Lana, that's... It doesn't work like that."

"It does if you want it to." Lana looked into her eyes. "You want to eat healthy and stay thin. I get that, and I think it's great that you're taking good care of yourself. But is boxing yourself in with rigid rules really the

101

way you want to live your life? Can't you make an exception every now and then?"

Claire groaned. "It's been a long day, Lana. Can we have this questioning-the-way-I-live-my-life conversation when it's not so late?"

A grin curled up Lana's lips. "It's not late." She tapped Claire's wrist. "It's five o'clock."

If Claire had learned one thing about Lana in the month she'd known her, it was that Lana was as stubborn as she was. One of them had to give in, or they'd still be staring each other down across the kitchen island by the time dawn broke. "Okay, I'll make an exception and eat a few bites. Just this once." She held up her index finger. "Happy now?"

"Yep." Humming off-key, Lana took plates out of the cabinet and cutlery from a drawer.

Minutes later, they sat at the kitchen island and dug into the—admittedly delicious—tuna noodle casserole. Claire ate every last bite Lana had served her and only her good manners stopped her from licking the plate.

Luckily, Lana didn't comment or tease her about it.

When Claire got up and carried the dishes to the sink, Lana stopped her with a touch to her arm. "Just put them in the sink. I'll put them in the dishwasher tomorrow."

"No, they're easier to clean if you do it right away, and that casserole dish needs a good scrubbing, so I might as well wash the plates too while I'm at it." Claire filled the sink with water and added over her shoulder, "You can go to bed if you want. I've got this."

But instead of leaving the kitchen, Lana reached for a dish towel. "You wash, I'll dry."

As Claire scrubbed the casserole dish, she had to smile at the picture they probably made, doing the dishes in their elegant dresses. They stood side by side at the sink, and their fingers brushed whenever she handed Lana something to dry.

Who knew that doing the dishes could be this nice? For a while, Claire allowed herself to get lost in the pleasant domesticity of the task. If she had ever shared moments like this with Abby, she couldn't remember them.

Within a short amount of time, the dishes were clean and the sink gleamed.

Claire turned off the light, and they walked down the hall without turning on the hallway light, only the faint glow of the moon from the skylight illuminating the house.

In front of the guest room, they paused and turned toward each other.

"Good night," Claire said.

"Good night."

Neither of them moved toward their respective room.

"Thanks for the casserole and for everything you did tonight," Claire added, "especially for being such a good sport about...um, the kiss."

"No problem." Lana grinned. In the dim light, her hazel eyes looked dark like sinful chocolate mousse. "I didn't suffer too much."

Was that Lana-speak for *I liked the kiss too*?

Well, it didn't matter. It had been a necessary part of their ruse, nothing more, nothing less.

Claire lingered next to her. *Come on. You thanked her, now go to bed.* She shouldn't have mentioned that damn kiss. Now crazy images danced through her mind. Images of leaning toward Lana and—

Are you out of your mind? This is just pretend, and good night kisses aren't in the contract! What the heck was wrong with her? Maybe all those late-night carbs had gone straight to her head.

"Um, sleep well." Abruptly, she backed away, whirled around, and fled to the safety of her own bedroom.

Chapter 10

WHEN CLAIRE GOT HOME FROM work on Monday evening, her cell phone rang just as she got out of the car.

Her agent's name flashed across the display.

"Hey, stranger," Claire greeted her. She had barely heard anything from Mercedes since before Renata's party two weeks ago.

"Sorry I made myself so scarce the past couple of weeks," Mercedes said. "I don't know what it is, but suddenly, all of my clients are getting book deals at the same time. Maybe it's something in the water."

"Well, whatever it is, I hope it'll happen for me too," Claire said.

"It will. Don't worry. The photos you sent me will help too. They're great." Mercedes let out a wolf whistle.

Claire hummed in agreement. Even several of her colleagues had commented on the new photo on her desk.

"But I hope you know that once I send them to Wishing Tree, there's no way out."

"Way out?" Why would she want a way out?

"Yeah. Once I hit send, you can't replace Lana with another actress, no matter how crazy her messes drive you."

"Oh. That. Right." That phone call when she'd complained about Lana seemed like ages ago. What a difference a month could make! "I don't want to replace her."

"Are you sure?" Mercedes asked.

"Yes. I didn't think I'd ever say so, but her impulsivity isn't always a bad thing."

For several seconds, only silence filtered through the line, then Mercedes asked, "Who are you, and what have you done with the real Claire Renshaw?"

"Hahaha. Seriously. I'm not saying I love the way my kitchen looks any time she cooks, but I have to admit that Lana's impulsivity helps in situations when we need to improvise. Her quick thinking saved our butts a time or two at Renata's party."

"I'm glad to hear it. Maybe she could teach you some of her improv skills. They might come in handy for the interview I arranged for you."

"What interview?"

"I arranged an interview on a popular call-in radio show in New York for you, right before you meet with Ms. Huge. It'll give you a better bargaining position if you show her that you're willing to heavily promote your book."

Claire rubbed her temple with her free hand. She'd have preferred to focus on the meeting with the acquisitions editor, but she trusted Mercedes's expertise. Another bargaining chip couldn't hurt.

"Don't worry," Mercedes said when Claire failed to respond enthusiastically. "The radio host is an acquaintance of mine, and she's great. She's actually a psychologist too. She used to have a late-night show here in LA before moving to New York."

"Can you send me a link to her show so I can check out what kind of questions she might ask?"

Mercedes laughed. "And here I thought Lana's spontaneity might have rubbed off on you."

"Um, no. I prefer to be well-prepared."

"Okay. I'll send you the link—and I'll send off the photos."

They said goodbye, and Claire entered the house.

Faint sounds came from the living room, announcing that Lana was back from her shift at the coffee shop.

Claire had to admit that it was kind of nice not to come home to an empty house. Instead of going straight to her room, she diverted to the living room and leaned in the doorway.

Lana certainly seemed to feel at home in the house, after living here for only a month. She was stretched out on the couch, wearing a gray pair of cut-off sweatpants that revealed her scar and her tan legs. A faded, purple T-shirt hugged her generous breasts. Bold letters across the chest said, *Pilates? Oh, I thought you said pie and lattes.*

Claire suppressed a chuckle. She had to admit that there was something unexpectedly sexy about a woman who indulged herself without worrying about the fact that she was more curvy than others.

Apparently, Lana was about to indulge her sweet tooth now. She had set up everything for a cozy night in. The scent of caramel popcorn drifted over, and a bottle of beer sat on the coffee table.

"Oh, hi." Lana looked up from the remote control and caught Claire studying her. "You're home early."

Claire directed her gaze away and pretended to check whether Lana had used a coaster—which she had this time. "My last patient of the day canceled."

"Great," Lana said. "Then you can come watch the movie with me."

"Um, I brought some files home with me to catch up on my documentation." Claire lifted the leather briefcase in her hand.

"Can't it wait?"

Claire hesitated. "It could, but—"

"I'm about to watch *The Philadelphia Story*."

"Really?"

"Yeah, why not? Since it's one of your favorites, I thought I'd see what I've been missing." Lana dangled the remote control in front of her like a carrot in front of a donkey and lowered her voice to a seductive purr. "Come on. You know you want it."

Claire had seen the movie dozens of times, but it might be fun to watch it with Lana, so she finally nodded. "All right. If you give me five minutes so I can change…"

"Sure." Lana jumped up from the couch with childlike enthusiasm. "I'll get you a glass of wine. Pinot Noir?"

So Lana had already figured out her favorite wine as well as her favorite movie. She was amazingly attentive and a keen observer. "Yes. Thanks."

Claire hurried to her room and slipped out of her pencil skirt and silk blouse. After a moment of hesitation, she put on brand-new sweatpants and a T-shirt she usually wore during her rare visits to the gym.

By the time she made it back to the living room, a glass of red wine and a plate of cheese, grapes, celery, and carrot sticks with two different kinds of dips were waiting next to her recliner.

Claire's mouth watered. She slid into the recliner with a contented sigh. "Thank you," she said as she reached for the glass. "I really appreciate it."

106

She didn't just say it to be polite. Since Lana had moved in, there were always fresh vegetables and fruit in the fridge, without her having to ask if Lana could swing by the store on her way home.

"You're welcome." Lana flashed her a grin. "Can't have my girlfriend starve, after all."

Claire popped a grape and a bit of cheese into her mouth. "Fake girlfriend," she said as soon as she had chewed and swallowed.

Lana waved the remote control and started the movie.

"Jesus," she said after a while around a mouthful of popcorn. She waved her hand at the screen. "She sets impossibly high standards for herself, doesn't she? Kinda reminds me of someone I know." She gave Claire a meaningful look.

"Me?" Claire pointed at her own chest.

"Certainly not me." Lana gestured at the way she was lounging on the couch in cut-off sweatpants.

Claire considered it for a moment. "Okay, I do have high standards, but they aren't as unrealistic as Tracy's." She gestured at the TV. "I was never as hard on Abby as Tracy was on her ex-husband. At least I don't think so."

She thought about it while the movie played on. Had she expected Abby to be perfect?

A ding from the iPhone she had placed on the coffee table provided a welcome distraction.

She peeked over at the device and then reached for it, but Lana was faster and snatched it away.

"Oh no. No email. We're watching a movie."

"But it might be work-related." Claire tried to take back the phone, but Lana moved it out of reach. "I told Tanya to email me if any of my clients—"

"No work. We are watching a movie."

Claire got up, rounded the coffee table, and lunged for the phone, which Lana held off to the side. She missed by several inches and landed sprawled across the couch—or, rather, across Lana's lap. Popcorn flew everywhere.

Overly aware of the warm thighs beneath her, Claire scrambled back to the other end of the couch. "Lana, come on. I've seen this movie fifty-three times already, as you recently pointed out."

"But I haven't, and you're the one who kept saying I'm missing out by not giving the great black-and-white classics a chance, so…"

"Of course you're missing out! You're an actress, and you have never seen *The Philadelphia Story*, for crying out loud!" Claire shook her head. "We can't have that."

"Which is why *we* are watching it to remedy that grand oversight."

After one last glance at the phone in Lana's hand, Claire slumped against the back of the couch. Instead of moving back to her recliner, she pulled her glass and plate closer and nibbled on one of her carrot sticks, while Lana picked up the popcorn that had spilled all over her lap and shoved a handful of it into her mouth.

Claire hadn't really seen the movie fifty-three times, but often enough to nearly know each line by heart. Watching it with Lana made it a completely new experience, though.

Lana laughed at some of the funny scenes, booed when it seemed that the main character would marry the wrong person, and even threw a piece of popcorn in the direction of the TV.

Claire watched her with a smile and marveled at how involved Lana got in the movie, as if she had completely forgotten that it was only a film and these were just actors, not real people.

As long as you don't forget that Lana is just an actress and this isn't real. She studied Lana. Was she acting now? Was this, hanging out on the couch together, work for her?

Lana seemed to feel her gaze because she turned her head and gave her a curious look. "What?"

"Um, nothing." Claire directed her attention back to the TV, but now she could feel Lana looking at her. She glanced back. "What?"

Lana regarded her for another moment, then her face creased into a smile, and she leaned toward Claire.

Claire's breath caught. *What is she...?*

"You've got a little..." Lana gently disentangled a piece of popcorn from Claire's hair and popped it into her own mouth.

"Oh. Thanks."

They stared at each other, then Lana directed her attention back at the TV. She cocked her head. "Ooh, I see. So that's why you like the movie so much!"

"Uh, what?"

Lana pointed one of her sticky fingers at the screen.

Claire turned her head.

On the screen, Katharine Hepburn was parading around in a swimsuit.

"Is she the kind of woman you like?"

Was she? Claire couldn't help comparing the actress's thin, elegant body and her tiny waist with Lana's full hips, her ample breasts, and her well-rounded butt. A few weeks ago, her answer might have been different, but now she found that Lana's more curvy body held a greater appeal.

But it wasn't just her body that made Lana attractive; it was her attitude toward life, people, and herself. She seemed so genuine and comfortable in her skin—including her curves, her scars, the messes she left everywhere, and the fact that she wasn't very successful in her career and didn't have much money.

"Uh, no, she's not really my type," Claire said when she realized Lana was still waiting for her reply. "At least not the way you think."

Lana put the popcorn bowl down. "What do you mean?"

"I admire her, that's all. She was a very independent, headstrong woman who refused to conform to the expectations society had of women." A bit like Lana, actually, just in a different way. "She wore pants at a time when it wasn't seen as fashionable for women, and she never gave in to the pressure to pad her chest."

"Oh wow. I had no idea." Lana gave the actress on the screen a respectful nod. "Kudos to you, sister."

"What about you?" Claire couldn't help asking.

"Me?" Lana chuckled and patted her generous breasts. "Never needed to pad my chest."

Oh yeah. I noticed. Claire bit her lip. "No, I mean, is she your type?"

"I don't think I have a type," Lana said. "Well, other than someone who's kind, smart, honest, and has a great sense of humor."

Honest. Claire swallowed. Well, she was lying to pretty much everyone she knew, so that ruled her out. Not that she was angling for anything but a fake relationship with Lana, of course.

When the closing credits rolled across the screen, Claire sat up from where she'd half-reclined against the back of the couch. "So, what did you think?"

"I didn't think I'd enjoy it, but I really did. Are her other movies as good?"

"Most of them. All her successful ones kind of follow the same pattern: a stuck-up high-society woman is brought down from her high horse by a more down-to-earth partner."

Lana chuckled. "Sounds familiar."

Claire arched her brows. Was Lana implying that she was stuck-up?

The thought fled from her mind when Lana unselfconsciously licked her sticky fingers.

The temperature in the living room seemed to rise several degrees. Claire bit back a groan. *Cut it out. You're paying her. That's like lusting after an employee.* "Um, stains," she blurted out.

Lana paused mid-lick. "Excuse me?"

"You'll leave stains all over the couch if you're not careful," Claire managed to say. "Why don't you go wash your hands?"

Lana rolled her eyes. "Fine, Mom."

Good thing she had no idea that Claire's thoughts hadn't been motherly at all. God, she really had to get a grip. The last thing she needed was Lana calling off this arrangement—or suing her for sexual harassment—because she couldn't keep her hormones in check. She'd never had this problem before, not even as a teenager. It had to be one of those crazy rebound things some of her clients kept describing, so it would pass if she kept ignoring it.

To distract herself, she reached for her phone as soon as Lana had gotten up from the couch.

"Ever heard of a work/life balance, Doc?" Lana called on her way to the bathroom.

At the moment, nothing about her life was in balance, so Claire ignored her and checked her email. It wasn't a work-related message.

It was an email from Darlene, a friend of hers. Well, maybe more of an acquaintance, since they hadn't seen each other in months. What did she want now?

Claire clicked on the email.

Hi, Claire,

How are you doing? I haven't heard from you in a while, so I hope you are okay and not working too much.

I just wanted to drop you a quick note and let you know that I would completely understand if you didn't want to attend the gallery opening after all. I know Abby might be there, and I don't know if she'll bring anyone, but I understand if it would be too awkward or painful for you.

No hard feelings if you'd rather stay away.

Take care,
Darlene

Oh God. The gallery opening. Claire had completely forgotten about that, even though it had been on her schedule since the beginning of the year. Back when she and Abby had still been engaged, they had planned to attend together. But now, everything was different. With a few words, Abby had cut her life into a "before" and an "after."

Darlene had given her an out. She could stay home and avoid running into Abby.

But somehow, that thought didn't sit well with her. Staying away would mean people would talk about her absence and the possible reasons for it. She could almost hear their whispering: *Poor Claire, she's probably at home, crying her eyes out.*

Or maybe Abby would even paint her as the bad guy, the one to blame for their breakup, behind her back.

No, Claire decided. She couldn't let that happen. She'd have to go, hold her head up high, and show everyone that she was fine without Abby in her life.

But she couldn't do it alone. Not if there was a chance that Abby would show up with a new girlfriend in tow. She put the phone down and stepped out into the hall.

"Lana?" she called through the closed bathroom door. "Do you like art?"

The water shut off, and Lana opened the door, the towel still in her hands. "Art? You mean like Monet and Picasso?"

"More like Appel and Rothko," Claire said.

"I have no idea who that is." Lana flung the towel over the towel bar. "You're not just asking to get to know me better, are you?"

Claire reached past her and straightened the towel, which had slipped halfway down. "No. That email I got... It's a reminder about a gallery opening next week." She hesitated but then decided that Lana deserved the whole truth. She couldn't blindside her again, the way she had done when she'd told Vanessa that Lana was a lawyer. "Abby might be there, and she might bring someone."

"So you don't want to go alone and look like a sock without its mate."

Claire tilted her head. "Something like that. So, would you come with me?"

"I'm game. But there's one problem."

"Don't worry," Claire said quickly. "I won't kiss you again."

"Uh, good to know, but that's not the problem. I lost some weight after... Anyway, I haven't had the time—or, to be honest, the money—to replace some of the items, so my formal attire is a little limited. Very limited. Actually, the dress I wore to the party is pretty much it."

"That's a problem easily remedied. We'll go clothes shopping on Saturday. You need something to wear for New York anyway. I'm paying, and you get to keep whatever we buy once our arrangement is over. How does that sound?"

"That's very generous of you. Thank you." Instead of beaming in delight as Claire had expected, Lana looked as if Claire had promised her an afternoon of scrubbing toilets.

Claire studied her. "You don't need to feel like you're accepting charity. It's all part of our deal."

"That's not it. It's just that clothes shopping is on my list of favorite activities right after having a root canal." Lana shrugged and put on an almost convincing smile. "But I guess I'll survive it if it means I finally get to meet the infamous Abby."

Claire groaned, suddenly no longer sure taking Lana to the gallery opening was a good idea.

The scent of freshly brewed coffee and hot chocolate greeted Claire as she pulled open the door of the Mean Bean. It immediately catapulted her back to a time, about a year ago, when she'd written *The Art of Lasting Relationships*. Whenever the words refused to come, she had grabbed her laptop and headed to the nearest coffee shop to write there.

"How can you focus with all that hustle and bustle going on?" Abby had always asked.

But to Claire, the background noise of conversations and clinking porcelain was stimulating. If she'd known about the Mean Bean back then, she might have even come here. The coffee shop wasn't part of a big chain. With the small, round tables along two walls, bunches of fresh flowers everywhere, and mismatched armchairs in the corners, it had its own charm.

Lana was behind the counter, wearing a cute apron with a coffee-bean cartoon character. She was sliding two cups toward a customer, saying something to him that made him laugh.

The tall, black woman behind the cash register noticed Claire looking. Her tightly curled hair danced around her shoulders as she nudged Lana.

Claire straightened and crossed the room toward them, just as the only customer at the counter left.

"Thanks for coming to pick me up," Lana said. She nodded toward the woman next to her. "Avery gave me a ride when my car didn't start this morning, but now I'm stranded here."

"I told you that piece of shit you call a car—"

"Hey!" Lana flicked a dish towel at her. "Don't insult Dorothy."

Claire watched them. She couldn't imagine interacting with her colleagues in such an irreverent way.

"Oh, sorry. Where are my manners?" Lana gestured. "Avery, this is Claire, my girlfriend."

Oh. Claire hadn't been sure what Lana had told her colleagues about her. Should she have greeted her with a kiss?

Avery shook Claire's hand. "So you're the mysterious new girlfriend."

Claire squirmed beneath the curious gaze.

"Yes, that's my sweetie." Lana leaned across the counter and planted a kiss on Claire's lips.

It wasn't much more than a platonic peck, but Claire flushed anyway.

"And this is Avery, my boss and favorite sister," Lana said.

Claire looked back and forth between them. "Uh, sister?"

Avery pressed her dark cheek to Lana's lighter one and grinned broadly. "Don't say it. We look like twins, right?"

Lana bumped her with one hip, nearly tossing the thinner woman against the counter. "Stepsister, actually."

As soon as Avery had regained her balance, she bumped her right back. "I can't believe you didn't tell your girlfriend that I'm black!"

Lana shrugged with an impish smile. "It didn't come up."

Claire watched them. They certainly interacted like siblings. "So you are one of the lucky seven who had to suffer through Lana's tickle attacks."

"Tickle attacks?" Avery gave them both a curious look.

A flush rose up Lana's neck. "Uh, long story." She untied her apron and lifted it over her head.

"Oh, I get it now. You just said that so you wouldn't have to be the one being tickled."

Lana flashed her a mischievous grin. "What can I say? Weak bladder."

"Then you'd better hope you don't lose control of it during our loooong shopping trip."

Lana groaned, rounded the counter, and threw a glance back at her stepsister. "If I'm not back by the time my shift starts on Monday, send out the dogs."

"Oh, no, no, no. You're not leaving yet," Avery called. "Let's have some coffee. I want to get to know Claire."

"You mean interrogate her," Lana answered. "Maybe next time. It'll take us forever to get to that boutique Claire wants to drag me to."

Avery sent Claire an impressed glance. "You seriously got her to go shopping with you? Wow! She really must be head over heels for you."

More like for my fifty thousand dollars. But before Claire could think of an answer, Lana waved and dragged her through the door.

Sometimes, Claire's follow-the-rules personality was a good thing, Lana decided as Claire guided the Audi through the bumper-to-bumper traffic inching toward Santa Monica. Claire never violated traffic laws or tried risky maneuvers to get to where she was going faster, so Lana felt safe in the passenger seat—or as safe as she'd ever feel in a car.

Lana stroked her fingers over the dashboard. "So, I guess you didn't name yours?"

"Mine what?" Claire asked without looking away from the street.

"Your car, of course. She needs a name."

"Why would it be a *she*?"

Lana chuckled. "My first stepfather, Avery's father, always said anything that costs so much money and takes so much time to maintain is clearly female."

Claire arched her eyebrows. "What did your mother say to comments like that?"

"Not much. He was actually not a bad guy. The ones after him were the assholes." But she didn't want to get into that topic with Claire, so she asked, "What about Sophia or Blanche? As a name for your car, I mean."

The driver behind them honked as Claire braked at a light that had just turned red instead of trying to make it across the intersection. Claire ignored him and turned toward Lana. "Let me guess. You like the Golden Girls."

"Sure. What's not to like?"

A new song started on the oldies station Claire had tuned in to.

Lana recognized it immediately. It was The Beach Boys' "Good Vibrations." *Oh please no. Not that song.* Cold sweat erupted all over her body and trickled down between her shoulder blades. She wanted to reach out a hand to turn off the radio or switch to another station, but she couldn't move. A car horn blasted behind her, making the world around her blur.

Stop! Make it stop!

Fear sank sharp claws into her chest, squeezing the air out of her lungs. *Can't…breathe!* Her heart beat so rapidly that it felt as if it would give out any moment.

Everything twisted around her like a carousel, but she could still see every detail in crystal clarity as a handful of seconds seemed to stretch into an eternity: the wide-eyed face of the driver in the oncoming car, the airbag exploding toward her, the hood of her car crumpling, glass shattering.

Worse than those snapshots were the sounds. Brakes screeched, horns blasted, metal crunched. Someone screamed. It might have been Lana.

Every muscle in her body stiffened, prepared for the pain of metal slicing into her.

The seat belt snapped taut, pinning her in place.

Crushed! She'd be crushed alive.

Pain flared through her arm, her leg, everywhere.

Then came that awful silence, worse even than the sounds. The only thing she could hear was the hiss of oil spilling over a hot engine and the drip, drip, drip of blood splashing onto the floor mat.

She clawed at the seat belt with numb, trembling fingers, then grabbed hold of something. Something warm and soft. Something that didn't belong in this world of sharp metal and pain.

"Breathe, Lana," a soothing voice said. "Take a deep breath. Slowly in and out through your mouth. That's it. Now another."

She wasn't alone in the car. Someone was there, breathing along with her. Oxygen trickled into her screaming lungs.

"You're safe," that voice said softly. "Just focus on your breathing. Stay in the present. Stay with me, Lana."

Slowly, the hissing and dripping sounds faded away, and the smoke wafting in through the shattered windshield dissipated.

Lana's stiff muscles went limp. She stared from the windshield—which wasn't broken or even scratched—to her arm. The scar itched, but there was no blood.

No blood. You're safe.

Someone rubbed her arm, right above the scar, where the blue and green tail feathers of the phoenix curled across her skin. Her previously numb fingers began to prickle as feeling returned.

Lana turned her head.

Claire was leaning over her, peering down at her with her eyebrows pinched together in concern, not even a hint of her professional mask in place.

The soft, warm thing that Lana had grabbed hold of was Claire's arm.

Oh shit. That would surely leave marks. She snatched her hand away. "I'm sorry. I...I..."

"It's okay." Claire took a bottle of water from the center console, unscrewed the cap for her, and pressed it into Lana's shaking hands.

The taste of blood and chemical dust from the airbag still seemed to linger in Lana's mouth, so she gratefully gulped down some water and then pressed the bottle to her sweaty brow.

116

Slowly, the shaking stopped, as did the ringing in her ears. Only now did she realize that the radio had been turned off, and Claire had performed a miracle by finding an open parking spot. They were parked in front of a trendy yoga studio somewhere in Santa Monica.

A couple with a stroller and several people with shopping bags passed by, giving them curious stares.

Oh God. Lana wanted to hide behind that plastic bottle forever.

"What was that?" Claire stopped rubbing Lana's arm and slumped back into her own seat. "Scratch that. I know what it was. You were having a full-blown panic attack."

"No," Lana said, wishing her voice sounded stronger. "I don't get those. Not anymore," she added more quietly.

"Lana. Please. Something just triggered a panic attack. Tell me about it." Claire's tone managed to be soothing and firm at the same time.

It sounded too much like the psychobabble tapes Lana's mother used to listen to.

"What happened?" Claire asked. "Was it...an accident?"

"You graduated summa cum laude. I bet you can put two and two together without me having to spell it out for you."

"Of course I can, but—"

A car horn blared in the distance, threatening to shatter Lana's fragile composure. She had to get out of here. Now. Blindly, she fumbled for the door release and swung her legs out of the car, ignoring the stiffness in her left thigh. "We're here to shop, not to play therapy." She slammed the passenger-side door shut with more force than intended and strode toward the boutique next to the yoga studio, trying not to limp.

An ocean breeze cooled her hot cheeks, and the scent of flowers and watered grass trailed on the air. Lana sucked it in greedily, hoping to get rid of that smell of burned oil and blood that still seemed to cling to her nostrils.

Claire followed her. "Running away won't help you deal with the trauma."

"Who says I haven't dealt with it?"

"If you had, you wouldn't still be having flashbacks." Claire caught up with her but thankfully didn't try to grab her arm. "This is very treatable, Lana. EMDR or cognitive behavioral therapy can—"

Lana stopped and whirled around so abruptly that they collided.

Claire took hold of Lana's shoulders to keep them both upright.

"I wasn't kidding when I said I wanted to amend the contract to no quack talk. Besides, isn't it unethical to counsel people you're involved with in your private life? So stop psychoanalyzing me!"

"I'm not psychoanalyzing you," Claire said. "I'm trying to help you. Not as a—"

"I don't need your help. If I had wanted a therapist, I would have gotten one." Lana shook off Claire's hands and continued marching toward the boutique.

Claire rushed after her and pulled her to a stop in front of the boutique's door, forcing Lana to look into her eyes. "Forget about me being a therapist for a second, okay? Can't I just be a friend?"

The soft, pleading look in Claire's eyes was nearly Lana's undoing. "If you want to be a friend, let it go. All I want is to find something to wear for the gallery opening and to forget about the last few minutes. Can we do that?"

Claire sighed and ran a hand through her hair, which had come loose from her chignon. "All right. If that's what you need." She twisted her hair into a new knot and reattached the clip.

If only Lana's jagged emotions could be put back into order that easily. But she was an actress, someone who pretended for a living, so she might as well pretend to be fine. She held the glass door open for Claire and followed her into the boutique on slightly unsteady legs.

Immediately, she wanted to apologize to the sales staff and back out in a hurry. Rows of designer skirt suits and tops from high-end brands lined the walls. Tables presented purses with price tags that made Lana gasp. She could never afford this upscale place in a million years, and even if Claire would be paying, was it really necessary to spend so much on an outfit that she wouldn't get to wear very often?

But a stylishly dressed saleswoman with too much makeup was already headed toward them, so it was too late to retreat.

"Are you sure you want to shop here?" Lana whispered out of the corner of her mouth.

"We're here now," Claire said. "Why not try something on? If we don't find anything that is worth the money, we can always leave."

"How may I help you?" the saleswoman asked.

Claire faced her. "We're looking for a dress for a gallery opening."

"Certainly." The saleswoman eyed her. "You're wearing a size six?"

"Yes, but it's not for me." Claire half turned and wrapped one arm around Lana.

Lana hoped she couldn't feel the slight trembling that still hadn't stopped entirely.

"It's for my fiancée," Claire added.

For a second, Lana's mouth gaped open. She would have bet money on Claire introducing her as a friend in this posh establishment.

To her credit, the saleswoman didn't bat an eye. Apparently, once you exceeded a certain number of zeroes on your price tags, sexual orientation no longer mattered, only how much money the customer was willing to pay. With her power suit and the discreetly sexy silk camisole peeking out from her blazer, Claire certainly fit into this upscale boutique.

Within short order, the saleswoman had guided Lana toward the fitting room, while she and Claire went about the store, picking out things for her to try.

Lana undressed behind the curtain and eyed herself in the full-length mirror. Did this store even carry anything that would fit a woman with real curves? Her gaze trailed down to the scar on her thigh. She gently touched it, following its raised contours with her fingertips. Other accident victims that Lana had met in the rehabilitation center had looked at their scars with disdain or had tried to avoid looking at them altogether, not wanting the reminder of the day they'd nearly lost their lives.

But for Lana, having the scars was nothing to be ashamed of. They reminded her that life was precious, and they were proof that she was a survivor. Her wounds had healed. *You're fine. Just fine.* The little voice in her head sounded like Claire, and Lana had to admit that it was soothing.

A soft throat clearing made her move her hand away from the scar.

"Um, here's the first one," Claire's voice came from the other side of the curtain. She pulled it back a bit and, without peeking in, held out a black dress on a hanger through the gap.

Well, that answered Lana's question about whether the store had anything in her size.

A pantsuit, two dresses, and several elegant tops later, Lana noticed two things: First, there was something to be said for shopping in expensive boutiques. The saleswoman had a great eye for sizes. Everything Lana tried on fit her to perfection. No squeezing into tops that seemed to be made for women without boobs, no frustrating struggles with zippers, no dropping pants back to the floor because she couldn't even pull them up past her knees.

If clothes shopping were always like this, she could almost come to like it.

Almost.

Because the second thing she noticed was a pattern in regards to what Claire was handing her: everything covered both of her scars.

The long-sleeved scarlet dress she'd just put on was no exception. Lana smoothed her hand over the satin hem, which ended below her knees so no hint of the scar would peek out.

Lana slid back the curtain with more force than necessary and stepped outside.

Claire, who stood by right outside with the saleswoman like a dutiful spouse, looked up. Her gaze slid over the dress and lingered on the hint of cleavage on display before moving on to Lana's face.

"You should definitely go with a dress, not a pantsuit," the saleswoman said. "You look wonderful in dresses." She sounded almost sincere, not as if she was just angling for a commission.

"Yes," Claire said quietly, still looking at her, "yes, you do."

Her gaze seemed to warm Lana's skin through the layers of satin. For a moment, she nearly forgot her annoyance with Claire.

"You don't like the dress?" Claire asked when Lana kept staring at her.

"I do, but…" Lana's gaze flickered to the saleswoman. "Would you excuse us for a second?" Not waiting for a reply, she tugged Claire into the fitting room with her and pulled the curtain closed.

A flush that outshone the color of Lana's scarlet dress rose up Claire's neck. "Um, you do realize that she now thinks I'm doing more than helping you out of the dress?"

Lana ignored the remark. The saleswoman could think whatever she wanted; she didn't care. "Tell me one thing. Is it my body that you dislike so much that you want to cover it from head to toe, or—"

"What? No!" Claire's eyes were as wide as Lana's when she'd seen the price tags. "I told you, you look gorgeous."

A flush of pleasure rose up in Lana's chest, but she suppressed it. "Then it's the scars that bother you." She made it a statement, not a question, and caressed the scar and the tattoo above it through the fabric of the sleeve, as if preventing the bird from angrily taking flight.

A fine line dug itself between Claire's brows. "Who said that?"

"Your choice of outfits does!" Lana gestured at the long sleeves and the below-the-knees hem.

"Nonsense! I don't care if you want to proudly display the scars and the tattoo."

Lana snorted. "Who's talking nonsense now? I saw how you looked at me during the audition, the very first time we met."

Claire deflated a little. "Okay. I admit it. I thought the tattoo was a little...much. I didn't get it then, but I think I do now. Your tattoo... At first I thought it was an overly colorful eagle. But it's a phoenix, symbol of rebirth, isn't it?"

Lana nodded and rubbed the bird's wings through the satin.

"So, show it off if you want. I don't care, but if you do, there'll be questions. About the tattoo. About the scars. Questions I won't be able to answer because you refuse to talk about it. You can't have it both ways, Lana."

Damn. Lana hadn't thought of that, even though she probably should have. She sank onto the stool in the corner of the fitting room.

Silence spread through their tiny refuge.

From the corner of her eye, she peeked at Claire. Would it really be so bad to tell her? Yes, Claire was a psychologist, and that made Lana want to pull up her mental drawbridges, but she was also a decent human being, someone who was trustworthy, private, and reliable. Despite their slightly rough start and the complicated nature of their relationship, Lana sensed that Claire's offer of friendship was genuine—and every fiber of her being urged her to accept it.

Lana opened her mouth, not yet sure what she was about to say or if her vocal cords would even work.

"Abby broke up with me five minutes before our engagement party started," Claire said, speaking very quietly. She didn't look at Lana. Instead, she sat on the second stool in the opposite corner, picked up Lana's T-shirt that had fallen to the floor, and folded it. Then she did the same with her capri jeans.

Lana closed her suddenly dry mouth. *Wow.* And she had thought Katrina leaving her the day she had been released from the hospital had been low. "And you had no idea it was coming?"

Claire huffed out a breath. "You'd think I would, right? I mean, how can a relationship expert be so blind to not see the signs?"

"Forget about that. In your private life, you're a woman, a mere mortal like the rest of us."

"Apparently." Claire smoothed wrinkles from the T-shirt on her lap. "I was as clueless as all those heartbroken women leaving comments about sudden breakups on my podcast. I sat on my high horse, giving them tips on how to get over it and find lasting love, while my own fiancée was planning to call off our engagement."

Lana slid her stool closer. "I don't get it. Why propose to you if she had her doubts about the relationship?"

"I was the one who proposed." A weary smile ghosted across Claire's face. "After seven years together, I thought it was time."

"Okay, but then why would she accept your proposal if she had her doubts?" Before Claire could answer the question, something else occurred to Lana. "Wait. That's why you asked her to marry you? Because you thought it was time?" And that from a woman who loved romantic black-and-white flicks.

"No. I... I thought she was the one. I thought we were happy." Claire let out a sigh. "Apparently, Abby didn't think so."

Lana moved even closer. Now their shoulders were brushing. They sat in companionable silence for a while. Then Lana asked, "Did she tell you why? I mean, was there someone else?"

"Abby said there wasn't."

"And you believed her?" Lana asked. Katrina had sworn up and down that the breakup didn't have anything to do with another woman before admitting that she was going back to her ex.

"Yes," Claire said without hesitation. "Abby isn't the type to cheat. She's one of the most loyal people I know. She supported me when I went back to school to get my doctorate and when I cut back my work hours to write my book."

Why, then? Lana wanted to ask, but she held herself back. No sense in digging deeper into a wound that obviously hadn't healed yet, especially since Claire might not even know why Abby had ended their relationship.

Finally, Lana reached over and squeezed Claire's hand. "I'm sorry."

Claire squeezed back.

Lana's fingers chose that moment to stop trembling. She smiled wryly. Who knew? Maybe therapists had that magic touch after all. Then she lightly shook her head. No. Not therapists. Claire.

She hesitated for another second. *Come on. One wound for another. It only seems fair.* "I was on my way to an audition when it happened. I was singing along to 'Good Vibrations' on the radio, hoping the song would send some good vibrations my way for the audition. I never saw it coming. Guess we have that in common."

Claire's fingers tightened around hers, but she didn't say anything, just let her talk.

"An SUV shot out of some side street and sideswiped me. My car spun and bounced around like a ball in a pinball game. By some miracle, I missed an oncoming car and smashed into the guardrail." She recited it like an accident report she read in the newspaper, trying not to let it touch her, but the technique didn't seem to help much because her hand was trembling again.

Or maybe it was Claire's, which was still holding hers.

"I think I might have passed out for a second or so. When I woke up, there was smoke, shards of glass, and twisted metal everywhere. The driver's side door was crushed against my left side." She pressed her left arm against her side as pain seemed to flare through it. "I couldn't get it to open. I tried to crawl out over the passenger seat, but my legs were trapped beneath the crumpled steering column. I couldn't get out. I couldn't—"

Spots danced in her vision, and a roaring sound filled her ears.

A sharp squeeze to her hand brought her back to the present. "You're not there. You're here, with me. Safe."

Claire was now kneeling in front of her, holding Lana's hand with both of hers. Her gray eyes, gentle and intense at the same time, peered up at Lana from only inches away.

Was this what she did for her patients when they were having flashbacks? For some reason, Lana didn't think so.

The pressure on her chest eased. She blew out a breath. "I'm fine. I'm fine now."

"Yes, you are." Claire rubbed her thumb across Lana's knuckles.

Lana hoped she wouldn't let go anytime soon, because that soft touch gave her the strength she needed to go on. Now that she had started, she needed to get it out. "I don't know how long I was in the car, trapped and bleeding, but it seemed like an eternity until the firefighters finally managed to cut me out."

Claire swallowed audibly. "Were you hurt badly?"

"The cut on my arm wasn't too bad, but my leg was pretty mangled. Shredded muscles, torn ligaments, the works."

Claire looked down at Lana's lap. Carefully, as if touching a spooked animal, she placed her hand on Lana's left leg, right over the scar.

A tingle shot up Lana's thigh, reminding her that she was very much alive—and so was her libido. She cleared her throat. "I spent three months in the hospital and a rehabilitation center, and even after that, it took me six months to walk without a limp. Well, more or less without a limp. It still acts up when I'm on my feet for too long."

"So you were out of work for a long time. And I imagine the medical bills piled up quicker than you could pay them." Claire's hand still lingered on Lana's thigh. "Is that why you agreed to be my pretend fiancée?"

Lana nodded.

Claire rubbed the back of her neck with her free hand. "Damn. Now I feel like I took advantage of you when you were in a very vulnerable position."

The words stirred something deep inside of Lana. It was exactly what she had believed of therapists and self-help gurus: that they took advantage of people at their most vulnerable, just for their own gain. But if Claire felt bad about it, she clearly wasn't one of them. "You didn't. It was my decision." She forced a smile. "And like I said, so far, I haven't suffered too much."

"Still." Claire got up from her kneeling position and slid back onto the stool next to Lana's but kept hold of her hand. "Thank you for telling me."

"Thanks for biting your tongue and not suggesting therapy again."

Claire tilted her head and studied her. "What is it with you and therapists?"

Lana shrugged as casually as possible. "I don't like them. Present company excluded, of course."

They smiled at each other.

A soft cough came from the other side of the curtain, interrupting their eye contact. "Excuse me?" the saleswoman called. "Is everything all right in there?"

"Everything's fine," Claire answered. "But we decided that we want to see a few more dresses."

Lana grimaced. She was suddenly bone-tired, and the last thing she wanted was to try on more dresses.

"Something with a shorter hem or maybe one with capped sleeves," Claire added.

Lana's fingers spasmed around Claire's. "Are you sure? If you'd rather your acquaintances not see—"

"I'm sure if you're sure."

Again, their gazes connected and held.

Finally, Lana nodded. If Claire wasn't afraid to let people see her scars and the tattoo, she sure as hell wouldn't shy away from it either. Like the phoenix tattoo, her scars were a symbol of survival and strength, something to be proud of, no matter what Hollywood wanted to make her believe. "I'm sure."

"No problem," the saleswoman said from the other side of the curtain. "I have the perfect dress in mind." She bustled away.

"Um, I'd better go too." Claire pointed toward the curtain. Her fair skin revealed a hint of a blush. Belatedly, as if she had forgotten she was still holding it, she let go of Lana's hand and slipped out of the fitting room.

Lana slumped against the mirror and stared at the swishing curtain. She'd talked about her accident before, especially with Jill and Crash, but even then, she had avoided going into too many details. Now she had told Claire, of all people, everything. Admittedly, it hadn't been as bad as she'd expected. In fact, it felt as freeing as the moment the crushed dashboard had been lifted off her.

Did Claire feel the same about finally opening up and telling her the details of her breakup?

Emotional confessions in a fitting room. She shook her head and laughed shakily. *Who would have thought?*

~~~~~~

"I can't believe you paid that much for a single dress," Lana said.

Claire put the garment bag into the Audi's trunk and shrugged. "It's beautiful."

"Yeah, but still… Just looking at that price tag made me dizzy."

The price of the dress wasn't what made Claire dizzy—although Lana had looked breathtaking in it. What made her mind reel was what had happened in the fitting room.

She really shouldn't feel so out of sorts. It wasn't as if she hadn't heard something like this many times before. Over the course of her nine years as a therapist, she had treated several patients with PTSD, panic disorders, or traumatic pasts. Once, she'd even had a patient with a story very similar to Lana's.

What was different was her own reaction to it. Her patient's suffering as he had recounted his accident hadn't left Claire cold, but there had been a professional distance that had protected her and enabled her to do her job without being paralyzed by her patient's pain. With Lana, that therapist's shield was thin as an eggshell—and it had crumbled entirely when she had told her about the breakup.

I can't believe I did that. During her therapy sessions, it was all about her patients, never about Claire as a person. If she revealed bits and pieces about herself, it was only as a carefully used tool.

And maybe she had thought that's what it had been in the fitting room—just a tool to get Lana to open up too.

But the moment she had started talking, that illusion had disappeared like a mirage.

"You okay?" Lana asked quietly.

Claire realized that she had climbed into the car and was sitting behind the wheel but hadn't started the engine. "I should ask *you* that question," she said, not willing to lower that eggshell-thin shield all the way again. She gestured at the car. After a horrible accident like that, she wouldn't have been surprised if Lana had avoided getting into a car at all costs.

126

Many of her patients who had suffered traumatizing experiences developed avoidance behaviors like that.

"I'm fine." A fine sheen of sweat gleamed on Lana's forehead, but her gaze projected strength. "But maybe…"

"Yes?" Claire wouldn't hesitate to do whatever Lana needed.

A ghost of a smile creased the corners of Lana's eyes. "Maybe we could leave the radio switched off, just in case."

Claire pressed a button on the car's touch screen, starting one of her '90s pop playlists. "How about this? No Beach Boys, I promise."

"Perfect," Lana said. "Thank you."

Claire sensed that she meant much more than only the music. She smiled and pulled out onto the street. "You're very welcome."

Chapter 11

As they walked toward the entrance of the art gallery, Lana tried to unobtrusively wipe her damp hands on her knit jersey gown.

Claire leaned toward her. "Don't worry. You look stunning."

A chuckle escaped Lana. "Well, with what this dress cost, I'd better!"

She peered down at herself. The one-shouldered blue dress left both of her arms bare, and the sheer mesh insets across the bottom gave teasing glimpses of her legs. Normally, she wasn't one for dressing up, but she had to admit that the dress was beautiful—and it made her feel beautiful.

Or maybe it was Claire's gaze, which sometimes lingered on her.

What did you expect? Abby is supposed to be here, so of course Claire is going to play the role of the smitten lover. Nothing better to make your ex jealous than to show her that you've moved on. That was the reason Claire had asked her to come and had bought this expensive dress after all.

The gallery was packed—full of people in cocktail dresses and tailored suits. Waiters wandered around, offering flutes of champagne and canapés on silver trays.

Lana swallowed. Even with her beautiful dress, she felt as out of place among all these rich, glamorous people as a snake at an arm-wrestling competition.

Claire took Lana's hand and placed it in the bend of her elbow. "Just follow my lead," she whispered into Lana's ear.

Her warm breath against the shell of her ear made Lana shiver. She ignored it. "So you're the lead actress tonight?"

"Let's not try for an Oscar," Claire said, her voice so low that only Lana could hear her. "All we need is to make it through this evening without Abby or anyone else suspecting that we're as fake as…"

"My grandmother's teeth," Lana said when Claire paused, looking for the right comparison.

A grin lit up Claire's tense face, and Lana was struck again by how attractive she was when she smiled.

"Something like that," Claire said.

Lana didn't need to act to cling to Claire's arm. With her free hand, she reached for a glass of champagne one of the waiters held out to her on a tray.

When he offered a glass to Claire too, she shook her head.

She had declined the champagne at her boss's party too, Lana remembered. "Don't you like champagne?"

"I do, but I don't want to drink tonight."

Because she wanted to keep a clear head while meeting Abby again, possibly for the first time after the breakup? Or because she was driving and wanted Lana to feel safe in the car with her? The longer Lana knew her, the more she could glimpse the kind, compassionate person behind that proper, uptight facade.

They walked around the room with its blindingly white walls, stopping every now and then to look at a painting or so Claire could exchange air kisses and small talk with one of her acquaintances. In the blur of introductions, Lana soon lost track of who was who, but she doubted that it mattered. None of these people seemed like close friends of Claire's.

Lana kept looking around, scanning the room for any blonde who could be Abby. She had gotten only a glimpse of the photo on Claire's nightstand before she had snatched it away to hide it from Jill. The gallery was full of beautiful, sophisticated women, so Lana wasn't sure she would recognize Abby if she saw her.

"She's not here," Claire said as if sensing what Lana was doing. Claire's relief was almost palpable.

Lana lightly patted her arm. "Maybe she's heard that you're dating someone new and wanted to avoid running into you and your stunning new girlfriend."

"Don't forget *modest* new girlfriend," Claire added with a smile.

"Hey, you were the one who said I look stunning."

Claire tilted her head in silent acknowledgment.

"In case I haven't mentioned it before, you clean up pretty well yourself," Lana said.

That was the understatement of the century. Claire was wearing a strapless black satin dress that showed off her smooth shoulders, delicate collarbones, and toned arms. Her blonde hair was pulled up into a sleek chignon, but a few strands were strategically left curling around her face and elegant neck, keeping her from looking too austere. Lana wasn't surprised to see her draw gazes from the art lovers all over the room. She had to admit that she was struggling not to stare too.

It wasn't just the dress that caught her attention. The way Claire moved—that characteristic mix of efficiency and grace—fascinated her too.

"Thank you," Claire said in a clipped tone.

Did she think Lana was complimenting her only because she felt their contract required her to do so? Or was she just tense because Abby might show up?

They wandered over to the middle of the room, where a large painting hung on a detached white wall. The canvas was painted in a blood-red color, with ugly green and brown splashes spilling over the red.

Lana stared up at it. That thing was supposed to be art? "Um," she whispered out of the corner of her mouth, "what is the artist trying to say? It looks like a cat threw up all over a red carpet or something."

Claire sent her a disapproving glare, but one corner of her mouth twitched, giving away her amusement.

Before she could answer, an older woman stepped next to them and gazed at the painting too. "Isn't it amazing?"

"Yes." Lana made good use of her acting skills to produce an enthusiastic smile. "It's so…" *Um…red?* What else could she say about this painting?

"Expressive," Claire threw in.

Did you get a list of vocabulary to use in situations like this once you earned your first million or something? Not that she had any clue if Claire had that much money.

Lana nibbled on a stuffed mushroom and some smoked salmon crostini from a tray while Claire talked about art with the stranger.

Finally, the woman walked away.

Phew! Lana nearly wiped imaginary sweat off her brow, but then she remembered that she was wearing makeup and let her hand drop back down.

"Think you can brave this crowd alone for a minute?" Claire asked. "I need to use the bathroom."

"Sure." Lana let go of Claire's arm. "I'll stay here and, um, enjoy this amazing work of art." Grinning, she pointed at the cat-vomit-on-red painting.

"You mean enjoy the stuffed mushrooms." Claire gave her a teasing nudge.

"That too."

"All right. Enjoy the food. Be right back."

With her back to the painting, Lana watched her cross the room, admiring the graceful way she moved. Once Claire had disappeared into the crowd, Lana turned toward the tray with the stuffed mushrooms.

"What's a woman like you doing in a place like this?" someone said from behind her.

Lana turned.

A stunning stranger stood in front of her. Blonde hair fell in shimmering waves down onto shoulders left nearly bare by the spaghetti straps of her slim-fitting green dress.

Lana squinted at her. Was this stranger flirting? Usually, thin, attractive, well-off women like that didn't give her the time of day.

"I mean, you aren't looking at the painting, so you're obviously not here for the art," the woman added.

Lana shrugged. "To be honest, I'm more of a pears and horses woman."

"Pears and horses?"

"Yeah, you know, paintings of pears or horses that you can actually recognize as pears and horses."

"Ah. So you're not into abstract art." The woman smiled. Her blue eyes twinkled.

"Not really. Plus it's pretty hard in here to even see the paintings without being hit in the face by a twenty-pound Prada bag." Lana gestured at the packed room.

The woman's smile became an all-out laugh.

Something about the way she looked when she laughed seemed strangely familiar. Had they met before? Lana didn't want to ask, because it might come across as if she were flirting. Not that she was opposed to flirting with this beautiful stranger, but she was supposed to be Claire's doting girlfriend.

Nope. If there were any flirting tonight, it would be with Claire. Just for show, of course.

When the woman stopped laughing, she offered her elegant hand. "Abigail Gardner."

"Lana Hen—" She froze with her hand halfway extended. *Abigail... Abby! Holy hell!* That's why the woman had looked so familiar. She'd been talking...nearly flirting...with Claire's ex!

Claire had tried to make a beeline from the restroom back to Lana's side, but her friend Darlene had intercepted her before she had taken even three steps in that direction.

Immediately, Darlene started to go on and on about her work and that of the other artists being showcased tonight. She swept her arm in a broad arc as she explained her use of layers in one of her paintings.

Had gallery openings always been so boring? Claire listened politely to Darlene's explanations while secretly peeking at her watch.

Now that she'd talked to Darlene and shown her support by making an appearance, maybe she and Lana could get out of here. Traffic shouldn't be too bad at this time of the evening, so perhaps it would still be early enough to watch *It Happened One Night* once they got home. Maybe she'd even be daring tonight and allow herself a handful of popcorn.

"I saw you looking at *Triumph of Nature*." Darlene waved toward the center of the room, where the red painting with the green and brown splashes hung. "What did you think?" Then, not waiting for Claire's verdict, she added, "It's amazing, if I say so myself."

Oops. That was one of Darlene's? Somehow, Claire managed to keep a straight face. "It certainly is. Even Lana commented on it."

A pleased smile spread over Darlene's face before it gave way to a frown. "Lana?"

"My girlfriend." Claire was proud of how natural that sounded, as if she had referred to Lana that way a thousand times already. "You've probably seen her. She stood next to me when I looked at *Triumph of Nature*. She's still standing in front of your painting, in fact. Couldn't tear herself away." *From the stuffed mushrooms.*

Darlene's eyes widened. She tugged on her pearl choker as if it were suddenly restricting her breathing. "That's your girlfriend?" she got out in a squeak.

"I know some people might think it's too soon to already be in a new relationship." In fact, she advised against it in her own book. Thankfully Darlene didn't know that. "But I met Lana, and she just…she swept me off my feet."

"Well, that's…um, wonderful."

"It is." Claire beamed like a smitten fool. "If you give me a minute, I'll get her and introduce the two of you. I'm sure she'd love to discuss *Triumph of Nature* with you," she surprised herself by saying.

Who knew she had such an evil streak? She hadn't expected to relax enough to have fun and tease Lana tonight.

"Sure," Darlene said but didn't look overly enthusiastic.

"If you're too busy tonight…"

"Oh, no, no, that's not it. It's just…" Darlene grabbed a glass of champagne from a nearby waiter's tray and took a long sip. "I'm just a bit surprised. Excuse me for saying so, but she doesn't seem like your usual type."

Her tone made Claire bristle. Darlene hadn't even met her yet, so clearly, she judged her solely on her colorful tattoo, her scars, or maybe the fact that she was the only woman in the room who didn't avoid the canapés because she was on a perpetual diet.

Claire plastered on a smile. "Oh, I didn't know you already met her."

"I didn't. I just meant… I'm sure she's a lovely person, but I had the impression that you prefer women who aren't quite so…well…"

Claire frowned at her. Darlene was the second person to comment on her type. Was she really that much of a snob that she wouldn't have considered Lana dating material in the past?

She looked around the room, searching out Lana, and found her, as expected, next to the tray with the stuffed mushrooms.

But she wasn't alone. Some blonde who had her back to Claire was chatting her up, if her body language was any indication.

Claire stiffened. Not because she was jealous, of course, just because appearances were important to her. If her new girlfriend was seen flirting with another woman, people would instantly judge it as another doomed relationship.

Poor Claire, they would say, *can't keep a woman. Guess the old saying is true: Those who can, do; those who can't, teach.* She could almost hear their mocking laughter.

"I prefer Lana," she said firmly. "If you'll excuse me now…"

Darlene paled. "I didn't mean anything by what I said. It was just an observation."

Sure. Just be glad I'm not sharing the observation Lana made about your painting, Triumph of Cat Vomit. "Oh, don't worry. I knew you didn't mean anything by it. You don't even know Lana, so why would you form an opinion?"

"Um, I didn't."

"I'll see you later. Thanks for giving me a heads-up about Abby possibly being here, even if she ended up not showing."

Just when Claire wanted to walk away, Darlene said, "Oh, she's here. Didn't you see her? I thought you were the one who introduced them."

She's here! Waves of hot and cold rushed through her. She'd known she'd likely run into Abby here, but now she felt entirely unprepared. Good thing she had Lana to cling to. If words failed her once she faced Abby, she knew Lana would jump in.

Then her panicked mind finally processed Darlene's words. "Um, introduced whom?"

Darlene waved her hand at something behind Claire. "Abby and your new girlfriend. They're over there, talking."

Claire whirled around. The blonde… Of course! She should have known her anywhere, even from behind, but Abby had cut a good eight inches off her hair.

What the hell was she doing, talking to Lana? Without saying goodbye, Claire marched toward them.

Abby tilted her head in a way that reminded Lana of Claire. "Something wrong with my name? It's usually only opposing counsel who react like that when I introduce myself."

Opposing counsel? So Abby was a lawyer? Was that why Claire had told her colleagues she—Lana—was a lawyer too? Did she still compare every woman she met to her ex and find that no one could measure up, as Katrina had done?

"Your name's fine, but…" Lana hesitated. But why not tell her? Claire would want her former fiancée to know she was with someone else. "Um, I think we have more in common than just a sense of humor about art."

"Your name is Abby too?" Abby smiled. "Didn't you say it's Lana?"

Lana shook her head. "Not the name. Claire. That's what—or who—we have in common." She drew herself up to her full height, which still couldn't match Abby's, especially since Abby was wearing four-inch Gucci stilettos and Lana couldn't wear high heels since her accident. "I'm Claire's girlfriend."

Abby stared, her blue eyes like the twin flames of a Bunsen burner. "I heard she had a new girlfriend, but I didn't want to believe it," she murmured as if talking to herself. "Maybe I should have. It's typical Claire."

"What's that supposed to mean?" Lana didn't have to rely on her acting skills to sound defensive.

"Oh, just that we can't have the big relationship expert show up at functions like this one all alone, can we? People might think she's actually human if she showed up without a trophy girlfriend. If you really knew Claire, you'd know she would pay a lot of money to avoid any public humiliation."

Damn. Is she on to us? Lana had to do something to convince Abby that their relationship was real. But what? She couldn't very well leave Abby behind, march across the room, and lay a passionate kiss on Claire, could she?

The thought made her cheeks burn as she remembered the hot kiss at the office party, but she discarded it immediately. Even though it might have worked for Vanessa, she had a feeling with Abby, they'd need a little more subtlety.

"Do I look like a trophy girlfriend?" Lana gestured at her tattoo and the extra pounds around her middle. She wasn't normally one to put herself down like that, but she knew it was exactly what people like Abby usually thought of her.

That seemed to trip Abby up for a moment. She sighed. "Maybe I'm wrong. Maybe she actually likes you. But let me give you a piece of advice from someone who's been there. Don't delude yourself into thinking that this honeymoon phase will last forever, no matter what the title of her book implies. She won't be this attentive for long. You'll spend most of your time in this relationship waiting for her to come home from work or to finally shut down that damn computer."

Was that the reason why their relationship hadn't worked out—because Claire had been too busy writing about relationships to actually have one?

"Thanks for your advice," Lana said with the most sincere smile she could manage. "I'm sure you mean well, but I've got my ways to make her shut down the computer in two seconds flat." She lowered her voice to a sensual rasp, the one that made casting directors shift in their chairs.

Someone stepped next to Lana, and Claire's spring flower scent washed over her seconds before Claire's warmth pressed against her side. Claire gave her a quick sidelong glance as if to ask what she and Abby had talked about. Something close to panic gleamed in her eyes.

When Lana gave her a tiny, reassuring nod, Claire turned toward her former fiancée. "Hello, Abby."

"Hello, Claire."

The two stared at each other, and the tension in the room seemed to ratchet up in leaps and bounds.

Did they hate each other's guts after their breakup, or did they still feel something for each other? Lana couldn't tell, but one thing was clear: there was a lot that remained unresolved between these two.

"You cut your hair," Claire said when the silence was starting to become uncomfortable.

Abby trailed her hand through her shoulder-length mane. "I thought it was time for a change. Apparently, that's true for you too." She flicked her gaze in Lana's direction.

Suddenly shoved into the spotlight, Lana shifted her weight in her uncomfortable shoes, wrapped her arm around Claire's waist, and laid her other hand on Claire's flat belly in a possessive gesture. That was what people would expect of someone who was meeting her girlfriend's ex for the first time, wasn't it?

The muscles beneath her fingers tightened as Claire sucked in a breath, either because she hadn't expected such an intimate touch or because of her ticklishness.

Just when Lana considered withdrawing her hand, Claire relaxed and wrapped her arm around Lana too. She faced Abby with a challenging tilt of her chin. "Are you going to tell me that she isn't my type, like everyone else did?"

"No." Abby didn't flinch away from Claire's gaze. "I wasn't even sure you still had a type, other than the women on your couch and the case interviews for your book."

Again, Claire's belly muscles tensed beneath Lana's hand.

"She does," Lana said softly before the situation could escalate. "She just had to rediscover it. Like she says in the manuscript: rediscover yourself to know what you need in a relationship."

It was a wild guess, based on her mother's audiotapes. Abby's pinched brows made her think she'd guessed wrong and Claire had no such passage in her book. *Oh shit. I messed up.*

"She...she let you read her book?" Abby stammered, her composure crumbling.

"Of course." Why was that so out of the ordinary? Surely Claire had requested lots of input while working on the first draft of her book, including feedback from her own partner, hadn't she? She peeked over at Claire, whose lips had compressed into a thin line.

"I can't believe it! She wouldn't even let me touch one of her sacred pages."

Lana hid her surprise. "What can I say?" She trailed the index finger of the hand resting on Claire's belly across the smooth satin, only a few inches beneath her breasts, giving the motion a slow sensuality that Abby wouldn't be able to miss. "Claire lets me touch *everything*."

A breathless gasp whooshed from Claire's lips.

Wow. That had sounded pretty convincing, nearly making Lana gasp along with her. Claire's acting skills clearly had improved since they had started this ruse.

Abby's bottom lip trembled.

For the first time, Lana wondered if they were doing the right thing. Lying to her sister and to Jill was bad enough, but this…

Then a mask slid over Abby's face, and she looked at them with the haughty high-society gaze that Lana had encountered more than once tonight. "You'll have to excuse me now. If I stand here any longer, Claire will start rumors about me begging her to take me back."

Before Claire could say anything, Abby stomped away on her velvet Gucci stilettos.

The urge to hurry after Abby nearly overwhelmed Claire. But acting on impulse had never been her thing. Besides, this was what she'd wanted, wasn't it? For Abby to believe that she was happy with someone else.

Then why would that lump in her throat not dissolve?

Lana slid her hand from Claire's belly and loosened her hold on her waist. "Did I overdo it? When I touched you…"

That touch had been a little much, but not the way Lana was thinking. Apparently, her very confused libido hadn't gotten the message that this was all a pretense. Thinking about that slow slide of Lana's finger across her middle made a new wave of goose bumps ripple over Claire's skin.

She sighed. "I don't know. I guess there's no handbook for a situation like this."

A hint of a smile danced around the corners of Lana's mouth. "Maybe you should write one."

"No, thanks," Claire murmured. So low that she wasn't even sure Lana could hear her, she added, "I'm starting to doubt that I have any business writing about relationships."

Lana stared at her.

"Come on," Claire said. "Let's get out of here."

While they waited for the valet to bring the car around, Lana said, "You know, I didn't expect Abby to be like that."

"Like what?" Claire asked.

"So…nice. Well, other than that little parting shot."

"She was just hurt because she thought I'd let you read the manuscript." Wait a second… Why was she defending her former fiancée?

Lana turned toward her and studied her. "You never let her read it?"

Claire shook her head.

"Why?"

"Renata and one of my other colleagues read it, and they provided me with so much feedback that I didn't think it was necessary to let Abby read it. Having too many cooks in the kitchen spoils the broth, you know?" It sounded like a weak excuse, even to herself. Honestly, she had never really thought about why she hadn't let Abby read it.

Then why don't you think about it now?

That little voice in her head sounded very much like her own when she was talking to a client. *Damn, Lana is right. That shrink voice is annoying.*

Lana still looked at her, patiently waiting.

The valet arrived with the car, giving Claire a short reprieve.

She tipped him and opened the passenger's side door for Lana. Funny how natural that gesture came, as if they were dating for real.

She steered them through the streets of downtown LA for a minute or two before saying, "Maybe on some level, I already sensed that there were cracks in our relationship, and I didn't want Abby to start seeing them too once she read the book. Or maybe I wasn't ready to share those parts of myself with her. A book is a pretty personal thing, you know?"

"You were ready to share the rest of your life with Abby, but not those parts of yourself?"

Claire grimaced. Phrased like that, it sounded pretty bad. "Now who's sounding like a shrink?"

"Now who's deflecting?"

Claire couldn't help laughing, and at the same time, she marveled at Lana's ability to make her laugh when she was feeling so down on herself. She stopped at a red light and sobered. "Maybe I should ask the publisher for more time to revise the book before resubmitting it. I'm clearly not as good at relationships as I thought I was."

"Maybe what your readers need isn't a know-it-all expert who has a perfect relationship," Lana said. "Maybe they could learn much more from someone who's made the same mistakes."

It sounded almost reasonable.

The light turned green, and Claire softly accelerated across the intersection. "No," she said after thinking about it for several seconds. "I've seen it in my practice. People want someone to give them guidance who knows what she's doing. Otherwise, they could ask the next person on the street."

She turned right onto the I-10 on-ramp.

Once she had merged into the lane, Lana asked, "Do you still love her?"

Claire tried to recall the exact emotion she had felt when she had seen Abby from across the room, standing there with Lana. Mostly, she had felt helpless and uncomfortable because there was no way for her to know or control what they were talking about. "I don't know."

If Lana suspected that she was deflecting again, she didn't say so.

"What did she say to you before I joined you?" Claire asked.

"She warned me that your workaholic ways would break my heart."

That wasn't exactly unexpected. "What did you say?"

Lana chuckled. "I told her that I had ways to get you off the computer in a hurry."

Her words, paired with her low, sexy voice, nearly made Claire swerve into the other lane. She gripped the wheel more tightly. "Jesus, don't say things like that when I'm driving."

Next to her, Lana was breathing too fast and white-knuckling the middle console. "I'll shut up now."

"No, no, you can talk, just don't…" *Don't what? Don't use that sexy voice?* Maybe not talking really was a good idea. She needed to focus inward and get her chaotic emotions back into some semblance of order—and not only where Abby was concerned.

Chapter 12

ON TUESDAY THE NEXT WEEK, Claire sat at her center island. The kitchen had undergone an amazing transformation, but she wasn't sure if it had become heaven or hell. While her mind said *hell*, her grumbling stomach and her nose said *heaven*.

The scent of fresh mint, ginger, garlic, and roasting cashews wafted through the room.

Watching Lana cook wasn't exactly a hardship either. She was poetry in motion, frying shrimp in a pan and chopping the lettuce, the herbs, and a cucumber without missing a beat.

Splashes of sesame oil and lime juice spattered over the counter as she whisked the almond butter dressing.

Claire winced. This was where hell was coming in. She bit her lip and forced herself to remain seated, even though every cell in her body itched to clean up the mess.

"Here." Lana poured a glass of white wine and set it down in front of her before returning to her cooking. "To soothe your nerves."

Was she that transparent, or had Lana gotten to know her so well in the six or seven weeks they'd lived together?

Claire took a sip of wine and licked her lips. *Mmm. A dry Riesling. Great choice.* "How did you know what wine goes well with the shrimp?"

Lana turned the shrimp in the pan, somehow managing to get oil over the backsplash. "I asked Chef Google."

Wow. Lana had gone to great length to prepare a healthy low-carb dinner and pick out the right wine for her.

"You know, I don't expect you to do this." She gestured at the Thai shrimp salad in the making and the fridge, which was full of the groceries Lana had bought today. "It's not a requirement in the contract."

"I know. But cooking is my go-to activity when I'm stressed, like cleaning is yours."

"Cleaning isn't anything like that to me," Claire protested. "It's merely a necessity."

"Oh yeah?" Lana turned and leaned against the stove. "So you coming home today and cleaning the bathrooms in your power suit, even though the cleaning lady was just here, doesn't have anything to do with you being stressed because we're flying to New York the day after tomorrow?"

Claire snapped her mouth shut. "Maybe a little. This is it: my one big chance to secure this publishing deal once and for all. If the editor sees through our charade or we manage to fuck it up some other way, I'm toast. I've talked about my book and the deal with Wishing Tree Publishing so much that I'd totally lose face if this doesn't go through."

"Great," Lana muttered. "Now I'm even more nervous. If you're not careful, you'll raise my stress levels so much that I'll be forced to make you a brownie sundae or some other high-calorie dessert."

Claire laughed and held out both hands in protest, even though her stomach gurgled at the mention of a brownie sundae. "Oh no, please don't."

Lana playfully raised the spatula she held. "Then you'd better—"

The ringing of Claire's cell phone interrupted her midsentence.

"Want to bet it's work-related? You really should consider shutting that thing off every once in a while." Lana shook the spatula, making drops of oil splash onto the kitchen floor.

Claire winced and picked up her phone. For once, Lana was wrong about the call being work-related.

The word *Mom* flashed across the display.

Her stress level shot through the roof. She'd just talked to her mother two days ago during their weekly Sunday phone call, so getting another call from her was unusual. Had something happened?

She swiped her finger across the screen to accept the call and lifted the phone to her ear. "Mom?"

"Hello, darling. How are you?"

Claire hesitated. "Um, I'm fine. How are you and Dad? Is everything okay?"

"We're actually a little upset at the moment," her mother answered.

A growl rose up Claire's chest. "What has she done now?"

"Um, who?"

"Steph, of course!" Who else was the number one source of upset emotions in her family?

"Your sister hasn't done anything," her mother said stiffly. "But is there by any chance something *you* want to tell us?"

Claire gulped and gripped the edge of the island with her free hand. What on earth was going on? She couldn't have done anything to upset her parents. She'd called them at eleven thirty on the dot on Sunday, had reported everything was going well at the center and with her book deal, and hadn't had any contact with her parents since.

A spike of fear drove through her. *They couldn't have found out about my fake new relationship, could they?* Her gaze darted to Lana, who apparently had picked up that something was wrong, because she'd turned off the stove and came over to her.

"Um, could you be a little more specific?" Claire asked. No way would she confess anything without making sure her mother really knew and wasn't just fishing.

"Is there any news regarding your relationship status that you want to share? Is that specific enough?"

Oh God! They knew. Claire gave Lana a panicked glance that made Lana grip her arms with both hands as if trying to prevent her from falling off the stool.

"How...?" Claire croaked out.

"How did we find out? Sadly, not from you," her mother said. "Your father ran into Darlene's husband on the golf course."

Darlene. Dammit. Claire covered her face with her free hand. Maybe Darlene should have named her painting *Triumph of Gossip.*

"I don't understand why you didn't tell us, Claire. You talked about what you were planning to have for lunch on Sunday, but you didn't think to tell us about your new girlfriend?"

"Oh, Mom. I didn't mean to make you feel excluded." It had been hard enough telling her parents about Abby breaking off their engagement. Her parents hadn't said it, but she knew they viewed it as a failure. She hadn't intended to tell them about Lana because now they would think she'd failed again when she and Lana went their separate ways.

Their entire lives, her sister Stephanie had been the one who made every mistake in the book—getting caught smoking weed in school, dropping out of college to become a stand-up comedian, getting involved with a string of men and women their parents didn't approve of—while Claire had always been the perfect daughter.

How could she explain this sudden deviation from her spotless track record?

"It's… It's complicated."

Her mother pointedly cleared her throat. "Since when are we allowing such lame deflections in our family?"

Claire pressed her hand on her mouth and groaned into her palm.

"What can possibly be so complicated about your relationship?" her mother asked.

You've got no idea.

"Is it because she's obese?" her mother asked.

If Claire hadn't still had her hand pressed to her mouth, her jaw would have gaped open. "What the…? She's not…" She cut herself off and glanced up at Lana, not wanting to repeat that word in front of her.

"Well, I wouldn't know because I've never met her," her mother said pointedly. "Not that I'd care one way or another. I'm just repeating what Darlene said."

Claire's vision went as red as the paint on *Triumph of Nature.* "Darlene doesn't know what she's talking about. Lana is beautiful, kind, and genuine, and she goes through life with positivity and a sense of humor that Darlene can only wish she possessed!" Her cheeks went hot, and she ducked her head, overly aware that Lana was listening to every word she said.

"Lana," her mother said. "So that's her name."

How typical. Darlene had commented on Lana's figure but hadn't even remembered her name. Claire mentally removed all of the art openings Darlene was involved in from her calendar.

"Yes," she ground out through gritted teeth. "That's her name."

"Well, then tell Lana that we're expecting her—and you, of course—for dinner on Thursday. Your father and I want to get to know her."

Oh shit. How could she get out of this mess? She threw Lana a panicked look, but of course there wasn't anything Lana could do.

"What's going on?" Lana whispered.

"The apocalypse," Claire whispered back. "I'll tell you in a minute." To her mother, she said, "We can't, Mom. We're flying to New York on Thursday, remember?"

"We? So Lana is accompanying you?" Surprise colored her mother's tone. Maybe there was even a hint of criticism.

Did she think Lana would fly to New York on Claire's dime and then go shopping while Claire met with Ms. Huge? Admittedly, with some of Claire's former girlfriends, she wouldn't have been far off, but if her mother knew Lana, she'd be aware of how ridiculous that thought was.

"The publisher specifically said they want to meet her." What they had really said, of course, was that they wanted to meet her fiancée, but Claire would rather devour two high-calorie sundaes than admit the entire ruse to her mother.

"Oh. It's very nice of her to support you like this," her mother said. "If Thursday won't work, let's have dinner tomorrow."

Tomorrow? Claire's mind raced, trying to come up with an excuse. "But...but...that's too short notice."

Her mother tsked. "Short notice? It's not like you need to prepare a speech or anything. You're just having dinner with your family and your girlfriend."

There was no *just* about it for Claire.

"So?" her mother prompted when Claire remained silent. "How about around seven? I should be home from the university by then."

Claire knew excuses wouldn't work. If she told her mother Lana was still working at that time, that would only lead to questions about what she did for a living, and Claire wanted to ask Lana about what she should say first. "Seven sounds good."

"Great. I'll see you then—you and Lana."

When her mother ended the call, Claire put the phone away, bent over the kitchen island, and pressed her cheek to the cool surface. A long groan escaped her.

"Claire?" Lana softly touched her back and rubbed it, easing the tension in her muscles a fraction. "Is everything okay?"

"No." Claire covered her head with her arms. "Nothing is okay. My parents found out about us, and now they want to have dinner with us tomorrow."

Lana sank onto the stool next to her, grabbed Claire's wine glass, and emptied it in one big gulp.

Claire got up to get a second glass and the bottle. They'd need it.

Lana fiddled with the chocolates and the bottle of wine on her lap, and this time, it wasn't just being in a car that made her nervous. In the past, she had usually looked forward to meeting her girlfriend's family, and they had always ended up liking her.

But today was different. This relationship wasn't real. She was playing a role, so how could she win over Claire's family if she wasn't entirely herself? Plus if Claire's passionate defense of her on the phone was any indication, Claire's parents were skeptical of her new relationship, to say the least.

She had a bad feeling about this. Her stomach twisted itself into knots.

Claire didn't seem to fare any better. She hadn't stopped drumming her fingers on the steering wheel since they'd left for her parents' house in Beverly Hills.

"So, what can I expect?" Lana asked when she couldn't stand the silence any longer. "The modern version of the Spanish Inquisition?"

"Oh no. No torture. My parents have much subtler methods."

Lana wondered what that meant but decided she didn't want to find out. That would probably make her even more nervous. "You and your parents...are you close?"

At a baseball field, Claire made a left turn from Olympic Boulevard onto a quiet, tree-lined street. "Kind of."

"How can you be kind of close? You either are, or you aren't."

Claire seemed to think about it for a second. "I guess we are."

"Then it's no wonder that they read you the riot act for not telling them about your new relationship." Her sister Avery had done the same when she'd found out.

"Yeah." Claire sighed. "That got their mental hamster wheels going. By now, they probably came up with a hundred different explanations for why I didn't want them to know."

Lana grimaced. So Claire's parents would watch her like hawks the entire evening, wondering what was wrong with her. "I guess we'll have to be extra convincing tonight."

Would that include more kissing? She raised her hand to her lips and traced them with her fingertips, then snatched her hand away when she realized what she was doing.

No kissing, she firmly told herself. If her parents were as formal as Claire, PDAs over dinner wasn't their modus operandi anyway.

"Um, about that… We have to be really careful."

"Careful?" Lana asked.

"Yes. There's something I should probably tell you about my parents before you meet them. They are…"

"Ax murderers?" Lana threw in to lighten the mood.

"Worse," Claire muttered. "Psychologists."

Lana stared at her. "Your parents are psychologists too? Both of them?"

"Yes. My mother mostly teaches at USC, and my father is an organizational psychologist, working with big, international companies."

Lana slumped against the back of the seat. "Poor you," escaped her before she could censor herself. "That must have been hell growing up."

"Oh no, not at all." Claire firmly shook her head. "We always had the most stimulating conversations at the dinner table."

Stimulating conversations? In Lana's opinion, that wasn't what a child needed most from her parents. *Jesus, I'm about to have dinner with three psychologists. I think I'd prefer the ax murderers over that.* But Claire already seemed nervous enough, so she didn't voice that thought. "I guess it won't be so bad." Was she trying to convince Claire or herself? She forced a smile. "After all, this isn't the first time I've had dinner with a psychologist."

"Having Thai shrimp salad with me is different, trust me," Claire said.

"Um, I wasn't referring to you." It escaped her without thought, and of course Claire immediately picked up on it.

"Oh?" She turned left onto Wilshire Boulevard, stopped at a red light, and glanced at Lana. "Don't tell me you were once dating a psychologist?"

"No!"

"Hey, don't sound so appalled. Psychologists can make great partners, you know?" Claire let out a sigh. "Unless they're workaholics like me."

Lana almost reached across the middle console to pat her leg but stopped herself at the last second. *Save the acting for later, when her parents are watching!* "I wouldn't know." Psychologists were firmly on her do-not-date list. "I never dated one—my mother did."

Again, it slipped out. God, she was becoming a little too relaxed around Claire, telling her more about herself than she had ever planned to. Somehow, this had stopped feeling like a simple business arrangement a while ago and started to feel more like a friendship.

The light turned green, and Claire steered the car across the intersection. "From your dislike of psychologists, I guess it didn't work out?"

"Depends on who you ask," Lana said. "My mother would insist that they're happy together, but I think she's deluding herself—and the APS's ethics committee probably wouldn't list their relationship as a big success either."

"APS?" Claire asked.

"That's the American Psychologists' Society, isn't it?"

"It's APA—American Psychological Association. Wait! You don't mean…? Your mother is dating her therapist?"

Now that she'd said this much, she might as well tell Claire everything. "She actually married him, but that was after her therapy was wrapped up."

"Wow. I don't know what to say." Claire wrinkled her nose as if smelling something foul. "That's a big no-no for any therapist."

"I know. But apparently, he didn't care, and she wouldn't listen."

"Wow," Claire said again. She was silent for a while. Once she turned onto a palm-lined avenue with luxurious mansions and stately one-family homes, she asked, "Is that why you no longer talk to her?"

"That's part of it, but it's more her misogynist attitude in general."

"Misogynist?" Claire arched her brows.

"Maybe that's the wrong word. Men-centric might describe it better. My mother has really old-fashioned views of society. It's like women have no worth of their own, unless they are somehow connected to a man. She couldn't stomach being single for more than a week or two, and once she was in a relationship, she clung to it, no matter what, trying everything to make it work."

"Including devouring self-help books on relationships," Claire said.

Lana nodded. "Tons of them. She also shelled out thousands of dollars for improve-your-relationship workshops and listened to audiotapes pretty much twenty-four/seven. If you wanted to talk to her, you had to hide those damn things—well, come to think of it, perhaps it was just me. She always had time to listen to my brother. God, she spoiled him rotten. You'd think he was a prince or something."

Once she had started, all of her childhood frustrations came spilling out. It felt strange, but not necessarily in a bad way. Somehow, it was freeing. That wasn't what therapy would feel like, was it?

Claire stopped the car at the side of the street and shut off the engine. She took one hand off the wheel and softly touched Lana's leg. "I'm sorry. You deserve more than such a self-involved mother."

Okay, that definitely wasn't like therapy at all. Lana was fairly certain that a therapist wasn't supposed to voice her own opinion—or to touch her patients—like that. But she liked seeing that furious fire in Claire's normally calm and controlled gray eyes. She put her hand over Claire's and squeezed. "Thanks. It took me a long time to come to that conclusion. When I finally did, I decided to cut her out of my life."

Claire nodded. "For what it's worth, I think you did the right thing, even though it must have been hard."

A sigh escaped Lana. "Yeah."

"What about your father?" Claire asked quietly.

Lana swallowed. "He died when I was little."

"I'm sorry." Claire's hand remained on Lana's leg, its warmth helping to soothe the old grief.

"Maybe that's part of why my mother can't stay single for long. She's trying to recreate what she had with him." Okay, now she sounded like a psychologist. Time to change the subject. "Is your mother anything like that?"

"God, no! My mother never relied on my father or any other man to feel good about herself. If anything, she's the boss in the family."

"So if she accepts me, I'm golden?" *Wait a minute...* She didn't really need Claire's mother to accept her as the new prospective daughter-in-law. If the meeting with the editor later this week went well, she might not even have reason to see Claire's parents a second time.

"Basically, yes. So, are you ready?" Claire took her hand away and nodded toward the house to their right.

Lana swallowed heavily. She felt about as prepared as she was for a triathlon, but she nodded anyway. "As ready as I'll ever be."

They got out of the car, and Claire led her through an open gate up a long driveway, flanked by cone-shaped bushes and manicured stretches of lawn.

Lana knew she was gaping, but she couldn't help it. This two-story mansion made even Claire's house look like a shack in comparison. "Oh my God. How much money do psychologists make?"

Claire sent her an amused smile. "Most of us aren't exactly starving, but my mother actually inherited the house from her parents. Her grandfather made a fortune in laxatives."

Laughter bubbled up, easing Lana's nervousness. "Did you just say... laxatives?"

"Yes," Claire said. "My mother prefers to tell people he was in pharmacology, but the truth is that he, as my sister likes to put it, got rich making people shit."

Lana bent over, laughing, and after a second, Claire joined her. They stood on the snow-white porch and giggled like two teenagers.

The front door, which could be more accurately called a portal, swung open.

Abruptly, Lana stopped laughing and straightened.

She stared at an older version of Claire, dressed in a pale pink pantsuit that might as well be straight out of Claire's closet. Her fair, unlined skin and her intelligent gray eyes were so much like Claire's that it was eerie, and she wore her hair in the same elegant chignon—the only difference being that her blonde hair was streaked with silver.

Claire's mother smiled at her daughter. Affection warmed her eyes as she regarded Claire. Then she turned toward Lana, and her gaze sharpened. "You must be Lana." Two air kisses were planted on Lana's cheeks. "It's so nice to *finally* meet you." She sent a glare in her daughter's direction. "Come on in."

After a look back at Claire, Lana stepped inside, into a two-story-high foyer. The dark hardwood floor reflected the light from several chandeliers, and the majestic staircase leading to the second floor looked like something out of *Gone With the Wind*.

Had Claire grown up in this house? No wonder she was so stiff and didn't know how to relax and have fun. There had probably been no running or roughhousing in this mansion.

God, I hope they won't think I'm some kind of gold digger, who's only after Claire's money. She bit back a nervous chuckle when she remembered that she *was* only after Claire's money, even if it wasn't the way Claire's parents might imagine.

She handed over the box of chocolates and the bottle of wine, glad to have brought something, even if it wasn't much. "Claire said you like reds."

"I love them." Claire's mother gave the bottle an appreciative look, even though she likely had much more expensive wines in her collection. "Thank you so much."

"You're welcome." Lana followed Claire's example and left her shoes by the door.

When Claire's mother led them deeper into the mansion, Lana reached for Claire's hand, more for reassurance than because she wanted to play the loving girlfriend.

Claire's fingers entwined with hers in a tight grip as if she needed something to hold on to.

"Your father is outside, by the pool," Claire's mother said. "Why don't you join him, Claire, while Lana helps me get the food on the table? You don't mind, dear, do you?"

Lana stood frozen. Claire's mother wanting to get her alone couldn't be good. But what could she say? "Uh, no, I don't mind at all."

"I'll help too, Mom," Claire said quickly. "That'll be faster."

Her mother kissed Claire's cheek. "That's nice of you, but your girlfriend and I can handle it, can't we, Lana?"

"Oh, yes," Lana said with all the fake enthusiasm she could muster. Good thing she had starred mostly in commercials, so she was used to sounding excited about things like soap and cough syrup.

Reluctantly, Claire let go of Lana's hand and mouthed "sorry" before disappearing down the hall.

Lana's heart pounded as if she were being led to the slaughterhouse.

The kitchen was as impressive as the foyer. It was the most pristine kitchen Lana had ever seen—and that included Claire's. Not a drip of sauce marred the granite counter tops, and the stainless-steel appliances were as shiny as if they'd recently been polished. The enormous six-burner gas range would have made any professional chef go green with envy. The state-of-the-art oven looked as if it could do anything except give massages.

Not that it got to show off its skills at the moment—and neither did the gas range. On the large center island sat half a dozen insulated containers and a large bag that hadn't yet been unpacked. The logo on the bag said *Culinary Delights Catering Service*.

Apparently, Lana hadn't hidden her surprise very well, because Claire's mother gave an unapologetic shrug. "I was never much of a cook, so I prefer to leave the food preparation to the professionals when it counts."

Lana had to chuckle. She liked that Claire's mother hadn't tried to hide the bag and containers and passed off the food as hers. "So that's where Claire gets it."

"Probably. She's a lot like me in some regards."

They started to unpack the bag and distributed the food into porcelain bowls and onto platters.

Lana tried hard not to grimace as she saw what each container held: kale casserole, vegan meat loaf, quinoa, baked yams, bean-sprout-and-asparagus salad, and roasted Brussels sprouts with smoked tofu. *Oh boy.* She'd definitely have Claire stop at a burger place on their way home.

"I noticed Claire gained a little weight," Dr. Renshaw commented.

Was that a good thing or meant as a criticism? Lana couldn't tell. Dr. Renshaw had the same therapist's poker face that Claire sometimes put on. "I didn't notice, but she does seem healthier. Can you believe she was only having an apple and a smoothie for dinner before I moved in? She really needs something more substantial after her long workdays."

Claire's mother arched her perfectly manicured eyebrows. At first Lana thought she didn't agree with Claire's new eating habits, but then Dr. Renshaw said, "She asked you to move in with her already?"

Oh shit. "Uh, Claire didn't tell you?"

"It seems she doesn't tell me much nowadays." Dr. Renshaw sighed.

"It's not that she doesn't want you to know. It just happened so fast." Lana put on her best smitten smile. "We had a bit of a whirlwind romance."

Claire's mother tossed the empty Styrofoam containers into the trash. "Good," she said firmly.

Lana nearly spilled quinoa all over the center island. "Uh, that's good?"

"It is. Don't get me wrong. I liked Abby—Claire's former fiancée. I really did, but that relationship was too cerebral. I mean, they shared the same values and interests, and that's certainly important, but as I said: Claire's a lot like me—too stuck in her own head sometimes. She needs someone who can get her to let go a little."

"Amen," someone said from the doorway. A slender blonde of about Lana's age swept into the kitchen, hopped up onto the counter, and popped a piece of broccoli into her mouth. Then she grimaced. "God, now I'm craving a cheeseburger and a large order of fries."

Lana bit back a laugh and a *me too*. Curiously, she studied the stranger, who was wearing jean shorts and a T-shirt with a tie painted on it, as if mocking the Renshaws' formal dress code.

"Hi." The stranger stuck out her hand and eyed Lana just as curiously. "I'm Steph."

"My younger daughter, Stephanie," Dr. Renshaw added.

This was Claire's sister? Claire had mentioned her in passing once, but Steph wasn't what Lana had expected. Except for their hair color and their slim figure, they didn't resemble each other at all. "I'm Lana, Claire's fiancée."

The two Renshaw women stared at her, then at each other.

Shit, shit, shit. For one critical second, she'd lost track of what story to tell whom, probably because she'd practiced introducing herself as Claire's fiancée to the acquisitions editor all week. Lana pressed her hand to her mouth, but it was too late to hold back the words.

"Fiancée?" Stephanie echoed. "Is Claire into speed-proposing now or what?"

"No, no," Lana stammered. Oh God, how could she get them out of this? Claire would kill her. "Claire, um, she doesn't know yet."

"She doesn't know that you're her fiancée?" Steph arched her eyebrows, and finally Lana could see the family resemblance to her mother and sister.

"I didn't mean fiancée fiancée...like we're already engaged. I meant to say..." Sweat broke out along Lana's back. "I know we haven't been together for long, but I just know that she's the right one for me."

"So you're planning to propose?" Steph asked.

The Renshaw women exchanged glances.

Finally, Steph shrugged. "Good luck with that. Don't be surprised if it takes Claire a while to make up her mind. She's not exactly the spontaneous let's-elope-in-Vegas type. It took her and Abby ages to get to that point. If you ask me, it was a clear sign that deep down neither was eager to tie the knot."

"Uh…" She couldn't say no now, could she? Not without making them think she wasn't serious about Claire. "Yes, I'm planning to propose."

"Well," Claire's mother said, drawing the word out as if it had five syllables, "you might want to wait a little."

"Wait a little with what?" Claire asked from the doorway.

Lana prayed for the gleaming kitchen floor to open up and swallow her whole. She was in deep, deep shit now—more shit than even Claire's laxative-inventing great-grandfather could have produced.

Claire looked from her mother to Lana. "Wait with what?" she repeated when no one answered.

"With dessert after dinner," Steph said. "Mom got carob-stevia brownies, so it'll be hard to control ourselves."

Claire narrowed her eyes at her sister, who was sitting on the counter like a little kid. "What are you doing here?" Claire winced. She hadn't meant it to come out so harshly, but having Lana in the kitchen with her mother made her tense.

Steph dangled her feet. "Having rabbit food with my family, it seems."

"Yeah, sure, you're here for the leafy greens and the quinoa." Claire snorted. "What do you need this time? Money or material for your comedy show?"

"What would you know about my shows?" Steph shot back. "You've never been to one."

"Girls, really!" Their mother positioned herself between them. "What is Lana supposed to think if you talk about each other like that?"

But Lana didn't seem to even be listening. She leaned against the center island as if needing it to hold herself up. Her face was as pale as it had been during the panic attack in the car.

Claire gritted her teeth. Had Steph or their mother said anything that had upset Lana? She vowed not to leave her side for even a second for the rest of the evening.

Striding past Steph, she went to Lana and put one arm around her shoulders.

A tremor went through Lana, instantly making Claire wrap her other arm around her too. "You okay?" she asked quietly.

Lana nodded but looked everything but.

Oh shit. If Lana's acting skills failed her, whatever had happened had to be bad. Claire itched to find out what was wrong. "If you'd excuse us for a moment," she said to her mother and sister, "I'd love to show Lana the pool." With one hand on the small of Lana's back, she guided her to the door.

"Oh, no." Her mother's voice stopped them. "You can do that later, or dinner will get cold." She pressed a bowl of Brussels sprouts and tofu into Claire's hands, then distributed bowls and platters to Lana and Steph before shooing everyone to the dining room.

"What's going on?" Claire whispered to Lana as they carried the food through the hallway.

"I made a horrible—"

"Claire!" Her mother shook her head disapprovingly. "No whispering! You know we strive for open, honest communication in this family."

Claire suppressed a groan. Maybe Lana was right. Having psychologists as her parents could be a pain in the ass.

A refrain of *shit, shit, shit* echoed through Lana's mind as she accompanied the three Renshaw women to the dining room. Somehow, Claire's hand that protectively rested against the small of her back made her feel even worse. What would Claire say when she told her what she'd done?

She wasn't the type to get angry and shout; Lana knew that much about her already, but would she take it as proof that Lana wasn't able to play the role required of her and dissolve the contract?

Don't panic. With all the back-and-forth between pretending to be Claire's girlfriend to some people, while calling herself Claire's fiancée to others, it had been a legit mistake to make. Claire wouldn't hold it against her. Lana vowed to make it up to Claire by playing her role perfectly for the rest of the evening.

In the formal dining room, a long table had been set for five. The gleaming silverware and the expensive china made it look as if they were hosting the queen of England.

Lana glanced around the room. White-washed beams formed a high ceiling. French doors led to a parklike backyard, where the evening sun glittered on the turquoise water in an oval pool.

A tall man stepped through that door now. Something about him identified him as Claire's father, even though they didn't resemble each other much physically. A hint of silver tinged Dr. Renshaw's raven-black hair at the temples. His tanned face was as unlined as his wife's—either they had great genes or a great plastic surgeon. He was wearing a pair of three-hundred-dollar jeans and a starched white shirt, but no tie.

When he saw Lana, he immediately held out his hand and engulfed hers in a warm grip. "Hi. You must be Lana."

She nodded. "Nice to meet you, Dr. Renshaw."

He laughed and held up his free hand. "Please." He glanced at his wife. "Didn't you tell her to call us by our first names? I'm James, and this is Diane."

James. Not Jim or even Jimmy. Diane had also called Claire's sister Stephanie, not Steph. Clearly, the Renshaws weren't big on nicknames.

They put the food down on the table.

Claire pulled out one of the white, high-backed leather chairs for Lana and then sat down next to her. Lana found herself catty-corner from Claire's mother and opposite her sister. She sat ramrod straight as they passed around the bowls and platters.

The disgustingly healthy food hadn't exactly made her stomach growl to start with, but after her faux pas in the kitchen, her appetite had gone on hiatus. She put a tiny bit of baked yams and Brussels sprouts onto her plate and passed on the rest.

"Don't be shy," Claire's mother said. "Having a healthy appetite is okay in this family."

Not from the way you all look. Lana smiled politely and took two stalks of asparagus.

156

Stephanie barely took anything either. "I'm holding out for the chocolate fudge sundae."

"What sundae?" her mother asked.

"The one I'll get on my way home." Steph grinned over at Lana as if sensing that Lana would have rather had a sundae too.

Her mother heaped bean sprouts onto her plate. "You're thinking of eating ice cream this late? You know you'll wake up with sugar pangs in the middle of the night, don't you?"

Steph rolled her eyes. "My mother has this thing about not eating carbs after—"

"Six," Lana finished the sentence.

"Yeah. So Claire does it too?"

"I'm sitting right here," Claire grumbled. "No need to talk about me in the third person. And just for your information, Lana has seduced me into eating carbs after six a time or two."

Steph swirled her fork through her quinoa and looked from Claire to Lana and back with a knowing grin. "Seduced you, hm?"

Claire looked as if she wanted to throw a Brussels sprout at her, but, of course, the Renshaws wouldn't stand for such uncivilized behavior. "You're just jealous because I'm in a happy relationship with a wonderful woman and you aren't."

Her words warmed Lana from the inside out. *She's just saying that to one-up her sister, you idiot.*

"Why would I be jealous of that? I'm free to sleep with any hot guy and any beautiful woman in Los Angeles."

"Yes, and at the rate you're going, you'll—"

Before she could basically accuse her sister of being a slut, Lana kicked her beneath the table.

"Ouch." Claire reached beneath the table to rub her shin and glared at her sister.

"Wasn't me." Steph smiled at Lana. "Thanks."

Dr. Renshaw...James...cleared his throat. "So, Claire, tell us about your meeting with the people from Wishing Tree Publishing. Do you think they'll be able to make a final decision right away?"

Lana somehow made it through dinner despite her knotted stomach. Once the dishes were done, Claire grabbed her hand and dragged her outside under the pretense of showing her the garden and the pool.

They settled beneath the poolside pergola, on a two-person lounge chair.

"Let's look all snuggly so that no one will disturb us," Claire whispered into her ear.

The warm breath bathing her ear made Lana shiver despite the rays of the setting sun. She cuddled against Claire's side and once again marveled at how well their bodies fit against each other, despite how different they were.

"What did my mother say to you in the kitchen?" Claire asked. "I swear if she said anything like Darlene did…"

So closely pressed together, Lana could feel Claire tremble with suppressed fury.

Her protectiveness felt good, but she didn't deserve it. "What did Darlene say?"

"Nothing worth repeating. So, what happened in the kitchen?"

Lana stared out across the pool. The water shimmered in the orange hues of the sunset, and the warm June breeze stirred the leaves of the fruit trees at the edge of the property. If circumstances were different, she would really enjoy sitting here with Claire. "I…I made a mistake. A really bad one."

Claire reached up with one hand and massaged one of Lana's shoulders. "You're as tense as a rock. Relax. It can't be that bad."

Lana sighed. "You've got no idea."

"What?" Claire laughed a little, but she sounded apprehensive too. "You told them you're an actress who gets fifty thousand dollars to pretend to be my loving partner?"

"No, not quite as bad, but not that much better. I accidentally told them—"

"Ah, there you two are." Claire's mother stepped outside. She shaded her eyes with one hand and looked at them.

Instinctively, Lana pressed closer to Claire, who did the same.

"Do you have a minute, Claire?" Diane asked. "I'd like you to take a look at the leftovers and decide what you want to take."

Try none, Lana thought.

"Just give me whatever you don't want," Claire said.

"No. Come pick your own." Her mother waved her hand in a way that brooked no refusal.

After a soft touch to Lana's thigh, Claire reluctantly got up from the lounge chair. "Be right back."

Lana watched them leave with a sinking feeling in her stomach. Diane wouldn't tell Claire anything about her supposed plan to propose to her, would she?

The lounge chair felt too wide and lonely for just her, so Lana stood and rolled up her best pair of slacks. She sat at the pool, close to the end, and put her feet on the top step. At least she'd get to enjoy this little bit of the pool during what would surely be her first and only visit to this house.

Someone sat next to her, and without having to look, Lana knew it wasn't Claire.

"Hey." Steph dangled her legs into the pool, making Lana wish she'd worn shorts too. "Mom kicked me out of the kitchen. Seems like she wants to talk to Claire alone."

Lana squeezed her eyes shut. Should she charge into the kitchen, making up some excuse about not feeling well, so she could rescue Claire from this situation?

"Don't worry." Steph nudged her. "I've been through a lot of these one-on-one conversations with Mom when I was younger. They're not so bad. It's when Mom and Dad gang up on you that you know you're about to be grounded until the day you retire."

Lana had to smile at her words and the dramatic gesturing that went with them. "Did that happen a lot when you were growing up?"

Steph laughed. "Sometimes it seemed like every other day."

"To Claire too?" Lana asked, even though she could already guess the answer.

"Nah. She was always Miss Goody Two-Shoes and never did anything she wasn't supposed to."

"You know, it's not that she thinks she's better than anyone else," Lana said. "She just can't help setting very high standards, especially for herself."

Wait a minute… Why was she defending Claire, whose perfectionism had annoyed her from the day she'd moved in with her?

Because that's what a girlfriend would do. And because she'd gotten to know Claire better since then and had come to like her, annoying little quirks and all.

"Yeah, I know," Steph said. "It's still annoying as hell. Do you have any siblings?"

"A younger brother. He can't do any wrong in my mother's eyes either, but unlike Claire, he doesn't have many redeeming qualities."

Steph swirled her toes through the pool. "Hmm."

"Did I understand that correctly earlier? You're a stand-up comedian?"

"Sure am. With two parents and a sister who're all psychologists, it was the obvious choice," Steph said with a straight face. "I mean, family dinners like tonight... That's pure comedy gold."

Lana wondered whether she'd somehow make it into one of Steph's routines. "Well, you've got my respect. Live audiences are tough."

"Oh yeah. I've been booed out of so many backrooms of pizza places that the smell of pizza still triggers my flight reflex." Steph withdrew one leg from the pool and half turned to study her. "You've got some experience with live performances too? Claire never mentioned what you do for a living. Not that she mentioned you at all."

God, this really wasn't her day. She'd made a second mistake, but this one could be corrected. "Oh, no, the stage isn't my thing." And after her failures tonight, maybe that was even the truth. "I just know a bit about stand-up comedy because one of my exes was a comedian."

That was true. She and Katrina had met when Lana had done a few open mics to improve her comedic timing.

"What's her name?" Steph wrapped her arms around her drawn-up knee and leaned her chin on top. She seemed so relaxed and comfortable in her skin that it was hard to believe that she and Claire were related. "Maybe I know her."

"Katrina Villanueva."

"Oh. Um, yeah, I've seen one of her routines."

Steph might be a comedian, but she was definitely not a good actress. "You think she's not very funny, don't you? I told her the same thing when she tossed all my clothes out the window."

Steph laughed. "You should be a comedian. You've got the dead-pan face down pat." She paused. "Did she really toss your stuff out the window?"

"No. I managed to end all my relationships in a more or less civilized manner."

Claire's sister sobered and regarded Lana with a serious expression.

For the first time, Lana realized that her eyes were the same gray color as Claire's.

"Good," Steph said. "Claire and I often don't see eye to eye, but that doesn't mean I want to see her hurt."

Oh shit. She had gotten herself into an if-you-hurt-my-sister-I'll-kill-you conversation without even realizing. Lana swallowed. "I don't want to ever hurt her either."

Her tone must have conveyed the right amount of sincerity, because the intensity of Steph's gaze lessened and her carefree grin returned. "So, how did the two of you meet? You don't seem like someone who'd attend those boring events that Claire goes to."

Finally they were back on solid ground. At least she and Claire had rehearsed that part of their plan. "Our first meeting wasn't boring at all. I ran her down with my roller skates."

Steph laughed and leaned forward. "Tell me more."

When her mother had sent Steph outside to keep Lana company, Claire had started to become concerned, but what really set off her alarm bells was when her father entered the kitchen.

Her parents stood side by side in the middle of the room, gazing at her with serious but carefully neutral expressions.

Uh-oh. Claire knew what that meant. Not that she had ever personally experienced it, but she'd watched it happen to Steph often enough as a child: her parents thought it was time for an intervention and wanted to present a united front.

Claire swallowed heavily and fought the urge to grab the leftovers and run. Finally, she decided to take the initiative instead of waiting for them to make the first move. "Let me guess… You don't like Lana and think she's all wrong for me."

"Oh no," her mother said immediately. "She's…well, different, but I really like her."

It sounded sincere, not like one of her carefully diplomatic replies.

Claire relaxed a little. She couldn't help shaking her head at the irony of it all. It wasn't that her parents had ever openly criticized any of her girlfriends, but neither had they ever told her they really liked one of them. Even Steph seemed to like Lana, and that was definitely a first.

"What is it, then?" Claire asked.

Her parents exchanged a long look, communicating in that silent way that had always fascinated Claire.

"Do you remember the letters to Santa that you and your sister wrote when you were kids?" her father asked.

Where was he going with this? Claire eyed them, but then answered, "Sure. I remember the year Steph wrote down that what she wanted most for Christmas was a —"

"Uh, yeah, we remember that too." Her mother cleared her throat. "What your father is trying to say is that Stephanie was usually done within two minutes, but it always took you days to finish your letter."

Claire shrugged. "I wanted to get it right."

"Exactly," her father said. "You were like that in everything, even ordering in a restaurant. It took you even longer than your mother to make up your mind because you studied every single dish on the menu before making a choice."

"That's why we are a little concerned now," her mother took up the thread. "It's not like you to rush into a relationship."

So that was where this was going. "I'm not rushing into anything, Mom." She knew it was a lame attempt to convince her parents it wasn't that out of character for her, but what else could she say? "I just decided that I don't want to miss out on having a chance at love with Lana because society expects me to mourn the end of my engagement for a year or something."

"It's not about societal expectations," her mother said. "I don't want you to make the same mistake twice."

Ouch. Claire winced. There it was: mistake. So they did think she was to blame for the end of her relationship with Abby. Claire clenched her teeth. "I'm not. Lana isn't anything like Abby."

"I didn't say she was," her mother said. "Lana seems to be a lovely woman. This isn't about her. It's about you and where you are emotionally. Four months ago, you were planning your wedding to another woman, and now you're nearly wearing the r—"

162

Her father cleared his throat and gave his wife a warning glance.

Claire's mother snapped her mouth shut.

Furrowing her brow, Claire looked back and forth between them. "Am I missing something? Yesterday, on the phone, you seemed shocked and hurt—and I totally get that—but you seemed open to the idea of me dating someone else. But now that you've met her, you're suddenly convinced I'm moving too fast."

Her father sighed. "All we're asking you is to make sure you're making the right decisions for the right reasons—and at the right time. If what you and Lana have is the real deal, waiting a little to make any life-altering decisions won't make a difference."

Life-altering decisions? What the heck were they talking about? It wasn't as if Lana could get her pregnant, even if they were having sex.

It was all a moot point anyway because what she and Lana had wasn't the real deal; it was—in Lana's words—as fake as her grandmother's teeth. So why was she having this standoff in the kitchen, defending her pretend relationship to her parents?

"The only life-altering decision I'm about to make is hopefully signing that publishing deal," Claire said.

Her mother exhaled as if she'd been holding her breath. "Good. Just make sure Lana understands where you're coming from and doesn't take it as a rejection."

"Rejection...of what?"

"You'll understand when the time comes." Her mother patted Claire's arm. "Now tell me which of the leftovers you want."

Claire stared from her mother to the kale casserole and back. She still had no idea what was going on, but it probably didn't matter. They'd make it out of here—hopefully within the next ten minutes—and once the book deal went through, she'd wait a few weeks before telling her parents they had split up.

Since her parents were already concerned about her moving too fast and making the wrong decisions, they'd definitely believe that Lana had only been a rebound girlfriend, not meant for life.

When they finally left the house with a bag full of food, Claire breathed a sigh of relief. In contrast, Lana still seemed as tense as when they had arrived. Was it because Steph had left the house with them, so they had to keep up their roles for a little longer?

Claire furrowed her brow, squeezed Lana's hand, and sent her a questioning look.

"I'll tell you in a second," Lana mouthed with a meaningful glance at Steph.

They walked down the driveway. Steph's turquoise metallic Mini Cooper convertible was parked behind Claire's car.

As Claire deposited the leftovers in the backseat of her Audi, Steph lingered next to them. To Claire's surprise, her sister hugged Lana. "It was great to meet you."

"Likewise," Lana said, sounding sincere.

"Maybe you can work a miracle and drag my sister to one of my shows."

Claire grimaced. "To hear you make a comedy routine out of our family or my private life? No, thanks. I'm not into public humiliation."

Steph regarded her with a shake of her head. "You really should learn not to take yourself so seriously."

"Or maybe you should learn to take some things more seriously," Claire countered.

Lana stepped between them. "Girls, don't make me separate you."

Steph laughed and hopped into her car. "See ya, sis. Bye, Lana."

"See you later," Claire said.

She opened the passenger-side door for Lana, but instead of getting in, Lana dug in her heels and kept hold of Claire's hand. "Um, can we…?" She glanced at Steph, who was still behind them, putting down the soft top of her convertible. "…go for a walk before we drive home? I'd love to see the neighborhood where you grew up."

"Now? It's dark. You won't see much."

"Doesn't matter," Lana said. As if for Steph's benefit, she added, "Who knows when I'll get you away from work again."

"All right." Claire closed the door and relocked the car.

They were still within Steph's line of sight, so neither let go of the other's hand as they strolled down the street. The warm breeze rustled through the palm trees to their left and right.

Maybe a short walk hadn't been such a bad idea before the craziness of New York City started tomorrow. This was actually nice.

Lana didn't say a word, not even after Steph had driven past them, honking and waving.

"What is it?" Claire asked softly.

Lana kept her gaze on the sidewalk. "I didn't want to tell you in the car."

The tension returned to Claire's muscles. "Tell me what?"

"What happened earlier, when your mother kidnapped me."

Claire squeezed her hand and only then realized she was still holding it. With Steph no longer watching, she could let go now, but did she really want to?

No, she decided. Lana's fingers felt nice in hers. Besides, some of her parents' nosy neighbors might be peeking out of their windows to see who'd been honking on their quiet street.

Claire waited, giving Lana the opportunity to say whatever she had to say in her own time. She had learned to remain composed in her years as a therapist, but now it was admittedly hard to be patient.

"I made a mistake," Lana finally said.

"So you said earlier. What happened?"

"I…" Lana peeked over at her like a puppy who'd piddled on the carpet and now wanted to see how angry its owner was. "Meeting your sister kind of threw me off my game, so I got my stories confused and accidentally introduced myself as your fiancée."

In the sudden silence, the sound of the neighbors' sprinkler seemed to become louder.

Claire's jaw moved, but she needed several seconds to make her vocal cords work. "You…what?"

Lana ducked her head but didn't repeat it. "I'm so sorry." She tried to withdraw her hand from Claire's, but Claire held on.

Yes, Lana had messed up, but making her feel even worse about it wouldn't improve the situation. They had to deal with this—as a team. "What did they say?"

"Um, at first, not much. They were too busy staring at me openmouthed. I tried to backtrack and told them I was planning to propose but hadn't done it yet."

A short, humorless laugh escaped Claire. "Now I understand that strange little intervention they staged in the kitchen and them going on and on about my Christmas wish list and us rushing things!"

"I tried to tell you by the pool, but your mother…"

"I know." Claire sighed.

They walked on in silence for a bit.

"What do we do now?" Lana asked quietly. "Do you want to cancel our contract?"

"What? No!" Claire realized she'd called it out more loudly than intended. She lowered her voice and repeated, "No. That's not what I want. There's too much on the line to stop now. It probably doesn't matter that my parents think you want to propose. We'll break up long before they expect to see a ring on my finger."

Lana's grip on her hand tightened until it became nearly painful. "Oh shit."

"Ouch. Hey, don't panic. I just said it doesn't matter what my parents—"

"No, no, that's not what I meant." Lana pulled her to a stop beneath a streetlamp and half turned to face her. "A ring! The publishing people will expect at least one of us to wear an engagement ring!"

Now Claire was the one who clutched Lana's hand. *Shit.* She glanced at her wristwatch. Where on earth could they get an engagement ring in the next ten hours?

An image of the two rings hidden away in the bottom drawer of her nightstand flashed through her mind: the one she'd bought for Abby and the one Abby had later given her. While Abby had left her ring behind along with her keys when she'd moved out, Claire hadn't yet brought herself to send Abby back her ring.

Maybe they could put the rings to use now.

But the thought of sliding Abby's ring on Lana's finger seemed wrong, as if she was trying to give her a hand-me-down from a previous relationship. Lana deserved better than that.

Oh, come on. Lana isn't really your fiancée. It's not like her feelings would be hurt.

Still, she didn't like the idea. Besides, the three-carat ring she'd bought Abby wouldn't be Lana's style at all. She'd have to come up with a plan B—and she'd have to do it fast.

Chapter 13

GOD, CLAIRE COULDN'T BELIEVE THE lengths she was willing to go to secure this book deal. This was possibly the most embarrassing and humiliating thing she'd ever done.

She peered through the glass door of the jewelry store.

Mr. Watson was behind the counter, polishing a ring or some other piece of jewelry.

Claire took a deep breath and lifted her hand to knock on the glass.

Lana's fingers wrapped around her hand. "Are you sure you want to do this? I can see how uncomfortable this makes you. We can tell the acquisitions editor I accidentally dropped my ring down the drain or something."

"Oh no." Claire firmly shook her head. "That's the oldest excuse in the book. Ninety percent of my patients use it to explain why they no longer wear their wedding ring."

"Then we tell them we've decided not to wear rings because we don't want to copy heteronormative ideas of what an engagement has to look like."

"But what if the editor likes those heteronormative ideas?"

Lana looked at her with a helpless expression. "Then we'll...um..."

"It's okay." Claire turned her hand around and gave Lana's fingers a soft squeeze. "I appreciate that you want to spare me the embarrassment, but I don't think there's a way around it. We need a ring, and Mr. Watson is the only jeweler I know who'd be willing to open early for me."

Slowly, Lana nodded and withdrew her hand.

Claire immediately missed its soothing warmth. She curled her hand into a fist and knocked.

Mr. Watson looked up. A smile spread over his face. He crossed the room and unlocked the door. As he opened it, a bell tinkled. "Good morning, Dr. Renshaw. Good to see you again."

Claire wished she could say the same. "Thanks for opening early for us. I wouldn't have called you, but we've got a plane to catch."

"No problem." He let them into the air-conditioned store. "How are your parents?"

"They're doing well, thank you. But if you could please not mention this visit to them…"

He mimed zipping his lips shut. "Confidentiality is a given in my profession, just like in yours. But now you've made me curious. What brings you here? Is there something wrong with the ring I sold you last December?"

"Oh, no, it's fine." Okay, here came the embarrassing part. She stiffened her shoulders. "I need another engagement ring."

"Um, surely you mean wedding ring, don't you?"

"No. I do mean engagement ring."

Mr. Watson's gaze went from her to Lana and back. "Oh."

Not wanting to see the judgment on his face, Claire strode past him to the glass-covered counter. Diamonds, sapphires, emeralds, and other gemstones sparkled beneath the glass.

"What kind of ring did you have in mind?" Mr. Watson asked, his voice carefully neutral. "A solitaire or a cluster? A gold, white gold, or platinum band?"

"I don't know yet. Can we see a few?"

"Certainly." Mr. Watson unlocked the lighted showcase, pulled out a black, velvet-lined tray, and set it on top of the counter.

Claire rubbed her chin as she studied each ring, taking in the different cuts and bands and imagining how each one would look on Lana's hand. Lana wasn't the flashy type, so a five-carat ring was definitely out. Claire eyed a ring with a smaller—but not too small—diamond, flanked by four tiny ones on each side.

"This one is nice, don't you think?" Claire said to Lana. Glancing at Mr. Watson, she asked, "How much is it?"

"It's a one-point-seven-carat ring," he answered. "It comes to eleven thousand dollars, plus tax."

Half a step behind Claire, Lana sucked in a breath.

Claire bent closer to study the ring. It came with a white gold band. *Hmm.* Would yellow gold be better? Or platinum? She compared the different stones and bands and massaged her temples. Had deciding been this hard when she'd picked a ring for Abby?

Lana cleared her throat. "Um, Claire..."

"What do you think?" Claire waved her closer. "Do you like it? Or do you want to see a few more?" She looked at Mr. Watson. "Could we?"

"Of course." He set two more trays on top of the showcase.

"Claire!" Lana tugged on her sleeve until Claire turned. "Can I talk to you for a minute?" Without waiting for a reply, she dragged Claire a few steps away.

"What is it?" Claire asked. "We don't have much time."

"Which is why I need to cut this short." Lana faced her with a fierce expression. "We're not getting one of these rocks."

"Come on. It's not the Hope Diamond. Eleven thousand is a reasonable price for an engagement ring. Besides, the price shouldn't matter as long as you like it."

Lana glanced at Mr. Watson and leaned closer. "Jeez, Claire! I won't keep the ring, you know that! Or have you forgotten that we're not really engaged?"

"Oh. Um, no, of course not." She hadn't. Not really. Okay, maybe for a second or two, but she would never admit that momentary lapse. "It's just that anyone who knows me would expect me to buy a nice ring for my fiancée."

"Yeah, but the editor doesn't really know you. Maybe she wouldn't even know the difference, so let's get a cubic zirconia or something cheap."

A cubic zirconia. Something as fake as their relationship. That thought was like a punch to the stomach. Every fiber of Claire's being protested. "No, that doesn't feel right. I don't want anyone to think I don't value you."

Lana sighed. "That's sweet, but my worth...anyone's worth can't be measured in money."

"I know. I just..." Letting Lana walk around with a cheap imitation on her finger wasn't right, even if it was only for a few days.

"Claire, please. We're going to miss our plane if you keep this up. We don't need the perfect ring. We just need a ring—preferably one that doesn't cost a kidney."

They were at a standoff. Lana was as stubborn as she was—if not more. She wouldn't budge. "Okay. Let's try chapter four of my book."

Lana quirked a smile. "Sex on the kitchen table...or rather, the glass counter? You'd have to be awfully good for me to give in and let you buy that expensive ring."

"Sssh." Claire's face grew hot. Her entire body, truth be told. She threw a glance at Mr. Watson to see if he had heard, but if he had, he gave no indication of it. "No. There is no chapter on...that in my book. Chapter four is *Finding the Right Balance: The Art of Compromise*. So let's compromise."

"All right," Lana said. "What are you suggesting?"

"If you were to get engaged...for real, I mean...what kind of ring would you want?" Claire prayed that Lana wouldn't want them to get Celtic knots tattooed on their ring fingers or something like that.

Lana walked to a smaller showcase in one corner of the room and bent to look at the rings.

"Um, these aren't traditional engagement rings," Mr. Watson said.

"I'm not a traditional woman," Lana countered with a smile. She pointed at one of the rings. "This one."

Claire walked over and had her point it out again.

The ring would be a perfect fit; she had to admit that, even though it would be a rather unusual engagement ring. The platinum band was shaped like a delicate feather that would wrap around the wearer's finger. The broadest part of the feather quill held a small topaz, which shone like the blue of a summer sky.

Claire immediately understood the meaning the ring would have for Lana. "The feather," she said quietly. "It's like a part of your phoenix."

Lana nodded.

They looked at each other.

"We'll take this one," Claire said without looking away.

Mr. Watson told her the price—one thousand three hundred dollars—and she handed over her credit card.

"Um, maybe it won't even fit," Lana said, as if she considered even that price too high. "It might be too small for me."

"I can resize it if it doesn't fit," Mr. Watson threw in.

Claire glanced at her wristwatch. Would they have time for that? She gently nudged Lana. "Try it on."

Mr. Watson unlocked the glass case and held out the ring.

Lana took it gingerly and slid it onto the ring finger of her left hand.

As Claire watched, she found herself holding her breath.

The ring fit onto Lana's finger as if it had been made for her. She held it up for Claire to see.

"Beautiful," Claire whispered.

Their gazes caught and held until Mr. Watson cleared his throat. "Let me put it in a box for you." He looked from Lana to Claire. "I assume you want to do a proper proposal later and not just have her stick the ring on her own finger, right?"

Claire's cheeks heated. "Um, right," she said, not wanting him to think her unromantic.

For someone who had seemed ready to get a ring from a gum-ball machine, Lana appeared to be pretty reluctant to take it off. She threw one last look at it before sliding the ring off her finger and handing it over.

Claire smiled at her. "See? That chapter of my book isn't so bad, is it?"

"I think I still prefer sex on the kitchen table," Lana whispered, so close that her lips almost touched the rim of Claire's ear.

A bolt of fire shot through Claire's body. "Um…airport," she stammered out. "We need to get to the airport."

"What about a ring for you?" Lana asked.

Claire hesitated, but she didn't want another ring that she'd soon have to take off and put in a drawer. "I don't need one. I'm the one who proposed, so you are the one who gets the ring."

Lana nodded as if sensing the real reason behind her decision.

With the ring box clutched in one hand and her credit card in the other, Claire followed Lana out the door.

Buying an engagement ring for Abby had definitely *not* been like this at all!

Lana boarded the plane and settled into her comfy leather recliner in the first-class section. *Wow.* She peeked over at Claire, who had the window seat. Having a rich fiancée definitely had its advantages. She had never flown first class before. For once, she didn't need to squeeze into her seat and glare at the travelers in front of her when they reclined their seats and started to snore not even twenty minutes into the flight.

Yeah, just don't get used to it. It's only temporary. She bit her lip and touched the empty spot on her finger where the ring had rested earlier. How could wearing it feel so strange and so right at the same time?

"Ma'am?" One of the flight attendants had stopped next to their seats. "Are you okay?"

At first, Lana thought she was talking to her. Quickly, she took her hand away from her left ring finger.

But the flight attendant wasn't looking at her; she was focused on Claire. Lana turned her head.

Claire sat ramrod straight in her seat, one hand gripping the armrest closest to the window, the other pressed flat to her thigh. She was pale, and sweat gleamed on her upper lip.

As soon as the flight attendant's attention was on her, Claire put on her practiced therapist mask. Her smile probably convinced the flight attendant, but not Lana. "Oh yes, I'm fine."

"Would you like something to drink?"

"No, thanks," Claire said.

Lana asked for water, eager to send the flight attendant on her way so she could find out what was wrong with Claire. When the woman walked away, she reached across the wide armrest between them and put her hand on Claire's. "What's wrong? And don't try that I'm-fine routine with me. I know you better than that."

"Yeah, I guess you do. But I really am fine."

Lana gave her a skeptical look. "Do I have to tickle it out of you?"

"Ha! Here? You wouldn't dare!"

"Are you challenging me?" Lana formed her hands into tickle-ready claws and slowly moved them toward Claire.

"Okay, okay." Claire put up her own hands as a shield between them. "I admit I'm not fond of flying."

"A psychologist with a phobia?" Lana put her hands back into her lap and gave Claire a teasing grin, hoping it would relax her a little.

"It's not a phobia. I just don't like..."

"Not being the one behind the wheel...or the control stick or whatever they call that thing?"

When Claire shrugged, Lana knew she'd hit the nail on its head.

"Okay, I admit it. I'm a bit of a control freak." Claire held her index finger and her thumb a fraction of an inch apart.

A bit? Lana smiled, but since admitting it was a big step for Claire, she didn't tease her about it. "Why don't you distract yourself with something fun that will make the flight go by faster?"

"Fun? Like what? I swear if you suggest a technique from my sex-on-the-kitchen-table chapter, I'm going to—"

"I thought you didn't have a sex-on-the-kitchen-table chapter?"

"I don't. But now I can't stop thinking of that chapter without your unofficial subtitle popping into my mind." Claire threw her a disgruntled look. "I swear if I accidentally call it that during out meeting with Ms. Huge, you'll be in trouble."

Lana laughed. "Since there's no kitchen table in here anyway, how about a movie?" She pointed at the touch screen in front of Claire.

"No, thanks. But you are right. A distraction might work. I could work on my book." She pulled her printed-out manuscript pages from her bag.

"That's something you consider fun?" After a second, she couldn't resist adding, "Well, other than the chapter on—"

"Don't say it, or *I* will have to tickle *you!*"

Part of Lana was tempted to find out if Claire would follow through on her threat. How would it feel to have Claire's fingers run along her ribs and then slide...? *Stop it!* She squirmed in her seat. *This thing between us is just for show, remember?*

Claire wasn't even her type.

Oh, so you don't like smart, confident women in power suits at all. Right.

The flight attendant chose that moment to deliver Lana's water.

"Thank you." She took it gratefully, fished out an ice cube, and chewed it. Maybe it would help her cool off.

As the plane taxied down the runway, sped up, and then lifted off, Claire paused in her last-minute editing and white-knuckled her silver pen so tightly that Lana thought she might break it and make ink explode across the entire first-class section.

"Here." She reached across the wide armrest between them. "Hold on to me instead."

Claire hesitated for a second before latching on to her hand.

It forced Lana to sit at an awkward angle, but she didn't mind. "Why are you still working on the book?" she asked to distract Claire. "Isn't the manuscript already with the publisher?"

"It is, but if they accept it for publication, I figure getting a jump start on the edits won't hurt."

Lana leaned across the armrest to glance at the changes Claire had neatly written into the margins. The page on top was the intro to chapter two, subtitled *Playing First Fiddle: Make Your Relationship a Priority*. Claire had crossed out the last part and replaced it with *Prioritize Your Relationship*.

"Um, I'm not a writer by any means, but isn't that kind of the same?" Lana pointed at the subtitle.

"Well, as Mark Twain once said, 'The difference between the almost right word and the right word is like the difference between the lightning bug and the lightning.'"

Lana gave her a look. "Really? You're using Mark Twain to justify your perfectionism?"

"I'm not a perfectionist," Claire said.

"And I'm not twenty thousand feet above ground," Lana muttered.

Claire's grip on her hand tightened. "Don't remind me. I'd just forgotten about it."

"Oops. Sorry. But do you really think the book needs more work, or are you just driving yourself crazy before the meeting tomorrow?"

Claire rubbed her temple with her free hand. "Honestly? I don't know anymore. I used to be able to hammer out a chapter and could instantly tell if it was good or not—or at least I thought so. But now..."

"Now...?" Lana prompted when Claire trailed off and turned her head away to stare out the tiny window.

A low sigh drifted across the armrest. Claire continued to watch wisps of clouds trail by. Just when Lana thought she wouldn't answer, she turned back toward her. "Now I've lost trust in my own judgment." She spoke so quietly that Lana nearly had to hang over the armrest to hear her. "I mean, my seven-year relationship crashed and burned, and I had no clue until the very end. And now look at this subtitle."

Lana did.

"*Prioritize Your Relationship*." A bitter snort escaped Claire. "If you asked Abby, I'm sure she'd say I was a complete failure at that. So would I really know if this chapter...or the entire book"—she picked up the pages on her lap and shook them roughly—"is utter bullshit?"

Lana studied her. Claire looked as if she had a stomachache. This was really gnawing at her—and probably had been for some time. "That's why you want this publishing deal so bad, isn't it? It's not just because you need it to bolster your reputation so you can take over the counseling center one day. You want someone to tell you that your advice is sound and you still have what it takes to be a good therapist."

The muscles in Claire's jaw bunched as if she had to chew on that thought for a while. Finally, she gave a tiny nod. "I never thought of it that way, but you might be right. I mean, I wanted to get my book published before Abby...before she told me it was over, but afterward, the publishing deal became my main priority." She tilted her head to the side and regarded Lana with something close to admiration. "You're pretty insightful."

"For an out-of-work actress working as a barista," Lana added.

"I didn't say that—or think it." The look in her gray eyes seemed sincere. "You don't need a degree to be smart."

"Sorry." Lana forced herself to relax back against her seat and gave Claire a lopsided grin. "It seems I needed a little validation too. Two years with no acting gig can do that to you."

"Not that I'm an expert on showbiz or anything, but for what it's worth, I think you're a great actress."

Claire might not have been an expert, but her praise still felt good. "Yeah? How do you figure that?"

"You've certainly managed to convince the homophobic idiot across the aisle that we're a couple." Claire nodded in the direction of a guy in a conservative business suit, who glared at them as if they had ordered the last bit of whiskey on board.

"Me?" She hadn't even noticed the guy so far, much less talked to him.

Claire smiled. "Yes, you."

She pointed at Lana's arm, which was angled across the armrest so she could hold Claire's hand. Her thumb was caressing the back of Claire's hand without her having been aware of it.

"Oh." Lana stopped the motion. Should she withdraw her hand? "Sorry."

"No apology necessary. It felt really n... Uh, I mean, it's good practice for tomorrow."

"Yeah." The more comfortable they were holding hands, the more natural it would look if they did it in front of the editor. The thought should have eased her nervousness about tomorrow, but instead, it left a bitter taste in Lana's mouth. Should she let it go, or...? But she wasn't one to hold back. "I'm not acting," she said very quietly.

"Excuse me?"

Lana lifted their joined hands. "This isn't part of the act. This is me trying to be a friend."

Claire stared at her. "I...I know. You are turning out to be a pretty wonderful friend. I didn't mean to imply... I just meant..."

A stammering Claire was kind of cute. Lana squeezed her hand. "It's okay. You were trying to be a good friend too, saying something nice about my acting skills to cheer me up."

Claire firmly shook her head. "No. I really believe what I said. I have a feeling that if Hollywood gives you a chance, you would be fantastic in pretty much any role."

The words flowed over her like warm honey. "How can you know that? You've never seen me in a movie."

"True, but you've got that same vibrancy that all of my favorite actresses have. You put yourself into everything you do one hundred percent, no holds barred." Claire chuckled. "That's how my kitchen ends up such a mess whenever you're cooking. But if you bring that to your roles...wow."

Lana had always considered cooking an art form just like acting, something she could use to express herself, and it pleased her that Claire had somehow seen a connection too. "Thank you. I think that's the best compliment I've been paid for my acting skills since...probably ever."

Claire acknowledged it with a nod.

For a while, only the muted droning of the plane engines and the conversation of other passengers filled the space between them.

Claire glanced at her manuscript but didn't open her pen to make more revisions, as if she was now afraid to make it worse.

"Do you want me to read it…the entire book or just this chapter or whatever you prefer? I mean, it's a five-hour flight, and I forgot to pack a novel, so…?" Lana realized she was rambling and snapped her mouth shut. "If you'd rather not let me read it, that's fine too. I know you—"

"Okay," Claire said very quietly—so quietly that Lana wasn't sure she hadn't just imagined it. She was even paler than she had been when the plane had taken off. Her fingers trembled as she sorted the pages and held them out to Lana.

When Lana wanted to take them, Claire didn't let go.

"Are you sure you want to read it?" Claire asked. "You hate relationship books."

Lana shrugged. "That's good for you, isn't it? If I hate yours too, it'll be in good company. You don't have to be afraid it'll mean it's bad."

"Oh. I guess that's true." Slowly, Claire eased her tight grip on the pages and allowed Lana to take them from her.

Lana let go of Claire's fingers and cradled the pages in both hands as if they were the stone tablets inscribed by God. Claire had given her chapter two, the section on prioritizing relationships—either because it was the chapter she felt most insecure about or because she couldn't yet handle giving her the entire manuscript. This was already big for her; Lana knew that, and she valued Claire's trust in her.

She read the first paragraph, then had to reread it—not because it was badly written or confusing but because she could feel Claire's gaze rest on her, and it was seriously distracting. "Don't stare at me," she said without glancing away from the manuscript. "It won't make me read any faster."

"Maybe I like looking at you."

What the hell was that? Was she teasing…or flirting? Lana turned her head and studied her, but Claire had averted her gaze and busied herself by pulling more manuscript pages from her bag.

She's just getting comfortable with her role, Lana decided and returned her attention to the chapter.

Claire tried every relaxation technique she knew not to fidget in her seat. She peeked over at Lana.

Still reading.

Was she a slow reader or trying to be thorough, or was the book that hard to read for someone who wasn't an expert? Claire had tried to leave out the psychologist jargon, but maybe those terms were so familiar to her that she had used them without realizing. Maybe—

"Stop driving yourself crazy," Lana said. "It's good."

Claire slumped against the back of her seat and beamed. "It is? Really? You're not just saying that to boost my confidence before the interview and the meeting with Ms. Huge tomorrow?"

"It's good," Lana repeated. She actually looked stunned, as if she hadn't expected to like it.

Claire bounced once in her seat, making Lana giggle. She grinned back. God, she could have kissed her. *Don't you dare!* Claire reined in her out-of-control emotions with a tight grip. "Give me details. What did you like about it?"

"It's amazingly well-balanced."

"What do you mean?" Claire asked.

"When I saw the chapter subtitle about prioritizing your relationship, I immediately thought this would be like the tapes my mother used to listen to. They always told women to sacrifice everything for love and to relegate their interests and their careers to a lower priority than their husbands'."

Claire snorted. "When were those tapes recorded? The fifties? A relationship needs a good balance to work. One partner's goals can't be more important than the other's. They might take precedence for a while, if there's a crisis or a time you really need to focus on them, but in the long run, it needs to balance out."

"Did it balance out in your relationship with Abby?" Lana asked quietly.

The question surprised Claire, but she still found herself answering honestly. "I thought so, but I guess Abby didn't feel the same." She tapped the pages on her lap. "I bet she would say we didn't have even one of the seven keys of lasting relationships. Guess that's why we didn't last."

It was painful to admit that, but now she was able to do it—at least to Lana since she knew Lana wouldn't judge her. "What about you?"

"Me?" Lana smiled, but it seemed a bit forced. "If someone asks me, I will of course say that my amazing fiancée," she playfully fluttered her lashes at Claire, "and I are batting a thousand on each of the seven keys—even though I have no idea what the other six are."

"Communication, compromise, honesty, sharing, trust, and making an effort." Claire rattled them off without having to think about it. "But that's not what I was talking about, and you know it. What about your last relationship? When we met your friends at the Persian restaurant, they indicated that your relationship with Katrina hadn't ended well either."

"You can say that again," Lana muttered. "She trampled all over my heart, then backed up, and ran over it again to make sure she'd done maximum damage." She rubbed her chest as if soothing her battered heart. "I should have seen it coming, but I ignored all the signs. Guess we have that in common."

Claire reached over and took her hand. "What happened?"

Lana sighed. "She had just broken up with someone when we met. I was hesitant to get involved with her at first, but she swore up and down that she was completely over her and only loved me." She hung on to Claire's hand as if that helped her get out the painful words. "Guess what? She lied. While I was in the hospital, recovering from the accident, she packed her stuff and prepared to move out. So much for the key principle of honesty."

"Ouch. Maybe she just didn't know her own feelings very well," Claire said softly, wanting to ease Lana's pain in whatever way she could.

"Whatever. It's not important."

Claire opened her mouth to tell her that minimizing her own feelings wasn't a good way to cope with a painful experience. But Lana didn't want a therapist, so she squeezed her hand instead. "I'm sorry. If she didn't appreciate what she had with you, she didn't deserve you."

The grim expression on Lana's face slowly faded away and was replaced by a smile. "So I'm not so bad after all?"

"You're…bearable."

Lana laughed. "Thanks. You're bearable too."

Claire took chapter two from Lana and put the manuscript back into the right order. If only she could do the same for her life so easily.

"There's something else that has you worried, isn't there? Something besides this chapter."

Claire stared at her. Was she that transparent? That didn't bode well for her interview and the meeting with Ms. Huge.

"It's the way you're straightening the manuscript." Lana pointed at the neatly lined up pages. "If you could, you would ask the flight attendant for cleaning supplies and go scrub the toilet or something."

The thought made Claire wrinkle her nose. "Ugh. No. I wouldn't go that far, no matter how stressed I am."

"So you admit there's something else stressing you out."

"You should have become a psychologist," Claire grumbled.

"Hey, no insults!" The grin curling Lana's lips took the sting out of her remark.

Claire was too tense to return the smile, even though she appreciated the attempt to cheer her up. "What I said earlier...about feeling like a fraud..."

"You never said that."

"Maybe not in so many words, but..." Claire swallowed. While she encouraged her patients to reveal their deepest secrets, fears, and self-judgments, she had never done it herself. Who knew it could be so hard? "I do. Feel like a fraud, I mean."

"That's exactly what I thought all therapists were—frauds," Lana said. "Quacks who sell snake oil to vulnerable people without believing a word of what they're saying. Are you telling me I was right...that you're preaching these seven keys without believing in them?"

"No, of course not. I believe in them." Claire paused and forced herself to think about it—really think about it instead of clinging to old beliefs because they were familiar and soothing in this new, chaotic post-Abby life. Slowly, she nodded. "I believe in them," she repeated with more vigor. "And that's exactly why thinking of the interview tomorrow is giving me a stomachache."

"The interview?" Lana echoed. "Not the meeting with the editor?"

"That too, but I think with her, it'll be about the conditions of the contract and about meeting me in person, not so much about the content of my book. But at the radio station, I'll have to sell my book. I'll have to talk about the key principles of lasting relationships."

Lana kicked off her shoes and pulled one of her legs under her. "What's so bad about that? I thought that's exactly what you wanted—to get a chance to talk about your book."

"Four months ago, I would have been ecstatic, but now…" With a grimace, she opened the folder that held the manuscript and showed her the subtitle of chapter three: *Honesty Is Always the Best Policy.* "How can I advocate honesty while I'm lying through my teeth, pretending to be engaged to you?"

"To be honest…"

Claire tensed in expectation of what Lana would say next but tried not to show it. "Go ahead. That's what we're talking about after all—honesty."

"Honesty is important to me. If I were one of your readers…maybe a real fan…and I'd later find out you'd lied about your own relationship…" Lana shook her head. "I wouldn't like it."

"Yeah. I know." Claire stared at her knees. "But if I'm honest and tell the publisher that I'm no longer in a relationship, this book will never see the light of day. No reader will ever get to read it. That's the irony of it."

"Hmm."

They were both silent for a while, then Claire said, "I guess if the radio host asks me to elaborate on the honesty factor, I'll just have to hope I don't sound forced and inauthentic when I answer." She sighed.

"Or tell them that you can't give everything away and they'll have to buy the book to find out more," Lana said. "If you can pull that off in a tone that is the right mix of teasing, sexy, and professional, it might work." She lowered her voice to the kind of tone she had described.

Claire shivered. She doubted she could pull that off the same way, but it was certainly worth a try. "That's good advice. I might use that answer. Thank you."

Lana nodded. "You're welcome."

Now that the immediate problem was solved—at least as much as it would ever get solved, Claire wanted to go back to her revisions, but Lana was still studying her.

"What?" Claire asked.

"Can I ask you something?"

"After everything I confessed to you today and over the last two months, you still need to preface a question with that?" It had surprised even Claire herself how open she'd been with Lana.

Lana smiled softly. "I guess I don't."

"So what's your question?" Claire asked.

"If you manage to get that publishing contract, the publishing house would expect you to do more promotion once the book is out…give more interviews, right?" When Claire nodded, Lana continued, "But that would mean you'll have to go through the same questions about honesty and the other key factors again and again. Are you sure you want to do that to yourself? Is it really worth it?"

"Yes," Claire said without having to think about it. "This is the book I wanted to write pretty much since the moment I became a psychologist. I'm not ready to give up that dream, just because it won't always be easy. Can you understand that?" She looked into Lana's eyes, searching for approval or at least acceptance. It amazed her how important that was to her.

"Oh yeah. If anyone can understand that, it's me. I never gave up on my dream to become an actress, even though everyone told me someone who looked like me would never make it in Hollywood."

Claire bristled. "Nonsense. If Hollywood stopped hiring only super-thin actresses, maybe not so many of my patients would suffer from self-worth issues and eating disorders."

"Amen." Lana nearly sang it out.

The guy across the aisle looked over again.

Claire decided to ignore him. "About having to face all the same questions during book promotion… I guess I'll have to cross that bridge when I come to it. From what my agent said, it might take a year or more until my book is out. A lot could happen in that time."

A lot that would no longer involve Lana.

She shoved that thought away and continued, "Not that I'm planning to rush into a new relationship or anything, but I figured by then maybe I would have met someone new and wouldn't have to lie when I tell them I'm in a happy relationship."

How strange it felt to say that! Wrong somehow, as if she were betraying what she had with Lana. *You don't have anything with her. It's all just a show you're putting on to get the book deal.*

182

Lana stared into her almost empty cup and swirled the half-melted ice cubes around. Tiny wrinkles furrowed her brow. "Yeah, I guess that could happen. I mean, a good-looking woman like you…" She paused and peeked from the ice cubes to Claire. "But could you be sure you're with her because you really want to be…or because it's good for the book promotion?"

What? How could Lana think that of her? It felt as if Lana had tossed that ice-cold water into her face. "I would never tell a woman I love her just because I want to use her as a promotion tool!" Claire struggled to lower her voice. "I know you don't have the best opinion of psychologists, but do you really think that of me? If I were the type to do things like that, I wouldn't have had to hire you."

Lana abruptly gulped down the contents of the cup, ice cubes and all. "That's not what I meant. But how can you be sure you're not tricking yourself into believing you love her when what you really love is that she makes you one half of a perfect couple? My mother had that down to an art form. She always deluded herself into thinking she loved her boyfriends, just so she didn't need to be alone. How can you know you're not doing the same?"

"I…" She wanted to say that it wouldn't happen to her, but then again, she had deluded herself into thinking that she and Abby were happy together. *Honesty, remember? At least be honest with Lana, even if you can't be honest with everyone else.* "I…I don't know. I hope by then, I'll be able to trust my own judgment again."

Lana studied her now-empty cup for what seemed like a full minute. Finally, she nodded. "I'll keep my fingers crossed for you. Until then… Do you want to borrow some of my judgment and have me read more of the book?"

Claire stared down at the folder on her lap. She was tempted to shake her head and tell her it wasn't necessary; feedback on one chapter was enough. But deep down, she knew it would have been a cop-out. Slowly, she took chapter three from the folder and held it out across the armrest.

Lana took it, and for a few moments, they held on to it from both sides of the armrest. "It's the chapter on honesty, isn't it?" Lana said without having looked at it.

"Yes."

"Thank you," Lana said.

Claire nodded and let go.

Chapter 14

THE SIGHTS AND SOUNDS OF New York City were still familiar, even after thirteen years on the West Coast. While Lana preferred the more laid-back pace of life in California, she'd kind of missed this too.

Just not the smell of trash, exhaust fumes, and urine wafting up from the subway grates—and especially not the blaring sirens and the car horns rising over the din of traffic and loud cell-phone conversations.

The honking and sirens made her break out in a sweat despite the air-conditioned cab that was taking them to their Midtown hotel.

Claire threw her a concerned look and leaned forward. "Could you turn off the radio, please?"

The cabbie grunted and turned off the radio.

"Thank you," Lana said, more to Claire than to him.

Claire tilted her head. "No use taking chances, right?"

Lana nodded.

As they crossed Fifth Avenue and caught sight of the Empire State Building to their left, Claire craned her neck and looked out the side window closest to her, then through the one on Lana's side, as if not wanting to miss a thing.

Despite her tension, Lana had to laugh. "You look exactly like Avery did when she accompanied me to an adult store and saw a strap-on for the first time!"

A blush shot up Claire's neck, making Lana grin even more. She was too cute when she flushed like this, so Lana could never resist teasing her.

"Hush." Claire peeked at the cabbie, who was now glancing in the rear-view mirror, all ears. "I don't look like...like that."

"Oh yes, you do. Just as curious and fascinated, but not sure it'll actually be your cup of tea. Haven't you ever been to New York?"

"No, never. You?"

"I lived here for about a year when I was fifteen," Lana said.

Claire, who'd turned back to the Empire State Building, swiveled around. "Really?"

Lana nodded. "My mom moved us here to be with one of her boyfriends."

"Did you like it?" Claire asked.

"Not at first since moving to New York meant I had to leave the love of my life behind." Lana sighed dramatically. "Ms. Fisher. My drama club teacher."

Claire laughed. "Was she aware of your undying love?"

"Nope. Thank God my mother dragged me halfway across the country before I could embarrass myself with a love letter or something like that."

Their cabbie slowed because a construction site blocked one lane. Soon, traffic came to a complete standstill, and the honking behind them became nearly constant.

"You can let us out here," Lana said. "The hotel is right around the corner. Just pop the trunk for a moment."

Claire raised her brows.

"Come on." Lana nudged her. "Be a little adventurous."

"Okay, okay." Claire paid the cabbie and then followed her as she climbed out of the cab.

The scent of hot dogs, Chinese food, pretzels, and candy apples hit Lana, mingling with some less-pleasant odors.

They grabbed their suitcases and squeezed past the honking cars.

Their hotel was a brick-glass-and-steel building that didn't look very big, but when they entered through a set of sliding glass doors, an impressive lobby with a long bar awaited them. Fire flickered in wood-burning ovens visible through the open restaurant kitchen.

Lana nearly let out a low whistle. *Wow.* Had the publisher sprung for this, or was Claire footing the bill?

With their suitcases in tow, they crossed the lobby, past brown leather couches, toward the marble-topped reception desk.

The man behind the desk greeted them with a smile. "Good afternoon. May I help you?"

"Yes, please," Claire said. "We'd like to check in."

"Do you have a reservation?"

"Yes. My name is Claire Renshaw, but the reservation might be under Wishing Tree Publishing since my publisher did the booking for us."

The receptionist punched in several key strokes and glanced at his computer screen. "Here it is. One room for Renshaw."

"One room?" Claire repeated.

Lana and Claire exchanged a look.

Duh! Lana couldn't believe they hadn't expected it. *Of course they'd reserve just one room for us. They think we're engaged!*

"Um, yes." The receptionist's brow furrowed. "Is there a problem with that?"

"Should we try to get another...?" Claire whispered to Lana.

"No. It's fine," Lana answered for both of them. She had shared a room with various stepsisters and friends over the years, so sharing a room with Claire for two nights should be fine.

The receptionist made an entry into his computer and then slid two key cards across the desk. "Room 1108. On the eleventh floor. The elevators are that way." He pointed to the left. "Do you need help with your luggage?"

"No, we can handle it," Claire said.

"Enjoy your stay, and let us know if you need anything."

As soon as the elevator doors closed behind them, Claire slumped against the mirrored wall. "Damn. I should have paid more attention to the confirmation email they sent me."

"Even if you had, it's not like you could have told them to book a separate room for me." Lana gave her an encouraging nudge with her shoulder. "Now we at least don't need to lie when we tell people we slept together."

"I'm not in the habit of telling people about my love life or lack thereof anyway," Claire muttered.

Once they arrived on their floor, she slid the key card into the lock and held the door open so Lana could enter with her suitcase.

"Thanks." Lana stepped past her.

Their room was small, but tastefully decorated. Exposed brick walls gave it a warm, old-time charm, which was balanced by the modern look of the forty-two-inch flat-screen TV and the Nespresso machine on the desk.

The view from the floor-to-ceiling window immediately drew Lana's attention. "Oh wow. Look!" She went to the window and pointed at the Empire State Building a few blocks to the south. It seemed almost close enough to touch.

Claire didn't say anything, even though she had marveled at the sights of New York earlier.

Her lack of response made Lana turn around.

Instead of enjoying the view, Claire had stopped in the middle of the room and was staring at the bed with its studded headboard.

The only bed.

Oh.

Now they were both staring at the piece of furniture.

Come on. It's a king size. It's not like we'll be lying on top of each other all night. The thought brought heat to her cheeks. *Hey, I said not!*

Finally, Claire cleared her throat. "Are you still fine with sharing a room?" She pointed at the bed. "I mean, this wasn't in the contract."

"Relax. It's fine. We're both adults, and it's a big bed. I call dibs on the side closer to the bathroom." Lana plopped down on that side of the bed. *Mmm. Nice mattress.* Not that it would get any action or anything. She bounced a little. "So, what are we doing with the rest of the day?"

"I thought I'd go over the manuscript again, then we could have dinner at the restaurant downstairs and make it an early night," Claire said.

Lana stared at her. "You're in New York for the first time and want to make it an early night?"

"Um, yeah? Tomorrow is a big day for me."

"What if I promise to have you in bed by eleven?"

Claire hesitated.

"Okay, ten," Lana offered.

"I really should look at the manuscript again..."

"You read it about three dozen times on the plane, Claire. All you're going to do is drive yourself crazy and be a nervous wreck by tomorrow." Lana got up, rounded the bed, and grabbed Claire's hand. "Come on. Let me show you a bit of the city."

"Okay, okay. Can I use the bathroom and get changed first?"

Lana laughed and let go of her hand. "All right. But hurry. There's a lot to explore." She couldn't wait to show Claire some of the sights and see that look of almost childlike amazement on her face again.

———⟲———

Claire couldn't remember when she'd last walked so much—or had so much fun. She'd assumed Lana would drag her toward nearby Times Square with its hustle and bustle, but instead, Lana had shown her several beautiful hidden spots in the Garden District.

They had wandered along rows of long oak tables in the Rose Main Reading Room of the New York Public Library, staring up at the chandeliers and the mural with its floating clouds on the high ceiling.

When they got hungry, Lana led her to a hole-in-the-wall food counter that Claire would have completely missed if she'd been alone. It was tucked into the loading dock of an office building and had only five faux-leather-covered stools in front of a counter. The light from fluorescent tubes flickered over weathered concrete.

Claire skeptically eyed the place and the food that was being served on paper plates and eaten with plastic cutlery. "Um, are you sure about this?"

"Very sure. Their food was to die for thirteen years ago, and I bet that hasn't changed."

Claire pointed at the beans and the salsa on the paper plates of the people eating at the counter. "Not the best idea. I want to impress the radio host and her audience with my book tomorrow morning, not with my… um…"

"Noisy digestive system?" Lana suggested with a grin.

"Something like that, yes."

"Let's get some empanadas to go, then. I already know where to take you for dessert."

Each with a cheese empanada in hand, they ventured back outside.

Claire took a careful nibble, then a more enthusiastic bite. The cheese and the warm pastry seemed to melt in her mouth.

Lana elbowed her while they walked. "Admit it. It's great."

Busy chewing, Claire hummed her agreement. "I don't think I need dessert after this," she said once she'd swallowed.

"You say that now. Wait until you see what I have in mind." Lana hooked her arm through Claire's and guided her past boutiques and gift stores to a little café with a white-and-pink awning.

Claire hastily finished her empanada before Lana pulled her inside.

Hundreds of macarons in all colors of the rainbow were displayed behind a glass counter.

"What can I get you?" one of the women behind the counter asked. She was wearing a French maid outfit with a white apron and a lacy headpiece.

Claire stifled a laugh as she remembered a couple she had counseled last year. They had described using the same kind of uniform to spice up their sex life.

"What?" Lana asked.

Claire opened her mouth to explain, then snapped it shut. *Wow.* She had almost told Lana about something that had occurred in a therapy session. That had never happened to her—not even once in her seven years with Abby. "Sorry. It's work-related, so I can't share."

Lana gave her a knowing grin. "I think I can guess what it is."

The French maid cleared her throat, so they both turned back toward the counter.

Lana ordered a rose lychee and a honey lavender macaron, while Claire studied the menu posted behind the counter, which explained the different flavors. So many to choose from... Finally, she remembered what her father had said about her childhood habit of taking forever to order food in a restaurant and just went with vanilla and pistachio.

"It took you half an hour to pick that?" Lana bumped her with her hip. She leaned closer and whispered, "So you're the vanilla type, huh? Should I expect to get bored sharing a bed with you tonight?"

Good thing Claire hadn't taken a bite of her macaron yet, or she'd have choked to death. Her cheeks heated. "Sleep," she said firmly. "That's what you can expect tonight." She turned to the woman behind the counter. "She's paying."

Laughing, Lana pulled out her credit card.

They left the café and wandered toward the Hudson River while sharing their macarons. Claire had to admit that the more adventurous flavors Lana had picked were better than the traditional ones she had chosen, even though she would never openly acknowledge that.

The sun started to sink lower, and Claire realized with regret that their afternoon of exploring New York was coming to an end. She glanced at her wristwatch.

"Oh no, Cinderella. It's not time to leave the ball just yet." Lana covered Claire's wrist with one hand so she couldn't see the time. "There's one more thing I want to show you." She hooked her arm through Claire's again and pulled her around a corner, beneath a railroad overpass, and then up a winding metal staircase.

"Where are we going?" Claire asked. "Aren't there train tracks up there? Um, I really think we shouldn't…"

Lana paused on the step above Claire and turned toward her. "Do you trust me?"

Claire looked into her eyes. "Yes." It came out with no hesitation, which amazed her.

"Good. Then come on." Lana reached for her hand and pulled her up so they were on the same step before she continued on her way.

Side by side, they climbed the remainder of the stairs.

Instead of gravel and rusty train tracks, Claire encountered an elevated steel walkway set beneath a canopy of magnolia trees and shrubbery she didn't recognize. Two old warehouses to their left and right created the feeling of standing on a bridge leading through a canyon. Some people sat on benches, reading, while others stood at the railing of a platform overlooking the street thirty feet below.

It was as if they had suddenly been transported into another world— still part of the city, but removed from it at the same time.

Claire realized she was gaping. "What is this?"

Lana grinned. "This is the High Line."

"I bet it was one of your favorite spots when you lived here."

Lana gave her a moment to look around, then hooked her arm through Claire's again and set them off along the walkway, which led north for more blocks than Claire could see.

"This didn't exist when I lived here. Well, it did, but it was just abandoned railroad tracks. My friends and I hung out here sometimes."

Claire's steps faltered. "Wasn't that dangerous?"

An impish grin curved Lana's lips. "That was half of the fun. Didn't you ever do anything like that when you were a kid?"

"No. But I like this little adventure."

"Me too." Lana squeezed her arm.

People passed them continually, going in the opposite direction, so they had to walk pressed close together, almost as if they were cuddling.

Of course, Claire acknowledged, they could have let go and walked single file, but neither seemed inclined to lose contact. With the setting sun, temperatures were going down, so Claire was grateful for the warmth emanating from Lana.

Yeah, sure. The warmth. That's the only reason you're enjoying having her so close. Right.

The steel beneath their feet slowly became a concrete walkway that started to gently curve to the left, with grass and wildflowers growing on both sides. On their left, a long teak bench followed the curve of the High Line, while rusty train tracks ran in the grass on their right as a reminder of what the park had once been. Every now and then, they passed a sculpture or a mural painted on the side of a building.

When they reached the point where the walkway turned west more sharply, they slowed. This was where they would have to return to street level and head east to get back to the hotel.

Claire wasn't in a hurry to have their time on the High Line come to an end, and apparently, neither was Lana. As if by an unspoken agreement, they stopped on the side of the walkway and leaned on the railing elbow to elbow.

To the west, the rays of the setting sun turned the Hudson River into a bronze band, while a shadowed line of Midtown skyscrapers rose on the other side. What a magical moment!

"You cold?" Lana whispered.

"No," Claire answered, her voice just as low. *Why are we whispering?*

"You were shivering."

"Was I?"

Lana nodded.

"I'm not cold." She wasn't. Lana's body heat against her side was keeping her warm. Even if she had been cold, she would have wanted to stay here for a while longer.

"Good." Lana directed her attention to something below them. "Oh."

Claire followed her gaze.

On what looked like an empty parking lot, an outdoor roller-skate rink had been set up beneath the High Line. Orange-and-white plastic barricades formed an oval, in which people skated around in circles. Top-forty music drifted up.

Claire half turned and watched Lana as she watched the roller skaters.

The look on her face was one of longing and bittersweet memories. It reminded Claire of the way some of her clients looked when they talked about the half-forgotten happy days of their marriage.

She peeked from her wristwatch to the slowly fading light. *We really should be going. You have to be at your best tomorrow.*

But despite that mental admonishment, she couldn't ignore the look on Lana's face. Gently, she touched Lana's shoulder. "If you want to take a quick spin…"

Lana stared at the skating rink below but shook her head. "It's getting late, and I promised to have you in bed by ten."

"And I'll be. Once around the rink won't take long."

Now Lana was the one hesitating to start a new adventure. "I haven't been on skates since…since my accident," she said quietly.

"Could you re-injure your leg?" Claire glanced down to where Lana's scar peeked out from her jean shorts.

"Nah. It should be fine, as long as I don't try any crazy tricks."

"Then come on. Let's rent you some skates, and I'll root for you from the sidelines." Claire tugged on Lana's arm to get her to move toward a set of metal stairs leading down to street level.

But Lana dragged her heels. "Oh no. If I'm doing this, I'm only doing it with you."

"Me?" Claire squeaked. "No way! I'd end up breaking something and showing up for the meeting with Ms. Huge tomorrow with a bulky cast or two!"

"Nonsense. We'll take it nice and easy." Now Lana was the one who dragged her toward the stairs.

With every step down, the sinking feeling in Claire's stomach increased. Images of what could happen if she entrusted her fate to those spinning rubber wheels tumbled through her mind. But if she refused to at least try it, Lana wouldn't put on skates either, and Claire sensed that she really wanted to. This might be an important part of the healing process for her, and if Claire had to get on those wheels from hell to help her with that, she would do it.

They got in line at the booth that rented out skates. Claire pulled two twenty-dollar bills from her wallet. "Let's get protective pads too."

Lana was wise enough not to protest. "Want a skate mate too?"

"Uh, aren't you my skate mate?" Claire asked.

Lana's laughter filled the space between them. "Yes, but I meant one of those things." She pointed at the rink, where a little kid was hanging on to a plastic support thingy that looked like a walker on wheels.

An adult hanging on to that thing would look ridiculous. "No, thanks. I'll just grab you instead. Uh..." Heat shot up her neck. "I mean, I'll hang on to you when I feel like I'm starting to fall."

Lana laughed again. "Relax. I know what you mean. Feel free to grab me any time."

That offer brought even more heat to Claire's cheeks. God, Lana was a hopeless flirt, and teasing Claire seemed to be her new favorite hobby.

They rented skates and protective gear and left their shoes in a locker. Lana had put on her old-school roller skates and the pads in no time, but Claire fiddled with the unfamiliar laces and straps. Halfway through, she realized she should have put on the pads first, before lacing up her skates. Now she had to balance on those eight little wheels while struggling with the protective gear.

Lana chuckled at her predicament. "Let me help you." She took the pads from Claire and went down on one knee.

Was it the ring they had left in the hotel room that made Claire think of a proposal?

She held on to Lana's shoulder so she wouldn't lose her balance on the roller skates.

Gently, Lana slid the elastic strap around Claire's leg. Her fingers brushed the inside of Claire's thigh as she fastened the strap. A bolt of desire spiked through Claire, making her suck in a breath.

Lana looked up, and their gazes met.

The air between them seemed to heat up, and Claire nearly forgot what they had been doing.

Roller-skating. You're here to roller-skate, not to gaze adoringly into each other's eyes. Leave that for tomorrow. Claire wrenched her gaze away and stood stock-still while Lana fastened the other knee pad, then the elbow pads, and finally helped her strap on the wrist guards.

Claire felt like a knight in armor—a knight who had no idea how to control the mount she found herself on. The few yards to the rink seemed like an insurmountable distance. "Are you sure you wouldn't rather do this alone? I don't want to spoil your fun."

"You won't," Lana said firmly. "Hang on to me."

Claire latched on to her arm and tried to hobble over to the rink's entrance on the stoppers at the tip of her roller skates.

Lana laughed. "Oh no. The toe stops are for stopping, not for walking." She demonstrated a stop by dragging one rubber stop over the asphalt behind her. "Here's how you skate: you bend your knees a little, push off with your left leg, put the left skate back down, then push off with the right."

She demonstrated, skating away from her, then coming back. To Claire's untrained eye, she didn't look rusty at all.

"Now you." Lana offered Claire her hand.

She took it and held on tightly as she counted to three and then pushed off carefully.

Lana skated next to her, stabilizing her whenever she wobbled. "Don't stiffen up. Even if you fall, it won't hurt. Usually, the fear of falling is much worse than falling itself."

That sounded like something from her book. Claire chuckled.

"What?" Lana asked.

"Just thinking that I never knew skating and psychology were so much alike."

"Ah." Lana laughed. "But skating is much sexier than psychology because you have to move your hips rhythmically."

Again, she seemed to delight in making Claire blush—and Claire's cheeks promptly obliged.

The first two rounds around the small rink felt like boarding a plane and entrusting her fate to someone else. But slowly, under Lana's patient guidance, Claire gained more confidence and stopped feeling as if she were on the verge of breaking her neck any second.

"Yeah, exactly like that," Lana called. "Want me to let go?"

Having Lana by her side, holding her hand, felt so much safer, even though she probably wouldn't be able to catch her if she fell. But she knew Lana was likely longing to try out her skills and to regain the part of herself that she'd nearly lost in the accident, so Claire slowly eased her grip. "Okay."

Lana squeezed her fingers and then let go but stayed by her side.

They skated along the barricade, with Claire on the outside so she wouldn't have to take such sharp turns.

"You don't have to stay with me," Claire said. Compared to some of the other skaters, they were crawling along, and she knew Lana had to be eager to skate at a faster pace.

"You sure?"

"Yes."

Lana hesitated but when Claire gave her an encouraging nod, she set off. She shot down the rink, turned in a tight spin, and raced back toward Claire. She wove between two other skaters as if she'd been born with those things on her feet. A broad smile split her face the entire time.

Claire knew she should pay attention to where she was going, but she couldn't look away from Lana. An answering smile spread over her face as she watched her. *I'm so glad I—*

A slight bump in the asphalt threw her off balance. Before she could grasp what was happening, she landed on her ass.

Lana was next to her before she'd even fully slid to a stop. She dropped to one knee pad. "Are you okay?" Her hands flew over Claire as if making sure there were no broken bones.

But Claire felt no pain—quite the opposite. Lana's hands on her legs and bare arms set off tingles all along her body. "Um, I'm fine. Just didn't see that bump in the asphalt." *Because I was busy watching you.* She didn't add that, of course. "Maybe it's time to quit."

"Oh, no. You should know that you need to get back on the horse, Dr. Renshaw." Lana pulled her up. "Come on. Let's do one last round together."

Claire's knees felt wobbly, but she wasn't sure if it was from the adrenaline rush of falling or from Lana's soft touches. She tried to ignore it as they skated side by side.

They approached the gap between the barricades that led to the lockers, and Lana took the turn first. She skated ahead of Claire and then came to a stop.

Oh shit. Claire wanted to copy her and use the toe stop to slow down but didn't dare put her foot behind her, afraid that it would unbalance her. "Lana! I can't stop!"

Lana whirled around. She barely had time to brace herself and hold out both hands before Claire crashed into her.

Her momentum carried them back several yards, but somehow, Lana managed to keep them both upright. They slid to a stop together, arms wrapped tightly around each other, legs tangled, bodies pressed together.

Claire gasped for breath. Her heart raced, but it wasn't just fear that made her pulse pound. Lana's closeness made her as dizzy as if she had done a series of pirouettes on her skates.

Her gaze strayed down to Lana's lips, which were only an inch or two from her own.

The music faded away, and all she heard and saw and felt was Lana—her warm breath on her face, her body against her own, her hands on her back.

"Claire," Lana whispered.

Then lights flared—not sparks of pleasure, Claire's dazed brain realized after a second, but spotlights that had been set up around the rink to illuminate it as twilight set in.

Claire jerked back. "Uh, we really should head back."

"Yeah." Lana let go and moved back so abruptly that Claire nearly fell a second time.

She caught herself, but her emotional balance wasn't as easy to regain. *Stupid, stupid, stupid.* She'd almost violated the conditions of their contract—on the evening before one of the most important days of her life, when she needed to keep her head together most.

What the heck is wrong with you? Giving in to a spontaneous urge was not like her. At the lockers, she pulled the roller skates off with so much force that her socks came off with them.

It had to be this crazy, out-of-control day, which had started with buying an engagement ring and then sharing parts of her manuscript with Lana. *Just get back to the hotel and go to sleep. Tomorrow you'll meet with Ms. Huge and everything will go back to normal.*

But first, she would have to make it through the night sharing a bed with Lana. *Oh God.* What had she gotten herself into?

───────⌇───────

Lana lifted her face into the warm spray and squeezed her eyes shut. The hot water did nothing to ease the tension in her muscles, and neither did it wash away the images playing through her mind on auto-repeat or the impressions of Claire's body against hers that seemed to linger on her skin.

What the hell was that? Had they really been about to kiss?

When she had signed that crazy contract two months ago, she hadn't wasted a thought on how to deal with any feelings of attraction she might develop. Back then, Claire had seemed like a cool, uptight shrink who looked down on her. Never could she have imagined roller-skating with her—or ending up in her arms, about to kiss her.

But now it had happened...well, almost happened. How would they deal with it? Was Claire waiting for her to come out of the bathroom so they could talk about it? But what was there to say?

They had stopped before anything could happen. And wasn't it normal to be attracted to a beautiful woman when you spent so much time with her, especially when you spent half of that time pretending to be in love? It didn't mean much, other than that her libido was finally over Katrina.

She wouldn't allow things to go any further, and judging from Claire's rigid posture and her silence on the way back to the hotel, she had come to the same conclusion. With the important meeting and a stressful interview tomorrow, Claire's emotions were probably all over the place, and she clearly wasn't over Abby either.

One more reason to stay away from her. Having her heart broken once by a woman on the rebound was more than enough.

With determination, Lana shut off the water, reached for her towel, and dried off. She hadn't packed anything special to sleep in since she hadn't expected to share a room with Claire.

So what? You'd have worn a negligee and sexy lingerie if you'd known? Please!

She shook her head at herself and put on a pair of panties and her baggy sleep shirt. For a moment, she eyed the complimentary bathrobe the hotel provided. *Oh come on.* Claire had seen her in her sleepwear several times at home, and besides, it wasn't as if she'd want to jump Lana's bones as soon as she saw a bit of skin.

But somehow, she felt exposed. She took her time brushing her teeth, not in any hurry to leave the bathroom.

Claire had taken quite some time too. One glance at the counter revealed what had taken her so long: she had straightened the stuff that Lana had spread all over as soon as she had unpacked. Now her makeup, lotion, toothpaste, and hair moisturizer were neatly lined up next to the sink—a sure sign of how stressed Claire was.

Finally, Lana couldn't delay it any longer. She opened the bathroom door and peeked out.

Nothing moved.

The only sound was that of the air conditioning, which Lana had put on full blast when they had entered the hotel room earlier.

Quietly, Lana stepped out of the bathroom.

Claire was already in bed, facing away from Lana, toward the window. Was she asleep?

Lana tiptoed around to Claire's side of the room so she could see her better.

Claire had switched off the lamp on her bedside table, but the illumination from the Empire State Building bathed her features in soft light. Her eyes were closed, and her face relaxed in deep sleep. Her normally controlled features looked so vulnerable that a wave of protectiveness welled up in Lana.

Wow. She's really sleeping? Lana doubted that she would be able to fall asleep after what had almost happened earlier. But maybe it hadn't affected Claire as much. Or was she faking sleep so she wouldn't have to talk to her?

Lana watched the slow rise and fall of her chest.

No. Claire was asleep. All the tension of the day and the flight had probably exhausted her. She had the covers drawn up to her chin, but one leg was sticking out, and the hem of her buttery-yellow silk nightshirt had hiked up.

Lana tiptoed closer and pulled the covers over the smooth skin of Claire's leg—not because she'd otherwise be tempted or anything, but because she knew that Claire got cold easily. More than once, she had complained about Lana setting the AC to temperatures that would chill a polar bear.

Claire sighed in her sleep as if sensing her presence.

Bullshit. She's just relaxing now that her leg is no longer freezing off.

She watched her face for a few seconds longer, then tore herself away. On the way to her side of the bed, she turned up the AC.

Quietly, she pulled back the covers and climbed into the bed, careful not to brush against Claire or to jostle the mattress in the process. She stiffly lay at the edge of the bed and stared at the ceiling.

God, she really hated all this unresolved tension after the great day they'd had. Should she wake Claire so they could talk about it and clear the air between them?

No. Tomorrow was Claire's big day. She needed every bit of sleep she could get.

In the grand scheme of things, their little moment wasn't important anyway. So what if they'd both become a bit confused for a second? Their arrangement would be over soon, and during the time that was left, Lana would carefully remind herself that Claire was a woman on the rebound.

It was as easy as that.

Then why did it take forever for her to fall asleep?

～～◊～～

Lana turned up the volume of the radio, tapped the rhythm on the steering wheel, and sang along as loudly as she could to make up for knowing only half the lyrics of the Beach Boys' song.

Another voice mingled with her own, singing much less off-key and getting all the words right.

Figures. Lana grinned. Of course her little perfectionist would know the lyrics by heart.

The sharp blaring of a car horn interrupted their cheerful singing.

Something slammed into their car with the force of a tank, and suddenly, they were spinning across the street.

Lana tried to counter-steer, to brake, to do something—anything—but the car spun out of control. All she could do was clutch the steering wheel and stare at the wide-eyed faces of drivers in oncoming cars.

Vehicles crazily veered around them, honking, tires squealing.

Then, with the sound of a tin can being crushed, they slammed into the guardrail. Shards of glass hailed down on her, and twisted metal pierced her arm and leg.

Blood spurted everywhere, but she felt no pain.

Smoke curled up from the crumpled hood.

"We have to get out!" Lana shouted and turned her head to see if they could escape through the passenger-side door.

Claire was slumped over, held in place only by the seat belt. A large piece of metal had drilled through her chest, and blood drenched her blouse.

Claire's blood.

"No, no, no, no!" Lana screamed out her despair. It wasn't supposed to be like this. She pressed her hands to Claire's chest and tried to hold back the stream of blood. "Claire! God, no! Not you!"

A sound wrenched Claire from deep sleep. She blinked into the dim light provided by the Empire State Building and other high-rises next to the hotel and brought one hand out from under the covers to wipe her brow.

God, what a nightmare!

Hazily, she remembered dreaming that she and Lana had met with Ms. Huge. But instead of making small talk and discussing the terms of the contract, the acquisitions editor had put them through an interrogation about their relationship, as if she suspected that they were just pretending to be a couple.

Endless questions had been fired at them: When had they met? Where had their first date been? How had their family reacted to their engagement? What was their favorite thing to do in bed?

Claire rolled her eyes. Ms. Huge definitely wouldn't ask that. It was a stupid dream, nothing m—

A whimper from next to her made her jerk upright.

Lana!

She was tangled beneath the covers, groaning and gasping. Clearly, she was having a nightmare too, but hers seemed to be about something much worse than intrusive questions about her sex life.

A constant string of moans tore from Lana's throat, and she mumbled something Claire couldn't make out. Was it *oh God, oh God*?

Claire's gaze darted around as if looking for help.

You are a trained psychologist, for Christ's sake! Do something! But as much as she tried, she couldn't remember whether you were supposed to wake a person from such an intense nightmare or not. When it came to Lana, all her training went out the window.

Then Lana sucked in a shuddery breath that almost sounded like a sob, and Claire couldn't bear it any longer.

Gently, she touched her fingertips to Lana's shoulder. "Lana? Wake up. It's just a dream."

Lana woke with a gasp, like a diver who'd just made it to the surface after nearly drowning. The white of her eyes gleamed in the light from outside as she wildly looked around, not quite awake.

"It's okay," Claire whispered. "I think you had a nightmare."

A groan rose from Lana's chest. Before Claire could react, Lana threw herself into her arms and buried her face against the curve of her neck.

"Uh." Slowly, Claire lifted her hands. She hesitated with her fingers hovering over Lana's back. All of her concerns—keeping a professional distance, sticking to the terms of the contract—weren't important right now. Lana needed her. She lowered her hands and gently stroked Lana's back.

Shudders racked Lana's body. As Claire repeated her soothing touches again and again, they slowly ebbed away until Lana lay still in her arms and the tense muscles beneath her fingers relaxed.

Lana sniffled once, then exhaled.

Her warm breath made goose bumps spread over Claire's skin. *Stop it,* she told her rebellious body. Lana needed a friend; her stupid confused libido had no place in this.

"Sorry," Lana mumbled and tried to pull away.

Claire didn't let her. She gently held her with one arm while she lifted the other hand and brushed a strand of sweat-dampened hair away from Lana's face. "Don't apologize. Want to tell me about it?"

Lana turned onto her side and nestled against Claire like a giant koala bear. "It was the same stupid dream."

"You're dreaming about the accident?" Claire tried hard not to switch into therapist mode, because she knew Lana would withdraw if she sensed it. Truth be told, with Lana cuddled against her, it was easy to keep her inner therapist at bay.

"Yes. It's always the same. But this time—"

"This time?" Claire prompted when Lana didn't continue. She fanned her fingers over Lana's shoulder. "Don't worry. I'm not psychoanalyzing your dreams."

"I know. That's not why I…" Lana nibbled her bottom lip. "I thought these nightmares had stopped. I don't know what's triggering them now."

Claire trailed her fingers soothingly across Lana's back again. "Maybe all this stress. If you'd rather not come to the interview and just meet me at the restaurant where we'll have lunch with Ms. Huge…"

It wouldn't be ideal. Since the interview was scheduled to last until eleven and noon was the only time Ms. Huge could meet with them, they would have to go from the radio station directly to the meeting with the editor. That was why she had wanted Lana to accompany her to the interview so that Ms. Huge would see them arrive at the restaurant together. It would bolster Lana's image as the supportive fiancée who would help promote Claire's book in whatever way she could.

"No," Lana said immediately. "I want to come. I'll be fine. Don't worry. I won't let you down."

"That's not what has me worried. I'm worried about you, not about the book deal. Okay, not *just* about the book deal."

"I'll be fine," Lana repeated. "Really." She yawned widely. "We should try to go back to sleep, or we won't be at our best tomorrow."

Claire nodded.

Neither of them let go or moved away.

"Is…is it okay if we stay like this for a little longer?" Lana sounded almost childlike. She searched Claire's face in the semi-darkness. "Maybe… until I go back to sleep?"

"Sure." Normally, Claire preferred some space while she tried to fall asleep, but if a bit of physical contact soothed Lana and helped her get some rest, it would be a good thing for the book deal.

If she was honest with herself, that wasn't the only reason she allowed Lana to keep clinging to her. Having Lana's warm, curvy body close was as sensual and relaxing as a bubble bath.

At least for now the awkward tension between them seemed to have eased

"Sleep well," Claire whispered. "And if you have another nightmare, wake me."

Lana chuckled. "If I have another nightmare, I'll be asleep and won't be able to wake you."

"True. Then you'd better not have another nightmare."

Lana pressed her cheek to Claire's shoulder. "I don't think I will." She wiggled her toes against Claire's feet and yawned. Soon, her breathing grew deeper.

Claire watched her for a while, going nearly cross-eyed because Lana was so close. Holding her while she slept, protecting her, filled her with a warm feeling that she didn't want to examine too closely.

To her own amazement, it wasn't very long until she felt herself drift off to sleep too.

Chapter 15

CLAIRE STARED INTO THE MIRROR above the sink. Her makeup was immaculate, but she still didn't feel as if she had her game face on.

Last night, she had fallen asleep almost immediately—first while she waited for Lana to come out of the bathroom, then after Lana's nightmare had woken her. Both times, it had been as if her exhausted brain had put the emergency brakes on before everything that had happened could overwhelm her and keep her up all night.

But now all her thoughts were back—thoughts of their magical evening on the High Line, which had ended with Lana in her arms.

She really should be focused on her interview and the meeting afterward, but no matter how often she tried to guide her thoughts toward interview questions and publishing discussions, they always returned to that moment on the roller-skating rink and to the way it had felt to hold a trembling Lana in her arms last night and waking up with Lana still cuddled against her.

Get yourself together! You hired Lana to help you get the book deal, not to distract you from it.

A soft knock on the door made her flinch.

"Yes?" Claire called.

The door opened an inch. "Are you decent?"

Claire peeked down at her scoop-neck silk camisole top and the Armani skirt suit. "I would hope so."

Lana opened the door more fully. Her gaze swept Claire's body in a way that made her tingle all over. "Wow. You look great. If book deals were awarded based on the looks of the author, your book would be in print already."

The compliment warmed her down to her toes. "Thank you." She regarded Lana, who was wearing an ankle-length, chocolate-brown skirt and a white wrap top that emphasized her curves rather than hiding them. "You look wonderful too."

"So this is okay?" Lana tugged on her top.

"Very okay. But there's one important thing missing."

"Makeup?" Lana asked. "I put on a little. Can't you tell?"

"No. Not makeup. I'm talking about this." She squeezed past Lana, ignoring the sensual scent of her perfume, and went to her purse, which sat on the desk. She reached inside and pulled out the small, black box.

Lana joined her and peered over her shoulder to see what she was holding.

Her closeness made Claire warm all over. She turned toward her and snapped open the lid.

The delicate feather ring with its sky-blue topaz sparkled against the black velvet.

"Oh," Lana said. "The ring. Of course."

Claire pulled the ring from its velvet bed. Gently, she took Lana's hand. Her gaze flickered up to her eyes, then her lips, then back to her hand. Jesus, why did this feel so real? As if she was about to put an engagement ring on Lana's finger for real, one that she'd later exchange for a wedding ring before they would go off on a honeymoon.

Oh, no, no, no. Don't go there. You've got to share the bed with her again tonight. No honeymoon thoughts! Think platonic thoughts. Unsexy thoughts.

But that was easier said than done with Lana's soft hand in hers, her body so close, and her trusting, almost intimate gaze on her.

Come on. You know what this is. You're latching on to the first woman you've met after the breakup. That's classic rebound. You should be stronger than that.

Just as she was about to slide the ring onto Lana's finger, Lana cleared her throat and pulled her hand from Claire's grasp. "Um, I can do it." She took the ring from her and backed away half a step before sliding it on her finger.

Oh. Yeah. That's what she should have done in the first place—let Lana put on the damn ring herself. She took a closer look at Lana's fingers. Were they trembling? "You okay? I mean, after last night..." The statement sounded too ambiguous, so she quickly added, "After the nightmare..."

"I'm fine." Lana looked up from the ring and studied her. "Sorry about last night. For latching on to you like that and for waking you up. I never realized I'm so loud." She flushed. "I mean, when I'm having a nightmare."

"It's okay," Claire said. "I'm just glad you didn't have any more nightmares after that. You didn't, did you?"

Lana shook her head. After hesitating for a second, she asked quietly, "Are *we* okay?"

Claire didn't know how to answer that. There wasn't even really a *we*, was there?

Before she could decide what to answer, the phone on the bedside table rang.

They both jumped.

Claire crossed the room and picked up the phone.

It was the front desk, telling her the cab she'd asked for had arrived. She thanked the clerk and hung up.

"The cab is here." Claire swallowed. *Showtime.* She put on the suit jacket and grabbed her purse and the manuscript so she could take another look at it in the cab.

Together, they walked to the door.

Claire opened it and held it for Lana. As Lana passed her, Claire said, "We're fine."

Lana stopped and looked at her. For a moment, Claire thought she might follow up with another question, but then she nodded, smiled, and led the way to the elevator.

Claire exhaled and followed her.

~~~~~~

Dr. Christine Graham, the host of the radio talk show, was exactly the kind of woman Lana suspected Claire would normally go for: a fellow psychologist with flowing, honey-blonde hair and a sexy Scottish lilt.

Truth be told, under different circumstances, Lana might have given those twinkling cornflower-blue eyes a second look too, but being attracted to one psychologist was already confusing enough.

Claire made no attempt to flirt either, as if she was too focused on the upcoming interview to even notice how beautiful the interviewer was. Or maybe she wanted to uphold the image of the faithful fiancée.

As Christine gave them a quick tour of the radio station, Lana kept touching the ring with her thumb. The metal had warmed and fit her finger as if it had been there for ages.

It's a prop, she kept reminding herself. *Just part of the act. Don't get used to it.*

Finally, Christine ended the tour in front of her soundproof, glass-enclosed studio. "Sorry," she said to Lana. "This is as far as you can go. But if you'd like, you can keep my producer company in the control room and watch from there." She pointed at the room next to the studio, separated from it by a wall with a large window.

"Thank you. I'd love that." She turned toward Claire, who'd put on her therapist mask, but Lana knew her well enough by now to glimpse the nervousness beneath. "Don't worry. You'll do great. The listeners will love you." For Christine's benefit, she added, "But, of course, not half as much as I do."

"Thanks, honey," Claire said.

Christine looked back and forth between them and grinned. "Last chance for a good-luck kiss."

"Uh..." Claire looked at her as if she'd been asked to perform a striptease.

Christine laughed. "Don't be shy on my account. I'm bi myself, so a wee snog between two women won't shock me."

Lana gave herself a mental kick and stepped forward. One quick good-luck kiss. It was what was expected of a loving fiancée. All part of the contract.

Claire stood rooted to the spot, clutching her manuscript with both hands. Her eyes widened as Lana approached.

Lana slid her hands beneath the lapels of Claire's blazer and smoothed her fingers over the silk of her camisole top right below Claire's collarbone. She tugged on her lapels. *Come on, Claire. Play along. We've kissed before. No big deal.* But after that moment at the edge of the skating rink last night, it somehow was.

Almost shyly, Claire slid her hand onto Lana's hip to keep her balance as they both leaned forward at the same time.

A quick, encouraging peck was all Lana had intended, just enough to make their couple status more believable and to give Claire a supportive send-off. But when their lips met and Claire's warm, soft mouth slid over hers, Lana's eyes fluttered shut. Her hands tightened on Claire's lapels on their own accord, pulling her closer.

Claire's low moan feathered over Lana's lips, and she parted them instinctively to meet Claire's smooth tongue.

She tasted like mint and passion and Claire, an intoxicating mix that made Lana's head spin.

Their tongues caressed each other with long, sensual strokes.

A throaty hum from Claire vibrated through Lana's body. Heat pooled between her thighs, and her fingers curled more tightly into Claire's blazer.

Christine loudly cleared her throat next to them, as if she'd done it several times already without them paying her any attention.

Blinking, Lana eased away from Claire's lips and stared into her smoky-gray eyes.

Claire stared back and then lifted her hand to her mouth and touched it as if she couldn't understand what had just happened.

Lana could barely believe it either. That kiss had taken method acting a little too far. *Acting? No.* That hadn't been an act, at least not for her. But what about Claire? Had she merely gone with the flow to convince the radio host she was in a happy relationship?

If that was what she'd set out to do, it had been a success.

"Phew, lassies." Christine fanned herself with both hands and grinned at Claire. "I can see that your agent hasn't exaggerated when she sold you as an expert on how to keep that spark in your relationship."

"Uh, I'm…"

"Happy to demonstrate your techniques, aren't you, honey?" Lana stepped in when Claire seemed to be at a loss for what to say.

"Aye, then let's introduce our listeners to those techniques." Christine pulled Claire through the door of her studio and left Lana with the producer, who was leaning in the doorway of the control room, grinning at her.

Guess he saw the kiss.

Everything happened very fast now, or maybe her brain was stuck in slow motion.

Claire didn't seem to have the same problem, or maybe she was just better at compartmentalizing things.

Through the glass, Lana watched her put on headphones and look down at the lit-up control board that Christine was pointing out to her.

"If you want to listen in, you can." The producer offered Lana another set of headphones.

"Thank you." She took them and put them on.

The red on-air light flashed, and then Christine's voice came through the headphones. "Good mornin', New York! You are listening to the *Morning Couch* with Dr. Christine. We've got Dr. Claire Renshaw as our guest today. Claire is a couples therapist and the author of a self-help book on successful relationships that she hopes to publish soon. Today, she's here to answer your questions on love, sex, and relationships."

Sex? Lana pressed her hand to her mouth, which still tingled. Claire would have to answer questions on sex? A short giggle escaped her. This she had to hear!

"Welcome, Claire," Christine said. "You and your lovely fiancée flew in from LA yesterday, didn't you?"

"We did," Claire answered.

Through the headphones, her voice sounded more intimate, as if only Lana could hear her instead of millions of listeners.

"So as an expert on makin' relationships last, did you do anything special last night? A romantic candle-light dinner at La Grenouille?"

"Um, no. Actually…" Claire looked up, and their gazes met through the glass. "We took a stroll along the High Line and then went roller-skating."

The simple words couldn't do their experience justice. It didn't sound romantic at all, more like two friends out for a fun afternoon. *That's what it was.*

"Ooh, the High Line! I love it," Christine said. "Looks as if you did your homework on the must-see spots before comin' to our lovely city."

"It was actually my fiancée who found it," Claire said.

"Ah, so she's the organized one while you go with the flow."

Lana laughed along with Claire, and again their gazes met through the window.

"No." Claire chuckled. "It's the other way around. But we complement each other well."

"Is that one of the secrets of lasting relationships?" Christine asked. "Finding someone who complements you?"

"It's certainly part of it. I think most successful couples have enough shared interests and values to give them a good common ground, but also enough differences to keep things interesting and to help each other grow and become more complete and well-rounded as human beings."

"Let's find out if our listeners agree." Christine flicked a switch on her control board. "Good mornin' and thank you for calling in. You are live on the *Morning Couch*. Who am I talking to?"

"Uh, my name is Eliza," a woman's voice came through the headphones.

"Good mornin', Eliza," Christine said. "So, what do you think is the secret to lasting relationships?"

"Uh, not throwing in the towel when things get tough." Eliza sounded as if she either had a cold or was trying not to cry. "My husband and I were about to give up on our twenty-year marriage, but then we attended one of Dr. Renshaw's couples workshops. We took away so much from that weekend, so I just called to say thank you."

Oh, wow. Pride flowed through Lana. Claire wasn't a quack who made fast money by selling her books and audio products to desperate people. She honestly helped patients, and that quiet glow that now emanated from her revealed how much the woman's call meant to her.

"You were the one who did the hard work," Claire said, her voice husky. "I only gave you a nudge in the right direction."

"Isn't it marvelous?" Christine said once the caller had said goodbye. "You've got your fans on the East Coast too. Let's see if our next caller has got a question for you." She flicked another switch on the control board.

"Uh, yeah, I actually do." The caller was another woman. This one sounded younger. "My boyfriend and I have been together for a while, and, um, he has repeatedly brought up wanting to have a threesome…"

Ooh, now the sex questions start! Lana zeroed in on Claire to see how she would handle it.

Instead of blushing, as Lana had expected, Claire looked completely composed, as if the caller had just talked about her boyfriend squeezing the toothpaste tube from the wrong end. "And how do you feel about that idea?" she asked.

"I...I don't know," the caller said. "I'm worried, I guess. I mean, what if he ends up liking the other girl better than me?"

"Have you talked to your boyfriend about your concerns?"

"Um, no, not really."

"You should," Claire said. "Threesomes can be tricky, and they only work with a lot of honest communication. You and your boyfriend need to be on the same page and have the same expectations about this experience. If you're only doing it to please him or because you think it'll fix your relationship, it won't work. You won't be able to enjoy it if you are constantly worried about him liking it a little too much."

Lana flashed back to the good-luck kiss. Liking it a little too much was a perfect description for what she'd felt.

She missed the rest of what Claire said to the caller and only started listening in again when Christine said, "You mentioned the importance of honest communication when it comes to negotiating a threesome. What role do you think honesty plays in making relationships last?"

Oh no. There it was: the question Claire had feared. Lana stepped closer to the window and laid one hand on the cool glass as if she could offer some support.

Both hands clutching the microphone stand, Claire stared at Lana with a get-me-out-of-here look.

Lana gave her an encouraging nod. *You can do this.*

"First of all," Claire cleared her throat, "you need to be honest with yourself—about your needs and wants. Do some soul-searching. Sometimes, you think you know what you want, but it might not be what you actually need from a relationship. If you don't know yourself, how are you supposed to communicate your needs to your partner?"

"Makes sense," Christine said. "What about being honest with your partner? Is there a thing such as too much honesty? Are there situations where a little...creative handling of the truth might be better?"

Damn. Claire's back was to the wall now. If she went on record saying that honesty was always the best policy, it would come back to bite her in the ass if their charade was ever discovered.

Claire made eye contact with Lana again before turning to Christine and giving her a tense smile. "Well, we can't give away all the secrets now, can we? Your listeners will have to read my upcoming book to find out."

She imitated the tone Lana had used on the plane perfectly, and the hint of playful seduction in her voice made Lana shiver.

Christine laughed. "I guess we've got to have you back on the show once the book is out."

The stiff posture of Claire's shoulders relaxed, and she grinned at Lana through the glass.

Phew. Lana grinned back.

"I've got one last question about something that I know a lot of our listeners might be struggling with," Christine said.

"Sure." Claire's tone was light, but Lana knew her body language by now and saw the tension returning to her shoulders.

Lana longed to reach through the glass and massage her stiff muscles.

"Nowadays, both partners usually have got a career and obligations outside of the relationship. How can they successfully navigate a relationship without giving up their other goals?"

Wow. Somehow, this woman seemed to target all the topics that were difficult for Claire to answer because they hit too close to home.

But Claire's face didn't give away any tension as she leaned toward the microphone. "First and foremost, get rid of your tunnel vision. Take a hard look at how you really spend your time. How often do you check your work email while you're watching a movie with your partner?"

Lana stared through the glass. Was that in Claire's book, or had she really heard Lana when she had pointed out that her cell phone and relaxing movie nights didn't go together?

"Keep work and your private life as separate as possible," Claire said. "When you're at work, give it your all. But when you're at home, be fully present. Otherwise, you're not doing your relationship or your job a favor."

"That sounds like good advice. Thanks for coming all the way from LA to talk to us," Christine said. "This was the *Morning Couch* with my guest Dr. Claire Renshaw. Watch out for her book *The Art of Lasting Relationships: Seven Secrets to a Thriving Love Life*, which will hopefully be in the book shops soon."

Some love song started to play, and Claire took off her headphones.

The interview was over, and as far as Lana could tell, it had been a success. Lana should have been able to relax a little now, but instead her hands were damp as she took off her own headphones.

Within the next few minutes, she would be alone with Claire, stuck in a cab, and she had no idea what to say to her after their good-luck kiss had turned a little too real.

One down, one to go. Claire shook hands with Christine, who then gave a friendly wave in Lana's direction and told Claire where to find a recording of the interview online.

Claire nodded and thanked her, but her thoughts were no longer with the radio show or its host. She stared past Christine to the woman in the glassed-in booth next door.

You're really making a mess of things. In less than an hour, they would sit at the table with Wishing Tree Publishing's acquisitions editor. She couldn't afford to have things between her and Lana be awkward or tense.

She needed to take her own advice: keep work and relationships separate. Lana was a professional actress hired to play a role. She needed to remember that.

They both stepped out of their respective booths and met up in the hall, where they lingered, not touching, not saying anything.

Lana's hair was adorably mussed from the headphones she'd been wearing, and Claire's fingers itched to smooth them back into some semblance of order. She shoved her hands into the pockets of her blazer to resist temptation.

Finally, Lana cleared her throat. "You were great."

"Yeah?" She knew she was fishing for compliments, but Lana's praise felt too good.

"Yeah. You handled that question about the threesome as if you got asked things like that every day."

Claire shrugged. "I do get questions like that every now and then." Her cheeks warmed as she realized how her words could be interpreted. "In therapy sessions, I mean, not in my own relationships."

"Of course not." Lana let out a possessive growl and wrapped one arm around her. "You're mine, and I'm not sharing."

"Uh…"

"The producer is right behind us," Lana whispered into her ear while pretending to nip it.

Claire's knees nearly gave out. Since when were her ears such an erogenous zone? *Get yourself together. You're a mature woman, not a teenager.* She was so out of it that she hadn't noticed that they weren't alone in the hallway. If something like that happened during the meeting with Ms. Huge, her book deal would be toast.

"Good." Claire's voice came out raspy, and she hoped that Lana would think she was just acting for the producer's sake. "Because I don't want anyone but you."

They looked into each other's eyes. Was it just her imagination, or was it overly warm in the radio station?

"Great interview," the producer said from behind them.

"Um, thanks." Claire tore her gaze away from Lana to give him a friendly smile. "And thanks for letting Lana listen in."

"My pleasure," the producer said. "Good luck with the book deal."

Oh shit. The book deal. They needed to go, or they'd be late to the meeting with Ms. Huge.

It seemed to take forever until their cab arrived. Claire didn't know what made her more nervous: possibly being late or waiting in front of the radio station, alone with Lana.

"Um, do we need to talk about…uh, earlier?" Lana asked quietly.

A lump the size of a basketball seemed to settle in Claire's throat. "If you want to."

"I think we should."

Claire sighed. She knew it was the mature thing to do. But how could she explain what she didn't understand herself? Her feelings made no sense at all, so it would be best to ignore them until she was sure she could trust her judgment again. "All right."

They looked at each other, each clearly waiting for the other to go first.

Considering Claire had been the one to talk about the importance of communication not even ten minutes ago, maybe she should start. "I…I'm really sorry. That wasn't appropriate. I don't know what to say. I guess I got caught up in our ruse for a moment and in that whole emotional roller coaster of the interview and the meeting and everything…"

Lana studied her for a while, as if searching for something. "It's okay," she finally said. "I guess I'm out of practice at slipping in and out of roles too."

Was that really all it was for Lana—a role? Or was she just giving her an out?

Before Claire could find an answer, the cab arrived.

On the trip across town, Claire leafed through her manuscript once more, but she barely registered what she was reading.

With two minutes to spare, they arrived at the Italian restaurant where they would meet with the editor. The hostess led them to a corner table, where Ms. Huge was already seated. Wishing Tree's acquisitions editor was in her fifties and had sharp, blue eyes that were constantly in motion. Claire had a feeling that she wasn't missing much.

"Dr. Renshaw?" Ms. Huge asked when they approached.

Claire nodded. "Call me Claire, please."

"Then feel free to call me Bridget."

As soon as Bridget stood, Claire realized two things: despite her name, the woman was tiny, and if her gaydar wasn't mistaken, she was a lesbian too. Claire wasn't sure if that would be to her advantage or not. It might mean that Bridget Huge wouldn't be fooled so easily because she was familiar with the dynamic in a relationship between two women. One more factor in this equation that she couldn't control. She was starting to sweat already, and she hoped her fingers weren't damp as they shook hands.

She wrapped one arm around Lana's shoulders and pulled her against her side, grateful for that bit of security and support. "And this is Lana Henderson, my fiancée. I hope we didn't make you wait. The interview went on longer than expected." It couldn't hurt to let Bridget know how dedicated she was to promoting the book, even in this very early stage.

But Bridget barely seemed to have heard that last sentence. "Lana?" she repeated. She shook Lana's hand while looking from her to Claire. "Didn't you say in one of your first emails that your fiancée's name was Abigail? I remember because it's my partner's name too."

The blood rushed from Claire's face, making her dizzy. *Shit, shit, shit.* They hadn't even sat down, and it was already over.

"It is," Lana said with a relaxed smile. "But you know how it is with first names. Any time my mother called me Abigail, I knew I was in trouble, and I have a sister named Gabby, so Abby as a nickname was out. I tend to go by my middle name most of the time."

Bridget laughed. "My Abby winces every time I call her Abigail too."

Claire discreetly wiped her brow. *Phew.* That was one disaster avoided. She threw Lana a grateful look, marveling at her quick thinking and improvisation that had saved Claire's ass time and again. *God, I could kiss her.* But since she was in enough trouble as it was, she settled for a quick squeeze of her hand.

They sat down at the table, and when the waiter came by, Claire ordered the first thing on the menu without even registering what it was.

"Thank you both for coming all the way from LA," Bridget said. "I know nowadays most things are handled via email, but a nonfiction publication is a huge investment for a boutique publisher like Wishing Tree, so we like to meet the authors before offering a contract. The author and her background are as important as the book itself."

Lana slid closer in the booth and covered Claire's hand on the table with her own. "Well, you don't need to worry about Claire. She's the real deal. She lives and breathes psychology."

"I know. I listened in on the interview on my way here." Bridget gave Claire an impressed nod. "I like how you handled yourself in front of a microphone. But there's one thing that made me curious."

Uh-oh. Claire swallowed, already sensing what would be coming. She tried to smile despite the tension in her jaw.

"That you'll-have-to-buy-the-book answer... I mean, you pulled it off in a charming way, but I work with PR people all day, and that's what they say when they have something to hide."

Claire's mind raced. Beneath the table, Lana's free hand found hers and squeezed it encouragingly. But this time, Lana couldn't answer for her, or Bridget would start to suspect that something strange was going on.

"Well..." Claire drew out the word to buy herself a few precious seconds to think. "You see, I didn't want to say too much because...um, because, well, to tell you the truth, I've come to believe that the chapter on honesty—and maybe the one on balancing work and relationships—could use a little more work."

Bridget leaned forward, her expression attentive, but completely neutral. "How so?"

"Getting engaged to Lana gave me a new perspective on life. I mean, I have always valued our relationship, but now that I put a ring on her finger..." She pulled Lana's hand onto the table and lightly trailed her fingertip along the piece of metal that was warm from Lana's body heat. "I've become even more aware of how little things can make or break a relationship. Things like turning off your phone every now and then or not working late all the time. I think I didn't emphasize that enough in the book."

"Interesting that you would say that." Bridget pulled out a leather-bound planner and opened it to a page full of notes. "Because I thought the same when I read those chapters. So would you be willing to work with one of our editors to revise them?"

"Of course," Claire said. "I'd love to get some constructive criticism."

The waiter appeared with their food. Bridget and Lana had ordered salads, and apparently, Claire had too.

Bridget pierced a bit of lettuce with her fork, but instead of eating it, she looked back and forth between them. "So, when's the big day?"

Big day? Was she talking about the publication date? Claire's brain couldn't keep up.

"She means for the wedding, honey." Lana laughed. "Isn't she adorable? She's such a wonderful psychologist, but sometimes she's got her head in the clouds." She gave Claire a loving smile.

"Oh. Yeah, the wedding date. Of course," Claire said. "Um, actually, we were talking about a June wedding."

"It's already June 29. Does that mean you're getting married tomorrow?"

"Um, no. I meant June next year." If she was lucky, the book would be out before anyone would start to expect photos of the happy brides.

"You see," Lana said, "my sister, Gabby, she's deployed overseas, and my mother would never forgive me if I got married without her, so we'll have to wait until she returns."

Claire decided then and there to pay Lana more than the agreed-upon fifty thousand for saving the day not once, but twice.

"Oh, really?" Bridget said. "Which branch is she in?"

"She's a medic in the Marines."

Lana's answer came so smoothly that Claire wondered whether one of her stepsiblings might really be a marine.

Bridget nodded respectfully. "Please thank her for her service."

In between bites of salad, she started asking questions: How much time would Claire be able to dedicate to promoting the book? What kind of contacts did she have to community centers, women's non-profits, or the press in the LA area? Was she willing to write articles for lifestyle and health magazines to get her name out there?

She seemed to like Claire's replies because she smiled as she scribbled down notes. Finally, she glanced from Lana to Claire and asked, "Would Lana be able to accompany you to some of the promo events?"

Claire wasn't hungry at all, but she popped a cherry tomato into her mouth anyway so she could think about her answer while she chewed. "She'll be there as often as she can." Hopefully, that was noncommittal enough while still making Bridget think she had her fiancée's full support.

Bridget put down her fork. "So, what do you do for a living, Lana?"

Damn. They should have talked about this beforehand. Should they stick to the lawyer story? But the last time Claire had lied about it, Lana had taken it to mean her job as a barista wasn't good enough.

Lana glanced at her, clearly not knowing what to say either. "Um, I'm a—"

"Barista," Claire said before Lana would be forced to lie.

Lana stared at her. Then a pleased smile curved her full lips.

Claire smiled back and held her head up high. If Lana really were her fiancée, that was what she would do—be proud of her, instead of trying to hide a part of her, be it her scars or her job. It was one of the things that Lana had taught her.

"Oh, that's great." Bridget sounded sincere. "We'll see what our PR department can do with that. I mean, coffee and books are a great combination, and we aren't targeting only women with degrees, so…" She scribbled down more notes.

What do you know? Claire grinned to herself. *Chapter three was right. Honesty really pays off. At least for the moment.* She tried not to worry about what would happen down the road, when she and Lana officially broke up. By then, she'd hopefully have a publishing contract, and Wishing Tree wouldn't be able to back out.

Finally, when the salads were gone and all questions were answered, Bridget closed her planner. "I don't want to make any promises I might not be able to keep, but things look really good. Of course, it's not just my decision. I still have to sell the project to the rest of the team, and our senior editor might want to weigh in on the decision too. I'll present the concept to the team during our meeting on Monday, and if all goes well, you can expect a publishing contract in your in-box before the end of next week."

Claire's beaming grin felt as if it would split her face. "That would be beyond great. Thank you."

Later, she barely knew what had been said after that, but she remembered with crystal clarity what happened once Bridget had left and they were outside, alone.

"You did it!" Lana wrapped her arms around her and twirled Claire around, making her squeal as the world around her became a blur.

"*We* did it." She felt a bit dizzy, but she suspected it had more to do with being so close to Lana than with being twirled around. Still she couldn't bring herself to let go, even once Lana had put her down. "Thank you, thank you, thank you." With each word, she planted a big kiss on Lana's cheek, dangerously close to the corner of her mouth.

Then both stopped laughing and stared at each other, arms still wrapped around the other.

"Uh, come on." Claire stepped back but allowed herself to keep hold of one of Lana's hands, pulling her toward their hotel, which was only a few blocks away. "Let's go get changed. I'm taking you out to celebrate."

"You don't have to. We just had lunch, and you're already paying me."

"You did so much more than what was required in the contract." She squeezed Lana's hand and gazed into her eyes. "Seriously, Lana. I admit that at first I wasn't too sure you were the right person for this role, but now I know I couldn't have done this with anyone but you. Let me say thank you in style."

Lana's eyes looked a little damp, as if Claire's gratefulness had touched her, but she was beaming. "Okay. What did you have in mind? Not roller-skating beneath the High Line, I take it?"

Considering how that outing had ended, a repeat wouldn't be a good idea. "Uh, no. Think high heels, not roller skates."

"I don't wear high heels," Lana said.

"I know. You can wear whatever you want."

"So where are you taking me?"

Claire had no idea. She hadn't thought of anything beyond this meeting with Bridget Huge. "You'll just have to wait and see."

Chapter 16

IN MORE CASUAL CLOTHES AND more comfortable shoes, they strolled down Sixth Avenue. Here, among the anonymous crowd of New Yorkers, there was no reason to hold hands and pretend to be a couple, and Lana missed Claire's hand in hers as much as she missed the fake engagement ring on her finger.

Was this what some of her colleagues went through after immersing themselves into a role for months? But she'd been Claire's pretend fiancée for only eight weeks, even though it felt longer somehow.

"So, where do you want to go?" Claire asked. "You pick."

Lana appreciated Claire, the control freak, leaving the choice up to her. She wasn't hungry yet, so she tried to think of something else they could do for an hour—something less romantic than a stroll along the High Line. A repeat of last night's almost kiss was definitely out, so an activity that screamed "two friends playing tourists" was in order.

She racked her brain, but all she could think of were activities for couples: rowing a boat underneath Central Park's Bow Bridge, a carriage ride, or a sunset sail to the Statue of Liberty.

A sight to their left helped her out. "How about the Empire State Building?" She pointed at the skyscraper. That should be safe. There was nothing romantic about the long lines they would have to brave to make it to the top. "Would you like to go up to the observation deck?"

"Yes!" Claire gave an uncharacteristic little hop that made Lana chuckle.

She loved seeing the usually controlled woman so enthusiastic and carefree.

Instead of the unromantic waiting in line Lana had imagined, Claire pulled out her phone and got them VIP tickets that allowed them to skip to the front of the lines. Soon, they were riding the elevator up to the eighty-sixth floor.

"I feel like I'm in *Love Affair*," Claire said.

Lana stared at her. "Uh, excuse me?"

"The 1939 movie, you know? Two potential lovers agree to meet at the Empire State Building six months after meeting on a luxury liner. The ending of *Sleepless in Seattle* was inspired by that movie."

"Oh." So much for the Empire State Building not being romantic. Lana nearly said they should watch both movies when they got back home, but Claire's house wouldn't be her home for much longer. Soon, she'd be back in her tiny studio apartment, and movie nights with Claire would be a thing of the past.

The thought gave her a queasy feeling in the pit of her stomach, and no matter how much she pretended it was from the fast-moving elevator, she knew it wasn't.

Finally, the elevator doors opened, and they stepped out onto the observation deck that wrapped around the building's spire.

"Wow." Lana turned in a circle and looked across the expanse of high-rise buildings below them.

"Haven't you been up here before?" Claire asked.

Lana shook her head. "I didn't do the tourist thing when I lived here."

"Then I'm glad we came."

"Me too," Lana said as she watched Claire make her way to the edge of the deck.

The wind whipped around her, playing with her hair that she'd not put up into a chignon for once. Her cheeks turned rosy, either from the wind or from excitement—or both.

"Look at that." Claire pointed at something.

"I am looking." Lana stepped closer and reluctantly looked away from Claire to gaze in the direction she was pointing. Past the One World Trade Center, they could glimpse the Statue of Liberty in the distance.

They walked around the observation deck, pointing out the nicest views to each other and snapping photos on their phones.

221

Finally, despite the humid June afternoon, the wind and the crowd on the observation deck became too much, and they took the elevator back down.

They strolled in the direction of their hotel, and again Lana had to stop herself from taking Claire's hand. She peeked over at her, wondering if she was having similar problems, but Claire's cheerful smile didn't give anything away.

They ended up having an early dinner at their hotel's restaurant. Lana decided that fate had conspired against her attempts to keep the atmosphere on their last evening in New York strictly platonic. A flower stood on their secluded corner table for two; the lights were low, and the waiter brought them two spoons so they could share the dessert Lana had ordered after the filet mignon.

Claire licked a bit of pistachio mousse off her bottom lip, and the sight definitely didn't inspire any platonic thoughts. "Ooh! This is good."

As she tried to cut off a sliver of the chocolate cake with the side of her spoon, Lana playfully pulled the plate to her side of the table. "Are you sure you want any?" She tapped her wristwatch. "It's after six."

Claire reached across the table. Their fingers brushed as she pulled the plate toward her. "I learned that some things are worth breaking the rules for."

She was talking about dessert; Lana knew that. Not about the no-real-involvement clause of their contract. But there still seemed to be an intimate undertone to her words.

They finished the mousse-topped cake, playfully fighting over every bite. Lana considered fighting over the check too, but Claire immediately snatched up the leather folder and slid her credit card inside. "My treat," she said as if guessing Lana's thoughts.

"Then thank you for a wonderful dinner."

Once the waiter had returned Claire's credit card, they made their way to the elevator.

Claire's finger hovered over the button for their floor. Was she as loath to end their evening as Lana, or did the thought of returning to their room make her a bit nervous too?

"How about a glass of champagne on the rooftop bar?" Claire pointed upward. "I hear they have a great view."

Lana grinned. "Carbs *and* alcohol after six? Wow."

"I'll make a one-time exception tonight. So?" Claire moved her finger back and forth between the button with the number eleven and the one with the number twenty-two.

Instead of answering, Lana put her finger over Claire's and pressed it on the twenty-two.

The elevator carried them up to the rooftop bar. Other hotel guests had apparently had the same idea, so the purple leather chairs at the bar were all occupied, but they claimed the last open table next to the chest-high glass railing.

The view was indeed stunning, with the Empire State Building directly in their line of sight and Midtown below them.

Claire ordered champagne.

Lana raised her glass and looked across the rim at Claire, who still hadn't put up her hair and looked beautiful with the wind in her hair and her cheeks flushed, either from the day's excitement or the sun she'd gotten earlier. "To you and *The Art of Lasting Relationships*." After a second, she couldn't help adding with a grin, "Especially the sex-on-the-kitchen-table chapter."

Claire rolled her eyes but laughed. "To our successful trip—and the actress who turned out to be the perfect person for this role."

Still looking into each other's eyes, they clinked their glasses together.

As they sipped champagne, the sun sank lower, painting the horizon in golden and orange hues. They watched as lights flickered on all over the city.

At the bar, couples huddled together as the temperature cooled up on the twenty-second floor.

"So," Lana leaned forward, "how does it feel? Having the publishing contract finally within reach."

Claire studied the bubbles in her glass before glancing up at Lana. "Surreal. I can't believe it's finally over. Well, almost over. The contract isn't in my in-box yet."

"It will be." There wasn't a doubt in Lana's mind. Claire deserved this contract, even though she'd lied to get it.

"From your lips to God's ear," Claire said, and her gaze seemed to linger on Lana's lips for a few seconds.

223

Lana's mouth went dry. She emptied her glass with one big gulp.

"What will you do once this is over?" Claire asked.

"Go back to wreaking havoc on my own kitchen, if you can call a hot plate and a mini fridge a kitchen," Lana said.

Claire chuckled. "I bet you'll miss my gas range."

"Oh yeah."

"And other than that?" Claire asked.

Lana held her breath. Was Claire asking her if she'd miss her too? She would, Lana admitted to herself. *God, I'd better stop at one glass.* Champagne apparently made her sentimental. She put on a brave smile. "Yeah, well, your cleaning marathons are a pain in the ass, but yeah, maybe I'll miss you a little too."

Claire stared at her, then gulped down the rest of her champagne. "Uh, I meant, what will you do other than wreaking havoc on your own kitchen…job-wise."

"Oh." Lana ducked her head and hoped the low light on the rooftop hid her blush. "I don't know yet," she mumbled, her head still down and her cheeks burning. "Probably what I did before. Keep putting steamed-milk hearts on lattes and go to auditions."

A gentle squeeze to her hand made her look up and into Claire's soft gray eyes.

"Now that you mention it, it's entirely possible that I'll miss you too," Claire said. "Just a tiny bit. The house will seem so empty without your stuff strewn across every available surface." She chuckled, but her gaze revealed that she wasn't joking. She would miss Lana too.

Lana couldn't look away, even though her inner alarm bells shrieked at her. This entire evening was heading into dangerous territory, blurring the lines between a thank-you dinner and a real date.

Claire abruptly got up as if she had been thinking the same. "I'm getting us a cocktail. What do you want?"

Lana opened the cocktail menu on the table and searched for a drink that didn't sound too potent. The way Claire looked tonight and the romantic mood on the rooftop were already intoxicating enough. "I don't know. I don't have cocktails very often." She slid the menu over to Claire. "What do you think would be good?"

"How about a Manhattan Fling?" Claire suggested.

Don't. Don't do it. But Lana couldn't help herself. Teasing Claire was like an irresistible drug. She tilted her head to the side and grinned up at Claire. "Does that mean you want us to ignore the no-sex clause for tonight?"

"What? I... You..."

Lana laughed. "I accept the offer...of the drink, I mean."

"I think I'd better order you a Cold Shower," Claire muttered. She whirled around and rushed to the bar as if she were dying of thirst.

Lana's laughter trailed off. What would she have said if Claire had answered that teasing question with a *yes*? She let out a snort. Claire would never do that...would she? She might be on the rebound, but she wasn't the type for a fling.

Claire returned and put a martini glass in front of Lana.

Lana eyed the pink drink. "That's not a Cold Shower, is it?" Was there even a cocktail with that name on the menu?

"No. It's the fling you wanted."

The first sip of the cocktail nearly went down the wrong pipe. The pomegranate juice burned in her throat, making her cough. "And what are you drinking?"

Claire swirled her straw through her rose-colored cocktail. "A Princess Charming."

Yeah. That was more Claire's style. She wanted a Princess Charming—a perfect partner for her perfect life, not a fling, and Lana had never been anyone's Princess Charming. She could barely take care of herself, much less rescue any damsels in distress. Besides, Claire was too much of a control freak to let herself be rescued.

Let's face it. We might have convinced everyone that we're a great couple, but it's all just for show. In real life, we'd never make it.

Claire had never liked that feeling of losing control that came with being tipsy, but somehow it felt different tonight. The constant background buzz of her thoughts—evaluating, analyzing, planning—was starting to fade, allowing her to enjoy the evening without reservation: the lights of New York City below them, the fresh, sweet taste of the prickly pear juice in her cocktail, and the sound of Lana's laughter.

Lana was still wearing the white wrap top but had now paired it with her beloved capri jeans that were worn in all the right places and looked soft to the touch. Her Roman-style sandals with the straps crisscrossing her calves drew Claire's gaze whenever Lana put one leg over the other.

She could imagine Lana wearing this very outfit on a date—and her date then slowly taking each article of clothing off her at the end of the night, revealing soft skin. In her imagination, it wasn't some stranger with Lana; her own hands were undressing her with confidence, as if Lana was hers for real.

Claire shook her head, but it did little to get rid of the mental image. Maybe being tipsy wasn't such a good thing after all. It made her thoughts head in directions where they had no business going.

She had no idea how late it was, but little by little the other guests left the bar until they were almost alone up on the rooftop.

"I think we should go before they throw us out," Claire said.

Lana chuckled and pointed to the street twenty-two stories below. "That could be painful, so yeah, let's go."

Claire couldn't remember moving her arm, but somehow her hand ended up on the small of Lana's back, guiding her to the elevator. This was their last night in New York, maybe even their last night together, so she allowed herself to keep her hand where it was.

Lana made no move to pull away from the contact either; quite the opposite, she seemed to lean in to the touch.

Two other guests, obviously a couple, stepped into the elevator right before they did.

Claire didn't know if she should be angry or relieved to not be alone with Lana in the enclosed space of the elevator.

"Which floor?" Lana asked them.

"Sixteen," the man answered.

Lana pressed button number sixteen and number eleven.

As the elevator carried them down six stories, Claire tried to keep her gaze on the illuminated floor numbers but couldn't help peeking at Lana's reflection in the mirrored walls. The greenish flecks in her hazel eyes glittered, and her light brown hair was attractively windblown. She seemed to glow with the success of the day.

Claire felt as if she had never fully appreciated how beautiful Lana was before this very moment. How stupid to compare her to thin, sophisticated women in cocktail dresses and makeup when Lana looked stunning in worn capris and with wind-flushed cheeks.

With a ding, the elevator doors opened on the sixteenth floor.

Claire had almost forgotten that they weren't alone. Quickly, she stepped to the side to let the couple get off the elevator. In the cramped space, she bumped into Lana, who wrapped her arms around her to keep her from falling, just the way she had at the roller-skating rink.

The elevator doors slid shut, but Claire barely noticed. She was too busy staring into Lana's eyes from only inches away. Her body heat seemed to draw her in.

She wasn't sure how it happened or who had moved first. All she knew was that her lips were on Lana's and they were kissing. Lana tasted of pomegranate juice and carefree laughter. Claire put both hands on Lana's shoulders, planning to push her away, to end this craziness, but instead her arms slipped around to pull her even closer.

For a second, both paused and moved back a few inches.

Claire stared into Lana's eyes, searching for any indication that Lana wanted to stop, but only saw her own desire reflected back at her.

With both hands on Claire's hips, Lana jerked her back into another kiss.

Urgency ignited deep within Claire. When Lana grazed her lower lip with her teeth, Claire gasped and tangled her hands in Lana's hair, needing her closer.

Their bodies molded together in a perfect fit. A slow burn started low in her belly and quickly began to spread.

One of Lana's hands slid down her back, leaving a trail of fire even through the thin silk of her top, and then squeezed her ass.

Claire groaned into Lana's mouth. Without breaking the kiss, she pressed her against the back wall of the elevator. It was almost as if she were no longer in control of her body, but she didn't care.

The ding of the elevator doors opening jolted her back to reality.

Both breathing heavily, they moved apart.

Claire licked her lips. She could still taste Lana. "Oh God. I'm sor—"

"If you say sorry, I'm going to slap you." Lana pierced her with a heated gaze that made Claire want to kiss her again. "We're both adults, and we both obviously want this, so stop apologizing and take me to bed."

A groan escaped Claire. She wanted nothing more, but sleeping with Lana would only complicate an already complicated situation even more. "But...but the contract specifically states..."

"Forget the contract. Like you said earlier: some things are worth breaking the rules for."

She had also said something about making a one-time exception for carbs and alcohol. Maybe they could make one for this too. She smiled tentatively. "So, you do want that Manhattan Fling?"

"Why not? If it's what we both want..." Lana grinned, but her gaze was serious, searching Claire's face for something. "Don't worry. I'm not going to insist you marry me for real just because you sleep with me once."

Claire was pretty sure that this was a bad idea, but for once, she didn't want to do the reasonable thing. She would deal with the consequences later.

Much later.

Without allowing herself time to reconsider, she grasped Lana's hand and pulled her out of the elevator and down the hall toward their room. Her fingers shook with both nervousness and desire as she slid the key card through the lock, and it took her three tries to open the door.

A smooth Princess Charming she was not.

But Lana didn't seem to care. She kicked the door shut behind them and drew Claire into her arms.

"I can't believe we're doing this," Claire whispered.

"Stop overthinking it, okay?" She brushed a strand of hair back behind Claire's ear and gazed deeply into her eyes. "Stop thinking at all, and just feel for once." And then, as if to help Claire with that goal, she kissed her.

Her lips were warm and soft, and when Lana traced the shape of Claire's lips with her tongue, Claire's knees went weak. She urged Lana over to the bed and pressed her down on it into a sitting position, which gave her back a bit of control.

Neither of them took the time to flick on the lamp on the bedside table, but the light from the Empire State Building illuminated the room.

Claire stepped closer, between Lana's legs, and cupped her face with both hands, trailing her thumbs along her cheekbones before she lowered her mouth to Lana's once more.

Their tongues probed and twisted together. Claire let her hands roam over Lana's shoulders, down her back, and up along her sides, brushing her fingers over the outer curve of her breasts. Heat rose beneath her fingertips, even through the fabric of Lana's wrap top, and she suddenly couldn't wait to feel her bare skin. She tore her lips from Lana's only for the second it took her to pull the top over her head, followed by her own.

Quickly, she folded both articles of clothing and set them on the bedside table.

Lana watched her with a mix of disbelief and affection. "What are you doing?"

"Undressing you." Claire touched her fingertips to the slope of Lana's full breasts and then slid them up along the straps of her simple, white cotton bra. She looked into Lana's eyes. "Is that okay?"

"Very okay. But you don't need to fold them."

"I know." Claire slid one of the bra straps down and kissed the soft skin of her shoulder, then trailed her lips down over Lana's flushed upper chest to her cleavage. *God, so incredibly soft.*

Shuddering, Lana buried her fingers in Claire's hair and guided her closer.

With Lana sitting and Claire standing, the angle was awkward, so Claire urged her to move back on the bed. She slid those sexy sandals off Lana's feet and set them aside. Her own shoes ended up neatly lined up next to them. After a moment's hesitation, Claire also took off her glasses and set them on the bedside table.

Lana watched, her hazel eyes more of a deep brown in the low light. "What would it take to get you to toss the rest of our clothes on the floor in a crumpled heap?"

A little smirk tugged on Claire's lips. "Feel free to try and find out."

"Ooh, a challenge! I like that." Lana knelt, tugged Claire closer, unbuckled the thin leather belt around Claire's hips, and pulled it from her belt loops. With a sexy grin, she dropped it to the floor.

Claire was tempted to pick it up—for exactly one second. Then she forgot all about the belt when Lana reached for her cotton shorts and undid the button.

Click, click, click, click.

Lana's fingertips grazed the silk of Claire's panties as she slowly slid the zipper down, one tooth at a time.

That ghost of a touch sent a jolt straight to Claire's center. She swayed on her feet and took half a step back. If she didn't take back some control, this would be over fast, and she didn't want that. Since this was supposed to be a one-time thing, she wanted it to last.

Very aware of Lana's gaze on her, she stepped out of her shorts, folded them, and blindly set them on the bedside table. Her bra and her panties followed until she stood in front of Lana completely naked. Cool air hit her overheated skin, making her nipples harden. She had never been shy about her body, nor particularly proud of it, but the way Lana looked at her—as if she wanted to devour her alive—made her tremble with a mix of desire and nerves.

Somehow, this didn't feel like an easy-to-control fling.

"God," Lana whispered. "You're amazing. Come here."

Claire longed to sink on top of her and lose herself in her, but she shook her head. She wanted—needed—to feel Lana's skin on hers. "First, we need to undress you."

Lana arched her hips and allowed Claire to drag her capris down and off. When Claire folded them and set them on top of the growing stack of clothes, Lana unhooked her bra, slid down her panties, and provocatively tossed them to the floor on the other side of the bed, where Claire couldn't get them.

Not that she wanted to.

She was too busy staring at Lana's ample curves and the light brown curls at the junction of her soft thighs. Her breasts were bigger than her own, with darker nipples. Instantly, Claire wanted to map every inch of her with her hands and her mouth and find all the spots that made her shiver or cry out in pleasure.

Lana let her look her share without attempting to cover herself, but for a moment, Claire thought she saw a flicker of insecurity in her eyes.

Claire wasn't sure what it was about—her scars, her more womanly body, or something else—but she immediately wanted to kiss that look of nervousness away. "You are the amazing one," she murmured and crawled onto the bed like a tigress stalking her prey. But her heart was hammering as if she were the one being hunted.

Part of her wondered what she was doing. This was Lana, not some one-night stand she had picked up at the hotel bar. Not that picking up strangers had ever been her style.

"You're thinking again," Lana whispered. "Stop it. The only thing you're allowed to think tonight is *oh God* and *more*."

"Oh yeah?" Claire's voice came out husky.

"Yeah." Lana lay back against the pillow, the colorful phoenix tattoo on her arm and her flushed cheeks a stark contrast against the white sheets. She looked so beautiful, so trusting, that it took Claire's breath away.

Claire hovered over Lana on her elbows, and they looked into each other's eyes. "Are you...?"

"Yes," Lana whispered before Claire could even decide how to finish her question. She wrapped her arms around Claire's shoulders and tugged.

Claire relaxed her arms and sank down on top of her. Her eyes fluttered shut at the feel of Lana's bare skin against her own and the softness of her breasts beneath her chest. She stopped thinking, stopped trying to make sense of what they were doing and where it would go. Instead, she lifted one hand and smoothed it along the curve of Lana's breast, marveling at the silkiness of her skin. "You feel so good."

"So do you." Lana trailed her fingers down both sides of Claire's spine and over her butt, lingering at the dip where her ass met her upper thighs.

The muscles in Claire's belly quivered. God, she was already wet. The self-control she prided herself on felt as if it was hanging by a thread. She buried her face against Lana's neck and moaned against her skin.

Lana's pulse pounded beneath her lips, so she gave it a lick, thrilled when it sped up even more.

With a raspy groan, Lana threw her head back, and Claire immediately took advantage by exploring the line of her throat, down to the slope of her breasts. "I feel like a kid in a candy store," she whispered against Lana's skin. She wanted to touch her everywhere at once, kiss her everywhere, even trace her scars with her tongue, but she wasn't sure if it would hurt Lana. Besides, it seemed too intimate somehow. "I don't know where to start."

Lana threaded her fingers through Claire's hair and guided her mouth to her breast. "This seems like a good place."

Mmm, a woman who knew what she wanted. Claire liked that. She dipped her head, nuzzled her face against Lana's breasts, and began to worship them. She cupped both of them, letting the soft flesh fill her hands.

Lana arched into her touch.

When Claire drew sensual circles around one nipple with her tongue, a throaty murmur of approval answered her.

I wonder what noises she'll make if I... She swiped her tongue directly across the nipple, then sucked it into her mouth.

"God!" Lana rolled her hips beneath her, bringing their bodies into even closer contact.

Her little gasps and moans spurred Claire on. She licked and suckled, trying to judge what Lana liked best from the way she arched up against her. *Fool.* There wouldn't be a next time, so she hardly needed to catalog Lana's reactions. But she couldn't help herself. The way Lana felt was too addictive. Lightly, she raked her teeth over the hardened nipple.

A long groan tore from Lana's throat. "You're killing me!"

Claire let go of her nipple to look up at her.

Lana's pulse visibly pounded at the hollow of her throat, and she gripped the sheet with both hands as if anchoring herself.

"Want me to stop?" Claire asked, half teasing, half giving her one last chance to back out, because if they continued, she wasn't sure she would be able to stop.

Instead of an answer, Lana let go of the sheet, clutched Claire's shoulders, and guided their mouths together. The kiss started out slow, almost tender, just their lips caressing each other. Then Lana slid her tongue across hers with a flutter that sent hot, piercing pleasure spiraling down Claire's body.

Their hearts thumped against each other, and they kissed until Claire had to pull her mouth away to draw in a ragged breath.

Lana used the opportunity to kiss and nibble along her jaw, then her neck.

Groaning, Claire tipped her head to the side to give her space.

Lana's warm breath caressed her ear, making her shiver. Then Lana took Claire's earlobe between her teeth and gave it a nip.

A shudder went through Claire. Her hips rocked down against Lana's in an instinctive rhythm. Lana's answering moan skyrocketed her own arousal. She pressed her thighs together in a struggle for control. *Focus on her, or this'll be over in three point five seconds.*

When Claire slid to the side so she was lying next to her, Lana let out a groan of protest and tried to pull her back on top of her. Her protest was cut short when Claire trailed her right hand down her body, pausing to caress the curve of her belly. *Mmm, so soft.* Eager to feel more of her, Claire slid her fingertips lower, into Lana's damp curls.

Both of them sucked in a breath at the same time.

"This okay?" Claire asked. She hardly recognized her own voice.

Lana nodded and opened her legs wider in a silent invitation.

Claire started a slow rhythm, keeping her touch light, sliding a finger to either side of Lana's clit but never directly across it.

"Claire!" Lana groaned out her name. She rocked against her touch, seeking more contact. Her breath came in short spurts already.

"So sexy," Claire murmured. Without stopping the motion of her fingers, she leaned over Lana to kiss her.

Lana made little noises in the back of her throat as Claire moved her tongue against hers in time with her fingers.

Claire's head spun. God, this was incredible. She stopped kissing her so she could look at Lana's face as she slid her fingers down, then paused and made eye contact.

"Yes!" Lana's eyes said the same, her pupils wide with desire.

Slowly, never looking away from Lana, Claire pushed inside.

Lana's long moan vibrated against Claire's mouth. Their lips met again as they started to move against each other. When Lana picked up the pace, Claire matched her, stroke for stroke. Soon, Lana tore her mouth away and panted.

Claire buried her face against the curve of her neck and sucked at her thudding pulse point. She had wanted to take this slow, to enjoy it, but she could sense that Lana was already on the edge, and with the pressure of Lana's thigh between hers, she wasn't that far behind. She curled her fingers up.

Lana cried out. Her nails dug into Claire's back, and the pinpoints of pain drove Claire's desire higher. Lana's hips lifted off the bed one last time, then her entire body stiffened against Claire and started to quiver before falling back to the bed.

Claire stayed with her, prolonging her pleasure for as long as possible. She didn't want this to end.

Eyes closed, cheeks flushed, Lana lay with her limbs sprawled, so open and vulnerable to Claire's touch that Claire immediately wanted to have her again.

But Lana seemed to have other ideas. She opened her eyes, her irises thin rings of brown and green, wrapped her arms around Claire, and rolled her over so she was on top.

One of her legs pressed between Claire's, making her moan.

Lana leaned over her on her elbows. She kissed Claire's cheek, her mouth, her throat, then her lips found her breasts. She nuzzled, licked, and suckled until Claire thought she'd go out of her mind. Then, after one last kiss to Claire's nipple, she slid lower and trailed her lips down her belly.

Hazy with lust, it took Claire a second to realize what Lana was doing. *No. Not that.* That was way too intimate for a one-time thing, and besides, she hadn't waxed or taken a shower all day. Even though her body protested, she grabbed at Lana's shoulders and pulled her back up. "You don't need to... Just touch me." She guided Lana's hand between her thighs and shuddered as Lana's fingers found her wetness. "This won't take long."

"That's what you think." Lana started to tease her with long, sensual strokes.

Claire's head fell back against the pillow. *Oh God.* She should have known Lana would be like this, not letting her have all the control. It was maddening...and totally hot.

Any time she was close, Lana slowed down or changed her rhythm, holding her at the edge of orgasm.

With the strength of frustration, Claire pushed her off and rolled her over until she was on top, straddling her. Lana's fingers sank deep.

Oh! Her hips bucked uncontrollably against Lana's hand.

Lana stared up at her and finally moved at the rhythm Claire wanted. "God, I can't tell you how hot this is...how hot you are."

Claire couldn't answer. She panted through parted lips. She wanted to keep watching Lana, to see the awed, passionate expression on her face, but her eyes fell shut. Sounds that she hardly recognized as her own fell from her lips. She grabbed hold of Lana's shoulders with both hands as she rocked against her.

Lana's other hand settled on her hip, urging her on. "Look at me. Look at me, Claire!"

Claire forced her eyes open. The pressure grew low in her belly, and as soon as their gazes connected, she bucked against Lana's hand once more and came—hard. Her vision went hazy, and her mouth opened in a soundless scream. Every muscle in her body went rigid with pleasure. She collapsed bonelessly on top of Lana, who caught her and held her and kissed her ear in a way that made Claire shudder.

When Claire's brain started working again, she was wrapped in Lana's arms, her leg across Lana's thighs. Her body was still pulsing around Lana's fingers, and Lana's heart pounded wildly against her chest as if echoing that rhythm. She held her fingers very still while her other hand caressed Claire's sweat-dampened back in calming strokes.

Finally, their breathing and heartbeats returned to a more normal pace, and Lana carefully withdrew her fingers.

One last ripple coursed through Claire's body. She bit back a moan.

"You okay?" Lana whispered.

"Yeah. It's just... That was..." She lifted her hand, gestured as if that would help her find the right word, and let it drop back to the mattress when her brain refused to form a more complex sentence.

"Oh yeah." Lana's cheeks were still flushed, her pupils wide and dazed.

They stared at each other.

What now?

Cool air moved across Claire's damp body, making her shiver. All she wanted was to cuddle up to Lana's constantly warm body, enjoy the feel of their bare skin against each other for a while longer, and then go to sleep.

But cuddling wasn't part of the agreement, was it?

She forced her pleasantly lethargic body up, away from Lana, and reached for the covers that had been pushed to the foot of the bed.

Lana's gaze was on her, almost like a touch, as she settled the covers over them and lay on her back, leaving several inches of space between them.

It felt like a chasm the size of the Grand Canyon.

She stared up at the near-dark ceiling and tried to get herself back together.

Lana lay next to her in a mirror position of her own.

They both turned their heads at the same time. When their gazes met, they quickly looked the other way.

Okay. This is officially crossing into stupid territory. She made her living counseling people how to successfully navigate relationships, and while this was by no means a relationship, she did care for Lana. This was no way to end this incredible night. "Lana?" she whispered into the silent room.

"Yes?" Lana answered quickly, as if she'd been hoping—longing—for Claire to say something.

"If we're making a one-time exception...do you want to extend it to cuddling?" Her cheeks went hot at the tentative offer, and she shook her head at herself. Only a few minutes earlier, they'd had possibly the hottest sex of her life, and now she was blushing because of a little cuddling?

Lana smiled in a way that made Claire want to kiss those full lips again, but she knew if she did that, they'd likely extend their one-time exception to, well, a two-time exception.

What's wrong with that? her body asked.

Everything, her head answered. She was already struggling to sort through her emotions as it was.

Lana opened her arms, and Claire immediately cuddled up to her warm, soft body. She wrapped one arm around Lana's waist, tucked her hand beneath her side, and settled her cheek on her chest. Lana's hand came to rest on her back, and her fingers drew lazy figure eights against Claire's skin.

They both let out a contented hum.

This felt right. As if this was where she belonged.

Don't be stupid. She had thought the same about Abby, but it had all been an illusion, so she certainly couldn't trust this...arrangement.

She closed her eyes and listened to Lana's heartbeat beneath her ear. It wasn't long until the soothing sound and Lana's soft caresses on her back lulled her to sleep.

Chapter 17

CLAIRE WOKE UP WITHOUT SHIVERING, despite the air-conditioned room. Her back was toasty warm, and the heat quickly engulfed her entire body when she realized Lana's breasts were pressed to her back. One of Lana's arms was wrapped tightly around her from behind, and her hand was cradling one of Claire's breasts.

Her nipple was as hard as a pebble.

Claire bit back a groan. Her body wanted to press Lana's hand more tightly against her breast—or to roll over and rub against her voluptuous curves.

Her mind, however, wanted to jump up and run from Lana, from what they had done, from her own jumbled mess of doubts and emotions.

Caught between those two conflicting impulses, she lay frozen.

When Lana stirred behind her, she held her breath. *Oh God.* She wasn't ready to face her. What was she supposed to say after last night?

But thankfully, Lana didn't seem to be waking; she just cuddled closer with a sleepy sigh.

Aww. It felt like one of the hardest things she'd ever done, but Claire gently lifted Lana's arm.

Lana mumbled a protest, and Claire's nipple echoed the complaint, not happy at the loss of contact.

Claire gritted her teeth, ignored her needy body, and slid out of bed.

Pain shot through her foot as she stepped on something hard and pointy. *Dammit!* She hopped around on one foot, clutching the other, and tried not to curse so she wouldn't wake Lana. What the heck was that? She never left anything on the floor.

Once the pain faded, she put her foot back down and picked up the offending object. It was her belt.

The memory of how it had ended up on the floor made her flee to the bathroom for a shower—a very cold one.

Safely behind the closed door, she leaned on the sink with both hands and stared at her reflection in the mirror. She looked the same as always, of course, yet also different. Her hair, which normally fell past her shoulders in smooth strands even in the morning, was disheveled, probably from Lana's fingers running through it, gripping it, last night.

The disordered look matched the chaotic state of her mind. Her emotions had been all over the place since the day Abby had broken up with her, and now she had made it worse by making lo— having sex with Lana.

The fastest way to get over someone is to get under someone else, her sister had once told her when Claire had caught her making out with a girl two days after breaking up with her boyfriend.

It might have worked for Steph, but Claire doubted it would work for her. If anything, she was more confused than ever.

A one-night stand wasn't like her. What the hell had she been thinking?

Yeah, well, you weren't thinking at all. But now, in the light of day, she had to. She wasn't ready for a new relationship, was she? Her own relationship book warned people not to jump into anything new too fast, especially not if you were the one being dumped.

No. She shook her head at herself in the mirror. She would stay single for a while and focus on her career. Only once her heart—and her pride— had fully mended would she start dating again.

No doubt one of her friends would set her up with a lawyer, a real-estate agent, or a doctor—someone with an impressive career, an elegant wardrobe, and a spotless kitchen. Someone like Abby.

But that thought no longer held any appeal.

She hadn't thought of Abby or a woman like that for even a second last night. There had been no comparison, no stray thought. Only Lana.

Could it be that her image of an ideal partner had changed—that the perfect woman for her was someone who wasn't perfect at all, at least not according to her old standards?

She stared at herself in the mirror, afraid of the answers lurking in her eyes. When it became too much, she tore her gaze away.

This is crazy. She and Lana were so different; how were they supposed to make it work—if Lana even wanted to make it work?

She gave herself a mental shake. This wasn't the time for woolgathering. They had a plane to catch.

Just as she was about to step into the walk-in shower, she realized that she hadn't taken any clothes into the bathroom with her.

God, where was her head this morning?

Still in bed, with Lana, an annoying little voice answered.

She shook it off and slipped into one of the complimentary bathrobes before tiptoeing back into the bedroom. It was stupid, really. Lana had seen—and touched—every inch of her last night, but now she couldn't help feeling exposed.

Lana was still asleep. She'd moved to Claire's side of the bed, her head on Claire's pillow and her arms wrapped around the covers as if she'd missed Claire in her sleep.

Claire stood stock-still next to the bed and stared down at her. She had never had a one-night stand in her life. Was this…this wave of affection… how it was supposed to feel the next morning?

Come on. Get a move on! She grabbed her clothes and her phone, slid out of her robe, and left it behind for Lana, in case she'd feel just as exposed when she woke up, and hurried back to the bathroom.

Lana woke cuddled up to something soft and warm. Without opening her eyes, she stayed very still and allowed herself to enjoy it for a little longer.

When the last fog of sleep lifted, she realized that she wasn't wrapped around Claire's smooth body. She was holding on to the covers, and the bed next to her was empty.

The sound of running water filtered into her consciousness.

Visions of getting up and stepping into the steamy shower with Claire danced before her closed eyes. She could almost feel the soapy skin beneath her fingers.

Then reality intruded as she opened her eyes and spied the stack of her neatly folded clothes on the bedside table. Claire's clothes were gone. Instead, a bathrobe that hadn't been there last night sat next to the stack.

A cold that had nothing to do with the temperature in the room crept through her. *Message received.* Clearly, Claire no longer wanted to see her naked. She was probably in there, washing the scent of their lovemaking off her skin.

Lovemaking? Oh, no, no, no, no. You did not just think that.

The sex had been good—okay, mind-blowing—but Claire had heartbreak material written all over her. It didn't take a degree in psychology to see that Claire was even more confused than Lana was—and that was saying something. Claire had been kicked to the curb by the woman she'd thought she would spend the rest of her life with not even four months ago. The dictionary entry for the word *rebound* probably had her picture beneath it.

Claire wasn't interested in pursuing something beyond their Manhattan Fling; otherwise, she'd still be in bed, cuddling, not in the bathroom, getting rid of the memory of last night.

Even if Claire were interested, did Lana really want to become involved with a control freak therapist on the rebound? Someone who'd paid her to play the role of her fiancée? How could she be sure that Claire wasn't on a subconscious level staying with her at least partially to save face and avoid a second breakup?

No. She couldn't live with that. Their relationship—if you could call it that—was built on a big, fat lie, and, as Claire's book said, honesty was key in relationships.

Now you of all people are quoting a relationship book? God, this thing with Claire had really messed her up.

She pressed her hands to her face and groaned—then groaned again when she caught a whiff of Claire's musky scent on her fingers.

When the bathroom door opened, Lana wrenched her hands away from her face. Lost in thought, she hadn't heard the water being shut off in the bathroom.

Claire stood in front of her, fully dressed. Her hair was pinned up in a chignon, and her face was flushed but otherwise gave nothing away, the therapist's mask firmly in place.

They stared at each other, and Lana became aware that, unlike Claire, she was completely naked. Whereas last night, Claire's heated gaze had made her feel desired, in the light of day she couldn't help feeling exposed and vulnerable. She reached for the robe.

Claire's blush deepened, and she quickly turned away and busied herself by shoving things into her laptop bag. "You should, um, probably get dressed. We'll need to take a cab to the airport in about thirty minutes."

Lana bit her lip until it hurt. *What did you expect? A dozen red roses and a love declaration? Don't be silly. We had our Manhattan Fling, but now we're leaving New York, so it's over. You knew that.*

"Sure," she said, trying to sound as casual as possible. She climbed out of bed and pulled the bathrobe tightly around her body before hurrying to the bathroom.

Once the door closed between them, she sank onto the closed toilet lid and put her head in her hands.

God. Maybe Claire had been right. Maybe they should have stuck to the no-sex clause of their contract. She had really enjoyed Claire's company the last couple of days, but now things between them were tense and awkward. The five-hour flight home would probably seem to last longer than a flight to Mars.

God, she hated flying! Claire clutched the armrest as the plane sped down the runway. What she hated even more was the awkward silence between Lana and her.

In a very short time, Lana had become a friend, someone who got Claire, tolerated her quirks, yet challenged her. Claire missed their easy conversation. She even missed the way Lana teased her. And she missed holding Lana's hand during takeoff.

They hadn't exchanged more than a few sentences while they had packed their bags and taken a cab to the airport. Was Lana going to pretend that nothing had happened between them? Was she used to one-night stands and casual flings? Was that how she could go on the next morning without attaching any emotional meaning to them?

You should do the same. But that was easier said than done.

Her stomach lurched as the plane lifted off.

Soft fingers closing around her own made her jerk.

"Sorry." Lana pulled her hand back. "I thought you might want…"

"No! I mean, yes." Claire's cheeks burned. "I mean, I'm not too proud to admit I'd love to hang on to something other than this armrest."

Reluctantly, Lana reached back across the armrest and laced her fingers through Claire's.

Amazing how hands so different from each other could be such a good fit. Claire immediately tightened her hold.

They sat in silence while the landing gear came up with a thump and the plane rose higher.

Claire clung to Lana's hand, even though, truth be told, her discomfort with flying wasn't at the front of her mind at the moment.

Finally, they reached cruising altitude. The plane leveled off, but Claire's tension rose anyway because she knew Lana would let go of her hand in a second and then the awkwardness between them would return.

"Better?" Lana asked softly.

Claire nodded.

Lana withdrew her hand.

Claire instantly missed the warm fingers. She curled her hand to a loose fist on her thigh and peeked over at Lana, who looked about as ill at ease as Claire felt. *Time to be an adult.* She took a deep breath. "Do you…want to talk about it?"

"Only if you don't use your shrink voice," Lana said firmly.

"Did I?"

Lana nodded.

"Sorry. I…" It had probably been an unconscious attempt to distance herself from her own emotions. She turned her head and studied Lana. "Did we make a mistake?"

"I don't know. Did we?" Lana angled her chin up in a silent challenge, but Claire could read the hurt beneath it loud and clear.

Yeah, being called a mistake will do that to a woman. Fix this, idiot. "I'm sorry. I didn't mean to imply…" She sighed. "I'm not good at this." She waved her hand back and forth between them.

Lana lifted her brows. "You're a relationship expert."

"We both know that doesn't mean anything when it comes to my own…" She cut herself off before she could say *relationships*, because that wasn't what this was, was it?

"Listen," Lana said after a few seconds of silence. She lowered her voice. "I think it's safe to say that we both enjoyed last night."

"Oh yeah." The two words escaped Claire before she could hold them back. Heat shot to her cheeks.

Lana chuckled, and the tension between them eased a fraction. "But that doesn't change anything." Her voice sounded mechanical. "We'll wait for Ms. Huge to send you the contract, then go our separate ways with no hard feelings at all, right?"

"Right." It should have been a relief, but somehow, it wasn't. With Lana's expectant gaze resting on her, Claire forced herself to add, "What happens in New York stays in New York."

In about a week, they would each go back to their own lives, with Lana fifty thousand dollars and Claire one publishing contract richer. They would both get what they wanted.

Then why did it feel as if she was about to lose everything?

Chapter 18

CLAIRE HAD NEVER BEEN so glad to have clients cancel a session as she was on this Monday morning. She couldn't focus on work, and that had rarely happened to her before. *Yeah, but you also never had a one-night stand before.*

After their return from New York, she'd spent the rest of the weekend revising the two chapters she and Bridget Huge had talked about. It wasn't just to get it done while it was still fresh in her mind, she admitted to herself.

Holing up in her home office also made it easier to avoid Lana and to distract herself from the constant slide show of images playing through her mind. Very erotic images that had no place at work.

With a grunt, she threw down her pen and closed the patient file. Maybe a coffee would help.

On the way to the break room, her gaze fell through the open door of the waiting room. It was empty at the moment. One of their patients had left two magazines behind on the small table instead of putting them back into the magazine rack.

Claire detoured and picked up the two magazines to return them to their proper place. *Wow.* The rack was a mess. Someone had put the newest issue of *Psychology Today* into the entertainment section. She pulled it out and put it back with the other health and psychology magazines. And what was *Better Homes and Gardens* doing next to *Sports Illustrated*?

She put down her empty coffee mug and started reorganizing the magazines.

A quiet "uh-oh" made her look up.

Renata leaned in the doorway, a stack of files under one arm. "Don't tell me they rejected the manuscript."

"What? No. Things went great in New York." Her annoying visual imagination immediately reminded her of just how great some of the things in New York had been. She hid her blush from Renata by turning back to the magazine rack to remove an issue of *Time* that was from last year. Only when the heat in her cheeks lessened did she turn back around.

"Really?" Renata beamed. "So they offered you a contract?"

"As good as," Claire answered. "The acquisitions editor said I'll have it in my in-box sometime this week."

"That's fantastic. I'm so happy for you." Renata came over, put her stack of files down on the table, and wrapped Claire in a motherly embrace.

"Thank you," Claire murmured against her shoulder. "And thank you for helping me with the book. Your support means the world to me. I hope I tell you that enough."

Renata let go and held her at arm's length to study her thoroughly. "You're very welcome. You know you're like the daughter I never had."

"You have two daughters."

"Oops." Renata flashed a grin. "Okay, then you're the office daughter I never had. Which is why it's my prerogative to be worried about you."

"Why would you be worried? I just told you the book deal will go through."

Renata tapped the magazine in Claire's hand. "Then why are you sorting the magazines?"

"Because they were a mess and needed to be put in order."

"Tanya could have done that. That's why we pay her the not-so-big bucks." Renata peeked out into the reception area and pulled the door closed. "Tell me what's going on."

"I, um…" Claire pressed her lips together. No use trying to pretend she was fine. She wanted to talk about it, but how could she without admitting that she had lied to Renata for the past two months and that she had secured her book deal only with a crazy charade?

"Is it Abby?" Renata rubbed Claire's arm.

Claire blinked. "Abby?"

"Yeah. I know you're in a new relationship now, but that doesn't mean you're completely over Abby. It's okay to be upset for a while."

Claire almost smiled. The funny thing was that she hadn't thought of Abby in days. Certainly not since Friday night. "I think I am."

"Upset?"

"No. Over Abby." It was the truth, she realized the moment she'd said it. "I think I've moved on."

"Wow. That's fantastic. I didn't think you had. I thought you just jumped into something with Lana to help you forget the pain."

Lana... Claire swallowed. She had jumped into something with her, but had it really been because of her breakup? "No," she said firmly. "That's not why I'm with Lana." At least that much she could say for sure. After all, she had hired Lana because of the book deal, not because of her broken heart.

"Are you sure?" Renata asked. "The last time we talked about it, you hadn't even sent Abby the ring back. Clearly, a part of you hadn't let go of the idea of marrying her."

That might have been true in the beginning, but lately, she had realized that she didn't want Abby and the life they'd had together back. She enjoyed the better work/life balance she had now—stopping to eat the lunch Lana had packed her, having dinner with her even if it meant bending her rule about carbs after six, and watching a movie together.

"Um, I still haven't sent back the ring." When Renata opened her mouth, Claire lifted her hands. "Not because I'm hanging on to the idea of a future with her. Maybe I did at first, but now..."

"Now?" Renata prompted.

"Now I actually forgot. With Lana and the book deal and everything..."

Renata smiled. "How's that working out?"

"Like I just said, the contract will—"

"Not the book deal. Your new relationship. I know you're usually very tight-lipped about your private life at the office, but I'd like to think we're more than just colleagues. You know you can talk to me about personal things, don't you?"

"Of course."

"So, how are things working out between you and Lana?"

Another blush rose up Claire's neck.

Renata chuckled and patted her arm. "That good?"

"It's... She's..." Claire gestured wildly, looking for a word that would explain without giving the true nature of their relationship away. *Whatever you do, don't say complicated to a psychologist.* It would be like waving a red flag in front of a bull.

A quick rap on the door interrupted her before she could say anything. Tanya opened the door and looked from Claire to Renata with a curious expression. "Sorry to interrupt your secret meeting, but I've got Mr. Hatfield from the magazine subscription service on the phone. It's time for our renewal, and he'd like to talk to someone about a new package they're offering. Do you want me to handle it?"

"No, thanks. I thought this time Claire might like to do it since she's so familiar with our magazine rack." Renata gave Claire a grin and a nudge toward the door.

Well, if she wanted to take over the counseling center one day, she'd have to handle things like this every once in a while. "I'm on my way."

And sometime this week, there was something else she had to take care of. She'd call Abby and arrange to finally give her the ring back. At least she would be able to resolve one thing before signing the contract and starting a new chapter of her life.

<hr>

Lana wiped her brow when the onslaught of the need-coffee-to-function crowd finally trickled down to one new customer every few minutes. If she had to prepare one more of these ridiculous orders such as *five pumps of hazelnut and five pumps of vanilla but hold the whipped cream because I'm watching my figure,* she'd have a screaming fit.

Avery pointed at the last customer Lana had served. "No little steamed-milk hearts on the lattes today? Our customers will think you don't love them anymore."

"I don't feel like little hearts today." Lana wiped down the steam nozzle of the espresso machine a little less gently than usual.

"Uh-oh." Avery waved at the employee working the morning shift with them. "Hey, Diego, can you take over for a minute? I need to talk to my sister." Not giving Lana a chance to protest, she tugged her into the storage room. "What's up? Trouble in paradise?"

Lana took a caramel cookie from one of the boxes, unwrapped it, and ate it while she thought about what to say. Denying that something was going on wouldn't do her any good. First, Avery knew her too well, and second, if she and Claire would officially break up soon, maybe it was a good thing if she indicated they were having problems to make it more believable later.

"Come on, sis. Talk to me," Avery said when Lana remained silent for too long.

"I don't think it's going to work out." She crumpled the wrapper in her hand.

"Why?" Avery crowded closer with a worried frown. "Did something happen when you were in New York?"

An image of Claire with her head thrown back in ecstasy flashed through Lana's mind. "Oh yeah. You could say that."

"What was it?" Avery asked. "Did you have an argument?"

Lana took another cookie and ate it to delay her answer. "No. Nothing like that. I just… I don't know. I don't know anything anymore."

"Want to translate that for me? Because it feels like you're talking in riddles."

Lana sighed.

"Well, whatever's going on, I know it's not about you realizing that you're not in love with her," Avery said. "I know that look on your face." She pointed. "That's how you looked when you fell head over heels for Jessica McPhee in eighth grade."

"Bullshit," Lana said, a little too loudly. "I'm not—" She bit her lip before she could add, *in love with Claire.* Avery was supposed to think that she was crazy for Claire. If she was honest with herself, her feelings were heading in that direction.

Yeah, and that's why it's a good thing it'll end soon before you're in over your head. How the hell had things gotten so out of control so fast?

"You're not…what?" Avery handed her another cookie as if bribing her to answer.

Slowly, Lana unwrapped the cookie and nibbled on it. "I'm not sure Claire and I are on the same page when it comes to our relationship. What happened between us…it doesn't mean the same to her as it does to me. You know," she said very quietly and stared down at the half-eaten cookie in her hand, "lately, I have started wondering if I'm like Mom, always falling for the wrong people and ending up getting hurt."

Avery snorted. "Girl, you're nothing like your mother. Yeah, okay, you didn't exactly win the relationship lottery with Katrina, but other than that, your track record isn't that bad. It sure as hell is better than mine. I kinda like Claire. Not that I got to see a lot of her."

Lana ignored the jab. "I kinda like her too," she murmured.

"Um, Lana," Diego shouted from the counter. "There's a customer who insists on having her latte made by you."

Avery nudged her. "Oooh. Looks like you have an admirer."

Lana tossed the cookie wrappers into the garbage can and stepped out of the storage room.

Her friend Jill was leaning against the counter, her sunglasses slid up onto her head. "Hey, stranger. Sorry, no admirer, just me." She grinned at Lana. "Not that I don't admire you, of course."

Lana chuckled, her mood improving at the sight of her friend. "Sorry I didn't call after we got back from New York. The weekend was a little... um, hectic. How are you doing?"

"I'm great."

Jill always said that, no matter how she was doing. But she did look great—not that the symptoms of MS were always visible.

Lana rounded the counter and gave her a hug.

"So," Jill said as Lana returned to the espresso machine to make Jill's latte, "how was New York?"

"Um, great. Claire's book is going to get published."

"Wow, that's great. Tell her congratulations. So, what else did you do in New York? Did you see any sights—or did you stay in your hotel room the entire time?" Jill gave her a teasing grin.

Lana fought a blush. "We were there for an interview and a meeting with the publisher, not for sightseeing or...other activities." After a pause, she added, "But we did manage to see a few things."

Images of Claire's naked body, stretched out beneath hers, rose in Lana's mind.

Jill laughed. "Judging from the nice color of your face, they must have been pretty spectacular things."

"Um, yeah, like the High Line and the Empire State Building."

Jill gave her a knowing look but mercifully let it go. "What are you and Claire doing for the Fourth? Crash and I are inviting some friends over— Laleh and Hope, Grace and Lauren, Jordan and Emma, and a few others. Everyone is bringing some food. The two of you are welcome to join us."

Lana bit her lip. Even if she and Claire were still together...um, pretending to be together the day after tomorrow, would Claire want to spend the Fourth with Lana and her friends now that the publishing contract was as good as signed?

Of course, she could always go alone, but she wasn't in the mood to mingle with all these happy couples and explain why Claire wasn't there.

"Sorry, we already have plans." Lana hated lying to her friend, but what else could she do? Since she still didn't feel like creating hearts, she put a foam fern on top of Jill's latte before handing it over.

Jill admired the latte art. "Nice. What do I owe you?"

"Nothing." Lana winked. "Just don't tell my boss. She's kind of stingy."

"Hey!" Avery protested from where she was refilling coffee beans.

Jill laughed and stuck her five-dollar bill into the tip jar. "I'll call you this weekend. Maybe we can catch up."

Before Lana could reply, she waved, slid her sunglasses down, and was out the door with her latte.

Lana groaned. Catching up meant Jill would try to get her to spill her guts about how things were going between her and Claire.

Chapter 19

ON TUESDAY MORNING, CLAIRE SAT at the kitchen island and checked her email on her laptop while sipping her first cup of coffee of the day. The two emails at the top made her groan. Both were from her mother, reminding her to bring a broccoli pasta salad to their Fourth of July family barbecue tomorrow—and, of course, to make sure to invite Lana too.

She had ignored her mother's first email yesterday, not knowing what to answer about Lana, so today she'd gotten another one, saying the same.

All she wanted was to have a nice day with her family and to bask in her parents' pride when she told them about the book deal and the successful radio interview. But if she didn't bring Lana, she'd have to face questions, maybe even tell them that they had split up. God, two breakups within four months. She would make even Steph look like the queen of long-term relationships in comparison.

You should have thought of that before you signed that crazy fiancée contract. Lana had a life to return to. Claire couldn't expect her to hang around forever. But maybe they could do this last outing together as a couple. *Uh, as a fake couple, of course.*

She was about to log out of her email account when a chime announced another message.

Probably another reminder from her mother.

But when she glanced at the sender, it was an email from Bridget Huge.

Her heart started beating faster. With trembling fingers, she tapped the track pad to open the email.

Dear Claire,

I've got good news: The team and our senior editor liked the concept of your book and your willingness to help with the promotion. We'd like to offer you a publishing contract.

Since it's the Fourth of July tomorrow, I lit a fire beneath the behinds of our legal department so you'd have another reason to celebrate. Attached is the contract for The Art of Lasting Relationships: Seven Secrets to a Thriving Love Life.

Please read it carefully, and let us know if there's anything you can't live with. I've sent it to your agent too, so she can go over it with you.

Once you have signed, we'll talk about the editing process and the publication schedule.

I'm looking forward to having your book published with us.

Welcome to Wishing Tree and best regards,
Bridget Huge

Her book would be published! Claire's mind spun with a dozen different emotions. Somehow, her brain couldn't seem to settle on only one. She opened the attachment and scrolled through the ten-page document, reading bits and pieces. Words such as *audio rights* and *royalty rates* jumped out at her, but she was too dazed to take in the information.

She stared into her coffee, which was probably lukewarm by now. This was it. The moment she had eagerly anticipated for the past two years. Somehow, it felt different than she had expected. Shouldn't she be jumping around, doing a victory dance, or calling all her friends and family members to tell them about the good news?

Instead, all she could think was: *Once I sign this, my deal with Lana will be over.* Lana would be gone from her life, probably forever.

So what? Meet her for coffee every now and then, but sign the damn contract. It's what you wanted, remember? Hell, it's the very reason you even met Lana in the first place!

The ringing of her cell phone startled her.

Mercedes's name flashed across the display.

As soon as Claire swiped her finger across the screen, Mercedes started screeching. "You did it! Have you checked your email? Wishing Tree just sent you a contract. Woohoo! Congratulations!"

Well, at least one of them was ecstatic. "Thank you."

"I need to take a closer look at it, but at first glance, the contract looks pretty standard. They don't even have an option clause."

"That's great," Claire said, even though she had only a vague idea of what an option clause was.

Mercedes remained silent for several seconds. "Is everything okay? You don't sound very excited. Were you hoping for a higher royalty rate? What they offer is pretty much what I expected, but if you want, I can try to negotiate—"

"No." Claire glanced at the contract on her laptop screen. "The royalty rates seem okay to me. I'm not in it for the money anyway."

"What is it then?"

"Nothing. It's great, really. I'm probably still a bit jet-lagged, and it hasn't sunk in yet. That's all."

"Ah. Then get some rest," Mercedes said. "We'll talk later, when I've had some time to read the contract more thoroughly. For now, just make sure you've got a bottle of champagne in your fridge."

Champagne… It made Claire think of the glass of champagne they'd had in the rooftop bar and the way Lana's eyes had twinkled when she'd teased her about alcohol and carbs after six.

"Will do," she said belatedly.

"Oh, and you can tell Lana that she can consider the agreement fulfilled. Make sure you get her bank information before she moves out."

"Uh, yes, of course. Bye, Mercedes. And thanks for everything you did to make this happen." Still in a daze, she slid the phone into her pocket and then went to pour her coffee down the drain.

Lana stepped out of her room, stood in the hall, and listened.

The house was silent. Claire had probably left for work already—right on time, as always. At first, her overly punctual, meticulous nature had driven Lana crazy, but over the past two months, Claire's little habits had grown on her. She had to admit that she might even miss the way Claire arranged her pantry by food group and the clothes in her closet according to color.

Oh, don't start moping again! Moving back to her own apartment would be nice. No one would complain when she dropped her keys or her jacket somewhere—not that she'd done that lately. Somehow, she had gotten into the habit of hanging them up by the door. But there also wouldn't be anyone grumbling when she made a mess in the kitchen. Of course, there would also be no one who complimented her shrimp dishes. Not that she would make shrimp dishes. Even with fifty thousand dollars in her account, she would use the money to pay off her medical bills and maybe cut back her hours at the coffee store so she could go to more auditions.

Speaking of coffee... She entered the kitchen to get herself a cup.

Her steps faltered when she found Claire in the kitchen, rinsing a mug while muttering to herself. Lana glanced down at herself. In panties and a sleep shirt that kept slipping off one shoulder, she wasn't exactly presentable.

But then again, Claire had seen her naked—touched her naked body—so it was a little late to worry about modesty. Lana shrugged it off and entered the kitchen, just as Claire turned and strode to the door.

They nearly collided and gripped each other's shoulders.

Mmm. The short-sleeved silk blouse felt nice beneath Lana's fingertips, and she had to fight the urge to slide her fingers over the smooth material— or over the even softer skin beneath it. Quickly, she let go and stepped back. "Good morning. I didn't know you were still here."

"Morning." Claire stared at Lana's legs and blinked owlishly. A hint of pink rose up her neck before she averted her gaze. "I was, um, just about to leave."

Lana smiled to herself. Friday night might not have meant the same to Claire as it had to her, but it hadn't left her completely unaffected either. "Have fun at the office, then, Dr. Freud." She barely held herself back from giving Claire a send-off kiss.

Claire chuckled. "Thanks. You too, Ms. Starbucks."

"I don't work at Starbucks."

"And I'm not a psychoanalyst."

They grinned at each other, and Lana nearly burst into song at how good it felt to get some of the old ease between them back.

Claire walked to the door but then stopped and turned back around. "Um, Lana?"

"Yes?"

"Do you happen to have any plans for tomorrow?"

"My sister will be out of town, so Jill and Crash have invited me to celebrate the Fourth of July with them. Why?"

Claire turned away. "Oh. Well, never mind, then."

Lana caught up with her and tugged on her sleeve. "Why?" she repeated.

"My family is having a barbecue, and my mother specifically told me to bring you. But, of course, if you've got plans with your friends…"

"Actually, the invitation was for both of us. But I didn't know if you'd want to go through another evening acting like a couple, so I told them we had other plans."

"Oh." Claire peeked over her shoulder at her. "So, would you go to the barbecue with me?"

"That depends," Lana said, trying not to give herself away by grinning. "On?"

"What will your parents be grilling? Tofu burgers on gluten-free buns with homemade ketchup made from beets instead of tomatoes?"

Claire laughed and turned fully to face her. "Probably. But don't worry, I'll get you a nice steak on my way home. Can't have my girl starving." She blushed again. "Um, I mean…"

Lana patted her arm. "I know what you mean. I'll be yours until you get the contract."

"About that…" Claire paused. She stared down at the kitchen tiles as if they had suddenly changed overnight, then peeked back up. "Bridget just emailed me the contract. I haven't signed it yet, but Mercedes says it looks good."

"Oh wow." Lana had known it would very likely happen sometime this week, but it still caught her off guard. "That's wonderful! Not that I ever doubted it." She engulfed Claire in a big hug, just stopping short of twirling her around again because she remembered that it had nearly ended with a kiss the last time she'd done that. Their bodies instantly molded together in that seamless way.

Claire brought her arms up too, returning the embrace without hesitation. It wasn't one of her polite hugs that Lana had observed at the art gallery or the office party but a full-body embrace.

Mmm. Lana's eyes fluttered shut as Claire's lilacs-and-spring scent wafted around her. "Congratulations," she whispered into Claire's ear.

Was it wishful thinking, or was Claire shivering against her?

"Thank you." Claire's voice seemed a bit raspy.

"I'm really happy for you." And she was. But a part of Lana couldn't help being a bit sad too. *Stop it. It's for the better. You know that.* Reluctantly, she let go and stepped back.

Claire's hands slid along Lana's back as she slowly let them drop away.

It felt so much like a caress that Lana bit back a moan. "So, you still want me to go to the family barbecue, even though you've got the contract already?"

"If you don't mind, I'd really appreciate it." Claire heaved a sigh. "I would really like to have my parents think everything in my life is going well for a little longer. They'll be flying to Paris for their anniversary next week, and I don't want them to spend half of the trip worrying about me."

For a moment, Lana thought about offering to extend their contract in some less time-intensive way, for example, accompanying her to family events for a year or so, but she could quickly see that snowballing out of control and being extended to promo events and office parties. Then they'd be back to where they were now.

No. If she wanted to avoid getting her heart broken again, she had to let go of this sham of a relationship.

"Well, you promised me a steak," she said with a smile that took some effort, "so I'll definitely be there for our last performance tomorrow."

~~~~~

Before she could stop at the butcher's to buy a steak for Lana, there was one other thing Claire had to do. The ring Abby had given her had burned a hole in her purse since she'd taken it out of her bedside table yesterday, but she hadn't had the courage to actually return it yet.

She knew Abby's new address from their mutual friends. She'd even seen the house before—at least from the outside. Once she'd found out where Abby had moved to, Claire had driven by twice, just to see if Abby's car was in the driveway.

Now she shuddered to think of how close she'd come to being a stalker. No wonder Renata had thought she wasn't over Abby!

She peeked into her purse to make sure the small, black box was still there before climbing out of the car and walking up the driveway.

At Abby's front door, she hesitated. Maybe she should have called first. After the way their meeting at the art gallery had ended, she should have given Abby fair warning.

Oh, come on. That's an avoidance tactic, and you know it! Ring the damn doorbell already! The worst that can happen is that she'll close the door in your face.

After one last deep breath, she pressed the buzzer.

It took a while, but finally, steps approached.

Claire's stomach tightened as the door swung open.

Abby stood in the doorway, wearing a spotless white apron over her slacks and blouse.

For several seconds, they stared at each other, neither saying a word.

"Uh, I'm sorry for not calling, but I was just in the neighborhood and…" Claire paused and squared her shoulders. *Oh, have some ovaries and cut out the lies. At least the unnecessary ones.* That inner voice sounded strangely like Lana's. "Okay. I wasn't in the neighborhood. I came to talk to you if you have a minute."

"Uh, sure. Come on in."

She should have known that Abby was too well-mannered to close the door in her face. Claire followed her through a spacious living area into a very clean kitchen that had all the latest gadgets. Abby's new home looked like a slightly smaller version of Claire's own house—or rather of the way her house had looked before Lana had moved in.

"Nice house," Claire commented because she wasn't sure what else to say.

"Yeah. Give me a second. I was just making pasta salad for tomorrow."

A pot of pasta was boiling on the stove, and ham had been cut into neat little squares. No dirty cooking utensils were littering the counters, and no sauce was splattered across the backsplash.

In the past, she might have found Abby's well-ordered method of cooking soothing, but now it seemed a little mechanical and less creative.

Abby poured the pasta into a colander waiting in the sink before turning back to Claire and eyeing her carefully. "So, what did you want to talk about?"

How sad that after a seven-year relationship that Claire had considered happy until the end, it had come down to this. She couldn't even tell anymore what Abby was thinking. "There's something that I need to return." She reached into her purse.

"My *Wonder Woman* DVD? You could have sent that by mail."

"Um, no. Not the DVD. This." Claire held out the little, black box.

"Oh." Abby wiped her hands on a dish towel and took the box from her. She snapped the lid open, and they both stared down at the three-carat diamond ring.

Unexpectedly, tears burned in Claire's eyes. Maybe Renata had been right. She hadn't fully dealt with the end of her relationship. Only now was she ready to admit that it had failed—that *she* had failed.

Claire cleared her throat. "I'm sorry it took me so long to give it back. It's just that I..."

"It's okay." Abby squeezed her shoulder.

When Claire looked up, she discovered that Abby's eyes were as damp as her own.

"I, um, I need to apologize too," Abby said quietly. "I shouldn't have ended it the way I did."

Claire stared at her. *Oh God.* Did that mean Abby regretted breaking up with her? The first week, maybe even the first month, she had halfway expected...had hoped for Abby to change her mind. But if Abby wanted her back now... Lana's image rose in front of her mind's eye.

"I mean, I still think that calling off the engagement was for the best," Abby added hastily. "But waiting until the day of our engagement party was a really shitty thing to do. I kept silent for too long, thinking it was only wedding jitters or something. But deep down, I knew that marrying you wouldn't have been right."

Four months ago, Claire had tried to convince her otherwise. Now she knew that Abby was right. Yes, they had a lot in common and never argued, and they would have probably had a pleasant marriage. But that true spark, that bone-deep connection, that feeling of being more complete would have been missing.

Abby would never have tickled her on the lawn, never gotten her to wear a pair of jeans and eat carbs after six, and never teased her about the sex-on-the-kitchen-table chapter in her book.

"I know that now," Claire said quietly. She raised her gaze from the ring to Abby's face. "But it was hard to accept."

Abby slowly closed the ring box. "Yeah, for me too. That's why I waited so long to tell you." She slipped the box into the pocket of her apron and studied Claire. "How have you been?"

"Good," Claire said.

Abby raised her brows.

"No, really. My book just got accepted for publication."

"Oh Claire, that's fantastic! I know how much that means to you. Congratulations." Abby beamed and, after a moment's hesitation, opened her arms and embraced Claire.

Abby's perfume and the feel of her slender body were still familiar. It felt like hugging an old friend—nice and comfortable—but it didn't make her want to never let go. She couldn't help comparing it to the hug she'd shared with Lana this morning. A sigh rose up her chest as she remembered how it had felt to sink into Lana's arms and be engulfed in her warmth. It was like immersing herself into a bubble bath, relaxing and exciting all at the same time.

Claire let go and stepped back. "Thank you." She nibbled her lip, then forced herself to say what was on her mind. "I'm sorry I never let you read it."

"It's okay," Abby said but folded her arms across her chest as if needing to protect herself from that hurt. "I guess I'll have to buy it once it comes out."

"I'll send you a copy." She studied Abby. "How are you?"

"I'm doing well." Abby wiped a drop of water off the counter with the dish towel. "I...I met someone." She peeked over at Claire as if afraid of her reaction. "I swear it only started after we broke up."

It would be weird to see Abby with someone else, but Claire realized she wasn't jealous. While she would always love her, she was no longer in love with her. She gave her a quick pat on the arm. "It's okay."

"Oh. I thought you might be upset or jealous. But, of course, you have Lana now."

Only for one more day. Claire bit the inside of her cheek and forced a smile. "I'm glad you found someone."

"Well, it's not like we're ready to move in with each other. But I really like spending time with her, and all of her grandmas and grandpas seem to like me, so we're off to a good start."

"All of her grandmas and grandpas?" Claire chuckled. "How many does she have?"

"Just the usual two sets, but she works in a retirement home, and the elderly ladies and gents there have adopted her, so…"

Claire imagined Abby being vetted by a dozen skeptical retirees and had to laugh. "Good luck, then."

"Thank you."

They looked at each other for a while, then Claire remembered that she still needed to pick up the steak for Lana. "I'd better go."

Abby accompanied her to the door.

Claire hesitated, unsure how to say goodbye. Finally, she lifted her hand in a wave. "Happy Fourth of July."

"Happy Fourth to you too," Abby said, one hand stuffed into her apron pocket.

Claire turned and walked toward her car.

Halfway there, she passed a blue-haired woman in her late twenties, who was heading toward Abby's house.

They threw curious looks at each other but walked on.

Could this be Abby's new girlfriend, the woman with the many grandpas and grandmas?

Claire climbed behind the wheel and chuckled as she stared toward the house, where both Abby and the blue-haired woman had now disappeared. *Looks like we're now both with a woman who's not our usual type.*

Then she froze with the key halfway to the ignition. *Christ. You're supposed to make other people believe it's real, not yourself!* Shaking her head at herself, she started the car and went in search of the juiciest steak in Los Angeles.

Chapter 20

LANA HADN'T EXPECTED TO SEE Claire's family a second time, but here she was. Had it really been only a week since she'd first met them? She couldn't believe how much had changed in those seven days.

Back then, walking into the house holding Claire's hand hadn't been a big deal. Strangely, little intimate gestures like that were getting harder instead of easier. The touch of Claire's hand against hers made her tingle all over, reminding her that while their relationship was fake, her feelings no longer were.

She was almost glad when Claire let go to hug her parents.

"Congratulations on your book deal, honey!" Claire's mother embraced her, while her father patted her back and added, "We're so proud of you."

Claire visibly glowed under their praise.

Then the Renshaws turned toward Lana and greeted her with a warmth that made her feel guilty. Would they be sad when Claire told them they had broken up?

"Stephanie is outside, *womanning* the barbecue, as she insists on calling it." Her mother nudged Claire. "Go say hello to your sister while Lana gives me a hand in the kitchen."

Claire eyed her with a wrinkle between her brows. "Is this going to become a habit? You stealing Lana from my side as soon as we arrive?" Then she pressed her lips together and fell silent, probably because she had remembered that this would be the last time they would visit her parents together.

"It's a distinct possibility," Claire's mother answered with a smile. She hooked her arm through Lana's and drew her toward the kitchen.

Lana was a little afraid of what kind of vegan health food she'd find there, but she couldn't help being touched by the way Diane treated her. Her own mother had struggled to accept Lana's sexual orientation and had never welcomed any of her girlfriends with open arms.

Bowls of spinach salad and kale salad sat on the kitchen counter, with the dressing already poured over them, ready to be served.

Lana turned toward Diane. "What did you need help with?"

"Nothing. To be honest, I just wanted a moment alone with you."

Lana gulped.

"Don't look at me like that." Diane chuckled. "I thought about our conversation a lot since the last time we saw each other, and I think I owe you an apology."

"Uh, an apology?" Diane wasn't talking about the food she'd served her, was she?

"I still think you and Claire are moving a little fast, but Stephanie pointed out that I was acting like my own mother did when James asked my parents for my hand in marriage." A sad smile flickered across Diane's face. "They thought he was a no-good hippie out for my money and wanted me to marry someone more respectable."

James had been a hippie? Lana couldn't see it.

"That couldn't have been further from the truth," Diane continued. "James and I had something very special from the start. When I just watched you and Claire get out of the car and walk up to the house... It seems there's something special between the two of you too. I've never seen Claire hold on to anyone's hand the way she clung to yours—as if she never wants to let go. I can tell she really loves you and that you love her too."

A lump lodged in Lana's throat, making it impossible to get out even a single word, even if she had known what to say.

"So if you really want to propose to my daughter, I'm not going to stand in your way."

Lana gaped at her. Claire's mother was giving them their blessing. If only she knew they were about to break up. *Jeez. You aren't about to break up! You were never really a couple in the first place.*

"Um, I..." Lana cleared her throat but couldn't get rid of the lump. "Um, thank you. I don't know what to say."

"You don't need to thank me or say anything."

262

Claire appeared in the doorway and looked from her mother to Lana. "Thank you for what?"

Diane shared a conspiratorial look with Lana. "For the food."

"Are you done interrogating Lana?" Claire asked. "Steph says the eggplant will get bitter if we don't eat soon."

Lana took the bowl of kale salad and went to her.

Claire wrapped her arm around her seemingly without much thought.

It felt so natural that Lana had to keep reminding herself that it wasn't real. Or was it? She didn't pull away as Claire guided her outside, where a long table had been set up beneath the pergola.

"Hey, Lana. Happy Fourth," Steph called from the gas grill, where she was turning the steaks, while her father kept an eye on the vegetables and burgers that were probably made of tofu.

"Hi, Steph," Lana answered. "Happy Fourth of July."

Claire pulled out a chair for her and took a seat next to her. "What did my mother say to you?" she whispered close to Lana's ear.

The feeling of her breath brushing Lana's ear never failed to send goose bumps all over her body. She had to consciously focus on the words before she could whisper back, "She gave her blessing for me to propose to you."

"What?" Claire hit her knee on the table and then bent over, clutching it with a moan.

Instinctively, Lana reached out and touched it to soothe the pain.

"Hey, you two lovebirds," Steph called. "Leave the rubbing and moaning for at home."

"Stephanie!" Their father threatened her with a pair of barbecue tongs.

Lana snatched her hand away from Claire's knee. God, it would be a long day. Instead of reminding herself to touch Claire to make everyone believe they were a couple, she'd have to focus on not touching her too much, no matter how drawn she felt to her.

That's what you get for lying. Karma was a bitch.

Claire carried the leftover grilled Brussels sprouts and the eggplant—which had indeed gone bitter—into the kitchen.

Her sister was at the sink, rinsing the plates.

Claire fell into the familiar routine they'd shared as teenagers and took each plate from her to put it into the dishwasher.

"Thanks for committing a sacrilege and bringing a steak for me too." Steph flashed a grin. "I have to say I really like our family dinners better since you're with Lana. Finally some real food!"

Apparently, their parents liked family dinners with Lana too—they were outside by the pool, showing her photos from their last trip to Europe. Truth be told, Claire was a little disgruntled at how much they monopolized Lana's attention. But, of course, they couldn't know that this was Claire's last evening with Lana and that she longed to be alone with her.

To do what? Hold hands? Kiss? If you were alone with her, you wouldn't do any of that. The irony of the situation was driving her mad.

When Claire didn't react to her comment, Steph turned, leaned against the sink, and studied her. "What's up with you?"

"I'm fine. Just thinking."

"About?"

Claire hesitated. She'd never really shared her thoughts with Steph since she had always considered her the annoying kid sister. Besides, Steph never seemed to take anything seriously.

But now she wasn't grinning or making jokes, as if sensing that something serious was going on.

Claire sighed. "Have you ever slept with someone you shouldn't have?"

A short laugh escaped Steph. "Hello? Remember who you're talking to. There were times when sleeping with people I shouldn't have was practically a hobby of mine." She sobered and squinted at Claire. "Wait a minute! You're not really talking about me, are you? Man, don't tell me you cheated on Lana!"

"What? No! I'd never... I mean... Argh!" How could she explain this without revealing what was really going on? She was tempted to just tell Steph to forget about it, but she needed to talk to someone, or she'd go crazy, and maybe Steph was the right person for that. After all, with all the shit she had done in her life, she wasn't in a position to judge her, unlike their parents or Renata.

She glanced toward the doorway to make sure her parents and Lana were still outside. "This has to stay between you and me, okay?"

Steph arched her eyebrows. "You're keeping secrets? You?"

264

"You've got no idea." Claire did a breathing exercise to gather her courage but still couldn't say it. She had always been the perfect sister that her parents had held up to Steph as a role model, and it was hard to give up that position. Apparently, keeping up the facade of having a perfect life had become too important to her. *Yeah, that's what got you into this mess in the first place, remember?*

"Come on." Steph waved her hand toward herself. "Out with it. It can't be worse than some of the stunts I've pulled."

Claire wasn't so sure about that. "Lana told you how we first met, right?"

"Yep. She ran you over with her roller skates. Pretty cute story."

"Yeah, but that's all it is—a story. We didn't actually meet like that."

Steph's forehead wrinkled. "You didn't? Why would you make that up?" She chuckled. "Don't tell me you met on some adult hookup site or something."

"No!" Although that might have been less embarrassing than what she was about to confess. "We... She... I hired her to pretend to be my fiancée so Wishing Tree wouldn't reconsider the book deal," she finally blurted out.

The dish towel Steph had held dropped to the floor. "You're shitting me."

Claire picked it up just so she didn't need to look into her sister's face. She pressed her lips together and shook her head.

Steph opened and closed her mouth several times like a ventriloquist's dummy. "So she's...what? Some chick from an escort service?"

"Watch your mouth!" Claire glared at her sister, ready to shake her should she say anything disparaging about Lana. "She's an actress."

"And apparently a pretty good one," Steph muttered. "God knows she had me fooled. And so did you." She eyed Claire for a while, then the tiny wrinkles on her forehead smoothed and she grinned. "Oh, now I get it! She's the woman you slept with, isn't she? You're not faking. You really are head over heels for her."

"Sssh, not so loud!" Claire looked around again. "Yes, I made...slept with her, but I'm not head over—"

"Oh, come on. Admit it." Steph grabbed the dish towel from her and flicked it in Claire's direction. "The only thing you're faking is that you don't feel anything for her."

Claire sighed. "I never said I didn't feel anything. I'm not a robot."

"Excuse me for sounding like you for a moment, but…how *do* you feel?"

"Scared. Helpless. Confused as hell." Claire ran both hands through her hair. It didn't help to order her thoughts or feelings.

Steph cracked a faint smile. "Sounds like you could use a good therapist."

"Yeah. But I can't tell Renata or any of my colleagues about this, so here I am, stuck with a comedian."

The humor of the situation made them both grin for a moment.

Then Claire sobered. "I do care for her. At first, I tried to tell myself that it's just rebound, but the more time I spend with Lana, the more I think it's not about Abby. It's about her—Lana. She's irreverent and maddening and…absolutely wonderful."

"So why don't you tell her that?" Steph asked. "Maybe leaving out the *maddening* part."

"It's not that easy. I've gotten myself into a pretty complicated situation. I mean, how do I tell how much is for real and what's part of the act? How can I be sure I'm not just fooling myself into thinking I love her because it would be better for the book promo or because I don't want to be alone?" Claire firmly shook her head. "Lana's mother was like that, and I can't do that to her. Besides, she's an actress. How can I even be sure that she's interested in me for real and not just immersing herself into her role a little too deeply?"

"Be sure?" Steph repeated. "You can't. Happiness can't be planned like your retirement fund, Claire. You put your heart on the line and hope for the best."

"That's your wisdom? Hope for the best?"

"Yep." Steph laughed. "There's a reason why you penned a relationship book and I entertain people with cracks at my miserable love life."

Claire looked at her sister—really looked at her for the first time in years. An unexpected maturity lay in her gray eyes, usually hidden by jokes and smart-ass comments.

"Thank you," Claire said quietly. "For listening. And for not judging."

"Oh, I will judge if you let Lana get away." Steph tilted her head and smirked. "Actually, I might snatch her up for myself if you don't."

Claire glowered at her.

"Snatch who up?" their father asked from the doorway.

Heat shot up Claire's neck, but Steph seemed unflustered. "No one, Dad. Are you done boring Lana with your vacation photos?"

"We're done *showing* her the vacation photos," their father said. "Your mother suggested heading over to the marina to see the fireworks show, but we'd need to leave soon to get a good place. Anyone up for it?"

Steph threw the dish towel onto the counter. "Not me. I've got a hot date later—with lots of fireworks of my own," she added with a grin.

Their father turned his attention to Claire. "What about you and Lana? Watching fireworks over the ocean...I bet it'll be very romantic."

A romantic evening. Just what she needed to make herself even more confused. Claire suppressed a sigh. "Ask Lana if she wants to go."

"She said to ask you."

"Guess you're going, then." Steph patted Claire's shoulder. "Have fun."

The fireworks show at the marina probably represented the longest and at the same time shortest twenty minutes of Claire's life.

While they waited for the display to begin, Claire shivered in the breeze from the ocean. Now that the sun had set, it was unexpectedly cool for July, at least for Claire, who got cold easily.

All around them, couples cuddled up. Even her parents were nestled close like two newlyweds.

Lana stepped closer. "Want me to...?" She mimed putting her arms around her.

"Um, well, it would look pretty strange if we didn't," Claire whispered back.

"Right." Lana moved even closer and wrapped her arms around Claire from behind.

Her warmth engulfed Claire like a blanket. She shivered, but this time it had nothing to do with being cold.

At exactly nine o'clock, the first firework rockets shot up and exploded, bathing the night sky in red, white, and blue. For a few seconds, the yachts and motorboats bobbing on the dark water below them looked like enchanted fairy-tale vessels.

The water reflected the colors of the fireworks as the sparks trickled down and then faded.

The crowd around them oohed and aahed.

"Beautiful," Lana whispered, her warm breath tickling Claire's ear.

Claire turned her head and caught a glimpse of Lana's face, illuminated by the golden starburst that now lit up the sky. "Yes."

Lana's arms around her tightened, holding her closer against her body.

Slowly, Claire relaxed. She put her arms over Lana's and leaned her head back against her shoulder.

They were surrounded by a crowd of strangers who had gathered on the dock, but with Lana's arms encircling her, she felt strangely isolated from them. Safe. She almost wished the fireworks show would go on forever.

But, finally, the display ended with a grand finale. Half a dozen rockets rose and burst all at the same time, creating circles of light that exploded outward and changed colors.

Sparks rained down like glittering waterfalls and then faded, leaving only trails of smoke behind.

The crowd applauded and cheered and, after a minute, began to disperse.

Claire and Lana didn't move for several seconds. Lana seemed just as reluctant to end their embrace and this last evening together. They both knew that tomorrow Claire would sign the contract—hell, Lana probably assumed she already had—and then Lana would move out.

Slowly, Lana dropped her arms from around her and stepped back.

Claire shivered when her back lost contact with Lana's toasty warm front. Her fingertips still tingled where she'd rested them against Lana's arms. She curled her hands into fists and stuffed them into her pockets.

"I didn't promise too much, did I?" Claire's father asked, his arm still wrapped around his wife. "Pretty romantic, hm?"

Claire nodded.

They set out for their cars, which were parked some distance away. After a few steps, Lana caught up with her, wordlessly pulled one of Claire's hands from her pocket, and laced their fingers together.

Was Lana merely keeping up the appearance of them as a couple in love, or was she trying to hang on to their last evening together too?

Claire had a feeling it was the latter, but maybe that was wishful thinking. With a lump in her throat, she squeezed Lana's hand but didn't know what to say.

They walked the rest of the way in silence.

Claire had no idea what the future had in store for her, but one thing she knew for sure: she'd never forget this Fourth of July.

Chapter 21

It was nearly midnight, and Lana was starting to feel like Cinderella. Their evening had been like a fairy tale, especially those moments at the marina, when she'd held Claire as they'd watched the fireworks.

But now they were back home—*at Claire's house,* she corrected herself—and the magic had ended, without Lana having the slightest chance of getting her Princess Charming.

She slid off her shoes—no glass slippers—and walked barefoot down the hall.

Claire followed silently. She lingered in front of Lana's room instead of continuing on to her own. "I've got the day off tomorrow, so I'll be home. Will I see you before you leave?"

"Of course. Did you think I'd leave without at least saying goodbye?" It hurt that Claire even had to ask. Did she really think what they had shared had meant so little to Lana?

"No. I just…" Claire slid her glasses higher up her nose and rubbed her eyes. "I'm just tired, I guess."

Lana wanted to reach out and caress her cheek so badly, but she held back, not knowing if an intimate touch like that would be welcome. "Get some sleep. I'll come say goodbye tomorrow morning."

"I could help you with the boxes," Claire said. "Or are Jill and Crash coming to help again?"

"No, not this time." She hadn't yet told her friends that she was moving out because she hadn't known how to explain.

"Then I'll help. I'll even put on some jeans this time," Claire said with a weak smile.

"I'd appreciate it. The help, I mean." *Well, and how your ass looks in a pair of jeans,* Lana added to herself.

They stood looking at each other for a few seconds longer, then Claire said, "Good night."

"Night, Claire."

Claire trudged down the hall.

God, she really looked tired. Or maybe sad. Lana wasn't sure.

She watched Claire until the door clicked shut behind her. Only then did she enter her room, where she dropped down on the bed and stared at the ceiling. No way would she get any sleep tonight, so she might as well pack.

She started with everything that was in her room, then tiptoed out into the living room and gathered her things from there.

Damn, her stuff was all over the house! No wonder it had driven Claire crazy in the beginning. She'd never realized what a slob she was, but two months of living with Claire had changed her perspective on a lot of things.

Maybe she would even consider looking for a therapist to finally talk about the accident once she'd settled back in at her apartment, although she doubted she could find one she would come to trust as much as she trusted Claire.

God, she'd miss her. Lana sniffed as she carried her armful of things into her room and dropped them onto the bed.

Something on the nightstand caught her attention.

The ring box. She'd taken the ring off after they had returned from New York. Of course, she'd have to give it back before she left.

The thought pierced her chest—not so much because of the piece of metal itself, although she did like the design, but more because of what it had come to represent: that Claire had listened to her, had *seen* her, so she had bought this unusual ring instead of a more traditional one.

When she felt as if she couldn't look at the ring box for a second longer without bursting into tears, she whirled around and marched to the kitchen to look for any of her stuff there. She didn't want to leave anything behind.

Just your heart, that annoying voice in her head commented.

Lana bit her lip. "Oh, shut up."

Claire lay in bed, but sleep was far off. In the light of the full moon shining into the room, she stared at the contract on her nightstand. She had read it in detail last night, and Mercedes had called to say she'd done the same and the contract was okay to sign.

Still, the line where Claire's signature belonged remained empty.

But it wasn't really thoughts of the contract that kept her up.

It was the quiet sounds that drifted through the closed door. Lana seemed to be "sleepless in LA" too, and she was walking around the house. Earlier, Claire had heard a suitcase click shut next door, so she knew Lana was packing.

By tomorrow, she would be gone. It was that thought that kept Claire awake.

With a grunt, she flicked on the lamp on the bedside table, sat up, and pulled open the top drawer to search for a pen. There was nothing she could do about Lana's leaving, but at least she could sign the contract. Maybe that would cheer her up.

She found three different pens and tried them out on a small notepad to see which one was nicest, not wanting to mess up this important signature by choosing the wrong pen. Once she'd decided on a pen, she flipped to the last page of the contract and stared at the two lines at the bottom.

Claire touched the pen to the paper in the spot that said *author signature*.

She had imagined this very moment a thousand times, but now that it had come, it didn't feel the way she had imagined. While she still wanted to get her book published and in front of as many readers as possible, it didn't fill her with an overwhelming sense of happiness and contentment.

Not the way she'd felt wrapped in Lana's arms at the marina earlier or strolling along the High Line with her or watching her make a mess of the kitchen.

If she signed this contract, she'd never get to feel any of that again. Not with Lana, who'd been burned by too many people who'd lied to her—lied to themselves—about their feelings, from her mother to Katrina. Even if Claire worked up the courage to ask her to stay and Lana agreed, there would forever remain a kernel of doubt in Lana's mind about whether Claire was really in love with her and not just with the idea of them staying together because it was better for marketing and for her reputation.

Claire lifted the pen from the paper, then lowered it again. What if she didn't sign the contract and Lana didn't want her anyway? Then she'd lose both the book deal and a chance at happiness with Lana. Wasn't it better to play it safe and not risk failing at both? A bird in the hand was worth two in the bush, right?

But there were other things tumbling through her mind, pushing back the pragmatic advice—scraps of conversations she'd had over the past week.

She remembered what she'd said when she'd been asked about honesty during the radio interview: *You need to be honest with yourself—about your needs and wants. Do some soul-searching. Sometimes, you think you know what you want, but it might not be what you actually need.*

Then Steph's voice added, *Happiness can't be planned like your retirement fund, Claire. You put your heart on the line and hope for the best.*

A long, pained groan rose up Claire's chest. She clicked off the pen and dropped it back into the drawer. Not giving herself time to think about it and reconsider, she took her cell phone from the bedside table and tapped out an email to Bridget Huge. She kept it short because she had no idea how she was supposed to explain what might turn out to be the most idiotic decision of her life.

Dear Bridget,

I'm really sorry to do this, especially since you fought so hard to convince your team of this project, but I can't sign the contract.

Best regards,
Claire Renshaw

When the *whoosh* sound of her phone indicated that the message had been sent, she pressed her hand to her mouth and struggled not to hyperventilate. *Oh God. I did it. I really did it.* A spiraling sensation started in her belly and then crept up her chest until she felt dizzy.

The creaking of a floorboard in the hall wrenched her from what felt like the beginnings of a panic attack—then threw her right back into it.

Lana was still up, which meant she had to go talk to her, take a leap of faith, and put her heart on the line.

Lana wasn't surprised to find her stuff all over the kitchen too. The lesbian mystery novel she'd been reading was on the island, her electric milk frother was plugged in next to the coffee machine, and several of her mugs were in the cabinets, even though she'd mainly used Claire's *I'm a psychologist, not a magician* mug lately.

Amazing how entwined their lives had become in only two months.

A noise made her turn away from the mugs.

Claire stood in the doorway in a dark blue satin nightie with spaghetti straps that revealed her smooth, fair shoulders.

Lana's mouth went dry. She reached behind herself and gripped the edge of the counter. *Maybe me leaving is a good thing. If I keep seeing her like this, I'll end up doing something stupid.*

"Hey," Lana said, her voice a bit raspy. "I hope I didn't wake you. I couldn't sleep and thought I'd start getting my stuff together."

Claire was holding on to the doorjamb with both hands the same way Lana was gripping the counter. She blinked as if her brain couldn't process a word of what Lana had said.

Lana took a step toward her. "Claire? Are you okay?"

"No, I'm not. I…" Claire let go of the doorjamb, took two quick steps, and gripped Lana's shoulders instead. "Don't go."

Lana swayed and squeezed her eyes shut. The words pierced her emotional shields, and she struggled to raise them back up to protect herself. "Claire… We can't keep doing this. *I* can't keep doing this. I know I said I'd be willing to stay longer if it becomes necessary for the publishing contract, but—"

"Forget the contract," Claire said. "I won't sign it."

"What? Why wouldn't you? You can't… That book deal means so much to you!"

"Yeah, but…" Claire's grip on Lana's shoulders tightened. "You mean more to me."

Now Lana was the one who had to reach out and take hold of Claire's shoulders as the floor beneath her feet seemed to tilt. "You…you want me? For real?" The words came out in a breathless whisper. She searched the glittering gray eyes only inches from hers. "Are you sure you're not confusing—"

"I'm sure," Claire said. "And I want you to be sure. I don't want you to think for a single second that deep down I might be asking you to stay because being in a relationship would be better for my career or my self-esteem. That's why I emailed Bridget and told her I won't sign the contract."

Lana gaped at her. For a second, she wasn't sure she was really awake and not just dreaming. Claire had thought up an elaborate scheme and was willing to pay her fifty thousand dollars to secure that book deal, and now she was giving it up—for her? For them?

"I know I'm probably the last person you expected to spend your life with, but...will you give us a chance?" Claire was trembling, her gaze as vulnerable as Lana had ever seen it.

Her throat choked up with emotion. Lana couldn't answer, at least not verbally, so she threw herself into Claire's arms instead.

"Uff." Claire obviously hadn't been prepared for that.

They staggered around the kitchen and ended up with Claire trapped between Lana's body and the kitchen counter, deliciously pinned. Not that she appeared to mind.

It seemed unreal for a second, like something that was too good to be true and might turn out to be an illusion. *It's real. Trust her.*

Their lips met in a long, urgent kiss. This time, neither of them held anything back. There was no audience, no pretending, no confusion, just them.

Claire melted into her in that amazing way and threaded her fingers through Lana's hair.

Lana wrapped one arm around her to pull her even closer and to protect her from the edge of the counter. She smoothed her other hand over the satin of Claire's nightie in a butterfly caress, then dipped beneath the fabric to feel the skin on her back.

In response, Claire's nails scraped over the nape of Lana's neck, making her shudder.

Her entire body transformed into a tight knot of wanting.

Claire's tongue stroked and caressed until Lana nearly sank onto the kitchen floor in a puddle of desire, and Claire clung to her as if her knees felt equally weak.

Finally, they pulled back and leaned their foreheads together, both breathing heavily.

"Is that a yes?" Claire whispered against her lips.

"Yes," Lana whispered back. "That's a *hell yes*."

Claire feathered kisses all over her face, each one closer to her mouth.

Lana's knees did that wobbly thing again. Rather than risk this turning into something that belonged in Claire's sex-on-the-kitchen-table chapter, she dragged her reluctant body away from Claire's. "Come on. Let's go to bed."

Before Lana pulled her out of the kitchen, Claire reached out and closed the cabinet door that Lana had left open after taking out her mugs.

Chuckling, Lana led her through the hall. What a neat freak. But Claire was *her* neat freak now.

As they approached the door to Lana's room, Claire slowed her step.

"What are you doing?" Lana asked.

"Uh, you said you wanted to go to bed..."

Lana stared at her. "You tell me you want me to stay, and you think I want to go to bed *alone*?"

"Uh, no?"

"Good. Because I'd really like to create some fireworks of our own, and I'd rather do that in your bigger bed."

Claire pulled her close and kissed her in a way that made a shudder ripple through Lana's body, all the way down to her toes. Then she took the lead and pulled Lana to her room.

The bed was unmade, and Claire blushed when Lana's gaze zeroed in on it. "I was already in bed, but I couldn't sleep because I kept thinking about you leaving."

"I couldn't care less about whether your bed is made or not. In fact..." Lana gently pushed Claire down on it. "Since we both have the day off tomorrow, I won't let you out of bed long enough to make it."

"You won't hear me complain." Claire laced her fingers behind Lana's neck and pulled her down with her.

Lana hovered over her on her hands and knees, staring into Claire's smoky-gray eyes. She couldn't believe she got to make love to her again.

"What?" Claire asked.

"Nothing." Lana smiled down at her. "Just feeling lucky."

"I'm the lucky one." Claire smoothed her hands down Lana's neck, over her shoulders, and then around to her collarbone. She traced the V-neck of her top with her fingertips. "Have I told you how much I like seeing you in wrap tops?"

Heat rushed to Lana's cheeks at the compliment. "No, you didn't. Compliments weren't part of the contract, I guess."

"Forget the contract," Claire said firmly. "Both contracts."

Lana leaned down and kissed the soft skin directly below Claire's ear. To her delight, goose bumps formed beneath her lips. "Does that mean I'm not getting my fifty thousand dollars?" she teasingly whispered into her ear.

"Of course you will."

"I don't want the money. I want you."

Claire, who'd just lifted up to kiss Lana, let her head drop down to the pillow and stared up at her. "You earned the money fair and square."

Lana thought about arguing, but when Claire looked at her with that intensity in her eyes, the last thing she wanted to do was talk. There'd be time for that later. Much later.

"The way I see it, we have two options. Option one: we could stay up all night and fight about the money or…" Lana nipped Claire's earlobe, knowing what that would do to her.

"Option two," Claire gasped out. "I vote for option two. Because as much as I like you in that wrap top, I like seeing you out of it even more."

Grinning, Lana sat up so that she was straddling Claire and pulled the wrap top over her head. Under different circumstances, she might have felt self-conscious, but the way Claire's heated gaze roved over her left no space for insecurities. Lana dropped the top next to the bed and reached for her bra.

Claire followed her every move with hungry eyes. As soon as the cups fell away, she trailed her fingertips over the outer curve of Lana's breasts as if admiring a work of art. She sat up beneath Lana, taking hold of Lana's hips with both hands so she wouldn't accidentally buck her off.

Lana took the opportunity to pull the satin nightie up over Claire's head. For several seconds, she sat still and admired Claire's fair skin and her firm breasts. "So beautiful."

Then Claire lowered her head so she could worship one of Lana's breasts with her mouth.

A jolt of sensation went directly from Lana's nipple to her clit. Her hips surged against Claire's belly.

They both groaned.

Every thread of fabric between them became unbearable. When Claire lifted her mouth from her nipple, Lana rolled off the bed and struggled out of her capris and her underwear with trembling hands.

Claire slid down her own panties, folded them, then reached for her nightie that had been tossed on the bed, probably to fold it too.

Lana watched her with an affectionate smile but didn't let her finish. She pressed her back to the bed, sank on top of her, and captured her lips in a passionate kiss.

The clothes dropped from Claire's fingers, and she clutched Lana against her with both hands. "I'm on to your evil plan," Claire said breathlessly when the kiss ended.

"Evil plan?" Lana kissed and nibbled a line down Claire's throat.

Claire shivered and writhed beneath her. "Yeah. Making me want to forget about—"

Lana licked the pulse point of Claire's throat. "About what?"

"Um…I forgot."

"Good." Lana's mission was to make Claire forget about everything but how it felt to be touched by her. She traced the hollow of Claire's throat with her tongue, tasting the faint aroma of sweat and her perfume.

One of Claire's hands came up and threaded through her hair, while the other trailed up and down her back. Every now and then, Claire's fingers grazed the side of her breast.

Lana moaned. How could a fleeting touch affect her so much? Her breasts had never been that sensitive. But tonight, everything seemed to be intensified. Every little sound from Claire made Lana shiver with desire.

Lana nibbled along Claire's collarbone, raked her teeth gently over the soft skin on her neck, and then sucked on it experimentally. It might have been an adolescent thing to do, but she wanted to leave a mark on Claire's perfect alabaster skin.

She started a slow journey down her chest, exploring Claire's upper body with her hands and her mouth. God, she wanted to devour her, inch by delicious inch.

Claire's hands tightened in her hair as Lana wrapped her lips around one hardened nipple and flicked her tongue across it.

A moan drifted up from Claire's chest.

After a while, Lana switched over to the other breast and caressed it with her hands, her lips, and her tongue until the little sounds coming from Claire had become nearly constant. Then she slid lower, planting kisses down Claire's sides.

Laughter exploded from Claire.

Lana looked up and smiled. "Oh yeah, clearly, you aren't ticklish."

"I'm not," Claire said.

Lana teasingly ran her tongue along Claire's side, making her giggle. "Yep, you're right. Not ticklish at all."

When Lana kissed and licked a path down her belly, Claire's giggles stopped. The muscles beneath Lana's lips tensed, and Claire's fingers in her hair tightened, preventing her from moving lower.

Lana remembered that Claire had stopped her from going down on her when they'd made love in New York too. She felt like a kid that had been forever banned from having her favorite dessert. "Don't you like oral?" she asked, trying not to let her disappointment show.

An enticing flush spread along Claire's body, and since she was naked, Lana's gaze could follow its path. "No! I like it. Love it. But I need some time to prepare. I mean, I took a shower, but I haven't shaved, um, down there in a couple of days." Claire reached between them and ran her hand through the very short curls at the juncture of her thighs.

The sight made Lana moan out loud. God, seeing Claire touch herself would be incredibly hot. But not this time. Tonight, she was all Lana's. "Okay. I'll give you fair warning next time." The fact that there would be a next time—many next times—filled her chest with a flutter of happiness. "But this time, I'd love to taste you just the way you are."

Claire hesitated. "Are you sure you don't mind?"

"Mind?" Lana echoed. "On the woman you love, a little bit of stubble can even be sexy."

Claire went very still beneath her. She didn't even seem to be breathing. "Really?"

Why was that so hard to believe? "Yeah. I'd find you sexy even if—"

"No, I mean, you...you love me?"

Now Lana was the one who stopped breathing. Shit, had she said that? It was too soon for saying *I love you*, wasn't it? Especially with the unusual way they had met. But she refused to take it back. *Honesty, remember?* She slid back up Claire's body and looked into her eyes, which stared up at her as if not wanting to miss a thing. "Um, yes." She gathered her courage. "I think I do. Love you, I mean."

Claire urged her up with her hands framing Lana's face and kissed her.

Their kiss started tender, full of wonder, and then quickly escalated into passion. Finally, both breathless, they broke the kiss and stared at each other.

Lana traced the smile on Claire's face with her fingertips. "Does that mean you love me too?"

"Yes." Claire kissed her again. "I love you."

A wave of euphoria swept through Lana. She wanted to shout out her joy but instead settled for returning Claire's kisses.

Finally, she leaned over her on one hand while she let her other hand trail down Claire's body. "So," she traced the hollow where Claire's belly met her thigh with her fingertips, evoking a shudder, "does that mean we can ignore the stubble? I'd really like to taste you. Everywhere."

With a moan, Claire let her head drop to the pillow. "Far be it from me to deny the woman I love what she wants."

"Oh, so you'll suffer through it for me?" Lana slid down, replaced her hand with her lips, and teasingly nibbled the soft skin on Claire's inner thigh.

"Yes." The word came out more like a drawn-out groan.

Lana placed a gentle kiss on each thigh and nudged Claire's legs apart. She deeply breathed in Claire's enticing scent and glanced up once more to make sure Claire was okay with what she was about to do.

Their gazes connected, and Lana was blown away not only by the passion in Claire's eyes but also by the trust. She knew how hard it was for Claire to hand over control, so she was determined to make this good for her.

Claire reached down and stroked Lana's face, then shifted her legs farther apart.

Slowly, Lana dipped her head, breathed her in, and teased Claire with a puff of warm air across her damp curls.

A shudder of anticipation went through Claire's body.

Lana inhaled again. Her mouth watered. She slid her palms up the outside of Claire's thighs, urging her to bend her knees, and then gently swept her tongue over the glistening folds

At the salty-sweet aroma, a moan rose from her chest. When she didn't hear an answering sound from Claire, she glanced up again.

Claire's face was flushed. She lay still, with one hand clutching the sheet, while the other rested in Lana's hair. Her teeth were clamped around her bottom lip, as if she was struggling to hold back her noises and emotions.

Oh, no, no, no. This tightly controlled version of Claire wasn't what Lana wanted. She longed to feel her come apart beneath her lips and her tongue. "Look at me, Claire. Don't hold back, okay? Stop thinking and *feel*. I want you to enjoy this."

Slowly, Claire loosened her grip on the sheet and caressed Lana's head instead. "I'll try," she said quietly.

Lana stroked her hip and pressed a gentle kiss to the top of her mound.

Claire lay beneath her completely exposed, and the trust she showed in her took Lana's breath away.

Slowly, Lana lowered her head again and slid her tongue against her.

Again, Lana moaned, and this time, Claire answered it with a shaky gasp.

The low sound sent shivers down Lana's spine. She immediately went back for more. "I love hearing you...and tasting you. Mmm." She hummed against Claire's wet heat, knowing that each word would vibrate through her. "This could easily become addictive."

"Not sure I want to...God...cure you of...oh!...that addiction," Claire got out between gasps and groans.

A teasing reply about a therapist letting an addiction go untreated ghosted through Lana's mind, but when Claire opened her legs wider, she forgot all about it. She directed Claire to lift one leg over her shoulder so she could press even closer and filled her senses with her.

Claire's fingers slid restlessly against her scalp, making her shiver, as Lana caressed her with languid strokes. "God. Lana. You are... Yes."

Lana circled her clit and then, when Claire's gasps and moans became more frequent, swiped the flat of her tongue across it.

The strangled sound that escaped Claire sounded like Lana's name.

Heat pooled in Lana's belly, and she squeezed her thighs together to stave off her own need and focus on Claire. She alternated between quick flicks and sensual strokes.

Claire arched beneath her and panted through an open mouth. Her other hand joined the one in Lana's hair guiding her to where she wanted her. "Right there."

Lana willingly followed direction. The way Claire showed her what she wanted was so damn hot. She clutched Claire's hips with both hands to keep her against her mouth, closed her lips around her clit, and sucked gently.

With a shout, Claire surged against her. Her nails clawed at the back of Lana's head.

The tiny pinpoints of pain translated into pleasure that sparked through Lana's body, urging her to suck harder.

Guttural sounds came from Claire, words that were impossible to understand, but Lana understood the need in them. She circled Claire's opening with her tongue, dipped in once, twice, before she went back to sucking.

One of Claire's feet dug into the mattress, pressing her up and against Lana, while her other heel ground against Lana's back. "La-na!"

Claire started to tremble beneath her. Her breath came in sharp bursts. *So amazing.* Lana's jaw was beginning to ache, but she ignored it. She held Claire to her mouth with both hands as Claire's thighs started to quiver.

Claire arched up once more; then her body went rigid. Her legs tightened around Lana before she collapsed back onto the bed.

Lana lightened her touch but kept caressing her, carrying her through wave after wave. When Claire's limp grip on her hair tightened, holding her still, Lana pressed her hot cheek to Claire's thigh. The ripples running through Claire's body sent answering quivers through her own.

When Claire tugged lightly, she lifted her head and wiped her mouth.

Claire looked down at her. A lovely flush covered her face, and a thin sheen of perspiration made her creamy skin gleam in the soft light from the lamp on the bedside table. Her blonde hair spilled over the pillow in wild tangles, and her eyes held a dazed expression. She looked as if she couldn't move, not even if Lana strewed the entire contents of her closet all over the floor.

Knowing she'd put that expression on Claire's face was like a powerful drug.

"God," Lana murmured, "you're so beautiful when you lose control. So sexy."

Claire's flush intensified. "I...I couldn't help it. It just felt so good."

A giggle rose up Lana's chest. "You make me feel like a sex goddess."

Claire weakly lifted her head off the pillow. "You *are* a sex goddess."

"No. It's you. All you." Lana slid up Claire's sweat-dampened body, covering every inch with kisses until they were face-to-face. Balancing over Claire on her elbows, she cradled Claire's face in both palms and looked her in the eyes. "Thank you for letting me do that."

Then she lowered her head and kissed her.

Life returned to Claire's limp body. She wrapped her arms around Lana and surged against her as she returned the kiss. Once they pulled back, both breathing hard, she got out, "You're thanking *me?* I should be thanking *you*. In fact..." She ran her hands down Lana's back, massaged her ass in a way that sent Lana's senses reeling, and then lightly scraped her nails down the back of her thighs. "Let me thank you now."

A heavy tightness settled low in Lana's belly. Her breathing was already coming fast, and she tingled all over at the thought of Claire touching her. "Well, as a wise woman recently said: far be it from me to deny the woman I love what she wa..."

Her last word ended in a strangled gasp as Claire slid her hand down between them and found Lana's wetness.

"Oh God." She pressed herself against Claire's exploring fingers, then rolled over so Claire was on top and could move more freely.

Claire immediately took advantage of the new position by lowering her head and placing a burning string of kisses down her throat. After grazing the outer edge of her breast with her lips, she caressed, kissed, and licked a path along Lana's shoulder and down her arm. When she reached the tattoo and the scar beneath, she paused. "Does it hurt?"

Lana shook her head. "Not anymore." The only ache she felt was a lot lower. She strained against Claire, who refused to be hurried and kept her fingers resting against Lana's swollen folds without moving them.

Claire licked along the wings of the phoenix, then pressed a tender kiss to the scar. "I wanted to do this in New York, but..."

Lana nodded. *Too intimate.* "Now you can kiss and touch it all you want. You can touch me everywhere."

"And I will." Claire cupped one of Lana's breasts with her free hand and nuzzled against it. "Mmm, so soft. I love your breasts." She flicked her thumb across it until the nipple hardened and then grazed it with the tip of her tongue.

Pleasure thrummed through Lana's body. She tangled her fingers in Claire's hair, pulling her even closer, and arched her hips against her to get her to move her other hand.

"Easy," Claire whispered against her breast. "We've got time, and I want to slowly worship every inch of your beautiful—"

"Next time." Desire coiled within her. "Now I need you too much to go slow."

Claire groaned. She kept her gaze locked with Lana's as she slid her hand deeper and entered her with one finger.

Oh yes. Oh please yes. Lana rocked against her, her hips rising and falling against Claire's hand.

"Beautiful," Claire whispered. Her eyes were smoldering as she watched Lana move. "So beautiful." Her breath bathed Lana's wet nipple, sending additional shivers through her.

She dug her fingers into Claire's shoulders and clung to her. A moan escaped her as Claire eased another finger inside. Her eyes fell half-shut, but she kept watching Claire through heavy lids.

Every twist of Claire's fingers drove her higher and higher. A ripple of pleasure curled her toes. Close. So very close. She gave herself up to the rhythm that Claire set and let the sensations engulf her.

Claire slid up a little and buried her face against her throat, her mouth hot and wet against Lana's skin.

Lana panted for breath. She was dimly aware that she was shouting something as she arched up against Claire one last time. Her mind went blank, and her vision blurred. The only thing she could hear was the roar of blood in her ears. All her senses focused inward, on the waves of pleasure pulsing through her.

Finally, when her brain started working again, she became aware of Claire softly kissing her face, her throat, and her upper chest, gently easing her down from her orgasm high.

Lana's body continued to shudder with aftershocks.

Once the last quivers had ebbed away, Claire carefully withdrew her fingers, evoking another groan from Lana.

Claire's skin slid against hers as she cuddled against Lana's side. It was the most sensual thing Lana had ever experienced. Claire invitingly opened her arms.

Feeling as if every joint in her body had turned into rubber, Lana sank into them.

Claire rolled onto her back and pulled Lana with her so she could hold her.

"I'm too heavy," Lana protested.

"Nonsense. You're perfect." Claire pulled Lana's head onto her chest. Her heart was thrumming a rapid rhythm against Lana's ear.

It was arousing to know how much touching her had excited Claire too, but for now, she was spent, and all she wanted was to hold Claire close.

After a while, she became aware of how dry her throat was. "Was I shouting?" she asked without lifting her head off Claire's chest.

"Oh yeah." The proud grin was obvious in Claire's voice. "My name. Repeatedly."

If she hadn't still been so dopey with pleasure, Lana would have lifted her hand and playfully slapped her for sounding so smug. But then again, Claire had reason to feel satisfied with herself—just as satisfied as Lana felt.

Claire kissed the top of her head before sliding out from under her.

"Hey!" Lana grabbed her arm and pulled her back onto the bed. "Where do you think you're going?"

Claire pressed a kiss to her shoulder, and Lana took the opportunity to lick the ridge of her ear. She grinned as Claire's breath stuttered.

"Getting you something to drink," Claire said, her voice husky.

God, that woman was attentive. Images of how else Claire could be attentive danced in front of her mind's eye.

Claire got out of bed again. This time, Lana let her. Claire took two steps on legs that looked a little weak. When she reached the door, she looked back. "I'll be right back. Don't move."

Lana pulled the covers over her cooling body. "Not going anywhere."

Their gazes met across the room, and Lana knew that it was so much more than just a promise not to get out of bed while Claire got them something to drink.

"Good." Claire's voice vibrated with emotion. "Because I like you right where you are."

"Me too," Lana got out through the lump in her throat.

Claire beamed, and Lana marveled at how much the smile transformed her normally serious face, making it look soft, beautiful, and happy.

She looks like she's in love. Lana knew she looked the same.

With Claire's scent surrounding her, Lana cuddled beneath the covers and listened to Claire's footsteps as they hurried down the hall.

While she waited, her gaze fell to the floor in front of the bed, and a chuckle bubbled up her chest.

In her haste to get back to her, Claire hadn't even paused to fold the clothes strewn around the bed.

Then Claire was back. She slid into bed—again without even seeming to notice the clothes on the floor—pressed her cool, naked body against Lana's, and offered her a bottle of water. "What's that smile for?"

"You." Lana took the bottle, but instead of drinking, she set it down on the bedside table and kissed her.

That water would have to wait for a while.

~~~

Just when they had finally fallen asleep after hours of exploring each other, the ringing of her cell phone wrenched Claire from a deep, satiated sleep. Groggily, she slid one arm out from beneath the covers and, with her eyes closed, felt around for the phone on her bedside table.

"Phone," Lana mumbled against Claire's shoulder blade.

God, she's cute. "I know. Go back to sleep." Claire finally found the phone and squinted at the display. *Oh shit.*

It was Bridget Huge.

For a moment, Claire was tempted to reject the call, but it would only postpone the inevitable. Not wanting to disentangle herself from Lana's warm, soft body that was cuddled against her back, she stayed where she was and accepted the call. "Good morning, Bridget," she said, her voice low so she wouldn't disturb Lana too much.

"I hope I'm not waking you, but I just read your email. What's going on, Claire? If you've got a problem with any of the clauses in the contract, we can talk about it and maybe negotiate a compromise. That's no reason to—"

"It's not that." Claire pressed the hand resting on her belly more firmly against her. "It's...personal."

"Personal? Like a sickness in your family or something? If we need to push back the publication date for any reason, we could. That's not a deal breaker."

"No, nothing like that." Claire sighed. How could she explain without blurting out the entire embarrassing story? "It's..."

"Tell her you'll take the book deal," Lana whispered into her ear.

Her warm breath in her ear made Claire shiver. Her body apparently didn't care that this was a business call. She rolled over, their legs still tangled, and caressed Lana's pillow-lined face with her fingertips. "No," she whispered back. "I don't want you or our relationship to be a marketing tool."

"So you'll just put your manuscript into the shredder?" Lana shook her head. "I won't have that."

"So I'll self-publish," Claire said, even though she hadn't given that idea a fleeting thought so far.

"But you said you wanted the prestige of a traditional publishing house."

Claire shrugged. "Prestige is overrated. I had my priorities all wrong with Abby, and I don't want to make the same mistakes with you. You mean too much to me."

Lana's gaze softened. "You mean the world to me too. But wouldn't self-publishing mean you'd have to invest your free time into getting your book out instead of being able to spend time with me?"

Damn. Claire hadn't taken that into consideration. Now that she had Lana in her life, she didn't want to go back to working around the clock.

"Claire? You still there?"

Shit. She'd forgotten that Bridget was still on the line. "Um, yeah. Bad connection. I, um..."

"Tell her you'll sign," Lana whispered. "I don't need you to reject the book deal to prove your love."

"But you said—"

"I know what I said." Lana took an audible breath. "But I trust you. I trust *us*."

Claire searched her eyes and found nothing but determination. "Okay." Into the phone, she said, "Bridget? I'm sorry for the back-and-forth. I'll do it. I'll sign. But I have one condition."

Lana tensed next to her.

"Name it," Bridget said carefully.

"I want one modification to the contract. I want to have final say in the choice of narrator for the audiobook."

Bridget paused. "That's highly unusual, but I guess we could do that—provided it's someone qualified. Do you have someone in mind?"

Claire glanced at Lana. "Yes, I do. She's very qualified."

"All right," Bridget said. "Let's talk about the details later."

Claire apologized again, said goodbye, and ended the call. She studied Lana. "Are you sure you're okay with me signing the contract?"

The corners of Lana's mouth curled into a smile. "Well, you seem to have a lucky streak with the contracts you sign lately, so…" Then she sobered. "You were willing to give up the book deal that you worked so hard to get—for me. For us. That's big. It occurred to me that I need to take a page from your book too—quite literally."

Claire cuddled against her, enjoying the slide of warm skin against her own. "What do you mean?"

"One of the chapters I read on the plane was chapter six—the one on trust. I can either make you—make us—suffer for something my ex and my mother did, or I can move forward and trust you."

"Wow." Claire searched for the right words without much success. Instead, she leaned forward and joined their lips in a tender kiss. When it ended, she tucked a strand of hair behind Lana's ear and grinned. "If chapter six got you to reconsider, maybe I'm a more brilliant writer than I thought."

"Yeah—and a modest one too." Lana reached out and tickled her. Then her tickling became a caress. She trailed her fingertips over Claire's hip and down the outside of her thigh.

Claire held on to the threads of her self-control to keep a halfway intelligent conversation going. "So, could I talk a certain talented actress into narrating the audiobook when the time comes?"

Lana's hand paused on Claire's thigh. "You mean…me?"

"No, I was thinking about having them hire Grace Durand." Claire nudged Lana's nose with her own. "Of course I mean you. Interested?"

Lana wrapped her arms around Claire and slid her leg between her thighs. "Very, very interested." She started nibbling on Claire's throat.

"I was talking about the audio… Oh yes!" Claire threaded her fingers through Lana's hair.

They could talk about the book later. Much later.

Epilogue

One year later

CLAIRE SWISHED THE WATER AROUND in her glass and forced herself to keep her back to the noises coming from the dining room, where the caterer was putting the last touches to the buffet table.

Soft footsteps approached, and then Lana slipped her arms around her from behind. "Hey. I didn't think I'd find you in the kitchen. I thought you'd be out there with the caterer, making sure everything is perfect."

Claire put down the glass and melted against her. Every bit of tension drained from her body as she settled her arms over Lana's. "I'm engaged to you. Everything *is* already perfect."

Lana's breathing hitched, and her arms around Claire tightened. "Yes, it is," she whispered. She buried her nose in Claire's hair, making her shiver as Lana's breath brushed along the rim of her ear. "You smell good—and you look spectacular."

The heat in her voice made Claire flush all over. "You look great too."

Lana chuckled, and the sound vibrated through Claire's body. "You haven't even turned around to take a look at my dress."

Claire would in a second, but for now, she didn't want to move an inch. "Doesn't matter. You would look fantastic, even if you were wearing sweatpants and that *abs are great, but have you tried chocolate-chip cookies* T-shirt."

"You might think so, but I doubt your parents would agree."

Claire snorted. "They wouldn't let me get away with it, but you probably could. They adore you."

Lana nestled her cheek alongside Claire's. "As long as their daughter adores me too…"

"Oh yeah, I know Steph is pretty fond of you."

Growling, Lana nipped Claire's ear.

An erotic tingle shot straight between Claire's thighs. With a moan, she turned around in Lana's arms, letting their bodies brush all along their lengths, and kissed her.

Lana's mouth met hers eagerly in a long kiss that made heat swirl through Claire's body.

She looped her arms around Lana's neck, while Lana tightened her hold on Claire's hips, pushed her backward, and pinned her against the counter with her body, all without breaking the kiss.

Claire gasped into her mouth. Her hands played over the soft material of Lana's top as their tongues slid against each other.

The ringing of the doorbell startled them apart.

Damn. Our guests.

Drawing in much-needed oxygen, they leaned against each other. "We need to open the door before they start thinking there's another called-off engagement," Claire said but couldn't bring herself to move away from Lana. "What is it with you and kitchens?"

Lana smiled, her lips only a fraction of an inch from Claire's. "It's not the kitchen. It's the woman. Although I wouldn't mind another encounter of the chapter five kind." Passion sparked in her hazel eyes.

Claire chuckled at the old joke between them. "You narrated the book. You know there's no sex in chapter five."

"Hmm, there should be." Lana whispered a kiss onto the corner of Claire's mouth.

The doorbell rang again.

"Yeah. Yeah. We're coming." Reluctantly, Claire slid out from between Lana and the counter. "I bet that's Vanessa. She always has to be the first."

"Well, if it's her, at least you can show off your author copies before the other guests arrive."

Claire took Lana's hand and kissed her fingers. Her lips skimmed the feather ring that Lana was once again wearing. Her own finger now displayed a ring with the same type of stone, but a more traditional band. "I'd rather show off my fiancée."

"Charmer."

They walked to the door together. About to open it, Claire paused and trailed her gaze over Lana, taking in the flowing, eggplant-colored skirt and the ivory-colored wrap top that framed her generous cleavage. "I was right. You do look stunning."

She had been right about something else too: with Lana by her side, life was pretty much perfect.

When Claire swung open the door, it wasn't her colleague Vanessa who stood in front of her. Instead, Jill held out a bottle of wine, while Crash waited half a step behind her.

"Hey, it's our favorite maid of honor," Lana greeted her.

"I bet you say that to Claire's sister too," Jill playfully grumbled. "But once you hear my news, I really will be your favorite maid of honor."

The two entered, and Claire closed the door behind them before hugging each woman in turn.

Jill seemed to vibrate with excitement. "I have a job offer for you," she said to Lana. "Grace is branching out from acting to producing, and I've shown her the web series you did a few months ago. She liked what she saw, so she's offering you the lead role in her first movie."

Lana stood stock-still, her eyes wide.

Claire squeezed her hand. "That's fantastic, isn't it?" In the past year, Lana had managed to work steadily as an actress, but she'd only had supporting roles so far.

"The lead role?" Lana gave a little bounce. "Wow. What kind of movie is it?"

"It's a romantic comedy about a relationship that starts out as fake, but quickly grows into true love." Jill cocked her head. "Think you can play that part?"

Lana and Claire looked at each other and laughed.

"You could say the role is tailor-made for me," Lana said, her eyes twinkling.

With a tiny wrinkle between her brows, Jill looked back and forth between them. "So you've played a role like that before?"

"Um, you could say that."

A year ago, they'd had a long discussion and had finally decided not to tell their friends about how their relationship had really begun. They didn't want to hurt their feelings or make them feel as if they didn't trust them enough to tell them the truth from the start. They'd told Claire's collegues that Lana wasn't really a lawyer; she was an actress who'd been preparing for a role as an attorney when they had first met her.

"Were you any good?" Crash asked with a grin.

Claire wrapped both arms around Lana and leaned in to her. "She was perfect. Simply perfect."

If you enjoyed *Just for Show*, you might want to check out Jae's Hollywood series, especially *Just Physical*, the novel in which Lana's friend Jill meets stuntwoman Crash and falls in love with her.

About Jae

Jae grew up amidst the vineyards of southern Germany. She spent her childhood with her nose buried in a book, earning her the nickname *professor*. The writing bug bit her at the age of eleven. Since 2006, she has been writing mostly in English.

She used to work as a psychologist but gave up her day job in 2013 to become a full-time writer and a part-time editor. As far as she's concerned, it's the best job in the world.

When she's not writing, she likes to spend her time reading, indulging her ice cream and office supply addictions, and watching way too many crime shows.

CONNECT WITH JAE

E-mail her at: jae@jae-fiction.com
Visit her website: jae-fiction.com
Like her on Facebook: facebook.com/JaeAuthor
Follow her on Twitter: @jaefiction

Other Books from Ylva Publishing

www.ylva-publishing.com

Something in the Wine
(2nd, revised edition)

Jae

ISBN: 978-3-95533-793-3
Length: 302 pages (108,000 words)

All her life, Annie suffered through her brother's constant practical jokes. Now he sets her up on a blind date with Drew, a lesbian winemaker, even knowing his sister is straight. Annie and Drew decide to turn the tables on him by pretending to fall in love. But what starts as a revenge plan soon turns their lives upside down as the lines between pretending and reality begin to blur.

Who'd Have Thought

G Benson

ISBN: 978-3-95533-874-9
Length: 339 pages (122,000 words)

When Hayden Pérez stumbles across an offer to marry Samantha Thomson—a cold, rude, and complicated neurosurgeon—for $200,000, what's a cash-strapped ER nurse to do? Sure, Hayden has to convince everyone around them they're madly in love, but it's only for a year, right? What could possibly go wrong?

Face It

Georgette Kaplan

ISBN: 978-3-95533-976-0
Length: 198 pages (70,000 words)

Ten years ago, Elizabeth Smile had one sizzling night with her roommate that left her craving more. Now her friend has reappeared with an odd request: Will Elizabeth play her fake girlfriend for a family Christmas in Ohio? The deal comes with a suspicious sister with her own agenda and the digging up of Elizabeth's old feelings. A twisty lesbian romance about getting more than we bargain for.

Just My Luck

Andrea Bramhall

ISBN: 978-3-95533-702-5
Length: 306 pages (81,000 words)

Genna Collins works a dead end job, loves her family, her girlfriend, and her friends. When she wins the biggest Euromillions jackpot on record, everything changes…and not always for the best. What if money really can't buy you happiness?

Coming from Ylva Publishing

www.ylva-publishing.com

Chasing Stars

Alex Thorne

For superhero Swiftwing, crime fighting isn't her biggest battle. Nor is it having to meet the whims of Hollywood star Gwen Knight as her mild-mannered assistant, Ava. It's doing all that, while tracking a giant alien bug, being asked to fake date her famous boss, and realizing that she might be coming down with a pesky case of feelings. A fun, sweet, sexy lesbian romance about the masks we wear.

Up on the Roof

A.L. Brooks

When a storm wreaks havoc on bookish Lena's well-ordered world, her laid-back new neighbor, Megan, offers her a room. The trouble is they've been clashing since the day they met. How can they now live under the same roof? Making it worse is the inexplicable pull between them that seems hard to resist. A fun, awkward, and sweet British romance about the power of opposites attracting.

Just for Show
© 2018 by Jae

ISBN: 978-3-95533-980-7

Also available as e-book.

Published by Ylva Publishing, legal entity of Ylva Verlag, e.Kfr.

Ylva Verlag, e.Kfr.
Owner: Astrid Ohletz
Am Kirschgarten 2
65830 Kriftel
Germany

www.ylva-publishing.com

First edition: 2018

Credits
Edited by Robin J. Samuels
Proofread by Laina Villeneuve
Cover Design and Print Layout by Streetlight Graphics

CPSIA information can be obtained
at www.ICGtesting.com
Printed in the USA
LVHW040803200219
608152LV00001B/33/P